John S. Hart

The Sunday-School Idea

an exposition of the principles which underlie the Sunday-school cause, setting

forth its objects, organization, methods and capabilities

John S. Hart

The Sunday-School Idea
an exposition of the principles which underlie the Sunday-school cause, setting forth its objects, organization, methods and capabilities

ISBN/EAN: 9783337272418

Printed in Europe, USA, Canada, Australia, Japan

Cover: Foto ©Andreas Hilbeck / pixelio.de

More available books at **www.hansebooks.com**

THE

SUNDAY-SCHOOL

IDEA:

AN EXPOSITION

OF THE

PRINCIPLES WHICH UNDERLIE THE SUNDAY-SCHOOL CAUSE,

SETTING FORTH

ITS OBJECTS, ORGANIZATION, METHODS AND CAPABILITIES.

By JOHN S. HART, LL.D.,

Senior Editor of The Sunday-School Times, Principal of the New Jersey State Normal School, author of "Thoughts on Sabbath-Schools," "The Golden Censer," "Removing Mountains," "Mistakes of Educated Men," "In the School Room," "Composition and Rhetoric," "English Grammar," etc., etc.

PHILADELPHIA:
J. C. GARRIGUES & CO.,
No. 608 ARCH STREET.
1871.

WESTCOTT & THOMSON,
Stereotypers, Philada.

PREFACE.

THE intention of this book is to give a general survey of the whole subject of Sunday-schools. I have considered, first, the object of the institution, in its relations both to the individual scholar and to the great work of Christianizing the world. Next, the organization of the Sunday-school has come under review, and the true basis for such an organization has been defined. After this, I have discussed at great length the varied duties and qualifications of the Superintendent and of the Teacher,—the men and women by whose labors and counsels the organization is to be carried on and made effectual. Besides the work to be done by these in their separate individual capacities, is that dependent upon concerted action, and this has led to a general review of the various associations of teachers, whether for their own improvement, or for the promotion of the cause at large. The important topic of Sunday-school literature has been discussed at considerable length, and suggestions have been made as to the best methods of selecting Sunday-school books and of managing the library. Sunday-school anniversaries, Sunday-school missions, the mode of starting a new school, the relations of the Sunday-school to the family, to the church and the minister, Teachers' Institutes, Teachers' Normal classes, with a large variety of other affiliated topics, have been passed under review.

The subject having for many years engaged no small share of my thoughts, there is in fact hardly any aspect of it which has not, at one time or another, come up for practical consideration. I have aimed accordingly in the present volume to give my whole rounded idea of what the Sunday-school is, and of what it is capable. I have aimed, however, to discuss principles rather than methods; and in those instances in which particular methods have been advocated, they have always been given in connection with the principles which underlie them and govern them. To the intelligent workman, here as elsewhere, the rationale of what he does is more important than the particular mode of doing it. Methods change or die out, principles are eternal. J. S. H.

Trenton, N. J., October, 1870.

CONTENTS.

CHAPTER I.

OBJECTS OF THE SUNDAY-SCHOOL.

PAGE

1. THE GREAT OBJECT—CONVERSION OF THE SCHOLARS. 14
   Building up the Converts in Holiness 15
   Instructing them in Bible Knowledge 16
   The Work before the Church 17
   Duty in regard to Religious Instruction.............. 18
   What the Church must do 19
   Alarming Deficiencies 20
2. THE MISSION WORK OF THE SUNDAY-SCHOOL ENTER-
   PRISE.. 21
   The Aggressive Work............................. 22
   More than Missionaries Needed 23
   Christianity essentially Aggressive 24
   Duty to those without 25
   Evangelization by means of the Sunday-school 26
   Duty of Churches as such 27
   The Sunday-school a Missionary Agency 29
   Supporting Missionaries 30
   Mission Work Everywhere 31

CHAPTER II.

SUNDAY-SCHOOL ORGANIZATION.

BASIS OF ORGANIZATION............................ 35
   Appointment of Superintendent 37

   PAGE

Appointment of other Officers...................... 40
1. The Secretary.................................. 40
2. The Librarian................................. 41
3. The Chorister................................ 42
Relation of Teachers to Superintendent 43

CHAPTER III.

THE SUPERINTENDENT.

1. The First Qualification—Earnest Piety................ 50
2. Executive Ability............................... 52
3. Things not Wanted............................. 54
    1. Not Fussy.................................. 54
    2. Not Fretful................................ 54
    3. Not Noisy.................................. 55
    4. Not a Talker............................... 56
4. Putting Forth a Personal Influence................... 57
5. Knowing what is Going on in the School............. 61
6. Knowledge of the Lesson 64
7. Bestowing Attention upon all 66
8. Sympathizing with all............................ 67
9. The Work of Classifying the School................. 69
    Principles of Classification........................ 70
      1. Age...................................... 71
      2. Size...................................... 72
      3. Social Condition 74
      4. Intellectual Progress...................... 75
      5. Individual Peculiarities.................... 76
10. Maintaining Order............................. 78
    1. Doing Things Quietly....................... 80
    2. Doing Things at the Right Time............... 83
    3. Keeping Things and Persons in Place 84
11. Exercising Government 87
12. Making a Programme............................ 93
13. Opening School Punctually 99
14. Preparation for the Opening...................... 100

PAGE

15. Giving out Notices in School 101
16. Giving out the Hymn............................. 103
  1. Waiting for the Scholars to Find the Place....... 103
  2. Care in Announcing the Place.................... 104
  3. Grammatical Blunders 106
  4. Reading just what is to be Sung................ 106
  5. Giving the Key-note........................... 106
  6. Looking while Reading......................... 107
17. Reading the Scriptures............................. 108
  1. Avoiding Formality............................ 109
  2. Being in Earnest 11C
  3. Studying the Passage 111
  4. Meditating over it 112
  5. Reading to One's Self......................... 113
  6. Number of Verses to be Read................... 114
  7. Keeping the School in your Eye................ 114
18. The Opening Prayer............................... 115
  1. An Example................................... 116
  2. Another Example 118
  3. The Superintendent's Manner in Prayer.......... 119
  4. A Devout Pause before and after............... 120
  5. Concluding Remarks........................... 121

CHAPTER IV.

THE TEACHER.

1. The First Qualification........................... 124
2. Winning Souls.................................... 128
3. Help from the Great Teacher...................... 131
4. Having an Aim.................................... 136
  1. To Secure Regularity of Attendance............. 138
  2. To Secure Study of the Lesson 138
  3. To Maintain Order............................. 139
  4. To Teach Something 142
  5. To Teach Something Additional every Sunday...... 143
  6. To Teach Something to every Scholar 143

PAGE

7. To make your Teaching Scriptural............... 145
8. To get the Scholars to Commit to Memory....... 146
9. To Secure the Conversion of your Scholars....... 147
5. Difference between Teaching in Sunday-school and in
   other Schools................................... 149
   1. None of the Ordinary School Penalties.......... 149
   2. The Subject of Instruction more Practical........ 150
   3. More Committing to Memory Required 152
6. Class-Teaching................................. 153
7. How to Question a Class......................... 157
   1. A Conviction that the Power is Attainable........ 158
   2. A Clear Idea of the Object of Questioning........ 159
   3. The Mode of Questioning 162
      a. The Teacher should not limit himself to the Book. 162
      b. He must be thoroughly at home in the Lesson.. 162
      c. He must make the Scholars give back all the
           ideas he gives them...................... 163
      d. He must Skip about the Class............... 164
8. How to Conduct a Recitation...................... 165
   1. Closing the Books............................. 165
   2. Reciting the Verses........................... 166
   3. Finding the References........................ 167
   4. Skipping about............................... 168
   5. Keeping all the Class engaged.................. 169
   6. Making the Scholars do the Talking............. 170
9. Teaching out of Book............................ 171
10. Holding the Attention of a Class................. 177
11. Keeping the Scholars busy....................... 184
12. Gaining the Affections of the Scholars............ 189
13. Reaching the Comprehension of the Scholars....... 193
14. Variety in Teaching 199
    1. In Manner.................................. 202
    2. In Topics.................................. 203
    3. In Illustrations............................. 204
    4. Necessity of Freshness....................... 205
15. Assigning a Definite Lesson..................... 206

PAGE

16. Preparation for the Lesson 210
    1. Committing the Verses to Memory............ 212
    2. The Parallel Texts......................... 215
    3. Use of the Question-Book.................... 215
    4. Finding Additional Illustrations................ 217
    5. Critical Study of Meaning.................... 217
    6. Providing Practical Thoughts.................. 219
    7. Beginning Early in the Week.................. 220
    8. Seeking the Aid of the Great Teacher.......... 220
17. Getting the Scholars to Learn the Lesson............ 221
18. Acquaintance with the general Contents of the Scriptures 229
19. Irregular Attendance of Teachers................... 230
20. Visiting Scholars................................. 233
21. Keeping up with the Times........................ 237
    1. He should take a Teacher's Paper............. 239
    2. He should have a Teacher's Library........... 241
    3. He should attend Conventions................ 241

CHAPTER V.

TEACHERS IN COUNCIL.

1. The Necessity of Social Gatherings................. 244
2. State Conventions............................... 248
3. County Conventions............................. 252
4. County Institutes............... 257
    Institute Programme............................ 260
5. Teachers' Weekly Meeting......................... 265

CHAPTER VI.

THE SUNDAY-SCHOOL LIBRARY.

PART I.—HOW TO SELECT THE LIBRARY.
    The Enormous Amount of Sunday-school Books....... 273
    Useless Lamentations not Recommended............. 275
    How shall the Selection be made ?.................. 277

PAGE

A Reading Committee.......................... 279
    How is the Committee to be Appointed?........... 280
Who are fitted to be on the Committee.............. 282
    1. Persons of Education and Culture............... 282
    2. Persons well acquainted with Christian Doctrine.. 282
    3. Persons having Sympathy with Children 283
What Sort of Books should be Selected 284
The Actual Selection........................... 286
What Books are Unsuitable...................... 288

PART II.—HOW TO MANAGE THE LIBRARY.
Difficulties in the Ordinary Methods. 292
    1. Books Disappear............................ 292
    2. Inconveniences in the Manner of Selecting Books
       from the Library............................ 293
    3. The Interruption to the Lessons caused by the usual
       Methods of Managing the Library............. 296
The Plan Proposed.... 298
    1. A Printed Catalogue to be used 299
    2. The Scholar's Library Card.................... 300
    3. The Use of a Register Number................. 301
    4. The Selection of Books to be made at Home..... 302
    5. Returning Cards and Books 302
    6. Giving out Cards and Books...................303
    7. Mode of Numbering the Books................. 303
The Work of the Librarian....................... 303
    1. The Use of the Checks 304
    2. The Use of the Register 305
    3. Recapitulation of the Librarian's Work.......... 309

CHAPTER VII.

RELATIONS OF THE SUNDAY-SCHOOL TO OTHER RE-
LIGIOUS INSTITUTIONS.

1. The Sunday-school and the Church 310
2. The Sunday-school and the Minister................ 318

3. The Sunday-school and Parents................... 324
4. Attendance of Scholars in Church................. 328
5. School Accommodations........................ 335

CHAPTER VIII.

MISCELLANEOUS TOPICS.

1. Sunday-School Music.......................... 340
   1. Mere Noise not Song...................... 342
   2. Mere Song not Sufficient.................. 342
   3. The Music of the School should be such as will be
     Continued in the Church................... 343
2. Sunday-school Anniversaries................... 346
3. Closing Schools in Winter..................... 355
4. Closing Schools in Summer 359
5. After Vacation.............................. 365
6. Treatment of New Scholars 368
7. Absenteeism............................... 374
8. Uniform Lessons............................ 379
9. How to Start a New School................... 385
   1. Seek Guidance from above................. 385
   2. Be Prepared to make Sacrifices 386
   3. Read on the Subject...................... 387
   4. Study the Ground 387
   5. Get together your Fellow-workers.......... 387
   6. Make a Family Visitation of the Neighborhood..... 389
   7. Secure a Place for holding the School........... 390
   8. The Cost of Starting a School................ 390
   9. Choice of Superintendent 392
  10. Opening the Meeting 392
  11. Classifying the Scholars.................. 393
  12. Method of Classification.................. 393
  13. The Teachers making themselves Acquainted with
     the Scholars.......................... 394
  14. The Superintendent to have a Class........... 394
  15. The Secretary and Librarian not to have a Class.... 395

PAGE

16. The First Session...................................... 395
17. Constitution and By-laws............................. 396
10. Are we making Progress?............................. 396
   1. A Better Theory of the Object of the Sunday-school. 397
   2. The Relation of the Sunday-school to the Church
        better understood................................ 398
   3. Greater Facilities in the way of Books, Maps, etc.... 399
   4. Improvement in Sunday-school Music 401
   5. Better Machinery for Improving the Character of the
        Schools.. 402
   6. Better Understanding of the Functions of the Sunday-
        School in Developing the Lay Talent of the Church 403
   7. A Hopeful Discontent with the Present State of
        Things... 406

THE

SUNDAY-SCHOOL

IDEA.

CHAPTER I.

THE OBJECTS OF THE SUNDAY-SCHOOL.

IN conducting any enterprise, it is important frequently to recur to first principles and to define clearly the objects for which the enterprise is undertaken. In the excitement of pursuit, it is not uncommon for men to forget what it is that they are pursuing, and to rush on from the mere love of the chase, regardless of the end. Few social agencies are more useful than the fire companies of our cities. Yet how frequently do we see more property destroyed by the exuberant and heedless energy of an excited fire company than by the fire itself!

I do not mean to compare the Sunday-school organization to the Fire Department. Yet Sunday-school teachers, equally with firemen, need to have clear ideas of what it is that they are called to do. The teacher, equally with the fireman, for the want of definite aims may beat the air, or may even do harm where he seeks to do good.

What then is the aim of the Sunday-school?

The First and Great Object.

The first, great aim, undoubtedly, is to bring the scholars to a saving knowledge of Jesus Christ—to secure their conversion. The teacher should aim at this just as steadily and fixedly as the fireman aims, above and before all other considerations, to save the life of a forgotten sleeper from the flames of a blazing dwelling. To the accomplishment of this his first end, all other ends are to the teacher subordinate and secondary. Until the accomplishment of this, all other results are nugatory. For this he labors, studies, visits, prays, agonizes. The burden of his thoughts and desires is, How shall I compass the conversion of my pupils? This, beyond all question, is the first and main end of the Sunday-school. The institution is not a missionary society, or a temperance society, or an anti-tobacco society, or a debating society, or a school for teaching history, geography, literature and antiquities, but a school to do for the young what the church is doing—to bring them to the knowledge of Christ. Nor is it an institution above, or below, or outside of, or in any way antagonistic to the church, but rather it is a particular mode in which the church itself is carrying out the behests of its Lord.

Building up Converts in Holiness. The church, while aiming primarily at the conversion of souls, does not stop at this naked result. When a soul is converted to God, the church does not then give up all care for it, and leave it to struggle on in its new career unaided and alone. As well almost might the mother abandon her new-born babe, and give her energies forthwith to other cares. The soul that is new-born into the kingdom needs continual watchfulness and fostering care. This is especially true of those regenerated in early youth. The tenderer the years at which they are converted, the greater the care and watchfulness required after their conversion. A teacher whose labors should be blessed by the conversion of all the members of his class would be strangely derelict in duty were he then to abandon his class as no longer needing his care, and go off in search of other scholars to be converted. Christ is glorified not only by the conversion of souls, but by their steadfastness in the faith and their growth in holiness. If a child, after being truly converted, is left to go astray and fall into sin, and to become through life a weak and puny Christian, though he may be finally saved, he yet misses much of the glory and brightness of the Christian life, and he brings much dishonor upon the cause.

We must aim, then, not only to bring the lambs into the fold, but to keep them there, and to give them due nurture and protection. The Sunday-school is an agency of the church specially suited to do this part of the Christian work. The young Christian needs to be thoroughly grounded in doctrine. When a scholar is converted and joins the church, our work with him is just begun. We must patiently and faithfully teach him the doctrines of the Bible. The truths of the Holy Scriptures are the aliment by which the Christian grows. What the young disciple especially needs is, not only exhortation, but teaching. The pastor who is wise will spend much time in simple, instructive discourses, having for their aim to build up the young of his flock in sound Christian knowledge, and he will regard with peculiar satisfaction those of his helpers and fellow-laborers who in the Sunday-school carry out in detail, and apply to personal and individual cases, the portions of doctrine which he from the pulpit distributes in the mass and to the whole congregation.

Instruction in Bible Knowledge. Nor should the teacher wait until a child is converted before beginning to instruct him in the truths of the Bible and the duties of the Christian life. The doctrines of the Bible, it should be remembered, are not only useful for growth in grace, but they are the most efficient means of conversion. While the teacher should not neglect the duty of personal appeal and exhortation, yet let him not forget that there is a mighty power in God's word to pierce the heart and conscience. Let him unceasingly plant this divine seed in the minds of his scholars. It may lie long before it is quickened. But in time it will take root and grow. The work of grace in a heart thus thoroughly indoctrinated in Scripture truth is much more glorious than that fitful excitement sometimes wrought by mere passionate appeals to the feelings.

The great aim of the Sunday-school, then, is the conversion of the young and the building up of its converts in holiness of heart and life, and its great means are the indoctrination of the young, both before and after conversion, in the truths of the Bible.

But this is confining our views to a single school. Let us endeavor to look beyond this single point, and get a view of the Sunday-school enterprise in its broader and more general aspects.

The Work Before us.

It is for Christians to Christianize the world. This is among the plainest postulates of the gospel scheme. Another truth equally fundamental is that education is the main agency to be used in the work of Christianization. Children believe what they are taught to believe. They are what they are trained to be. After all necessary deductions and abatements for individual cases, this is the great fact in human history. As the twig is bent the tree is inclined. Teaching and training make the man. Teaching and training make the nation. There are no means more used and blessed by the Holy Spirit in the work of

2 * B

turning men to Christ and of establishing his kingdom in the world than this of education.   The
church itself is only the school of Christ, in which all
are alternately scholars and teachers, ever learning
and teaching the truths which Christ has promul-
gated for the salvation of the world.

*Duty of the Church to give Religious Teaching
to the Young.*   The Sunday-school is not an institution by itself, having an independent existence and
organization of its own, but is only the church working in that particular way while carrying out its
appointed mission of evangelizing the world.   The
duty of giving a Christian education to the young has
been laid upon the church by the Master, and this
duty, it has been found, can best be discharged by
means of the Sunday-school.   Children *may* indeed
be taught the doctrines and precepts of the Bible
privately at home by their parents or by others specially employed for the purpose.   The same is true
of all parts of a child's education. He may be taught
the languages and the various sciences at home by
his parents or by private tutors.   Many persons pre-
fer this method of education.   But it is easy to see
that not one in a thousand, perhaps not one in ten
thousand, has the means to educate his children in
this way.   Few parents have themselves the education or the leisure to discharge the duty personally,
and still fewer have the wealth to enable them to
employ a private tutor.   Religious teaching is no
exception to this remark.   It would be a sad day for

the church and for the world if no children were to receive religious teaching and training but those who had educated and godly parents able and willing to do the work. To the mass of mankind, the ninety and nine out of the hundred, knowledge comes by schooling. The young learn the doctrines and precepts of the Bible most readily and effectually, just as they learn most readily the rules of arithmetic and grammar—namely: by going to school for the purpose, by making a business of it. Any other method is apt to be fitful, irregular and inadequate. If the great body of children in the community are to be instructed systematically and effectually in the doctrines of the Christian religion, and if this instruction cannot conveniently be given in the week-day school, then we must have a school especially for the purpose on Sunday, and this Sunday-school must be made as efficient as the talent, the education, the wealth and the fidelity of the church to her Master can make it.

What the Church must do.

The church must aim, first, to bring into the school all the children in her borders who are of school age, and secondly, to give to the school the very highest efficiency of which it is capable. The church is not acting up to the exigencies of the case until it is found willing to expend upon this work an amount of energy and liberality commensurate with that which the State spends upon secular education. The city of New York alone spends annually upon

her daily public-schools more money than is expended by all the Christians of the United States on
Sunday-schools. So long as such a state of things
exists, so long as the Sunday-school is sustained in
this feeble, half-hearted way, let croakers and unbe-
lievers cease to wail over its failings and short-com-
ings. The Sunday-school is not accomplishing what
it ought to accomplish. Nobody knows this more
fully, nobody bewails it more truly, than I do. But
I also as truly and fully believe that the Sunday-
school may be all that is claimed for it, that it may
accomplish all that is legitimately required of it, that
it may teach its pupils the doctrines of religion and
train them in habits of piety, just as thoroughly as
these same children on the other days of the week
are taught and trained in the daily schools how to
read, write and spell. But to do this the church
of course must use adequate means and must go
about the work in good earnest.

Alarming Deficiencies. There is no disguising
the fact that fully one-half the juvenile population of
the community is out of the Sunday-school, and of
this half all except the most inconsiderable fraction
are outside of religious instruction and influence.
The good people who go to church and to Sunday-
school themselves, and who see with their own eyes
the crowds of others who attend the church and the
school, can hardly be made to believe the portentous
fact which I have named. If they might with propriety on a Sunday morning, instead of going to

church, take a stroll in the fields in the neighborhood
of the village or town, and see the hundreds of idle
boys and young men on almost every open lot engaged in the so-called sport of base ball, which has
become such a national mania, they might perhaps
realize a little better the startling facts revealed by
the census. Is the church doing anything in refer
ence to this evil at all commensurate with its gigantic character?

The Mission Work of the Sunday-school Enter-prise.

The Sunday-school work of the country is clearly
divisible into two heads. The first contemplates the
perfecting of the schools which exist, particularly
of those which are connected with old and well-
established churches. This undoubtedly is a great
work. Of the more than one hundred thousand
existing schools, how few are accomplishing all that
they might accomplish! What a power to the
church this agency would be if its machinery were
all complete and thoroughly efficient! If our Sunday-schools had even the efficiency and the completeness of our week-day schools, though the latter
are far from being models, what an impulse would
be given to the healthful life and activity of the
church, and to the growth of godliness among men!
Most assuredly, the perfecting of our existing schools
is one great department of the Sunday-school work
in this country.

The Aggressive Work. But the aggressive work of the Sunday-school enterprise is still greater and more important. If the four millions or more of children who attend the Sunday-school are very imperfectly taught, and receive comparatively little benefit, let it not be forgotten that not less than five millions attend no school, and are entirely without the means of religious instruction. The very poorest school that was ever kept together is better than no school. The child who attends most irregularly, and has a teacher of the very smallest qualifications, is better off than the child who goes to no school and spends his Sunday in roaming through the streets or the fields. Every well-conducted inquiry develops almost uniformly the fact that more than one-half of the youth of the land are growing up in ignorance of God and of Bible truth, attending neither school nor church, many of them unable to read, and even these, by reason of the vicious and depraving literature with which young minds are poisoned, being for the most part better off than those who can read.

This, then, is the aggressive work of the Sunday-school enterprise. The people of God have in hand the invasion of this vast outlying mass of neglected ignorance and vice. They aim at nothing less than to bring into the Sunday-school, and under religious influence, every child who is willing, or can be persuaded, to come. The Sunday-school has become a leading agency by which the church seeks to fulfil its mission of evangelizing the entire population. It

is in the fullest sense of the word a missionary enterprise. It is a work in which every Christian who
is in bodily health may give personal service. Not
every one can personally preach Christ to the
heathen. The most of us must content ourselves
with giving our money to send others. But in
bringing neglected children into the Sunday-school,
almost the entire body of Christians can engage personally. It is a work which can be adequately
accomplished in no other way than by the personal
service of the great body of Christians.

More than Missionaries Needed. A few city
missionaries scattered here and there, a few scores
or even hundreds of missionaries in the West, cannot
accomplish this work. The work is too great, too
pervading, too widespread, to be effectually reached
by any mere partial, or local, or transient effort.
We must have, indeed, our city missionaries and
our Western missionaries, and we must multiply them
twenty-fold. But these, however multiplied, cannot
do the work. As well might a few gardeners, with
their watering-pots, undertake to supply the summer
rain. The great work of Christian evangelization
must be done by the great mass of God's people.
To bring into the Sunday-school five millions of
neglected children can be done only by the general
co-operation of the six millions of professing Christians. It is a work for all. It is a work for every
one. Deducting one-sixth for those physically dis-
abled by ill health and the infirmities of age, there

would still be left one professing Christian for every neglected child. What Christian loves his Lord so little, or is so poor in resources, that he cannot, by inquiry and persuasion and personal effort, in the course of a year, or of two years, or three years, bring one child into the Sunday-school? What church that will undertake this matter seriously and systematically cannot, in one, two, or three years, bring into the Sunday-school as many neglected children as it has church members? What Christian, what church, has not within reach neglected children on whom to operate? We need not go to Bedford street, or to the Five Points, or to the far West, to find children that go to no Sunday-school. They are all around us, within stone's throw of our dwellings, living in the next street, perhaps in the next house. We meet them every time we go to our places of business. We see them on every street corner. We can hardly avoid them if we would.

Here, then, is the aggressive work in which we are engaged. The six millions of American Christians must, not by gifts of money, not by sending substitutes, but by personal service, bring into the Sunday-school and under religious influence the five millions of neglected children among us who are growing up in practical heathenism.

Christianity Aggressive.

Christianity is essentially aggressive. The man who is a true Christian himself desires to see all other men Christians. To this he looks, for this he labors and prays. "Thy kingdom come" is the burden of his prayer. To speed its coming is the object of his labor and effort. It is not in the nature of the case that he should be indifferent to this object. Neutrality in the case is not possible. Our Saviour himself expressly says, "He that is not with me is against me." Christianity is not like a scheme of philosophy, or a dogma of science, which a man may receive as his own belief, with unconcern as to what others believe about it. If a man believes Christianity to be true, he must needs be anxious that others should have the same faith. He is, by his very nature as well as by his profession, a propagandist. The church is an organization for this very purpose, to spread the doctrine it has received. The church has been planted in the world, not for the purposes of self-defence, but for aggression. It aims at no less than to bring all men within its pale.

Duty to Those Without. If such be the nature of Christianity, and such the office of a Christian church, what should we expect in any community in which a number of churches are planted? Should these churches be contented with merely holding their own?—with merely taking care each of its own flock? Surely not. Every church should consider itself bound to make aggressions, not into its neighbor's fold, but into the territory not yet reclaimed from the enemy. There are few communities in which at least one-third of the population is not out-

3

side of any church. In the United States, the proportion of those who attend no church, and who are
openly of the number of the ungodly, is reckoned at
one-half the population. This may possibly be an
exaggeration. There may be particular communities in which the number of those who are outside
of religious influences and connections is far less.
Yet I have never known a community stirred up to
make a thorough exploration of this subject who
did not find the facts far more deplorable and alarming than they had imagined. The number of those
who in this Christian land live and die as heathens,
if not one-half of the entire population, is appallingly
large. The Christian church has a work to do in
regard to this element of society, which it must look
steadily in the face, neither disheartened by the
magnitude of the evil, nor on the other hand ignor-
ing its existence.

It is a dreadful mistake for a church to content
itself with merely looking after the families connected with its own organization. This undoubtedly
it should do. But there are other things which it
should not leave undone. No church is true to its
Master that is not continually and systematically
making inroads upon the kingdom of Satan.

Evangelization by means of the Sunday-school.
It has so come to pass in the providence of God, that
much of the work of evangelizing the mass of the
people, both within and without the pale of the
church, is now accomplished by means of the Sun-

day-school. Whatever, therefore, this institution may have been in its origin, it is now clearly a church institution—a part of the church, not a sanctuary outside of the church. It is one of the modes by which the church is doing the work assigned to her by her Lord. The Methodist Church moved in the right direction in the changes adopted a few years since in their Book of Discipline, in which the Sunday-school was formally incorporated as a part of the working machinery of the church, and as such subject to ecclesiastical supervision and control. I have long thought the institution one too important to be left to mere voluntary guidance and support. I hope the day is not distant when every ecclesiastical body will not only assume the charge of its Sunday-schools, but will give them that efficient and systematic support accorded to other acknowledged agencies of the church.

Duty of Churches as such. But there is a step beyond this even which our churches must take. They should not only look after the children of their own flocks, seeing that they are brought into the school, and that they are duly cared for and instructed, but they should systematically and with organized effort go out into the byways and bring in the neglected ones. Every conference, synod, convention, presbytery, classis, or church judicatory, having control in matters of discipline, should enjoin upon its members the duty of gathering into its Sunday-schools the children who have no church connection.

Much has been done in this way by voluntary associations of teachers, who have organized themselves into visiting committees for the purpose of visiting every family. But such associations are transient, and more or less spasmodic. Churches are permanent. They are the proper agency for aggressive work, as well as for the work within their own congregation. When every church shall have fully organized and equipped itself for this work, and shall have entered upon it with earnest zeal, and shall have reaped an abundant harvest as the fruit of its labors, there will still remain " much land to be possessed." There is enough for all to do. Let all engage in doing.

If a church may be interrogated by its supervisory body as to its faithfulness in regard to the children of its members and of the families worshipping with it, why should it not be interrogated also as to its faithfulness to those " which are without ?" If a church may assign to some of its members the duty of superintending and teaching in the Sunday-school, and of seeing that the children of its households are properly instructed either in the Sunday-school or elsewhere, why may it not also organize a stated and responsible machinery for bringing into the school and the congregation children and families that have no religious connection ?

" *Not to Leave the Other Undone.*" The current of thought among Sunday-school teachers all over the land at this time is strongly set upon improving the methods of teaching. On this branch of the subject I shall have much to say in the present volume. The greater part of my volume, indeed, will be devoted to this point. But there is another aspect of the case that is equally important, and that is for the time in some danger of being forgotten.

A Missionary Agency. The Sunday-school is of incalculable importance as a missionary agency of the church. As a means of reaching the destitute, those lying outside the pale of the churches, there is no agency comparable to it for efficiency, none that can supply its place. The improvements in teaching and training, and in the general management of schools, upon which the minds of Sunday-school men are now set, will contribute doubtless to the effectiveness of the institution as a missionary agency ; for the better and more attractive we can make our existing schools the more readily can we propagate and multiply them. But the mission work of the Sunday-school is, after all, something distinct, having motives, methods and agencies of its own, and is of primary and most urgent importance. The danger of the hour seems to me to be that this great work will unintentionally and unconsciously be made secondary in the thoughts and efforts of God's people ; and I take the occasion, therefore, in the very threshold of my book, to emphasize this feature of the Sunday-school enterprise.

More than half the Children out of Sunday-

3 *

school. The broad, patent, acknowledged fact which the church is called on to consider is that there, in our own land, more children are outside the Sunday-school than inside, and with all our efforts thus far we have not perceptibly reduced the proportion of those who are growing up godless and unchristian. Must these things be?

The duty of every Christian church and of every Christian in this matter is easily divisible into two heads. First, we owe something to the neglected children in our immediate neighborhood—those within reach of our own homes and churches, in the lanes and streets and alleys all around us. Secondly, we owe a duty to those living in sparsely-settled regions in the interior of the old States and in the ever advancing borders of the new States, where churches and Christian institutions are not yet fully enjoyed.

Supporting Missionaries. The duties of this second class cannot be discharged in most cases by personal service. We cannot go, but we may send. We must give of our worldly substance to those who are willing to act as missionaries in this work of planting Sunday-schools in pioneer regions. We should give a cordial and liberal support to those societies and agencies which have this work in hand. There is one society especially, national in its character and name, catholic in its principles, and venerable in its history and associations, which should share largely in the sympathies and the liberality of all Protestant Christians. I refer to the American

Sunday-School Union. As a Society, it has facilities for missionary work in pioneer regions such as no other benevolent agency has with which I am acquainted. It has, too, a noble record in the past, and I hope a glorious work in the future. I bid it most sincerely God-speed. I commend its missionaries and its work to the confidence, the prayers, the sympathies and the liberality of God's people. The Society should have ten missionaries in the field where it now has one. It should receive hundreds of dollars where it now receives ten. As a missionary agency its necessity was never so great, its opportunities were never so ample, its wants never more urgent. As a missionary agency it is comparatively inexpensive. The entire support of one of its missionaries is within the means of many a single school. There are at least five hundred Sunday-schools in our great centres of population, each of which might have its missionary, and every such missionary might gather in one new school on an average every week in the year. Could there be a more blessed privilege, a more imperative duty?

Mission Work Everywhere. But there is a vast amount of missionary work to be done that requires no intervention of any society, national, State or county. Every school, every church, every man, woman, or child, that loves the Lord Jesus, has missionary ground always within reach. Wherever there is a child whose religious interests are not cared for, who is growing up without a knowledge of God and the way of salvation, there is missionary work to be done. The strong, well-ordered, prosperous schools should count it a part of their indispensable duty, not only to aid in sending missionaries to remote settlements, but to engage personally in mission work in their own immediate neighborhoods.

A school connected with one of our large city congregations ought to place these three objects before it : First, to bring into itself, among its own classes, a continual stream of that class of children known as mission scholars, consisting of such as live near enough to attend the mother church. Secondly, to maintain one or more outlying mission-schools for such children as live too far from the church to attend there. Mission stations like this exist to almost any extent in our towns and cities. Thirdly, to maintain a missionary of its own on some distant field, using for this purpose the agency of some society.

A large school of this kind is not thoroughly organized for its work unless it has, in addition to its teachers, librarians, etc., a goodly number of laborers whose business should be to go out regularly every Sunday looking after children. When the teachers go to the school, let these visitors go into the streets. Let the work be a stated one, just as much as that of teaching, and let it occupy as much time. A school that has twenty teachers ought to have at least five of these child-hunters. Such an arrangement would enable the superintendent and pastor to utilize a large amount of talent that is now resting unemployed. Many pious persons might profitably engage in this service, and would be glad to do so, who have not the qualifications for teaching. What an impulse it would give to all our schools if for every four or five teachers one voluntary missionary visitor of this sort were engaged every Sunday, all the time of the session of the school, in exploring the streets and alleys for neglected children !

C

CHAPTER II.

SUNDAY-SCHOOL ORGANIZATION.

IN the remarks which I am about to make I refer, not to the institution as a general or national concern, but to a particular school. How shall a Sunday-school be organized? What ideas enter into such an organization? What officers are needed for its full efficiency?

In sketching such an organization, I have in mind the school of a large, well-appointed city church, a school numbering from two to three hundred scholars. Many modifications would be needed, of course, in organizing a city mission-school, or a small country school.

I would enter, also, one other important caveat. However decided may be my opinion in regard to the best method of Sunday-school management, or the true theory on which Sunday-school organizations should be based, yet if in any particular case I found an old, well-established school in successful operation conducted on some other plan, I should think it eminently unwise to disturb such organization just for the sake of realizing a theory. But

34

every year scores of new schools are coming into life, and there are also hundreds of old schools in a disordered, enfeebled condition, requiring reorganization. In all these cases the way is open for experiment, and one may enter the work with a reasonably fair chance of carrying out a preconceived plan without material or vexatious obstructions.

Basis of Organization.

The first question to be settled is, What is the true basis of the Sunday-school? Is it an independent, self-originating institution, like a Temperance Society, or a Society for Preventing Cruelty to Animals, or is it an offspring of the church?—a part of the machinery and working of the church? The answer given to this question will determine many others—most others, indeed, relating to the management of the school, and therefore it should take precedence of other questions. There is a tendency in many quarters to feel and act, if not distinctly to say, that the Sunday-school is something distinct and apart—an institution by itself. This notion, I am happy to believe, is not as prevalent as it was ten years ago. It still exists, however, and wherever it does exist it exerts a controlling influence in shaping affairs.

For myself, I have no sort of sympathy with any such feeling or notion. The Sunday-school, according to my theory, is a part of the working of the church, as much so as the prayer-meeting, or the weekly lecture, or even the Sunday sermon is. It is one of the ways in which the church shows its life. The religious training of the young is an imperative duty of the church, which it can neither ignore nor delegate. The instruction of youth in the principles of the gospel is one of the leading means by which God's people are to fulfill their great mission of Christianizing the world. It is therefore the duty and the interest of every Christian church, first to diffuse and foster among its households a disposition to train their children in the knowledge of the Scriptures, and secondly to supplement this family training by organizing and supporting a school wherein the Scriptures and the symbols of the church may be studied in some systematic and orderly manner. The school, according to this idea, is not something outside, springing up of itself, and coming in as a co-ordinate and collateral influence. It is rather, or at least it should be, the direct offspring and child of the church.

Holding this view of the subject, I am at no loss to determine what shall be the fountain of authority in the school. If a school is in a healthy condition, its teachers filled with zeal for the regeneration and conversion of their scholars, questions of authority and power and precedence will rarely arise. Still, in every organization where human beings work together, there must be a recognized centre and a recognized source of authority and control. The superintendent is the centre of control and authority in the Sunday-school. That is agreed on all hands.

But who clothes him with this authority? Whence does it spring as its source? Who appoint him and remove him?

Appointment of Superintendent.

"Why, the superintendent is elected by the teachers," says the reader; "how else should he be elected?"

That is just where we differ. The school, according to my notion, is not a little republic, or a ward meeting, or an arena for exercising the suffrage, but a place for work under the direction of the constituted authorities of the church. The church has a work to do, and they appoint a man to manage it for them, just as a railroad corporation appoint an engineer or a conductor. The teachers of a public school do not elect their principal; why should the teachers of a Sunday-school do so?

The opinions of nearly all Sunday-school teachers, and the customs of nearly all Sunday-schools, I know, are against me in this matter; and yet I am persuaded the common mode of proceeding has grown up by chance and through indifference, rather than from any well-considered theory on the subject, and I have good reason to believe that the method which I advocate is steadily and surely gaining ground. It needs but a sober and unprejudiced consideration to become general.

There are two ways of killing all life out of a school. One is to load it down with a complex

4

machinery of laws and by-laws—to " constitution" it
to death. The other is to make its offices a bone of
electioneering contention. When this sort of feeling
creeps into a school, it might as well close its doors ;
and how can this feeling be excluded when the position of superintendent is held up as a prize to be
scrambled for, and the aspirant feels that he must
cater for votes ?

The simplest, the safest, the most effective way of
organizing a school is for the session, or the vestry,
or whatever body constitutes the government of the
church, to select their man and say to him : Here
is a work which we want you to manage for us and
for the Master. Look through the congregation and
select your instruments. Invite one to teach, another
to be secretary, another to be librarian, and so on.
We wish the school conducted on certain principles,
but we leave the details of administration and the
selection of the instruments to yourself. When you
have your corps of teachers and assistants selected,
you will, of course, as every wise administrator does,
confer with them freely and kindly, and be thankful
for advice and suggestion ; but remember that you
are the overseer of the flock, and to you we look for
results.

In other words, the superintendent represents the
session, or whatever body, according to the usage
of the particular church, constitutes its governing
authority. The superintendent is appointed by the
church, to do a work for the church, under instruc-

tions from the church. Instead of being elected by the teachers, he invites the teachers to be his helpers in the work assigned him.

As I said before, where a school is already well established and in successful operation, and has been organized on the other plan, I would not break up the existing arrangements for the mere sake of theory. But where a new school is to be established, or an old one is to be revived or reconstructed, I would ask those interested to consider seriously and candidly the position which I have taken.

The character, almost the life, of the school depends on the superintendent. This is admitted on all hands. Are there not grave reasons why he should not be subject to an annual election by the teachers? or to an election by them at all? Suppose the superintendent, through some infirmity of temper, or want of tact, or lack of executive ability, is not succeeding, is it not likely that a change of administration can be effected with more discretion and with less friction, with greater quietness and at the same time with greater firmness, in the manner which I have indicated, than by the exasperating publicity of a popular vote? Many a school drags out a feeble and sickly existence for years just because the teachers wish to avoid a scene. They feel naturally timid about turning out an incompetent superintendent. Surely such things can be managed better by a few wise heads, having competent authority, than by electioneering intrigues.

This, then, is the first point in the organization of a Sunday-school ; namely, the appointment of the superintendent.   But suppose a superintendent appointed, what officers or assistants does he need in carrying on the work ?

Othe. Officers.

1. *A Secretary.* Many superintendents perform the duty of secretary themselves.   If the school is very small, and no suitable person can be obtained for the purpose, the superintendent may have to do this work.   But I am not now speaking of such schools, or of such extreme cases.   In the great majority of cases, where there is no secretary to keep the records of the school, it is because the superintendent is an immethodical man, with loose habits of business, and does not see the importance of a systematic and careful record of what is done in the school.   Clear and correct minutes of attendance and of proceedings add greatly to the efficiency of the school, and are as important to it as to other kinds of business.   Such minutes, if full and accurate, help not only to measure progress, but to guide in deciding practical questions.   But to be of any use they ought to be made with care and neatness, and from actual observation on the spot.   If the school is a large one, collecting the facts which ought to be registered and reducing them to record is work enough to occupy the time of one person during the whole session of the school.   The superintendent's time in school is

too valuable, and is too much needed for other purposes, to be occupied with these details. In almost
every congregation there is some young man of
quiet, gentlemanly habits, accustomed to business,
perhaps a clerk or accountant in a mercantile firm,
who, though not a member of church, and not willing or perhaps not suited to act as a teacher, yet
feels an interest in the school, and would take a
pleasure in thus making his good penmanship and
his business habits contribute to the promotion of the
cause. One of the special benefits of the Sunday-
school work is that it gives employment to much
precious talent that would otherwise go to waste.
Every young man that can be utilized by occupa-
tions like these is so much positive gain. The
superintendent, in selecting his secretary, ought to
have an eye to this, so as not only to secure a valuable assistant, but to bring into the field of usefulness
one who would otherwise be standing idle.

   2. *A Librarian.* The qualities needed in the
librarian are very similar to those required in the
secretary. One is needed who is a good penman
and a good accountant, trained to method and to
habits of business; one who is quiet, patient, con-
siderate and careful ; one who is not a mere routinist,
but who has some fertility of invention, so as to find
out ways of collecting and distributing books without distracting the teachers in the work of teaching,
and so as to secure the books from being destroyed
and lost. The librarian, in a school of any size,

4 *

needs at least two assistants, one for the boys' classes and one for the girls' classes. A third assistant is needed for the infant class. In very large schools as many as four or five assistants are needed. There is rarely any error in employing too much assistance in the work of the library. The common error is in the other direction. The library gives an opportunity of retaining in the school many of the young men of the church, and turning to good account their talents for business.

3. *A Chorister.* This office is not an indispensable one, like the two others which have been named. But wherever it is practicable, it adds much to the effectiveness of the music in the school to have some competent person whose recognized business it is to lead the children in the singing. Often the church chorister performs this office for the school. More commonly it is one of the teachers. The office is not incompatible with that of teacher, as the office of librarian or of secretary is. It is important, however, that the singing should not be left at loose ends, as it often is, but that some one of good judgment and competent musical talent should be charged with the duty of attending to the music. It needs some one, not merely to raise the tune when the time for singing comes, but to study the matter and devise the ways and means of improving the music. Sunday-school music has become a great power. But in order to the full development and the wise exercise of this power, there is needed a competent

knowledge of the subject, invention, tact, sound judgment, and no small amount of labor and thought outside of the school. The superintendent who is able to summon to his aid an assistant of this kind adds thereby largely to the effectiveness of all his other operations. Good music in the Sunday-school operates like the breath of the south wind in spring-time upon a bank of flowers—sending a pleasant warmth and glow to all the genial forces of nature.

4. *Teachers.* I shall have occasion, farther on in this volume, to go into a good deal of detail in regard to the duties and qualifications of teachers. The only point now to be considered is the relation of the teachers to the superintendent.

The general idea which, according to my view, lies at the basis of the whole Sunday-school organ-ization, must be our guide here. The pastor, the rector, the session, the vestry—whatever man or men constitute the ordinary authority of the church —appoint the superintendent, or invite him to carry out their views in organizing and conducting a Sun-day-school. The superintendent in like manner invites such persons in the congregation as he deems fit to be his helpers in this work. The teachers are assistants to the superintendent, acting in co-opera-tion with him, under his advice and direction, by his invitation.

In other words, so far as there is an election, the superintendent elects the teachers, not teachers the superintendent. I do not like this word election, anyhow, as applied to such matters. I would as soon speak of the minister's electing some one to pray at the Friday night prayer-meeting. As the minister conducts the prayer-meeting, so the superintendent conducts the school, calling to his assistance, and at his discretion, such members of the congregation as he needs and as are willing to co-operate with him in the work.

Such, I believe, is the ordinary and actual mode of doing things, whatever theory to the contrary people may have. I never yet knew a school that was thoroughly alive and efficient that was not conducted virtually on this plan, and I have known scores of good schools killed by attempting to carry the other plan into practice. If, whenever a teacher leaves the school, or a new class is organized, or a teacher becomes remiss or shows signs of hopeless incompetency, a teachers' meeting is to be called, and the matter of personal merits and demerits is to be discussed and a vote to be taken, how can it be possible to avoid heart-burnings, wranglings and alienations? The selection and the displacement of teachers in a work so purely voluntary as that of the Sunday-school are matters requiring the utmost delicacy and tact, and any attempt to manage them by means of public discussion and popular vote must end in disaster. Patriarchal government, not democracy, is the want of the Sunday-school.

It will be objected, perhaps, that I make the superintendent an autocrat, and that the plan takes away all self-respect and freedom of action from the teacher. But let it be remembered that the superintendent holds a similar relation to a power above him, from which he receives his own appointment and authority, and to which, in turn, he is amenable, and that in case of delinquency or incompetency of any kind he too may be dealt with, just as the incompetent or delinquent teacher is dealt with by him. Let it be remembered, too, by those who fear that our theory will lead to superciliousness, arrogance, or abuse of any kind, on the part of the superintendent, that the service is a purely voluntary one on the part of the teacher, and thus the teachers have it most effectually in their power to check any arbitrary or undue exercise of authority on the part of the superintendent.

My readers will excuse me for having dwelt a little on this matter. I feel persuaded that the efficiency of our Sunday-school operations has been much impared by the vague, ill-defined notions prevalent on this subject. Practically, superintendents and teachers have acted on the plan which I recommend, while their theory of action has been all the other way, and this difference between what, according to their theory, they ought to do, and what, by the sheer necessities of the case, they are compelled to do, has produced a state of hesitation and uncertainty entirely incompatible with the highest efficiency. No correctness of theory, indeed, will give to an incompetent superintendent common sense, tact, discretion, or executive ability. But supposing him to have these qualities, it certainly does add greatly to the ease and efficiency with which he can work the complicated machinery, to have his relations to its several parts clearly understood and recognized, not only by the church authorities, but also by the teachers.

It does not follow from the view which I have taken of the superintendent's relations to the teachers that, on taking charge of an established school, he will feel called upon to displace the existing teachers merely to re-appoint them or to appoint others. It is to be taken for granted that he has some few grains of common sense, and that he will be only too glad to retain in the service the faithful workers that he finds there. But when on full trial it is plain that any particular teacher is out of place, and the good of the school requires a change, or when the methods of any teacher are capable of being improved by wise and kindly suggestions, or when a teacher is wanted for a newly-formed class, I cannot doubt that such changes and choices are purely administrative, and come within the functions of the superintendent rather than those of the teachers' meeting. I can as little doubt that this putting into the superintendent's hands, distinctly and avowedly, the duty of calling teachers to his aid where needed, and of displacing or changing teachers when necessary, contributes as much to the harmony and good feeling of all concerned as it does to unity and efficiency of effort.

To sum up in a few words my whole theory of Sunday-school organization :

The church selects the superintendent ; the superintendent selects his secretary, librarian, chorister and teachers.

The secretary, librarian, chorister and teachers are responsible to the superintendent ; the superintendent is responsible to the church.

CHAPTER III.

THE SUPERINTENDENT.

THERE is not much exaggeration in the common saying that the superintendent is the school. Scholars and teachers of course are needed in making a school. But scholars and teachers are of little avail without a superintending head. A number of people, young and old, brought together without any organic centre of action, do not constitute a school. They are only a mass-meeting on a small scale. Chemistry gives us a good illustration of this idea. Two or three different kinds of materials put into a vessel make simply a confused mixture. But add another ingredient of exactly the right kind, and the confused mass becomes at once organic. It is forthwith converted into a crystal, every little molecule finding its appropriate place with all the exactness of a mathematical formula. The superintendent is the crystallizing ingredient in the Sunday-school, giving form and order to what would otherwise be chaos, changing into a school what would otherwise be a mere mass-meeting.

If the superintendent is the right sort of a man,

the school will flourish despite all adverse influences. If the superintendent is incapable or faithless, the school will languish and dwindle despite the best of teachers and the most favorable circumstances. The case can hardly be expressed too strongly. A good superintendent is a *sine qua non* of a good school.

It is not every one who is capable of being a good superintendent. Yet there are probably in every community more persons than is generally supposed who have the capacity if it were only properly developed, and many of those who are now exercising the office in a feeble and unsatisfactory manner might attain high excellence in it, if only they would take the necessary means. It is worth while, therefore, to make some special study of this important matter. Clear ideas in regard to the nature of the superintendent's office conduce greatly to its efficiency and to the success of the school. Some persons who have really all the substantial qualities needed in a superintendent fail through a mistaken notion of what a man in that position ought to do. I have one instance at this very moment in my mind, of a gentleman who presides over a large business concern with admirable success, managing its complicated affairs with system, order, and tact, and who, if he would only bring into the school the same methods that he applies to his business, would meet there with a like success; but unfortunately he has in his head a false theory of what a Sunday-school

superintendent should be, and in carrying out this
theory he is killing his school.   Let us soberly consider, then, what are some of the qualities needed
in a good superintendent, and what are some of the
things which he has to do.

1. *The First Qualification.*

Earnest Piety.   It is hardly necessary to say, the
superintendent should be a man of unmistakable piety.
In many respects the duties and qualifications of
the superintendent differ from those of the teacher.
But in one particular they are on common ground.
Both alike seek the renewing power of the Holy
Spirit for the salvation of the scholars, both need to
feel that power in their own hearts.   Whoever en-
gages in the Sunday-school work, in any of its departments, needs, above all other qualifications, that
of a renewed heart, thoroughly devoted to the Master's service.   There are emergencies, indeed, in
which, rather than let a class be disbanded, a teacher
may rightly be employed who is not a converted
person.   But no emergency seems possible in which
it would be right to place an unconverted man in
the position of Sunday-school superintendent.   In
regard to the other qualifications which are to be
spoken of, they are all desirable, and the person
should be selected who has the greatest amount and
variety of them.   But this one qualification is indispensable.   No matter what a man's abilities or attainments may be, he is not to be once thought of

for the office unless he is a real, earnest, devoted Christian.

There is such a unanimity of opinion on this point that it has seemed hardly necessary to name it, much less to dwell upon it. Yet I shall have to dwell so much upon other points, and especially upon those qualities which relate rather to one's ordinary business capacity, that there may possibly be the risk of misapprehension. Let me be understood, then, once for all, as holding not only that the Sunday-school superintendent should be a real, sincere, earnest Christian, but that this element of character is the very first, the principal, the main consideration in estimating his fitness for the office. The superintendent should not only be pious, but eminent for piety. He should be one who feels the burden of souls upon him; one who is much in secret prayer, crying mightily to God night and day for the outpouring of the Spirit; one who, without importunity or solicitation from others, from the mere yearnings of his own irrepressible desires, will make large sacrifices of ease, of time and of money for the promotion of the cause; one who yearns to see souls saved and the Master honored more than he longs or labors for success in any worldly business.

This earnest, whole-souled piety has a wonderful transforming effect upon the character, developing in every direction whatever other natural qualifications a man may have. It redoubles his vigilance, his punctuality, his labors of every kind; it gives

tact to the awkward, it makes the slow of speech
eloquent.   The man who has this earnest, burning,
self-sacrificing, self-consecrating zeal will find time,
even at the expense of worldly interests, to do something daily for his school.   He will deal faithfully in
private with the delinquent teacher.   He will visit
sick, or neglected, or truant scholars.   He will seek,
as for hid treasures, for every symptom of the work
of the Spirit upon the hearts of the children.   Every
teacher, every class, every scholar will be engraved
upon his heart; for every one of them will he make
statedly earnest personal supplication; not one of all
the crowd will appear before him on the Sabbath
whose name has not been on his lips at some time
during the week, as he has wrestled with God in
secret prayer.   Such a man, so coming before the
school, so mingling among the scholars, must needs
be a mighty power for good.   The superintendent
who has to the full this first, main qualification for
the office can hardly fail of a good measure of success, whatever other secondary qualities he may
lack.

2. *The Second Qualification.*

Executive Ability.   The superintendent should
have good executive ability.   It is not easy to define
exactly what is meant by this term.   The thing itself, however, is something that we all recognize
wherever we see it.   It is, to speak generally, the
ability to see clearly what agencies are needed for

success in any enterprise, combined with a certain inventive power in finding out such agencies and employing them in their appropriate work. A man of executive ability is not the one who attempts to do everything himself, but one who knows how to utilize the talents of other people. A man who is fit to superintend a railroad or a machine shop or a cotton mill, or to manage any large business in which the co-operation of many human wills is concerned, has the kind of executive ability required in superintending a Sunday-school. A man is wanted who knows how to make others co-operate harmoniously and efficiently to a common end. Such talent, though undoubtedly rare, is not so rare as is generally supposed. All the organized agencies of business require it, and so tend continually to develop it. What we want is to summon to our aid in the Sunday-school just that kind of aid which every extended business enterprise seems somehow to succeed in finding. The reason that this quality is so often wanting in Sunday-school management is that those who select the superintendent do not distinctly look for this as a leading and indispensable requisite. They forget that it is not the man who can make the best prayer, not the man who can speak with greatest glibness on anniversary occasions, not even the man who is the best teacher, that is wanted, but the one who combines with the first qualification I have mentioned, the best executive and administrative ability.

5 *

3. *Things Not Wanted.*

There are some things *not* wanted in the superintendent.

1. He should not be *fussy.* It is not easy to define in words what is meant by this epithet, but probably every reader understands it without a definition. Some superintendents make such an ado about every little thing, good or bad, that takes place in the school, as to keep the attention of the classes all the while distracted. The superintendent should study composure of manner in conducting the routine of business, and so far as possible avoid attracting the attention of either scholars or teachers except when he specifically wants their attention.

2. The superintendent should not be *fretful.* He needs especially to guard against this disposition, because in a large school there are, of necessity, many things to fret and worry him ; and if he yields to the temptation and loses his equanimity, he is sure to make matters worse. Some things *will* go wrong, no matter how well he may lay his plans. There will be noise in one class, a teacher absent in another, bad teaching or bad example in another. The librarian may be behindhand in his work, or the secretary not accurate enough in his entries, or ill feeling may show itself in scholars or in teachers. Let the superintendent resolve to do what he can to allay discontent and to keep the machine in good working order, not ashamed to profit by his

own mistakes, when he makes mistakes, and then receive with equanimity the result, whatever it may be.

3. The superintendent should not be *noisy*. He should learn to step lightly, to speak gently and to *keep his hand off the bell.* When will superintendents learn that making noise is not the way to stop noise? If the school is getting noisy, look quietly round the room till you see just where the noise is, and going there put your finger directly on the cause. Say to Mr. A., " Perhaps you are speaking a little louder than you are aware." Say to Mr. B., " Could you not get the boys in your class to answer in a rather lower tone?" Say to Mr. C., " The boys at this end of the bench are taking advantage of your back while you are turned round to talk to those at the other end." Say to the librarian, " Ask your assistants to be a little more quiet in the discharge of their duties." Find some one to take charge of that class which is running riot without a teacher. Go round thus from point to point, where the chief sources of noise exist, and use, in the most noiseless way possible, the means of suppression at your disposal. Remember that, for reducing a noisy school to order, one pair of eyes is worth twenty pair of lungs. If, instead of these quiet means of repression, you go rushing about the room as some superintendents do, bell in hand, rattling, ringing, shouting, stamping, snapping your fingers, pounding the desk, and making all sorts of frantic

gestures, you only make confusion worse confounded. Be quiet if you would have quiet.

4. The superintendent should not be *a great talker.* Frequent harangues from the desk are the bane of a school. Let not the superintendent mistake his function for that of the teacher. From the desk, as from the central spring of motion, he should indeed direct and penetrate all the general movements of the school—the prayer, the singing, the responsive reading, and so forth. But if he cuts short the time of the teachers for the purpose of haranguing the school, whether upon the lesson or upon anything else, he is a trespasser. There are times, indeed, when the superintendent should address the school from the desk. But to do so habitually and as a matter of course, on closing the school, is a grievous mistake. It is unfortunately a mistake made most frequently by those who seem least conscious of their inability to speak profitably to children. They seem to have no faculty of seeing that, while they are talking, not one child in ten is listening to them. When the superintendent has something special to say to the school — which will of course happen occasionally—the very rarity of it will draw attention. And let him know beforehand exactly what he is going to say. The extemporaneous fumbling in which some indulge in presence of a Sunday-school betrays a contempt for the institution which soon recoils on the per petrator.

The school is to be pitied that has a fussy, a fretful, a noisy or a talking superintendent.

4. *Putting Forth a Personal Influence.*

The word personality is commonly used to mean something said or written which refers, especially in a disparaging way, to the conduct or character of another. It is not that kind of personality of which I wish now to speak. What I refer to is that putting forth of direct, personal influence which constitutes in every enterprise one of the great elements of power. It is an indispensable feature in the work of the Sunday-school superintendent.

In the solution of a mathematical problem, or in the investigation of a metaphysical truth, one may be as impersonal as he pleases—the more impersonal and abstract the better. But in the management of affairs where human interests are concerned, and where living souls, with all their varied passions, prejudices, affections and wills are the factors in every problem that comes up for solution, mere reason and logic, separated from all personal considerations and influences, do not go far. The superintendent who wishes to accomplish anything substantial must throw *himself* into the work. It is not in mere rules to govern a school. Government of any kind should indeed act according to rule. But after all there is no vitality in a mere rule. Governing is in its essence a personal matter. Whoever moulds and manages the characters of others, especially in an organization like that of the Sunday-school, must do it, not by a code of rules which in themselves are so much dead paper, but by bringing his personal influence to bear upon the scholars and teachers under his direction.

It is a great mistake in a superintendent to be afraid of showing emotion. It is not in human nature to be greatly influenced by any one unless there is felt to be some bond of sympathy between the parties. The superintendent should be a man of a sympathetic nature, and should not shrink from giving expression to his sympathies. This is the Scripture method. The Bible does not set forth bald truth in syllogisms and logical statements like an algebraic equation, or like the formulas of chemical affinity, but teaches us doctrines and duties in their connections with human interests and passions. " The words of King Lemuel, the prophecy that his *mother* taught him." Here the affection of a loving boy for the mother that bore him is used to give force to the divine precepts. " My son, hear the instruction of thy *father*, and forsake not the law of thy *mother*." " Hear, ye children, the instruction of a *father*, and attend to know understanding. For I was my *father's* son, tender and only beloved in the sight of my *mother*." Thus, everywhere in Scripture, the tenderest and most endearing of earthly relations are appealed to in moving men to receive what is in itself true, or to do what is in itself right. It is even represented as one of the reasons for the incarnation that the Saviour, being himself a man, might be one who could be touched with the feeling of our infirmities—one who could sympathize with us—one to whom we could go in our troubles as we would go to a brother.

A superintendent who would make himself *felt* all through his school must continually put himself forth—not egotistically, not dictatorially, but by a warm, genuine, *manifested* sympathy. There is in the minds of many good men a constitutional shrinking from this process of sending out their feelings toward others. They are afraid of being too demonstrative. This natural timidity is increased by the unfavorable criticisms which they hear in regard to others who make a great show of interest in the work. But I am not advocating sham, or pretence, or a mere show of interest where the reality itself is wanting. If the superintendent has not this real interest in his scholars or his teachers, no make-believe will take its place. Even if he has a genuine feeling of interest in them, yet if his controlling motive in the matter is a love of display or a desire to show himself off, the weakness will make itself seen through all his attempted disguises, and he will not win the confidence and affection which he seeks.

But some superintendents, seeing instances of self-seeking and of pretence of this sort, make the mistake of going into the opposite extreme, and of not showing the love and sympathy which they really feel. When they speak to their school, it is always with a sort of diplomatic reserve. Surely this is not the kind of feeling which ought to exist between a superintendent and his school. The only remedy for a superintendent who feels this embarrassing shyness is to have such a personal interest in every teacher and every scholar that he cannot help showing it. And the true way to awaken this interest is, by continual visitation and inquiry, to make himself personally acquainted with every member of his charge. We cannot feel a personal interest in any one unless we know something about him—who he is, where he is, what are his surroundings, what has been his history.

To obtain this knowledge of all the members of a large school is no light matter. It implies a great deal of labor. One must take many weary walks, and give to the subject many hours of patient, plodding inquiry outside of the time occupied with the sessions of the school. The superintendent needs to have the same thoroughly familiar knowledge of his school that the teacher should have of the lesson, and this knowledge is to be bought by labor only. But once obtained, it is an element of power. It is the only thing that makes real sympathy possible or its manifestation easy and natural.

A superintendent who thus knows personally every member of his school can let his feelings of kindness flow forth toward them intelligently in all the little details of administration without the appearance of affectation, and he will almost certainly find himself doing so without so much as once thinking of it. His mind will be so much occupied with his scholars that he will forget all about himself.

This self-forgetfulness, in the very act of the most intense self-projection, gives to its possessor a sort of magnetic power. It gives him the utmost freedom in throwing his own personal wishes and opinions as a make-weight into the scale in all the number-less decisions which scholars and teachers are called upon to make. It helps them; it is wise and right in him. The superintendent should distinctly aim to put forth this kind of personality—to make him-self personally felt in every class and by every mem-ber of his school.

5. *Knowledge of what is Passing in the School.*

The superintendent ought to know thoroughly what is going on in his school. This is by no means an easy task. He ought to be able to gauge the mental attainments and the capacity of each of the teachers, to know what amount of preparation they make for the weekly lessons, what are their methods of teaching, and what they actually do teach or fail to teach. I once knew a lady who interested very much her class of intelligent girls, but on inquiry it was found that they were being indoctrinated in no-tions about religion and the Bible quite at variance with the standards of the church to which the school belonged. In another instance a class was ap-parently in a very flourishing condition, but the rapt

6

attention of the children, which gave such a pleasing appearance to a visitor or a casual observer, was due to the fact that the romantic young lady who had charge of it merely entertained the children Sunday after Sunday with a succession of captivating stories instead of indoctrinating them in Bible knowledge. Another teacher, a gentleman, who had a flourishing Bible-class for larger boys, kept it full by giving them entertaining bits of history and natural science.

Now it is the business of the superintendent, without playing the spy or the eaves-dropper, yet in some way, to know what his teachers are and what they are doing. It is not in rules to prescribe how this knowledge shall be acquired. No two men will acquire it alike. The man must cultivate a talent for observation. An eminent dry goods merchant of Philadelphia some years ago constructed a store with special reference to his idea of superintendence. His own private office was perched up midway between the upper and the lower floors, and every desk and counter in the establishment was so arranged as to come within the range of vision from this unseen observatory. There, spider-like, sitting at the centre of his web, he could look out upon every boy and girl and man and customer in the vast establishment without once showing himself. It was a mechanically perfect system of espionage. For my own part, after being made acquainted with this arrangement, I never entered the store without a feeling of degradation. I am very certain the system must have defeated itself by its debasing effects upon the minds of the employés. It begot eye-service instead of open-handed honesty. There is another large trading establishment with which I have been for many years familiar, in which no such mean and offensive tricks are resorted to, and yet it is evident that the gentlemanly proprietor, as he passes in and out through the various departments of his little kingdom, is thoroughly acquainted with the personal peculiarities and the modes of business of every employé.

The Sunday-school superintendent, of all men, must not play the spy upon his fellow-laborers. And yet, if he is to do his own work intelligently and well, he must know what they are doing and what they can do. He must have a similar knowledge in regard to the affairs of the librarian and the library. He must know as much as practicable of each scholar. I put in a qualification here, because in a large school it is hardly possible for a superintendent to be thoroughly acquainted with each scholar; yet the nearer he can approach this knowledge the better. A superintendent's power in the school is increased in proportion to the fulness of this personal knowledge. It would be well if he knew familiarly the name, residence and domestic circumstances of every scholar, as well as of every teacher. Many of the sad mistakes which mar his work would be avoided if through visitation in the different homes he acquired this knowledge.

6. *Knowledge of the Lesson.*

The superintendent must know thoroughly the lesson. I say "*the*" lesson, because I have in mind those schools which have a uniform lesson for the whole school. Whether there is or is not a teachers' meeting, in which the common lesson is studied and reviewed under the supervision of the superintendent, he ought in any case to prepare himself on the lesson for the week even more laboriously and minutely than those who have the direct charge of classes. The fact that the superintendent is thoroughly familiar with every minute point of the lesson exerts insensibly a wholesome influence on both scholars and teachers. Neither teachers nor scholars are ambitious of exposing their ignorance in the presence of one whose quick ear is sure to notice the least mistake, even though he may never mention it. Besides, the superintendent will be often appealed to for information upon different points in the lesson, and he ought to be able to resolve at once every such difficulty brought to him.

Moreover, though the superintendent should be sparing of his talk, as before intimated, yet occasionally at least, in closing the school, he may find it important to address the school upon something connected with the lesson, and nothing but an entire familiarity with the lesson will enable him to do so with the proper effect. Nothing is easier than for a superintendent to weaken his authority with both scholars and teachers by unpremeditated, injudicious talk from the desk.

KNOWLEDGE, then, is of transcendent importance to the superintendent—a knowledge of the lesson and a knowledge of his school—not vague, dreamy ideas, but specific, certain, direct knowledge—such knowledge as comes only from hard work, but always brings with it power.

In the various essays which I have read about the office of Sunday-school superintendent, it has always seemed to me that there was a good deal of waste of words. Talents of various kinds are enumerated, the necessity of which no one would question. The only difficulty is to find the man who possesses them. We must take for our superintendent the best man we can get in the congregation. If there are certain natural gifts which he lacks, we cannot clothe him with them by merely prescribing them as among the qualifications for the office. But there are requisites for the office which are within the reach of every man who will take the necessary pains, and these requisites we cannot insist on too much. Not every man has a pleasant voice or a winning address; not every man is gifted by nature with what we call tact. It is not in books, or essays, or convention resolutions to give these qualities to those from whom nature has withheld them. But every superintendent who wishes it, and who will take the necessary pains, may have that *knowledge* of his scholars and of what they are studying, of which I have been speaking.

6 *   E

The proper amount of labor will ensure him this great desideratum. It may cost one more labor than it costs another; but the knowledge will come if he will only pay the price, and it will assuredly make him potential in the management of his school. Instead of sighing vainly for things beyond his reach, let him set himself diligently to work at this which he can compass.

7. *Bestowing Attention upon All.*

Another point equally unambitious and unpretending, yet equally within the reach of honest endeavor, is to give every scholar and teacher, and to every part of the working of the school, some fair amount of attention. The work of the superintendent should be much more a work of detail than many persons imagine. It does not consist in making now and then a grand splurge, but in incessant and almost omnipresent labor—doing a little here and a little there, going round to all parts of the machinery, like the engineer with his oil-can, lubricating this joint, putting the screw on that, and seeing that every part is in good working order. Some men, of course, have a more natural aptitude for this kind of work than others have. But it is obvious that every one may fulfil this condition of the office who will take the necessary pains. Any superintendent who has fulfilled the preceding conditions—who knows every class, every teacher, every scholar, every part of the lesson, every book in the library—

can know perfectly well whether there is any class, scholar, teacher, or other part of his little kingdom to which he is not giving attention and help, and by increasing sufficiently his labor and activity he can supply the defect. He cannot, perhaps, be any more eloquent or persuasive as a speaker; he cannot command the dexterity and the winning address of some; but he can attend to the wants of Richard as well as to those of William; he can see that the children in that obscure corner of the room are cared for as well as those in a more conspicuous position; he can see that the librarians are doing their work without interfering with the work of the teachers; he can find some one to look after that sick child who is kept from school from illness, or that bad child who is playing truant. The superintendent, in short, if he will, may make himself pervasive — reaching and touching every part of the complicated machinery under his control — and it is this faithful, humble work of omnipresent detail, rather than shining and conspicuous gifts, which brings out great results in the end.

8. *Having Sympathy with All.*

Still another point, not requiring special natural endowments, but coming within the reach of every superintendent who is willing to pay the price, is that he have an active sympathy with every member of his school, whether teacher or scholar, entering with feeling into their joys and sorrows, their successes and their disappointments. Here, again, men differ in the facility with which they enter into the feelings of others. It is for some a very hard work to become sharers in the experiences of another. But there is no man who cannot feel this active sympathy if he will, and every time he allows his sympathies to be thus exercised, the exercise of them will become easier, until finally they will flow forth spontaneously and readily on every appropriate occasion. I am disposed to emphasize this point, because I am persuaded that it is a good deal overlooked and underrated. It makes a great difference in the success of a child in school, especially if it be one who, from ignorance, humbleness of position, or infirmity of any kind, naturally needs help and support, that such child in its troubles should feel sure of a ready sympathy from the superintendent. A man having a large-hearted and ready sympathy has in that very thing a mighty source of power. A man who has learned not officiously to meddle, but truly to sympathize with all those under his control, has therein one of the very best means of exercising that control. Here, too, as in the previous cases, it is a work of almost infinite detail. It is not by making a gushing speech on some grand occasion that the superintendent is to gain supreme ascendency over the hearts of his scholars, but by bestowing his sympathies as the occasions require, all the time, and on all alike.

No man can reach the full measure of success as a superintendent who does not make every scholar and every teacher feel that he or she is individually known by him, and has in him a ready sympathizer and friend; and no man need fail in producing this impression who is willing to give the necessary price.

9. *Classifying the School.*

Next to keeping order, the superintendent has no duty more urgent or imperative than that of making a proper classification of his scholars. The duty is not without its difficulties. Superintendents often enter upon their work with vague ideas of what they have to do. They have never distinctly settled in their own minds on what principles the classification should be made, if indeed they have fully settled the question that they have a positive and distinct duty at all in regard to it. So when the moment of action comes they hesitate and are at a loss, and let matters drift without any settled order. Some enterprising teacher has been missionating during the week, and has succeeded in bringing several new pupils into the school. Being the fruits of her own labor, she naturally wants to have them in her class, and they themselves, knowing perhaps no one in the school but her, and feeling timid and shy, wish to be with her. Perhaps they even stipulate this as the condition of remaining in school at all. Or perhaps the new-comers have been led into the school by some of the other scholars with whom they are acquainted, and they want to sit with their friends. Or there is some particular teacher in school of whom they have

heard, and they have come to join his or her class.
More frequently they have their dislikes, and they
are unwilling to sit with a certain pupil or in a certain class, or to be instructed by this or that teacher.
Or they are large and overgrown, and they claim to
be put in the Bible-class, no matter how deficient
they may be in knowledge. These are some of the
difficulties which the superintendent has to meet in
disposing of new scholars. In the case of pupils
already in the school who are found to have been im-
properly classified, the difficulty of a rectification is
greatly increased. Nowhere do children form such
tenacious attachments as in their Sunday-school
class. There is sure to be a scene whenever the
superintendent undertakes to remove a pupil from
one class to another, and not unfrequently the pupil
leaves school in consequence. Children have been
placed together because perhaps they happen to be
acquainted out of school, or because they are of
about the same age or size, and having formed a
part of the same magic little circle for a considerable
length of time, they cannot bear to be torn from it.

The superintendent who forms to himself a distinct plan for classifying his scholars, and who undertakes to carry it out by removing pupils who are out
of place to the classes to which of right they ought
to belong, and who exercises the same judgment and
prerogative in assigning new scholars to their appropriate classes, must expect to give dissatisfaction in
many quarters. He need not be surprised if some

of his scholars are so much offended as to leave him. Even at such a cost it is better to go forward. Should the school be permanently diminished in numbers in consequence of his insisting upon a proper classification, the evil would be more than counterbalanced by the improved condition of those that remain. More good can be accomplished in a school of one hundred pupils well classified than in a school of one hundred and fifty pupils thrown together promiscuously. But there is no danger of a school's declining in numbers in consequence of its being carefully and judiciously classified. For every pupil or teacher that leaves in pique on this account, two or three others will be added on account of the improved tone of the school which will result.

The points to be considered in classification are age, size, social condition, intellectual progress, and individual peculiarities. Let me say a few words in regard to each of these.

1. *Age.* The superintendent would of course be unwise who should be governed by age alone in making up his classes ; who should put all his nine-year olds into one fold, all his ten-year olds into another, and so on. Yet there is an extreme at the other end which needs equally to be avoided. Very often adults come into our Sunday-schools—grown-up men and women—who can scarcely read, if even they can read at all, who are not more advanced in their studies than are the classes just above the infant-school. Surely it would not be wise to put such

adults in with children eight or ten years old. The arrangement would be uncomfortable and unprofitable all round. Some regard must be had to the age of the scholar in assigning him to a place in the school. Other things being equal, scholars get along better together who are of nearly equal age. Some concessions, therefore, must be made on this point. If a scholar is not quite equal in attainments to the class in which you put him, it is yet worthy of consideration whether, on the whole, he will not do better there than he would among scholars much younger than himself. In a large school, also, it often happens that there are adults enough to form several classes, and in such a case the superintendent may have the means of forming an adult class, all of whom are deficient in book knowledge. Such opportunities should be eagerly embraced. The institution is never doing a more legitimate or a more hopeful work than when it numbers in its ranks entire classes of adults who can barely read, or even who cannot read at all.

2. *Size.* Some superintendents will smile and shake their heads when size is mentioned among the things to be considered in making a classification. Yet it is a point which cannot be disregarded entirely. It has to be put very much on the same footing as age. A great, overgrown bumpkin often does not know enough to keep up with the scholars of his own size, and yet he feels extremely uncomfortable if put among the little fellows who are his

equals in knowledge, and this feeling of discomfort and mortification, if not watched, will drive him from the school. If the superintendent has several scholars of the sort now described, he can form a class of them, and thus dispose of the difficulty. When, however, this is impracticable, the best way is to take a medium course. Put the scholar in a class about halfway between that suggested by his size and that suggested by his attainments. Though he will not profit there as much as he would in a class lower down, yet he may gain something, and the arrangement may be the means of preventing his leaving school altogether. If indeed such an over-grown scholar is entirely willing to go among the little fellows, the superintendent will of course so place him. It is best for the superintendent in such cases to be entirely candid. Say to the youth frankly, You could get along better in this class (pointing it out), and I would advise you for your own good to enter it. But perhaps you may feel uncomfortable among scholars so much smaller than yourself. I can, if you desire it, put you into such a class (pointing to one consisting of scholars rather larger), but you will find it a good deal more diffi-cult to keep up with them in their lessons, and per-haps not be as pleasantly situated as you would be among the smaller scholars. I will leave it to your-self to decide.

Not unfrequently, when the matter is presented in this way, the scholar will acquiesce in your views;

7

and when he does not, he is sure to be pleased with the evident consideration with which you have treated him.

3. *Social Condition.* The superintendent here is treading upon dangerous ground, and many well-meaning people cry out against all attempts in the Sunday-school to recognize in any way the condition of the scholar outside of the school. Here, if any-where, it is said, rich and poor should meet together, and any classification based upon social condition is unchristian and wicked. With due deference I would say, this kind of talk is mere idle clamor. The superintendent should not be frightened by shadows, no matter by whom conjured up. If the school is small, as in most country schools, intel-lectual attainments must be almost the only thing to be taken into account in making up a class. But in a large city school there may be forty or fifty, or per-haps a hundred, scholars about equal as to attain-ments, age and size. Surely in grouping such a number into classes the superintendent would be unwise who should not consider whether there were not other elements in the problem which would naturally draw some together and drive others apart. It is not a question of whether some are better than others or more worthy of consideration. In this respect they are all equal before the eyes of the super-intendent. The question is, What grouping of the scholars will most conduce to harmony, efficiency and comfort all round? Which arrangement will

produce least constraint and embarrassment? The child of the poor washerwoman who lives in some obscure court or alley is just as precious in the sight of the Master as the child of wealth who lives on Fifth Avenue. But the poor child has not the same opportunities of books and leisure as the other. The temptations of the one are different from those of the other. The entire current of their ideas is different. They do not feel at home with each other. The children of the poor particularly feel disobliged by being compelled to go into a class with children with whom they do not mix out of school, and not unfrequently this unnatural mode of classification drives away the poorer class of children from the school. I cannot doubt, therefore, that, other things being equal, and the number of scholars being sufficiently large to admit of it, some regard should be paid to the social condition of the scholars in assigning them to classes. Those scholars go best together in school who go most together out of school.

4. *Intellectual Progress.* It is not necessary to argue the importance of this point. All superintendents and teachers agree in this. Scholars do best together in Bible study who are about on a par with each other in their other studies. The superintendent, therefore, on receiving a scholar and canvassing the question as to which class to assign him, should always take into account the progress which the scholar has already made in other studies, so as to put him as nearly as may be with his equals in

this respect. The error of some superintendents is that they consider this point only, and make no allowance for the others which have been named.

5. *Individual Peculiarities.* Some scholars have peculiarities of temper or of manners or of mental action which require peculiar treatment, and these peculiarities have to be considered in determining their classification. Some scholars are full of life, with a natural buoyancy of disposition and a tendency to fun. They bubble over on the least occasion. If two or three such happen to be in the same class, they, without any bad intention, upset all order and study. The superintendent therefore may find it wise to separate them. So with other peculiarities. They cannot, indeed, have a controlling influence in the general arrangements of the school, but neither can they be entirely ignored by one who wants to get along comfortably.

The work of classification is to be performed chiefly in the act of admitting new scholars. Occasionally the superintendent may exercise his prerogative in this respect by transferring pupils from the class in which they now are to other classes for which they are better fitted. But this almost always produces friction, and it should be done, when done at all, with extreme caution, and after full consultation with the teachers concerned. But when a new scholar is introduced into the school, whether brought in by a teacher or by a scholar, or coming of his own accord, the invariable and inexorable rule should be that the scholar should be brought first of all to the superintendent before being taken to any class. If teachers or scholars bring in a new recruit, let them exercise entire freedom in expressing to the superintendent what they know in regard to the condition and character of the new scholar, and in expressing also their views in regard to the class to which he should be assigned. But at the same time let it be understood that in this matter the superintendent must be supreme.

The superintendent should have a bench or form in some convenient part of the room for the reception of new scholars. To this seat all new-comers should be conducted, and there they should remain until the superintendent is at leisure to dispose of them. He should, on receiving new scholars, inquire of them with much particularity their name, age, residence (street and number), and all the other items of information needed in guiding him in the classification, and these items should be entered by him in a book. Some superintendents, particularly where the school is large. leave it to the secretary to make these inquiries. But the little conversation with a child needed for eliciting these particulars gives the superintendent the opportunity of forming some opinion in regard to him. It is a kind of informal examination which cannot well be done by proxy. The superintendent needs for his guidance just the information and the impression which this personal interview gives. Let the secretary transfer to his permanent record these items, so far as needed, from the superintendent's note-book, but let the original inquiries and notices be made in all cases by the superintendent himself. It is an important and intransferable part of his personal duties.

No function of the superintendent requires for its exercise more sound judgment, good temper, and nerve than this duty of classifying his scholars. It will not do to adopt an iron rule in the matter, and follow out a theory regardless of consequences. The Sunday-school work is altogether a voluntary work, and a spirit of conciliation must be exercised. Large concessions must be made to prejudice, and sometimes even to whim and caprice. But by persistent resolution in a conciliatory spirit, and by knowing exactly when it is expedient to resist and when to give way, the superintendent will in the end carry his point, and will have his reward in seeing the school achieve results entirely unattainable on any other basis. A good classification will cost some tears, perhaps some heartburnings, and it undoubtedly requires some nerve. But it pays.

10. *Maintaining Order.*

Good order in a large Sunday-school is confessedly a difficult achievement. It is more difficult to maintain order in the Sunday-school than in the secular school. In the latter the teacher is vested with more official authority, and may enforce obedience if necessary by punishment and by other means of discipline that cannot be used in the Sunday-school. Attendance in the latter being voluntary, a child, if obliged to submit against its will, may leave the school altogether. The difficulties inherent in the case are aggravated by others not necessarily belonging to it, though actually existing in ninety-nine cases out of a hundred. Among these may be mentioned the fact that a large part of the teachers are young and inexperienced, without practiced skill either in teaching or governing. Another source of difficulty arises from the fact that usually a large number of classes are reciting at the same time in the same room. Still another difficulty is that the classes come together but once a week, and then only for a single, short session. In the daily school the teacher, by continuing the pressure day after day, has a better opportunity of confirming his authority. But in the Sunday-school, what is gained one Sunday is in danger of being lost in the six days intervening. Altogether, it is no easy matter to maintain order and quiet among two or three hundred children, or even among a hundred children, organized in a Sunday-school.

The business of maintaining order in a Sunday-school, as in every other school, belongs partly to the superintendent or principal and partly to the teachers. Neither of these parties can fully succeed in this point without the efficient and wise co-operation of the other. The duties of the two, however, though thus conjoined, are yet in their own nature

distinct and different. What the teacher has to do
in the maintenance of order is not only something to
be done by himself and by nobody else, but also
something different in kind from that to be done by
any one else. Of the teacher's duty in the matter of
order I shall have occasion to speak hereafter. My
remarks at the present time will be confined to the
duty of the superintendent in this respect.

Before proceeding to these remarks, however, it is
best to have some distinct understanding as to what
school order is and what it includes. Order in Sunday-school consists chiefly of these three points:
doing things quietly, doing things at the right time,
keeping both persons and things in their right place.
Disorder, accordingly, consists in being noisy, out of
time, out of place. This classification of course is not
exhaustive. Yet any one who will take the trouble
to consider will find that at least nine-tenths of what
may be termed disorder in school may be reduced
under these three heads. A few words upon each.

1. *Doing things Quietly.* Some noise is to be
expected in the Sunday-school—more, a good deal,
than in other schools; and this not only because the
reins of discipline cannot be drawn so tightly as in
other schools, but also and mainly because there are
so many classes in the same room reciting at the
same time. Twenty or thirty or fifty classes all reciting at once in the same room must needs make
some noise. The effort of teachers and of superintendent should be, not to suppress this noise, which

would be as undesirable as it is impracticable, but to keep it in check. Scholars and teachers should be trained to conduct their recitations in a subdued and quiet tone, just sufficiently above a whisper to make what is said distinctly audible in the class without being heard by those in the adjoining classes. Whenever the teacher or the scholars of one class raise their voices so as to be distinctly overheard outside of the class, they are becoming noisy, and need to be reminded of the error.

But there are other sources of noise besides that arising from recitation. The movements of the librarians and of the secretary often produce unnecessary noise. Scholars are noisy in coming in and going out. Chairs and benches are upset through carelessness; the doors fly to with a bang. The superintendent himself oftentimes is noisy—talking in a loud tone to those around him, moving about the room with a heavy tread, worrying scholars and teachers with the everlasting tinkling of the bell, or, worse still, shouting aloud for silence, as if the only way to stop a noise was to drown it by making a greater noise. The superintendent who would have a quiet school must first of all learn to be quiet himself.

A superintendent who is good for anything seldom sits at his desk. His place is on his feet; he should be moving continually about the room, and nothing is beneath his regard which can help him in reducing the amount of noise which his movements may produce. He should learn to set his foot down

F

lightly and to see that no " squeak-leather" is put into his boots. If he finds the classes becoming noisy, the way to stop the noise is, first to listen, that he may know exactly where repression is most needed, and then to go to the spot as quietly as possible and notify the teacher. A teacher and a class who are very earnestly engaged in the discussion of a lesson often forget themselves and make an undue noise without being aware of it. The superintendent, from the very fact of his general oversight of the room, is in the position to know when the noise in any quarter is becoming excessive.

Nine-tenths of the superintendent's time in school should be spent in thus passing round quietly from class to class, using his eyes more than his tongue, but ever ready to put in just the right word at the right moment, preventing disorder by removing its causes and nipping it in the bud before it becomes general. The superintendent should never scold. The moment he does so he begins to lose the respect of the scholars and his power over them. He should never show vexation, even if he cannot always help feeling it. Children do many things merely for the pleasure of seeing the irritation they produce. They love to tease you just as they love to tease a wasp. If no irritation is produced, there is no fun in it and they stop.

Scholars also are prone to engage in what is called " cutting up," which creates distraction if not noise. It is the business of the superintendent to keep his

eyes open for anything of this kind, and to arrest it
by the same process by which he arrests noise. Let
him, without attracting unnecessary observation, go
directly to the place where the disorder exists, and
there do whatever is needed with the least possible
noise or fuss. Whether he reprimands a scholar or
asks the teacher to do it, let him speak in a whisper.
The very worst way for a superintendent to suppress
disorder of any kind is for him to stand at his desk
and shout or ring his bell. There is but one use for
the bell in the school-room, namely, to give notice
of the general movements of the school—to notify
when lessons begin, when they stop, when school is
to be closed, and so forth. *It should never be used
for arresting noise and disorder.* To use the bell
for this purpose is a most pitiable and humiliating
confession of weakness on the part of the superintendent.

2. *Doing Things at the Right Time.* The
superintendent should make out an exact programme
of what is to be done in school, and of the time to
be allotted to each, and should keep the school up to
time with the same strictness with which a railroad
engineer moves his train from station to station.
The time for opening and for closing should be as
definite and certain as that for the departure of a
railroad train. There should be a certain time during the session for giving out notices, for taking up
and giving out library books, for distributing papers,
for making collections, for making reports of classes,

and these things should be done only at the time appointed in the programme. All this is a matter of order, and lies exclusively within the province of the superintendent. It requires on his part forethought, method, and decision. If an item of business of any kind has been forgotten at the right time, it is better generally to omit it entirely than to interpolate it out of its place.

In making the programme two points should be kept firmly in mind, namely, so to order the business of the school as first to secure for the devotional part of the service entire freedom from interruption of every sort, and secondly to secure a good, solid, unbroken period of time for the instruction of the classes by the teachers. Nothing short of the house being on fire, or the roof falling in, should interfere with this time. No speech-making, no ringing the bell to give a notice, no running about of the secretary or of the librarian for reports or books, no introduction of distinguished visitors. From the time when the bell notifies the teachers to begin their lesson to the time when the same bell notifies them to stop the lesson, interruption of any kind is as much an impertinence as it would be for a like reason to interrupt the minister in the course of his sermon. The time proper for the lesson is in fact about as long as that ordinarily occupied by a sermon, and it should be held just as sacred and as free from intrusion.

3. *Keeping Things and Persons in Place.* When

a child goes to school for the first time in his life, the first thing he has to learn usually is the necessity of remaining in his seat. Until distinctly told and trained otherwise, he will very likely move about from one part of the room to another just as he has been in the habit of doing at home. The necessity of sitting still must be drilled into him. Of course I do not mean that children should be immovable like so many statues. A little restlessness and twisting about and fidgeting is to be expected. The teacher is simply cruel who undertakes to stop it. What is meant by sitting still is the remaining in the same seat. A scholar should not be allowed to change his seat in the class, much less to go from one class to another, without the teacher's permission, and this latter only for the most urgent reasons.

Should a scholar in any case be allowed to go out into the yard during the session of the school? Perhaps it would not do to forbid such a thing absolutely, yet the prohibition should be as nearly absolute as may be. The Sunday-school lasts just about as long as the church service, and children are not allowed to go out of church during the service; why should it be necessary during the time of school? If the permission to go out is granted, only one should go at a time, and the permission should be hedged in with so many difficulties and formalities that it would be seldom sought. Perhaps the safest check would be to let no one go out except on a written

8

application from the teacher to the superintendent. If any one thinks some such stringent check is not needed, let him pass through the yard of almost any Sunday-school during the time of the session, and he will find that I am speaking not without cause.

But scholars are not the only ones requiring to be kept in place. Teachers sometimes commit the very great impropriety of leaving school during the session, or getting up from their classes to converse with other teachers, or with visitors, or going to the library. Surely such movements are an irregularity and a disorder, and require the interposition of the superintendent.

The superintendent should in this matter look to *things* as well as to persons. By things I mean whatever in the school-room is of a movable character—the benches, the chairs, the desks, the books, the wall maps, the ornaments. Any confusion in these things has a tendency to produce confusion of mind in scholars and teachers. On the contrary, there is a certain comely and even pictorial arrangement of the furniture and apparatus of a school-room which has a corresponding and unconscious moral effect upon the minds of the scholars and teachers. The superintendent is not indeed to be the janitor or housekeeper, but he should have an eye to these things, and see that no confusion or disorder prevails in the arrangement of even the furniture of the school-room.

11. *Exercising Government.*

A Sunday-school does not cease to be a school because it is an organization for religious purposes. Its prime function is that of teaching, and one of its necessary conditions is that of subordination and obedience, exactly as in every other school. There may be cases in certain bad neighborhoods where the best that can be done is to collect the children in a crowd and harangue them in a style suited to their rude natures, just as the politicians harangue a crowd of roughs at a mass meeting. We have children in our cities who can at first be reached in no other way, and we have men peculiarly fitted for this rough work; a good and important work it is too. But it should be clearly understood that such gatherings are not schools. A school necessarily implies subordination and government. The two correlated ideas of obedience on the one side and authority on the other lie at the basis of the whole superstructure, and these two ideas imply in turn some kind of sanction by which in the last resort this obedience may be secured and this authority asserted. There must be, even in Sunday-school, some *ultima ratio*, some final appeal, which shall be competent to enforce its own laws. Just so far as this power is wanting the school loses its living principle as an organization, and tends toward a mere disorderly mass meeting.

The fact that such a power exists and that a knowledge of its existence is clearly present to the minds

of scholars and teachers makes an appeal to it a rare
and exceptional occurrence. Indeed, it is a maxim
in all wise government that the penalty of the last
resort should be used with the greatest rarity, and
only in the most extreme cases, and that there should
be as many intermediate steps as possible between
the first slight check of a gentle admonition and the
full, final blow. But in order that these intermediate
and gradually increasing steps may be of any avail
as a check upon the thoughtless or the disorderly,
that these steps may be effectual in preventing the
necessity of appealing to that last resort, scholars
must feel that there is such a resort and that it is
fully adequate to the end. Just in proportion to the
clearness of this conviction will be the efficiency of
the lighter and more gentle class of restraints. Love
and tenderness and persuasive admonition have a
tenfold power when coupled with a wholesome fear.
Let a rude boy know that you have no means in the
last resort for enforcing respect and obedience, and
your kind words will be accepted by him as only so
many acknowledgments of weakness on your part.
On the other hand, a conviction in his mind that you
have all needful power at your disposal makes him
feel that you speak kindly to him because you feel
kindly—that your manner is not put on to coax and
wheedle him, but wells up naturally and instinctively
from a loving and sympathizing heart.

While insisting thus upon the necessity of power
as the true basis of all government, let us be careful

not to run into the extreme of making a constant show of authority. This needless flaunting of one's authority into the face of a scholar, like the thrusting of the crimson banner before the eyes of the enraged animal in the bull-fights of Spain, only provokes resistance. The human heart naturally rebels against whatever has the air of mere assumption, the needless and unprovoked show of power, as it naturally acquiesces and stands in awe of a power that is held in reserve. There should be in human government, as there is in God's, a wise " hiding of his power" (Hab. iii. 4) ; not an absolute concealment, but just sufficient intimation of its existence to let us know that it is there, and that it is there in ample measure, yet keeping a wise reserve in regard to the exact mode of its operation. Nothing so strikes awe into the heart as this calm, confident, mysterious " hiding of power." When the Duke of Wellington was at the head of affairs in England, there was at one time a violent insurrectionary spirit among the lower classes in London, and organized resistance to the government was threatened. The duke brought the troops into the city, and it was well known that he had given them orders, in case the final use of force should be necessary, to use the bayonet and solid shot, instead of blank cartridges. At the same time these troops were kept studiously out of sight, being drawn up behind blank walls, but ready to issue forth at a moment's notice. Not a soldier was to be seen, but every malcontent in that heated million

8 *

knew that the mysterious thunderbolt was there. Its
power was magnified ten-fold to their excited imag-
inations by this very concealment, and in less than
twenty-four hours their courage had so oozed out
that those hundreds of thousands of strong men were
quietly dispersed by a few resolute policemen.

But what is the power of final resort in the Sunday-school—the *ultima ratio* of the superintendent?

Here, it must be confessed, is the weak point in
our system. The ordinary methods of restraint and
correction used in other schools are necessarily excluded from the Sunday-school. The rod is out of
the question. We cannot " keep in" after school.
The one solitary punishment in the last resort is expulsion, and the scholar who merits expulsion is for
that very reason the one who most needs the benefits of the school. The Sunday-school teacher is a
missionary, and, like his great Exemplar, his errand
is not to the whole, but to the sick ; not to the right-
eous, but to sinners. He goes to seek the erring, to
save the lost. The child hardened in sin, with no
home influences to help him, the young outcast and
thief who has never known the restraints of parental
authority and who will not submit to yours, is just
the one of all others whose condition appeals most
strongly to your sympathy, who most needs your
help. It is so difficult to induce these young outlaws
who infest our streets and alleys to come to the Sunday-school at all, and we are so glad when we can
in any way succeed in bringing them in, that we

must needs pause before turning them out. Expulsion in such a case is virtually giving the child over to the unchecked dominion of the devil.

What shall the superintendent do?

Dreadful as the result may be to the individual scholar, yet when all other means have been tried and have failed, and when the example of the scholar is producing in the minds of others a defiant disposition which it is found impossible otherwise to quell, the superintendent is bound, in faithfulness to the general interests of the school, to remove a contumacious and persistently disobedient scholar. One such act of exclusion, if rightly performed, without heat and after full deliberation, will so improve the tone of a school as to induce others to attend. One expulsion sometimes brings in ten new scholars. Children love an orderly school. It draws them with a sort of fascination. Even the disorderly and the lawless like to see order. It pleases their natural sense of what is beautiful and harmonious. Hence it is always easy to replenish the ranks of a school where order reigns supreme. The better the state of discipline in a school, and the higher its general tone in regard to duty and order, the more dreadful will the sentence of banishment seem to the scholars. Expulsion from a disorderly school is no great terror to the unruly scholar. In most cases he would rather be turned out than not. It is part of the fun.

Expulsion is not a thing which should be done

publicly, with a pompous announcement from the
desk and an attempt at dramatic effect. Such a
course only gets up a scene and makes a hero of the
offender. When the superintendent finds such an
act of discipline necessary, the best way of proceeding is to visit the scholar privately at his home, and
there, without the presence and sympathy of his
companions, tell him that it has been found necessary to request him to discontinue his attendance.
Such an announcement will sometimes so work
upon the mind of the culprit as to change his whole
bearing and make it entirely proper to restore him
to his position. Even where this does not occur, a
good effect is produced upon the other scholars.
The cause of the non-appearance of the dismissed
scholar is sure to leak out. Some who are determined at all hazards to be disorderly will quietly
withdraw, and the others will be penetrated with a
wholesome and restraining fear. The writer, in the
course of a large experience in Sunday-schools, both
as a teacher and a superintendent, has been obliged
once, and only once, to proceed to this last resort.
The effect in that case was happy in the extreme.
It settled at once and for ever the question of authority in the minds of the scholars, and enabled both
him and his teachers to use with proper effect the
genial influences of love and kindness. It sobered
finally even the boy himself; not at once, for he continued for some months rebellious and defiant; but
in the end he came seriously to reflect upon his evil

course, and he then re-entered the school " clothed
and in his right mind."

12. *Making a Programme.*

One of the most important and responsible duties
of the superintendent is that of making a programme.
No one of his duties requires the exercise of a sounder judgment, no one affects a greater number of interests of the school. The making of the programme
is only another word for disposing of the entire time
of every scholar and every teacher during the whole
session, and that not for one Sunday merely, but for
a whole season, or as long as the programme continues in effect. Any error in judgment, therefore,
in making a programme is far-reaching in its consequences. On the other hand, however, almost any
kind of programme is better than none. Those superintendents who conduct the exercises of a school
in a loose, unpremeditated way, without any settled
order of business, have no idea what a waste of time
and of moral force is involved in their hap-hazard
proceedings. This is particularly the case with
" talking" superintendents. Half the time of the
school is wasted by their unpremeditated and profitless harangues.

The programme should be reduced to writing, and
a copy of it should be posted in some conspicuous
place where every teacher and officer of the school
can consult it. If the school is a large one, it is well
to have the programme printed, so that every teacher

may have a copy. The programme is to the school
what the time-table of a railroad is to a train,
and the superintendent, like the engineer, should
move exactly on time. The efficiency and comfort
of all his fellow-laborers depend upon his conform-
ing strictly to his own orders. The teachers, librarians, secretary, and others make their calculations
as to the time for completing their work, and the
superintendent has no right to break in upon the settled order of business for the purpose of indulging
in any sudden fancy or caprice. Extreme cases may
arise, of course, in which the superintendent is justi-
fied in interrupting the regular business of the school.
But in all ordinary cases the programme, once settled, should be supreme, and the superintendent
should not deviate from it for even a single minute.

How shall the time of the school session be divided?
What portion shall be assigned to each exercise?

Nothing so surely tests one's idea of what the
school is as this apportionment of its time. The
" talking" superintendent will naturally make ample
provision for his harangues. The " singing" superintendent will be equally liberal to the music. The
writer of the present paragraph confesses to a feeling of jealousy for the rights of the teacher. Let us
remember that the institution is not a prayer-meeting
or a debating society, but a school, and its principal
function is that of teaching. The time to be assigned
to the teacher, therefore, is the first and main consideration, and it should be religiously guarded.

Some time must be allowed of course for other things, but let not the teacher's time be sacrificed to those things which at the best are only auxiliary.

But to come to a practical point: What proportion of the whole time of the session should be given up to the exclusive possession of the teacher? I answer: If the session is for an hour and a half, give the teacher about an hour; if the session is only an hour, give the teacher about three-fourths of it. In other words, give to the teacher from two-thirds to three-fourths of the whole time, according to the length of the session. When the sessions are of the length usual in most of our schools, that is, an hour and a half, we can afford to be comparatively liberal toward the various incidental operations. But where the entire session is crowded into one hour, as it sometimes is, the superintendent must be sparing to the extent of meanness toward everything except the actual teaching time.

Next to the teaching time—next, I mean, in amount—is that which should be allowed for devotional exercises. A safe rule here is to divide into two nearly equal parts the time that remains after providing for the teaching, and to give one of these parts to the devotional exercises and the other part to all other operations.

Under devotional exercises I include: 1. The reading or reciting of portions of Scripture and perhaps also of some formula of doctrine, such as the Apostles' Creed; 2. Singing; 3. Prayer. These devotional exercises should be all together, either at the opening or at the closing of the school, and not divided, as they sometimes are, part at the beginning and part at the end. My own preference is to have the devotions at the opening. There is no need, as there is no time, for two prayers, one at the opening and one at the close, or for two singings. The scholars and teachers come together, not for a singing-school, not for a prayer-meeting, but to study God's word. All the singing, the praying, the public reading or recitation of Scripture should be closely knit together as one compacted, impressive act of solemn worship, by way of special preparation for the main work of the hour. This devotional exercise should in no case exceed fifteen minutes. It may include sufficient variety and be brought within ten minutes. In my own school the service includes: 1. The Commandments, recited in concert by the whole school; 2. Singing (two or three verses of a hymn); 3. The Apostles' Creed, recited in concert by the whole school; 4. The Gloria Patri, sung by the whole school; 5. The Scriptures (twelve to fifteen verses), read by the superintendent; 6. The Lord's Prayer, by the whole school; 7. Prayer by the superintendent. No part of the service is hurried; every portion is conducted with seriousness and deliberation; and yet the whole occupies just twelve minutes.

What time remains, after providing for the teaching and the devotional service, belongs to the superintendent for addresses, notices and other general business.

No time is here allowed for assembling. Scholars and teachers should expect to assemble and to be in their places before the time for opening. When the hour for opening has arrived the doors should be closed and locked, and remain so until the devotional service is over. Any, whether scholars, teachers, or visitors, who are late, should remain outside until the doors are reopened. By following this rule the superintendent is enabled to begin the service at once, without the loss of more than a minute. Some superintendents who follow this plan pause after closing the doors to call the roll of the teachers. But this consumes time, besides being irritating, and the end can be gained without either of these results. The secretary, without calling the roll, can notice by mere inspection the teachers who are present, and the fact that they are thus noticed and registered will have all the effect desired.

No time is allowed for the work of the librarian. All his work can be done without consuming the time of the school, as I shall show farther on.

No time is allowed for missionary collections. The collection should be made in each class by the teacher and enclosed in an envelope, with the amount and the name of the class on the outside, according to a form prescribed by the superintendent, so that all the secretary would have to do would be to go round and collect the envelopes, without interrupting any one, and without consuming any of the time of the school.

No time is allowed for notices. These the superintendent must give in the time assigned him for addressing the school.

Five minutes should be allowed for dismission, and this will have to be secured by abridging to that extent the hour or the three-quarters of an hour appropriated to teaching.

With these data before us, let me construct two imaginary programmes, one for a school of an hour and a half, the other for a school of an hour:

First Programme (90 minutes).

	Minutes.
Closing doors and coming to a pause..............	1
Devotional service	15
Change, and getting ready for teaching...........	1
Teaching the lesson............................	55
Change, and getting ready for the superintendent...	1
Superintendent's (or visitor's) address.............	10
Change, and getting ready for dismission..........	2
Dismission........	5
	90

Second Programme (60 minutes).

	Minutes.
Closing doors and pause........................	1
Devotional service.............................	8
Change, and getting ready for teaching...........	1
Teaching the lesson.....	40
Change, and getting ready for the superintendent...	1
Superintendent's (or visitor's) address....	4
Change, and getting ready for dismission..........	1
Dismission....................................	4
	60

The signal for closing doors, for change, and for dismission should be a single tap of the bell, and the bell should be used ordinarily for no other purpose.

13. *Opening School Punctually.*

Open exactly at the time agreed upon. Not fifteen minutes after the time, not ten minutes after, nor five minutes, nor three minutes, nor one minute, but *exactly at the moment.* If there are not half a dozen persons in the room besides yourself, still begin. If even you are as badly off as Dean Swift once was, when, according to the tradition, he had no one present but the clerk, begin. You need not make a joke of it, as he did, saying, "Dearly beloved Roger, the Scripture moveth you and me in sundry places." But if you have even "two or three" present, you have a quorum according to the Scripture rule (Matt. xviii. 19, 20). Waiting a few minutes for stragglers to come in is only an inducement to stragglers to continue in their bad habits. It is, moreover, a wrong done to those who come early and who want to use all their time. If your school begins professedly at nine, and it gets to be understood that you begin your services in all cases exactly at the stroke of the clock, you will have just as many present then as you would have a quarter of an hour later, if it is found that you usually wait a quarter of an hour for laggards to come in. There is a certain percentage of every school or congregation who may be relied on as coming in late under all circumstances. You will not diminish that percentage by habitually waiting. On the contrary, by the degree of uncertainty produced you will increase it. No opening services are so little disturbed by laggardism as those which are known to begin exactly at the moment agreed upon.

14. *Preparation for the Opening Service.*

Know beforehand fully and exactly what you are going to do at the opening. The superintendent has no right to waste the precious time of scholars and teachers by his extemporaneous fumbling. When he rings his bell it should be a signal not only for undivided attention on the part of the school, but for uninterrupted, connected service on his part. It is no time then for him to stop and hunt up a hymn, or to turn over the leaves of the Bible backward and forward in search of a suitable passage to read, or to consult with his fellow-teachers about any measures to be adopted in the school. Then is the moment of execution, not of study or deliberation. Whatever is to be then done ought to be determined on beforehand, even as to the minutest particulars. The superintendent, quite as much as the teacher, needs to make preparation for his work, and to make special preparation for every session of his school. He should select his hymn beforehand, and determine precisely whether he will sing all of it or only a part, and if a part, which part. He should in like manner select beforehand the passage of Scripture, and determine exactly the number of verses to be read. If there are notices to be given he should make a written memorandum of them, and determine in what part of the service the notices shall come in. When a superintendent is thus prepared, even to minute details, for the opening service of the school, he not only discharges the duty more effectively, but he gets through in half the time.

15. *Giving out Notices in School.*

I have spoken of notices. There is nothing in regard to which the conductors of public services, whether superintendents or others, make more grievous mistakes. Nothing in the management of any kind of public audience needs more care than giving a notice. Yet very many blurt out a notice without any premeditation, just as the thought comes into their mind, without reference to the time when it is given or the words in which it is expressed. Not only are the proprieties of the most solemn parts of public worship outraged by such a proceeding, but the object of the notice itself is totally lost when thrust thus unexpectedly upon the attention.

If you wish to give a school a notice on any point, and to have them remember it, you must first call deliberate attention to it. So far as practicable, have a certain time in the order of exercises when notices, if any, are to be given. It is well even to say in form, " I am about to give a notice and I wish your

9 *

attention," and then wait till every eye in the room is fixed upon you.

Do not ordinarily repeat a notice. When the children understand that it is your habit to do so, they only learn thereby not to listen to you the first time you say it, expecting you, as a matter of course, to say it over again. If you do repeat a notice, always give it in exactly the same words the second time as the first time. A variation of the form of words, instead of deepening the impression, only confuses. It is always safer to reduce your notice to writing. Those who are not in the habit of doing so are not aware how much uncertainty and vagueness there is in their notices as usually given.

As to the time for giving notices, there are two points in the school session when they are opportune, namely, one at the opening exercises, the other at the closing, and in both cases the notices should be despatched and off the mind of the superintendent and of the school before entering upon the devotional part of the service. They should never be thrust in between the singing and the reading, or between the reading and the prayer, nor is it well to tack them on after the prayer, thereby dissipating whatever of devout feeling may have been awakened by that exercise.

It may seem trifling to dwell so long upon these little things. But it is by attention to these little things that the superintendent saves the time of the school for greater things.

16. *Giving Out the Hymn.*

The rarest gift among public men is that of reading well. Superintendents are no exception. On
the contrary, it is most painful to listen to hymns as
they are usually read from the superintendent's desk.
It is a great misfortune that it is so. Good reading
would add wonderfully to the effectiveness of this
part of the service. How the style of reading is to
be improved it is not easy to say. But, in addition
to bad elocution, there are some glaring faults of manner which any superintendent may avoid.

1. *Waiting for the Scholars to Find the Place.*
In the first place, when a hymn is announced as
about to be read, immediately after the announcement there should be a pause. The superintendent
should wait a moment for teachers and scholars to
find the place, should look round the room to see
that they are doing so, and should not begin to read
until he sees every one in the room ready to follow
him. Some of my readers, I dare say, will smile at
my giving so simple a suggestion. You will think,
perhaps, that no one could be so ignorant as not to
know this; or perhaps you may think it trifling to
make so small a matter a subject of grave comment.
I can only say my experience differs from yours.
Nothing is more common than to see the leader of a
meeting give out a hymn and begin at once to read
it. If any one in such circumstances will watch the
operation, he will see the majority of the audience

occupied with hunting up the hymn, rustling the
leaves of their books, asking the place of some one
of their neighbors, or otherwise diverting attention
during at least one-half the reading. Indeed, all
that the auditors aim at in such cases is to be sure to
get the place by the time the reading is over. In
the case of children at school, it is still worse. If
the superintendent rushes on with the reading of the
hymn immediately after announcing it, it is practically telling the scholars that they are not expected
to hunt it up, at least not then. The majority of
them consequently will busy themselves with their
library books or in talking until the hymn has been
read through, and will then for the first time begin
to look for it. They do not seem to think that they
have anything to do with the superintendent's reading of it.

2. *Care in Announcing the Place.* There should
be some care in making the announcement of the
hymn. It should be done in a clear, deliberate manner, and loud enough for every one to hear. The
superintendent generally will unconsciously announce
the hymn in this way when he really expects and requires all the scholars at once to find the place, and
waits till they do find it.

In making the announcement, he should be careful also to make no mistake in the number of the
hymn. I once had an experience of this kind. A
superintendent, who was a man of decided abilities,
but who was negligent of these little matters, in-

tended to give out the 379th hymn. He announced the number and commenced at once the reading. Whether through not seeing clearly, or more likely in consequence of having his mind just at that moment mainly upon the hymn and not upon its number, he called it the 375th. I watched the effect. One person in front of me, finding there was some mistake, and happening to catch the first line, turned over to the index, and so was able, before the hymn was more than half through, to find it. Another not far off, finding that it was not the 375th, turned to the 365th, then to the 385th, then to the 395th, and then began to look round the room only to see others in a like bewilderment. Another person behind me, after trying the 365th and the 385th, concluded his ear had misled him as to the *first* figure, and so he industriously hunted up the 275th, and then the 475th, and so on. There was not one in ten anywhere in sight that succeeded in finding the place. All sat perplexed, waiting for the superintendent to get through, hoping to catch either the first line or the number when they should be announced a second time. By a little *extra* carelessness, the superintendent, after finishing the reading, announced the hymn to be not the 379th, but the 397th. But as he luckily read the first line over again, the majority of the audience succeeded at length in the object of their search. I repeat, then, my remark: Let the superintendent in announcing his hymn be careful to make no mistake as to the number. Be careful also to call out each several figure of the number distinctly. You can tell infallibly, if you will only look at the children, whether you have been rightly heard or not.

3. *Grammatical Blunders.* In giving out a hymn, some little grammatical blunders are often made which cause perplexity. Thus, the superintendent says, " Sing the first and last two verses." Does this mean three verses or four? If the former, he should have said, " the first verse and the last two." If the latter, the phrase should be, " the first two verses and the last two." There then would be no possibility of mistaking the meaning. I have heard a superintendent make the announcement thus: " Omit the 3d and 4th verses of the 125th hymn," instead of saying, " Sing the 125th hymn, omitting the 3d and 4th verses." This perhaps would lead no one astray, as we may naturally infer that the hymn is to be sung. But the expression is awkward. It tends to distract the mind.

4. *Reading Just what is to be Sung.* In reading the hymn, it is best to read just those verses, and those only, which are to be sung. Omit in reading those that are to be omitted in singing. Do every minute thing, in short, that will have any tendency to prevent distraction of mind.

5. *Giving the Key-note.* Besides the musical tune, there is in every hymn that is worth singing at all a *moral tune*, which the superintendent should endeavor to catch and give. This, I suppose, is the

real object in reading the hymn before singing. If the hymn expresses joy, or penitence, or faith, or hope—whatever emotion each particular verse is intended to convey—let the superintendent try to catch the very soul of it, and give utterance to it in his reading voice. It is the best possible preparation and guide for the expression of the same thought or emotion afterward by the singing voice. The reading of the hymn should never be a mere idle and unmeaning form. It may be a source of as much pleasure and profit to the school as the singing of it is.

6. *Looking while Reading.* In reading a hymn or a passage of Scripture the superintendent should give the school the full benefit of his eyes. There is something contagious in a look. Get your children as much as possible to look you in the eye, and let your eyes ever rest calmly and pleasantly on theirs. Say not that you cannot do this while reading. *You must do it.* You should not undertake to read a passage that you are not entirely familiar with. By following the passage with your finger as you read, so that when your eye returns to the book it will know exactly where to fall, you will only have to look at the page occasionally, just to take a fresh start every second or third line. By this means your eyes will be almost as free while reading as while speaking extemporaneously. A good reader, by means of his eyes and his looks, keeps himself just as fully in communication with his audience as

if he was speaking to them. The superintendent or the leader of a meeting of any kind who has not learned the knack of this should learn it without delay. He loses half his power with his audience by the want of it. The superintendent has never really read a hymn to his school unless, while giving it utterance with his voice, he has seen the scholars' eyes catching fire from his eyes, and has felt his own soul simultaneously taking new warmth from the reflection of theirs. It is this quick, warm interchange of soul by voice and look, and not the trappings of office, that gives the superintendent any real power among his children. In so small a matter as the mere reading of the opening hymn, the superintendent *may* put forth a power and influence that shall imperceptibly permeate and leaven the exercises of the school for the entire session. He gives therein the key-note to the whole service.

17. *Reading the Scriptures.*

No writings, if well read, are so impressive, none are so capable of high elocutionary effect, as the Holy Scriptures. Yet of all books that are publicly read for the edification of the people, none ordinarily is read so badly as the Bible. It is not merely that public readers fail to give to the words the fulness of power and beauty that is in them. It is not merely that the reading lacks rhetorical elegance and finish, and that Holy Writ as uttered by such persons ceases to charm and captivate. The bare meaning even is not rendered. The Scriptures are often read as one would read a formula in an unknown tongue, whose alphabet and pronunciation he had mastered, but without having the slightest idea of what the words meant, or whether they had any meaning. They are often read with an entire perversion of the meaning.

It is no part of my present purpose to lay down rules for reading. Yet I do wish to say to superintendents, and to all who are required to lead the devotions of others, Give earnest heed to this matter. You may never learn to give to the Scriptures the melting power which they had when coming from the lips of Dr. Mason or Elizabeth Fry. You may not have the natural gifts of voice and intellect, or the opportunities of culture, which those eminent persons had. But there is a certain degree of excellence which you may attain. There are certain faults of manner which you may avoid, and which you surely will avoid if you desire earnestly and truly to give effectiveness to this part of your public duties.

Avoid Formalism. It is unpardonable to read the passages of Scripture with which you open school in such a way as to give the children the idea that it is a mere form, something which is to be gone through with, but in which they have no interest. Children are quick reasoners, and do not often mistake in such matters. If they get the idea in any instance that the superintendent is reading a passage

10

in the Bible merely because such reading is in the programme, a part of the customary routine, and that it has no meaning or relevancy to them, the chances are that they are right in their impressions of the case. The superintendent will find, if he will go to the bottom of his own mind, that in his inmost thoughts this reading is really not a living process of his soul, as it is when he is talking his own thoughts to the children. He is doing exactly what the children suppose. He is going through a mere form.

Be in Earnest. Now it is not in rules to correct the evil of formalism, of which I have been speaking. The only remedy is for the man to realize better what it is that he is about. He must in some way learn to feel that it is really a serious thing to read to others the words of the great God. Reading louder or lower, slower or faster, putting an emphasis on this word or on that, affected starts and grimaces, measured cadences and solemn cant,—none of these things reach the case. What is wanted, the indispensable requisite, in order that the reading shall take hold of the audience, is reality, life. It must first take hold of yourself. The moment you really feel that you are reading the words of God, that you are communicating to your hearers a message from heaven, your feeling will infect them. Just in proportion as you feel they will feel. They will catch the tone instantly. Nothing is half so contagious. If a man is in earnest, whether he is reading or speaking, his hearers become earnest. It is a law of human nature.

Study the Passage. Study beforehand the passage which you intend to read at the opening. It is no easy matter to find out exactly what is meant, and all that is meant, by the written words of another. We are accustomed in every-day intercourse to leave a great deal of our meaning to be expressed and supplemented by the tone of the voice and by significant gestures and looks. When only the voiceless, inanimate words are before us, it requires for their full comprehension not merely practiced skill in verbal and grammatical analysis, but often much historical knowledge, and always a vigorous imagination, to bring the original circumstances fully and vividly before the mind. In the passage, John xx. 16, for instance, when Jesus turns and says "Mary!" it is evidently in that voice of familiar tenderness which says, by its very tone, "Do you not know me?" Mary's "Rabboni!" is in like manner an expression of surprised, joyful recognition. A mere study of the words does not bring out the meaning. Imagination must work. The scene must stand clearly out before the mind's eye. Then only will the voice do its office as a true interpreter of this most beautiful passage. Who that ever heard that almost despairing wail with which the venerable Dr. Archibald Alexander used to utter the cry, "Eloi, eloi, lama sabacthani!" but felt that he had received a new revelation of the meaning of that mysterious utterance? It was not that Dr. Alexander understood Hebrew better than thousands of others have done. It was because he had meditated upon the subject until he had the whole dreadful scene fully before him.

Meditate on It. Meditation implies something more than study. Begin, of course, by studying the subject carefully. Find out by studious examination and reflection the exact meaning of the passage and of each particular word in it. Then ponder it, until your mind has become fully possessed with the ideas and thoughts which it contains. Dwell upon it. Turn it over and over on the previous days of the week, as you would any grave and weighty message that you were preparing to deliver on some important occasion. Take as much pains and time in preparing yourself to read a passage at the opening of the school as a faithful teacher would take in preparing to teach it. Get your thoughts filled with the very things themselves which are spoken of, so that when you read you hardly think of the words— so that, in fact, you seem to yourself not to be reading the words, but only the meaning which lies beneath them. It is as when one looks through a window at objects in the street. The glass is only the medium through which, and unconscious of it, he sees something beyond. So by long dwelling upon a passage you learn gradually to forget the words in thinking of the meaning which they convey. You look with your mind's eye through the words, and, forgetful of them, see only the real objects which lie beyond.

When you rise at your desk to read to the school, with your own mind thus prepared, you need not fear that the exercise will be a dull and formal one, either to you or to those who hear you. The prime difficulty with superintendents, and with others similarly situated, is that they have no adequate conception of the importance and value of the exercise, and they make no adequate preparation for it.

Reading to One's Self. A member of Congress once made an attack upon John Randolph. It was a long, dull speech, to which no one apparently listened but the man himself who made it. Randolph began his reply as follows: "Mr. Speaker, while the gentleman was talking I was thinking of the first lesson in our old school-book, Corderius. '*Quid agis?* What are you doing? *Repeto mecum,* I am repeating to myself!'" It is exactly the case of many who read the Scriptures publicly. They stand up indeed in presence of others, but they are really reading to themselves. There is no communication of thought and feeling going on between them and the listeners. There is no interchange of looks. There is no play of sympathy back and forth. If the reader would not have the feeling that he is reading to himself, if he would not give the same impression to those who are listening, he must not confine his eyes to the book. He must learn to read, and at the same time to look his hearers in the eyes. Take the word of an old hand at the business. You will never feel any ease or comfort in this part of your duty, you will never perform it acceptably or profitably to others, until you get the knack of looking at the people that you are reading to.

Number of Verses. How many verses should be read at the opening of the school? The common error here is that of reading too long a passage. Rarely read a whole chapter. From twelve to fifteen verses is about the length. When the school, or a considerable portion of it, has a common lesson, it is often a good plan to read at the opening the verses which constitute the lesson. Where this is not done, but the superintendent selects a passage, take something which is complete in itself, a single parable, or the narrative of one particular event, something which will make an impression as a whole, and which will not produce a confusion of ideas.

Some superintendents require the school to read verse about. That is, the superintendent reads the first verse, the school reads the second, and so on, alternating as in the service in the Episcopal Church.

Keeping the School in your Eye. While the scholars are thus reading alternately, or repeating after you, use your eyes most diligently. Let that calm, quiet look of yours search out every little delinquent who, through indolence or inattention, fails to add his young voice to the general volume of sound. Do not distract the attention of the others by

stopping then to comment upon it, or by calling out
to the delinquent publicly. Only see him. If possible, let him feel that you see him. In the course
of the session you will have an opportunity of re-
minding him privately and kindly of his duty. See
that the teachers respond as well as the scholars.
Not only the example of the teacher is important as
an inducement to the scholars, but his voice is a
guide to them and helps to keep their voices together. Do not urge the school to respond loudly.
What you want is not noise, but concert. You
want every voice to join intelligently in the service.
While your own utterance is clear and distinct, yet
let there be a certain degree of tenderness, a subdued solemnity, in the tone of your voice. The
children will be very apt to catch it. They are im-
itative creatures. If you bluster, they will bluster.
If you are gentle and devout, they will learn unconsciously to be the same.

18. *The Opening Prayer.*

I do not propose to speak of prayer in general,
but only of that particular prayer with which a Sunday-school should be opened.

If time and forethought are needed to make the
service short, much more are they needed to make
it simple. The words must be such as children can
understand, the wants expressed must be such as
children feel. Avoid long sentences as well as long
words. Let each petition, so far as possible, be a

single sentence by itself. Beware of circumlocutions and euphuisms and cant phrases, such as are doled out unmeaningly in ordinary prayer-meetings. Every school, every class, has wants of its own—special, specific wants. Each week brings new wants. Have these fixed in your mind beforehand, so that you know exactly what you are going to ask for when you stand up to pray. If the list of wants becomes too long, select those that are most urgent, and arrange in your own mind the order in which the several petitions shall be presented. Think over the terms to be used in each particular request, so as not to degrade the subject by using words that are trivial and vulgar, and yet be not so refined and dainty in expression that the children do not know what you are talking about. Let one or more of the petitions always be connected with the sentiments contained in the hymn and in the passage of Scripture read. This knits together the whole opening exercise and gives unity and strength to the general impression.

An Example. Among the petitions which would be seasonable in almost any Sunday-school are such as the following :

"Help us to keep this Sabbath day holy. May we love the dear Saviour more and more. Give us new hearts. Make us true Christians. Help us to remember our lessons. Teach us the meaning of the Bible words. Teach us how to pray. If we live to grow up, may we become good men and women. May every child learn to obey his father and mother. May every child be kind to his broth-

ers and sisters. *Bless those children who cannot come to Sunday-school. Bless those children who have no one to teach them. Bless heathen children. Bless all Sunday-schools. Bless that dear boy whose mother died last week. Comfort his heart and be very merciful to him. May we all learn to be still and attentive during the school hours. May we always be glad when Sunday comes. Fill us with joy when we sing God's praises. We have just sung that children ' around the throne of God in heaven' praise thee; help us too to praise thee here upon earth. Forgive those who do not learn their lessons. Forgive those who swear. Forgive those who lie. Forgive those who play on the Sabbath. Forgive those who sometimes stay away from Sunday-school and run about the streets. Forgive those who use bad words. Forgive those who get angry and fight. May we all be sorry and learn to do better. May those two teachers who are sick soon get well. Bless all the teachers. Bless our dear pastor. Bless our fathers and mothers. We thank thee that Jesus died for us. We thank thee for this precious Bible. We thank thee that so many of us are able to come to school to-day. We thank thee that the sun shines, and that we have such a pleasant day and such a pleasant school-room. We thank thee that we have clothes to wear and food to eat. We thank thee that we know how to read. Give us more knowledge. Teach us how to do good. Help us to be gentle and kind. Keep us from being cross and ill-natured. Keep us from being idle. May we be a comfort to our friends. We have just read in the Bible that thou carest for sparrows; care for us. Care for our school. May somebody give us money to get a new library. Send us more teachers for those classes that have no teacher.*"

This is not given as a model prayer, but only to illustrate what is meant by simple petitions, such as will be likely to reach the understanding and the wants of children.   In the actual prayers of any particular school the petitions will often be much more specific than any here given, and they will vary from week to week, according to the varying wants of the school.   If the superintendent in his prayer thus comes to the "Father who is in heaven" with the actual wants of the school, expressed in a plain, straightforward manner, the children will follow him, and the exercise will be one that they will take pleasure in.

Another Example.   But suppose the superintendent begins in this wise :

"*O thou great and mysterious Being, who inhabitest eternity, whose are all the ends of the earth, who alone dwellest in light inaccessible and full of glory, whom no eye hath seen nor can see, who art, and there is none beside thee, King of kings and Lord of lords, look down in compassion upon us thy unworthy creatures, who have forsaken the fountain of living waters and have hewn out to ourselves broken and leaky cisterns that can hold no water; show us how vain and futile are sublunary joys and pursuits; let not these transitory interests and passions draw us away from those heavenly contemplations which ought to fill our thoughts; may we rise superior to earth and its allurements, the things of time and sense, which perish with the using, and may we cleave to those eternal realities which never fade away.   In the midst of deserved wrath remember mercy.   Send down thy blessing on those whom thou hast placed in the responsible position of instructors of the young and tender mind.   Bless him also who goes out and in before us and breaks to us the bread of everlasting life.   May his words be as a nail driven in a sure place, sending down its roots broad and deep, and sending out its branches like a green bay tree, fair as the moon, clear as the sun, and terrible as an army with banners"!!!*

How long is it likely that the children will follow such a prayer? Will not the superintendent be to them as one that beateth the air? Will he not be as one that speaketh in an unknown tongue?

The Superintendent's Manner. Besides the substance of the prayer, there are some things in the manner of it that deserve attention. In no one act of the superintendent should he be more careful of his manner than when he thus attempts publicly to lead the supplications of a youthful audience. To this end let his manner be subdued and gentle. Noisy vociferation, equally with flippant levity, is utterly irreconcilable with a devout and humble spirit. Above all things, never shout out the name of God in a sharp, loud tone of voice. Nothing that you can say to enforce the obligation of the Third Commandment will have half the effect upon the youthful heart that will be produced by your own tender, loving tone in breathing the sweet words, "Our Father which art in heaven." Though the petitions be brief and simple, do not, in uttering them, rush on hastily from one to another. When the late Dr. Ashbel Green was in the height of his popularity as a pulpit orator, one night, in returning home from church and mingling with the crowd, he unintentionally overheard various comments upon the sermon. Among other remarks, one lady said, "Oh, don't you admire his pauses!" The lady was right. There is often strange eloquence in a pause. In uttering simple, detached petitions, such as those quoted in the first example, there should be a slight pause after each, that the thought may rest for a moment upon the mind of the hearers, and as if in a sort of expectancy of its effect upon His mind to whom it is presented. A man will thus pause without thinking of it; indeed he cannot help doing so if he truly realizes what it is to present a series of requests to Almighty God. Each request will have a sober, separate, deliberate presentation.

A Devout Pause Before and After. In addition to this deliberateness of manner during the prayer, there should be a special, solemn pause before and after the prayer. Before beginning to pray, the audience rise, or kneel, or make some change of position. If the audience is large, consisting of several hundreds, and especially if they are children, the change of position, and the little adjustments of dress and person attendant upon it, necessarily take some perceptible time. The superintendent must wait quietly till the whole movement is completed, till the attention which has been thus momentarily diverted has returned once more to the service. Let him pause till every sound is hushed, and expectancy reigns supreme. Then let those wonderful words, " Our Father which art in heaven," begin to fall gently on the ear.

So, too, after the prayer, let there be a pause, as if teachers and scholars had been high up on the mount of vision, and it required some little time to break off from that solemn communing. Some superintendents and some preachers hardly have " Amen" out of their mouths before they are off full gallop upon whatever comes next in order. Before the audience have resumed their seats, or have had time to become composed, a chapter is begun, a text is announced, or there is a rush to business of some kind. It is needless to say, the solemnity produced by the prayer receives a rude shock from this indecorous haste. The silent prayer at the close of the service in the Episcopal Church is a most beautiful observance. How much more becoming is this than the rattling haste with which some congregations rush out of the house of God the moment the word " Amen" is pronounced !

But to return to the subject. Let the superintendent and the school learn to attain a quiet, cheerful, composed attention before beginning to address the great God, and let them also retain that composure for a brief space after closing the prayer, and before engaging in anything else. There should be no rude abruptness either on entering or leaving the presence of the great King.

Concluding Remarks.

If any superintendent, judging by the length of these remarks about opening the school, should infer the propriety of making his opening services equally long, he would make a grievous mistake. I have occu-

11

pied more than twenty pages in the description of a service which at the longest should not exceed ten minutes. But many people forget, or never find out, that what requires brief space in action often takes long and toilsome hours of patient preparation. In fact, the briefer the time for action, the greater and more minute must be the preparation. The speaker was not astray who apologized for his address being so long, by saying that he had not had time to make it shorter. Many people also mistake haste for speed. An expert will execute a movement with entire composure, and as if he was quite at his leisure ; and yet, if you time him, you find that he gets through it with extraordinary despatch. With what wonderful celerity some of the most critical operations in surgery are performed ! Yet the operator proceeds with all the steadiness and apparent deliberation of one taking an airing. It is because in these cases there is really no crude extemporization. Everything, to the minutest particular, is thought of and prepared for beforehand.

If the superintendent comes to his work of opening school without full and special preparation, he will be very apt either to spin out to an unreasonable length what he has to do, or to rush through it with a fatal haste that accomplishes nothing. Every mistake of the superintendent is, in its effect, multiplied by the number of those under his care. In a large school, say of three hundred scholars. every minute during which the superintendent detains the school unnecessarily makes a loss of three hundred minutes, which is five hours. He must study therefore the art of expediting matters. On the other hand, entire deliberation and steadiness are absolutely essential. A jerking, fitful movement is fatal. The scholars will detect at once whether the superintendent really knows what he is about, just as the steeds before a coach know who it is that handles the reins. As the skilful driver has the art of communicating his own impulses, of diffusing his very self, so to speak, through the dumb beasts that like a single living intelligence yield their wills to his, so when the superintendent takes the reins and calls the school to order, he must aim to make every one in the room feel his touch. He must diffuse himself through the entire mass. He must try to wield the thoughts and the willing attention of all. Children, no less than horses, delight to give themselves up to the control of a master mind. Like horses, too, they are not slow to kick out of the traces the moment they detect a want of skill in the driver. Let no one expect to wield this power who has not studied carefully what he has to do, and who has not every particular so perfectly and definitely settled in his mind that he cannot by any possibility be thrown into confusion and disorder.

Do not consider me prolix, therefore, if I have taken a good deal of space in canvassing the details of a service which in its actual performance occupies, or at least ought to occupy, a very little time.

CHAPTER IV.

THE TEACHER.

THE main work of the Sunday-school is that done by the teacher. The present chapter, devoted to the consideration of his various duties and qualifications, will necessarily be the longest, as it is the most important, in the book. It is not necessary to follow any particular order in this discussion, but the several topics connected with the subject will be considered, one after another, in such manner as shall seem most conducive in each case to some practical result.

1. *The First Qualification.*

Let the teacher ever remember that the great end of Sunday-school instruction is the salvation of the soul. We would bring the children to Jesus. This is the beginning, middle and end of our effort. The humble disciple who brings others to the saving knowledge of the Lord Jesus is doing a good work, though the teachings by which it is done are old-fashioned and quaint and behind the times, though the teacher may know nothing of the new methods,

124

though his class may make no show at anniversaries, and may have nothing about it that is novel or picturesque.

I am about to give considerable space to the discussion of Sunday-school methods. Teachers' institutes, model lessons, Sunday-school libraries, Sunday-school music, means of registering attendance, means of securing attention, means of visible illustration,—these and similar topics will be commended to the earnest attention of the reader. I feel that too much or too earnest attention cannot be given to these topics. At the same time, I desire at the outset to recall to the mind of the reader that these are but means, and that the end of them all is to win souls to Christ. The true, genuine conversion of one child by the most antiquated method of teaching, is a better result than the most brilliant and captivating display of skill which yields to the Master no harvest of souls.

I commend the new methods with all my heart. I earnestly exhort all Sunday-school teachers to avail themselves of every opportunity of studying the art of teaching. Observe others, read books on the subject, attend institutes, make experiments. Use your utmost diligence in these things. But forget not that infinitely greater preparation, the fresh baptism of your own soul by the Holy Spirit. Get your own heart all aglow with a burning love for souls. Get some realizing sense of the inexpressible value of the soul. Let it be no sham, no mere make-

11 *

believe, when you tell your children of your earnest desire for their salvation. This is the first qualification, before and beyond every other, for the office of Sunday-school teacher, that he have the same mind that was in Christ—an earnestness of love for the work that has in it something of agony.

Love is inventive. Its ends are so inexpressibly dear that it stimulates the mind to the highest exercise of its powers in finding out how those ends may be secured. A soul burning with a love like that which brought Jesus down to earth will by that very passion be raised to a degree of mental power of which it had before been deemed incapable. A man with this intense, almost consuming, fire of love in his bosom, does not, therefore, work without means or against means, but the very strength of his desires for the accomplishment of the end leads him to use with increased diligence all the means within his reach. This is the true incentive to invention, to study, to toil, to self-denial. The Sunday-school work is no mere pastime, no holiday entertainment, but real *work*, requiring for its propelling power something more than a love of novelty, or a love of applause, or a pleasurable excitement. To carry us through triumphantly to the end, to make us persevering and hopeful under discouragements, to give us courage in the face of obstacles and dangers, to make us tireless in effort and exhaustless in invention, ever willing to learn in order that we may teach, ever ready to try a new method when old methods fail, and never willing to yield so long as any method remains untried by which we may bring a lost soul back to the fold of Christ—to do all this we need to feel, as Christ did, that one soul is really and truly of more value than the whole world beside.

To have this conviction of the value of the soul, this burning love for the salvation of souls, is the first, the incomparably greatest qualification of the Sunday-school teacher. It can only be had in the closet of secret prayer, by the direct outpouring of the Holy Ghost. But it may be had by every one. We must get it, as we get our own salvation, by begging for it on our knees, and by continuing to beg until we get what we ask. The teacher needs to study, needs to read books instructing him in his duties, needs to attend institutes and normal classes and conventions, needs to talk over with his fellow-workers the work that he has in hand. But his first need, his greatest need, his most constant, paramount, indispensable need, is to pray. Prayer—secret, incessant, importunate prayer—is the one means which he may never neglect—prayer, not only for his scholars, but for himself, that he may have such a baptism of the Spirit as shall set his whole being aglow with new life, and shall make him feel all the length and breadth and height and depth of that awful question, "What is a man profited if he shall gain the whole world and lose his own soul? or what shall a man give in exchange for his soul?"

A true impression of the unutterable greatness of divine things is the teacher's first qualification. It is the gift of the Holy Spirit, obtainable by prayer, and free to all. The teacher who has this gift will be no laggard in acquiring the others.

2. *Winning Souls.*

The ultimate end of all Sunday-school teaching, and of all the means connected with it, as I have so often said, is to bring souls to Christ. Of this truth there is no serious doubt in any quarter. All Sunday-school men agree in regard to it. It is our common bond of union—the first article of our Sunday-school faith.

But in regard to this cardinal point there are two opposing extremes which we need to be guarded against.

The first is the mistake of those who have their thoughts so exclusively directed to the end that they seem to forget the means. They are like a man who expects to win a race by looking intently at the goal, while neglecting to see that his horse is properly bridled and saddled, and without paying heed to the various bends and inequalities of the track. There is a mode of dealing with children, in trying to convert them, which consists in what children themselves expressively call picking at them. Some pious people seem to think that they are doing nothing toward building up the kingdom of God unless they are incessantly exhorting somebody " to escape the damnation of hell." A teacher is not necessarily neglecting or forgetting the great end of his labors because that end is not perpetually on his tongue. A teacher may really and truly have the conversion and salvation of his scholars in view, who spends many an hour in labors in which that end is not once named. He has not necessarily lost sight of it because he is training his fingers to skill in the use of the crayon and the blackboard, because he is studying geography and history, because he is reading books on the theory and practice of teaching, and is attending teachers' institutes and normal classes. These things are among the means by which the Sunday-school workman is equipped for his work. Whatever can awaken a greater love for the work, or can improve the methods by which it is to be accomplished, or can remove obstacles from the path of the worker, is important as a part of the means.

But, secondly, there are those who become so absorbed in the study and use of the means that they virtually forget the end. This is the danger in the other direction. Let us, then, accept this exhortation, Never to forget what it is that we are laboring for. It is not merely to build up large and showy schools, it is not merely to have big meetings and eloquent speeches. The end of all our labors is to win souls for Jesus. Our new school-houses, our " normal" methods, our " blackboards" and " institutes," our books and pictures and papers, our consultations and gatherings and teachers' meetings, and our improved machinery of every kind, are all of questionable utility unless a holy ardor for winning souls pervades and animates them all.

If, with all our improved methods and machinery, no souls are converted, let us seriously re-examine our whole position. If, within the sphere of our observation, there is some humble laborer, some pious and devoted Mary Gardiner, who without any of these improvements is quietly and unostentatiously bringing in a continual harvest of souls, let us go and sit meekly at her feet as learners. We need not give up our improvements. But let us catch that living spirit without which all else is mere machinery.

The conversion of his scholars need not always be on the teacher's tongue, but it should be ever in his heart. Let it burn there as an unquenchable fire. The mistake of some teachers in this matter is, not in thinking and feeling too much about it, but in talking too much about it.

While we should not be so much occupied with the means as to forget the end, and while also we should not disgust and harden our scholars by that sort of pointless iteration which becomes wearisome, let us also avoid that other and worse extreme of never making religion a personal question. There is such a thing as being entirely too dainty in this matter. Our scholars ought to feel in their inmost souls that that which brings us to the class is not their amusement, but their salvation. If we fail to give them this impression, we are seriously derelict. There is something to be done which we have not yet done.

Besides this general impression, which is the combined result of our whole manner, the teacher should at proper times bring the subject of personal religion home to the conscience of each pupil by direct individual appeal. Let no natural timidity or conscious want of skill keep us from the discharge of this imperative duty. A few words, well timed and fitly spoken, may bring to a decisive point all the labor and preparation of months. For the want of such a direct appeal, all the general and indirect labor of weeks and months may be dissipated and come to nought.

3. *Help from the Great Teacher.*

Sunday-school teachers at the present day, more than at any previous time, are pondering the question how they may best qualify themselves for their work. Nothing is more evident than the fact that there has been among teachers a great awakening on this subject. The chief movement in Sunday-school matters for the last few years has been in this direction. Teachers are zealously studying how to teach. Maps, visible illustrations, natural objects, blackboards and chalk, model teachers' meetings, and model lessons of every grade, have become universally familiar. Anything which can help the teacher in his work is sought for and welcomed.

In this general inquiry for help there is one agency which should never be neglected. I refer to the influence of the Holy Spirit. In the meetings for prayer on this subject the aid of the Spirit is indeed often invoked, but not for the particular point now in view. He is asked to convert the children, to open their minds that they may understand and receive the truth. This is all very well. But teachers need his influence on themselves, and that not merely in touching their hearts and creating in them greater love for their work and for their children, *but in giving them skill.* We all too much ignore the fact that the Holy Spirit is the source of mental as well as of moral power. The teacher who will may have him as an instructor, to give wisdom and skill, just as surely and effectually as did Bezaleel of old in constructing the work of the tabernacle.

It is worth while for teachers to ponder well the memorable saying of Christ to his disciples just before leaving them, as recorded in the 14th chapter of John. Up to that time they had Jesus as their daily teacher. But now he gave them to understand that he was about to leave them, and they were filled with consternation, remembering on how many subjects they were still ignorant, and feeling that they would need continual guidance and instruction. Our Saviour assures them that when he has ascended to heaven, and is no longer personally present with them, another Person of the Godhead shall be sent, who will be with the disciples in the place of Jesus; "He shall teach you all things."

This is doubtless a great mystery—as great as that of the Incarnation. Yet it is none the less a fact, as sober and practical as it is momentous. God the Holy Ghost is in some way present to the hearts and minds of men, and does in some way influence them, helping them to think as well as to feel, guiding the judgment, quickening the invention and the memory (He shall " bring all things to your remembrance"), making clear what is obscure, giving us control over the attention, bringing right thoughts to the mind, right words to the lips. This agency of the Holy Spirit in its effects upon mental action needs to be pondered by teachers. I do not propose to explain it. The fact, indeed, does not admit of explanation. Yet perhaps an illustration or two may make it more appreciable.

Let it be remembered, then, that action of every kind, mental or material, is to be aided and accelerated, if at all, by force of the same kind with the primary force. If a certain amount of weight avoirdupois will not make the scale kick the beam, we may produce the effect by laying on the requisite number of additional pounds—that is, by adding force of the same kind with the original. If the flame of one candle does not produce the illumination required for a particular effect, the addition of a second or of a third will. If we wish to increase the speed of a locomotive, we do not whistle to it, or whip it, or say to it " get up ;" we add steam. If, on the other hand, we wish our horse to travel faster, we use a motive addressed to his nature. We appeal to his generosity, his pride, or his fear. So mental action is influenced and induced by forces of the same nature with itself. One mind operates powerfully upon another mind, working often, too, by mysterious influences that elude analysis.

The influence of mind upon mind, other things being equal, is in proportion to the completeness of these three conditions—the fulness of accord and sympathy between two minds that are brought into contact, the closeness of the contact, and the greatness and power of the influencing and controlling mind. A mind fully in sympathy with another is by that very circumstance in a condition to be powerfully influenced by that other. In like manner, as we all know by daily experience, the mind is lifted up, enlarged, enlightened, strengthened, by intercourse with one of powerful intellect. We all feel, too, when wishing to influence any one, that we could effect our end the better if we could but get our mind into actual contact, as it were, with his mind, if we could enter into the very chamber of his soul, so as to know certainly and exactly what he is thinking of. This indeed we can never do. We think sometimes that we come very near to each other. But, after all, we never touch. Between my mind and yours, between your mind and that of the most intimate friend you have in the world, there is a barrier, high as heaven, deep as hell, impenetrable as adamant. Thus far can we come and no farther. We can never enter into the soul of any human being. No human being can ever enter into ours.

Yet there is one Mind, and that a Mind of infinitely great and transcendent power, to which there is no such barrier, and this transcendent, all-knowing, all-powerful Mind is in direct contact with the very essence of our minds. Can I influence the thinking faculties of a fellow-man, and cannot the infinite God, who made those faculties? Can He who gives our bodies all their power of growth and strength not give growth and strength to our minds?

I do not profess to understand how the divine Mind acts upon the human mind. I cannot always understand how one human mind acts upon another. But of the fact, I make no more question than I do of the power of flame, of steam, or of gravitation.

In all earnestness, then, would I exhort teachers devoutly to invoke the aid of the Holy Spirit in the prosecution of study. If you would acquire that mental discipline which is to enable you to study and to teach in the very best and highest manner, PRAY! Call mightily upon God the Holy Ghost, who is after all the great educator and teacher of the human race. Carry your feeble lamp to the great Fountain of light and radiance. Put your heart into full accord and sympathy with that of the infinite Mind. Wrestle with him mightily in secret, as one that feels the burden of a great want.

There is sound philosophy as well as religion in
the utterance of the wise man : " The fear of the
Lord is the beginning of *knowledge.*"   Surely that
man is not wise who, in cultivating mind, whether
his own or that of another, neglects to invoke the aid
of the infinite Mind.

4. *Having an Aim.*

Much of the efforts of good people come to nought
because those efforts are put forth without deliberation or distinctness of purpose.   The fleet-footed
youth Ahimaaz is a fair representative of many well-
meaning people nowadays.   There had been a
great battle, and he was in all haste to carry the
news to the king.   In his zeal he actually outran the
more sober-minded Cushi, and was the first to enter
the royal presence.   But when asked his tidings, he
could only say, " I saw a great tumult, but I knew
not what it was."   So the king said to him, " Turn
aside and stand there."   Thus, too often, in their
zeal to be doing something, people rush out into the
thickest of the turmoil without knowing exactly
what it is that needs to be done, and without having
formed for themselves any definite plan of action.
Such proceedings are worse than a mere waste of
energy.   They are often positively injurious.   Paul
says : " So fight I, not as one that beateth the air."
When he gave a blow, he was careful to take aim.
He wished to hit somebody, and to hit the right one.
These people who thrust out at random not only

beat the air; they often hit and hurt the very ones whom they seek to befriend.

The teacher, of all persons, and the Sunday-school teacher, of all teachers, should seek distinctness of aims. The work is one in which mistakes are so easy and so mischievous. Children, in consequence of their inexperience and their pliability, are more easily led astray than grown people. The interests at stake are more momentous than those which concern merely the loss or gain of money. Another thing which makes it particularly important that care and right methods should be used, is that the Sunday-school work is not so well organized as the work of the week-day school. In a well-organized public school a bungler has not half the power of mischief that he would have in a Sunday-school.

It is the duty of every teacher, therefore, to spend some time in reflection. Less action and more thought is sometimes the true wisdom. If the teacher would have a full measure of success in his work, he should occasionally pause, and take time for consideration. He should fix upon certain definite ends to be accomplished, and then keep these steadily before him.

What are some of the aims that the Sunday-school teacher should have distinctly in view? or, to vary the expression, what are some of the things which he should aim to bring about? I will indicate some few of these, without undertaking, of course, to ex-

12 *

haust the list, and without reference to the relative importance of the topics named.

1. *Regularity of Attendance.* A teacher should aim to secure a regular attendance of his pupils. How this is to be done is another matter. The point I now make is that it should be one of the things at which the teacher should distinctly and deliberately aim. The means will vary with varying circumstances. That which will answer with one class will not answer with another class. One teacher has means at his disposal that another has not. What I urge upon every teacher is to fix this end in his mind, and exhaust every means at his disposal to accomplish it. One thing, however, may be assumed as certain : the end will never be accomplished by scolding. A gentleman of my acquaintance had a Bible-class in the city of New York. On assuming the charge, he adopted the following plan. Whenever a pupil was absent, he invariably called at the scholar's home to inquire into the cause, and if possible on the very day that the absence occurred. The consequence was that absences, except for serious and satisfactory causes, were entirely broken up. The plan was completely successful, and after the first few Sundays gave him very little trouble. The scholars got so into the habit of coming regularly that he rarely had calls to make.

2. *Study of the Lesson.* A teacher should aim to secure from every scholar a study of the lesson. The facts on this subject are discouraging, almost alarm-

ing. It is no exaggeration to say that more than half the children who attend Sunday-school go without any preparatory study of the lesson. I do not say that even in such cases they learn nothing or get no good. They may learn something from hearing others recite and from the explanations of the teacher, even if they have not studied the lesson at home. But the good accomplished is small indeed in comparison with what might be done were there the proper amount of home study. How this home study is to be secured I do not undertake now to say. All I say to the teacher is, aim at it. Persevere in your aim. If one method fails, try another. Give the matter some thought and consideration. Use your invention. One thing, however, you may depend upon. If you let the matter take its own course, unless you are more fortunate in your pupils than most teachers, you will rarely find your class decently prepared on the lesson.

3. *Maintaining Order.* The teacher should aim to keep order in his class. How this is to be done it would require many pages to show. Whole volumes, indeed, have been written upon it. One thing only I say about it now. The very first step toward the maintenance of order is for the teacher to make up his mind that the thing must be done. Necessity is the mother of invention. Let the necessity first of all be admitted, distinctly, fully. Means will follow. Many teachers unfortunately seem to be entirely purposeless on the subject. They leave the matter to

the chapter of accidents, or they leave it to the poor, overburdened superintendent. Let every teacher understand that in this thing aiming at the end is half the road toward reaching it. The first rule for keeping order is, resolve that you will have it. Fix it definitely in your mind as a thing to be done by some means; then revolve in your mind what those means shall be.

The burden of maintaining order does not rest on the superintendent alone. It is a joint responsibility. Each teacher ought to hold himself responsible for the order of his own class. Nearly all that has been said of the superintendent on this subject will apply to the teacher. The teacher, however, comes into closer and more immediate contact with individuals. His is a contest hand to hand, and he will soon find that either he or his scholars must rule. This rule must be real and no sham. But it need not be harsh. It need not be ostentatious. The less show of government, so there really is government, the better. In the asylum for the insane, the windows are secured by iron bars and the furniture is made of iron, so that it cannot be broken, and there is no possibilty of escape. But the furniture is all painted to look like wood, and the windows seem to have merely a light, graceful lattice-work. Let the teacher, even when he has to resort to what almost amounts to restraint, be as gentle about it and make as little show of it as possible. You may give a command without putting it in the imperative mood. "Will you please?" has the form of a request; and when the boy does please, he seems to be doing a favor, and yet there has been a real putting forth of authority on the one side and a yielding of obedience on the other. Remember, too, that the forms of politeness always inspire children with respect. But there must be no make-believe about it. A group of children have a wonderful quickness at seeing through any kind of shams.

It will help the teacher in keeping his class in order if he will be careful to sit in such a position that he can at all times see all the members of his class. In some schools, where semicircular benches are used, it is not uncommon to see a teacher place himself so near the scholars at the centre of the seat that those on the extreme right and left are entirely beyond the reach of the teacher's vision. In fact they are behind him.

The power to govern children does not come by delegation. Scholars mind you, if at all, not because the superintendent or their parents have told them they must mind you, but because it is in you to be minded. This power over children is a personal attribute, inherent, incommunicable. The first element in it is a strong will. You must resolutely determine to carry your point. The next element in importance is a persuasive manner, and the best way to bring about this persuasive manner is to cultivate a love for children in your heart. Without this love in your heart all your smiles and your bland words will be sham, and will be seen to be such by the children. These two ingredients, love and firmness, are the main sources of the teacher's power.

4. *Aim to Teach Something.* Let the teacher aim distinctly to teach something. This may seem a very simple rule, hardly worth uttering. Yet many make a serious mistake just here. They occupy the teacher's chair, they go through a certain routine of duty from week to week, but they do not teach. Let it be remembered that talking is not necessarily teaching. Hearing recitations is not teaching. Teaching is making some one know what he did not know before. Let the teacher, when the hour is over, ask himself this question: Do my class know anything which they did not know before? or have they merely exhibited to me what they had learned in preparing the lesson? Have they gone away with a distinct, positive addition to their scriptural knowledge? This will be found a searching and critical question, and the teacher who can answer it in the affirmative will find himself surely gaining a hold upon his scholars. Nothing so effectually secures good attendance as the consciousness on the part of the pupils that they are learning. But the teacher who would reach this end must aim at it with distinct purpose, and must habitually raise the question, whether he has really been teaching. If he does not, he may depend upon it that much of his labor is going to waste. He is working, but doing nothing.

5. *Aim to Teach Something Additional Every Sunday.* The mistake of some teachers is that they act fitfully. They get hold of a new thought now and then, and lavish their gifts of instruction upon the class for a while, but the stream soon runs dry. A dreary interval of drouth and dearth succeeds. I have known teachers, gifted and brilliant, who would thus hold a class delighted for a single Sunday, now and then, but who, for want of method and persistence, failed in the long run. It is not the large gains, but the steady gains, that make rich. There is a wonderful power in simple addition. The teacher must, in this sense, act on the principle of the miser. Every week have some new thought or fact or illustration for your class. Let them get unconsciously into the habit of feeling that they can never be absent without losing something. The amount of new matter contributed each week may not be large. You had better not attempt to make it large. Only be sure that each week you teach your class something that they did not know before, and you will be surprised at the end of a year to see how much they have grown in knowledge. You will find, too, that your own old stock of ideas is running out, and you will need to keep replenishing yourself. If you are to teach them something fresh every week, you must every week have something fresh yourself.

6. *Aim to Teach Something to Every Scholar.* This is the hardest point of all, and the one least frequently attained. Every class has some scholars

who are dull, inattentive, indolent, perhaps positively perverse. Every class has also some of exactly the opposite character to that just described. The temptation is strong to give one's time to these bright, studious, loving pupils, to the neglect of the others. It is such a pleasure to teach the one kind, it is such a toil to teach the other. But such a course is not wise husbandry. The farmer who would gather a large return from his acres does not content himself with having a few heavy ears here and there. What he aims at is to have some substantial returns from every foot of soil. The drooping and sickly plants are the ones which before all others receive his care. The hardy and vigorous plant will thrive anyhow. So with the bright scholar. You are almost sure he will learn. Bend your efforts, then, to get a good return from the dull boys and girls. If you succeed with them, you will not fail with the others. If, on the other hand, there is any child in your class who habitually learns nothing, depend upon it, that child will soon drop out of your class. The very best method for preventing the loss of scholars is to see that every scholar every Sunday learns something from you. A class in which this is done will be always full. Old scholars stick to it, new scholars are glad to get into it. But to secure such an end, the teacher will find that he has need not only of making it a special aim, but a subject of much special study. He must acquaint himself with the disposition and the intellectual condition of each scholar, so that even in presenting the same truth to his class, he must have various modes of doing it, one suited to one pupil and one suited to another, and he must keep at it until every one is reached.

7. *Aim to Make your Instructions Scriptural.* The Bible is our text-book in the Sunday-school. The teacher is not fulfilling his mission who occupies the hours of the Lord's day in telling anecdotes and amusing the children with entertaining stories. Children may be held in rapt attention all the hour, and yet go away no wiser in Bible knowledge. Where an apt story or illustration will not only gain attention, but make a Bible truth plainer to the child's apprehension, or fix it deeper in his memory, the use of such a story or illustration is commendable. But in our Sunday-schools we have a great deal of story-telling which has no end beyond merely keeping the children entertained. There is also occasionally a teacher who aims to gain the attention of his scholars by giving them curious scientific and literary information. The scholars are entertained and pleased, and the knowledge gained is of a kind that is innocent and even honorable. But it is not that for which the Sunday-school was instituted. The teacher should aim to see not only that his class is learning something, that they are learning something every Sunday, that every one of them is learning, but also that they are adding to their knowledge of the sacred Scriptures.

8. *Besides a Knowledge of the Meaning of the Bible, aim to get your Pupils to Store up a Portion of its Very Words.* In our Sunday-schools, and in all our schools in these days, we are going into the extreme of neglecting the cultivation of the memory. Childhood is the time when this faculty should receive special cultivation and development, and in the whole range of studies to which a child is called, there is none that gives so precious a field for the selection of passages suitable for this purpose. I do not advocate setting children to committing to memory whole books of the Bible. If it were practicable for them to know the whole Bible by heart, this plan would be less objectionable. But as the portion of the Bible which any child can commit is comparatively small, the portions thus learned should be selected, and the value of the acquisitions will usually depend very much upon the care and judgment of the teacher in making a selection. A teacher should go over the Bible for this very purpose, and mark passages suitable to be committed to memory, so that he can direct a child at once to a verse or verses proper to his particular case. It would be a great gain if we paid more attention than we do to the book of Proverbs. A few of these priceless maxims—worldly wisdom coined in heaven's mint—stored away in the mind of the child, might save the man from many a ruinous business mistake. Psalms, parables, the Sermon on the Mount, short summaries of doctrine from the Epis-

tles, etc., should be thus committed. The Bible is full of passages, sometimes a single verse, sometimes a paragraph, just fitted for storing in the memory. Teacher, do not neglect this precious opportunity. Aim to secure from every scholar, every week, the committing to memory of some portion of God's holy word.

9. *Aim at the Conversion of your Scholars.* Until this is accomplished the work is incomplete. Attendance, lessons, order, everything, is subordinate to this, and mainly valuable as an auxiliary to this. "How shall I bring this child to the saving knowledge of Jesus Christ?" is the burden of the true teacher's heart. Not "How shall I make him well-mannered?" or "How shall I, by inculcating habits of order and industry, improve his social condition?" or "How shall I preserve him from sickness or disease?" but, "How shall I save his soul from everlasting death?—how shall I snatch him as a brand from the burning?"

Teacher, keep this great aim ever before you. Seek the conversion of your children, not in the uncertain hereafter, not as something to be gained by them when they become men and women, but *now*. Every week, seek their conversion that very week. Seek it, not in the spirit of dictation to the Almighty, not in the spirit of discontent, but in earnest, importunate, agonizing prayer. Seek it with unutterable longing. Seek it in hope, as something to be expected. Seek it with persevering courage against every disappointment. Seek it in the use of every appropriate and available means.

Will Sunday-school teachers, will parents, will the church, ever really wake up to the fact that children may be converted just as easily as grown people, nay, far more easily? Will the time ever come when the means and energy put forth for the conversion of children shall be truly commensurate with the results which labors for the young ordinarily produce? We do something, indeed, in their behalf in the family and in the school. Yet after all, down deep in the heart of the Christian Church is the yet unshaken belief—not expressed, perhaps—that "Youth is *not* the time to serve the Lord." Notwithstanding all our sayings and preachings to the contrary, we involuntarily think of adult age as the time when people are expected to be converted. We admit that children *may* become Christians. But when a case does occur, we regard it rather as a marvel, as something out of the common way. Is there not an enormous practical delusion on this subject? Is it not one of Satan's most gigantic devices to cheat the church out of some of the richest parts of her inheritance? Has the church, have parents and teachers, anywhere, gone to work in downright earnest, as they would do in any similar case where a temporal or a worldly interest was at stake?

The several aims here pointed out are all plain and practical. No one who wishes can be at a loss to know whether or not he reaches them. I recommend to the teacher every Sunday evening to make a written register of progress. Let him interrogate himself honestly how far he has that day succeeded in each, and in what particulars he has failed. This record will doubtless show many failures. But it will help wonderfully to keep him to his work, and he will ere long find himself substantially and surely reaching what he aims at.

5. *The Difference between Sunday-school Teaching and Teaching in other Schools.*

In many things teaching is the same, whatever be the subject, the time, or the character of the pupil. The very essence of teaching—which is simply causing one to know—is and must be the same under all conditions. While admitting this to its fullest extent, I think it important also to note that, in many of its processes, teaching is a most variable art. One will make a woeful mistake who undertakes to teach children as he would teach adults, to teach in the Sunday-school exactly as he teaches in the weekday-school, or to apply to the teaching of religious truth all methods that may be proper and right in teaching arithmetic and geography.

What are some of the things in which Sunday-school teaching differs from other teaching?

1. In the first place, we can use none of the ordinary school penalties for compelling attendance, attention or study of lessons. Other teachers may

13 *

or may not have the affection of their scholars. But to the Sunday-school teacher it is essential. Without the love of his scholars he can do nothing. This is his only hold upon them. This is the silken rein by which he must draw them. He may curb them to some extent by that natural authority with which God has clothed some minds as their inalienable birthright. But beyond this he cannot go. He must make up his mind, therefore, to be content in many cases with intellectual results far short of what he obtains from pupils of a like grade on other days of the week. Not always, however. Love is a great worker. Under its influence, with no other promptings, a pupil will sometimes achieve a progress truly astonishing. But these are special cases. In the main, children will not learn their Sunday lessons with that fulness, exactness, and regularity which are expected, and which may be effectually *required* of their lessons on the other days in the week. Let the Sunday-school teacher aim, indeed, to secure lessons of the very best and highest character. But if he comes short of this high standard, let him not be discouraged, or think that his teaching is a failure.

2. In the second place, religious truth, which is the subject of Sunday-school instruction, is far more directly practical than the truth or knowledge which forms the subject of other teachings. A youth in the weekday-school studies a passage in Shakespeare or Milton for the sake of tracing its grammatical

construction, or its poetical beauty, or the force of its argument, or the derivation and power of particular words and phrases, or the historical allusions and parallels. He solves a question in algebra or arithmetic. It is a mere mental gymnastic. It has served its main purpose when it has given him intellectual exercise, and the intellectual strength and acumen which are the legitimate fruit of that exercise. But far different is the spirit in which he should approach the study of any scriptural subject. The parable of the Prodigal Son may, indeed, exercise his intellect and his fancy, and his power of taste and judgment, as much as any work of art. His main object and aim in the study, however, is not mental cultivation, but the practical application of the parable to his own conduct and condition. What does the great Teacher mean for *me* in this parable? Wherein am *I* like this prodigal? How am *I* to act in view of these teachings? Noah's flood, or the destruction of the cities of the plain, finds its chief interest as a Sunday lesson for us, not in its geological explanations or history, but in its character as a religious truth—an alarming demonstration to the conscience that God's Spirit will not always strive with man. All Scripture is intended for the instruction of man in practical godliness, and we miss the main intention of any Sunday lesson when we secure only an intellectual product. We aim, indeed, to secure this, but only as a means of securing something infinitely, transcendently greater.

Here is an important distinction which teachers would do well to ponder. Do not teach the Gospel, or the Acts of the Apostles, or any part of Holy Writ, as you would teach a page in geography, or a chapter in the history of the United States. A clear apprehension of the facts and of the import of the language used is, of course, the first requirement in Bible study. But that is only a preliminary step to the main lesson. The Bible student is not unlike a soldier on the field of battle who happens to be a foreigner unacquainted with the language. First of all, he must learn the import of the word of command. But the soldier does not rest there. The command is something to be done as well as known. So all Bible knowledge, so far as it is religious knowledge at all, and a fit subject for Sunday study, is practical knowledge. It is something to be done. It is something which employs the intellect only as an avenue for reaching the conscience.

3. In the third place, in the Sunday-school, care should be taken, more even than in the weekday school, to store the memory. This is not a difference so much in kind as in degree. In all teaching it is important, after certain results are reached and clearly established, to store them up in the mind in the form of rules, maxims or principles. It is well to commit to memory the exact words in which weighty truths have been expressed by the great, leading minds of the race. But in the Bible we have the most momentous truths expressed in the

words of God himself—the truths of salvation in the
words of Him who is the author of salvation. The
young cannot be too diligent in treasuring up these
precious words in the memory. What a fund of
practical worldly wisdom is contained in the proverbs of Solomon! What priceless texts for every
emergency of religious experience in the psalms of
David! What words of consolation, of warning, of
prayer, of faith, of hope, in the Gospels and the Epis-
tles! Everywhere in the Bible, tucked away often
among mere historical or ceremonial details, are precious phrases, like detached nuggets of virgin gold,
which should be seized upon and laid up for use.
Of course, in studying the Bible, we proceed in many
particulars as we do in other studies. But, in my
opinion, there is no study in which we should use
the memory so freely and so largely.

I fear there has been on this point a serious and
hurtful departure from the good old ways. I fear
there is not as much as there once was of committing to memory the sacred Scriptures. Will teachers
and parents look to this matter?

6. *Class-Teaching.*

By class-teaching I mean teaching a considerable
number at once, as distinguished from teaching one
at a time. It is not uncommon to see teachers with
large classes who yet never do any real class-teaching. Such a teacher will hear Johnny say his verses,
and perhaps give him some explanation of their

meaning, will then hear Jimmy say an answer in the catechism, then Charley say a hymn which he has learned, and so on, taking one scholar at a time, until the class is finished. This is teaching *in* a class, but it is not class-teaching. The distinction is something more than a mere play upon words. It involves facts of the gravest import. I fear there are more teachers following the individual method than superintendents generally are aware—teachers, I mean, who never teach a class as such, but give instruction successively and separately to one after another in a class.

I hold it to be the duty of the superintendent to look into this matter by personal observation, and wherever a teacher is found who can teach by the individual method only—that is, one at a time—I do not say the superintendent should dispense with the services of such a teacher, but he should feel bound, so far as this method is allowed to prevail in his school, to provide as many teachers as there are scholars. Every scholar has a claim to instruction all the time he is in school. If a teacher has ten scholars and follows this method with them, he has what appears to be a class, but it is really ten classes.

Class-teaching consists in making a unit of all the scholars, no matter how many, who are under one teacher. The ability of teachers differs in this. One teacher can make a unit of twenty, another of ten, another of five, another of three, while some, and their number is larger than is generally supposed, can teach but one, or at the most but two, at a time. Nothing is gained by assigning to a teacher more scholars than he can keep occupied all the time. The school may have a prettier appearance, perhaps, when the scholars are evenly distributed by sevens or eights all over the room. But for the real benefit of the scholars, it is better to assign to some teachers but one or two scholars apiece, and to others twenty or thirty, if thereby all the scholars are fully occupied all the time. A teacher is overloaded the moment he has a single scholar more than he can keep fully occupied. Every teacher should ascertain, or the superintendent should ascertain for him, exactly how many he can thus weld into one, and every scholar added to the class after it has reached that limit should be considered as so much material wasted.

Of course there may be real teaching and good teaching by the individual method. Rich people sometimes employ a private tutor to devote his whole time to the instruction of one child. But such instruction is enormously expensive. Besides that, except in special cases, it is less valuable to the pupil than instruction received in genuine class-teaching. In the latter, the pupil receives a stimulus from his fellows which is wanting in the other case. Reciting by one's self to a private tutor is dull and stupefying work compared to the brisk, breezy, bracing exercises of a class.

It is not an easy task to hold at all times the attention of an entire class, so that whatever the teacher says to one is said equally to all, and whatever any one scholar says is heard and shared in by all. Yet nothing short of this can claim to be class-teaching. The entire intellectual activity of both teacher and scholars is concentrated upon a single point, and this concentration, like that of the sun's rays brought to a focus by a convex lens, gives heat as well as light. Truths glow with brightness and shine into the soul with a certain piercing vigor when a considerable number of minds, all wide awake, are united as one mind in the examination of a subject. To produce this concentration, to weld five, or ten, or twenty, or fifty young minds into one, to arrest at once the least wandering of attention, requires no little skill. It is the first and most indispensable requisite in the teacher's art.

The object of classification in a school is to enable the teacher to do class-teaching. The more thoroughly this object is accomplished, the greater will be the general improvement and efficiency of the school. No teacher should rest contented until he has achieved some success in this line. It is a matter in which improvement is capable of almost infinite degrees. The best way for one who is conscious of being deficient in this respect is to begin with a small number and increase it as you acquire the power. When you have learned to control thoroughly the attention of five scholars, try six.

When you are master of six, try seven. Let it be
your ambition to see how many young minds you
can wield as one, remembering that you multiply
yourself by every one added to the number of your
scholars. If during the entire hour you can wield
the undivided attention of twenty pupils, you are
virtually making yourself twenty teachers. You are
at least making yourself equal to twenty of those
who teach by the individual method.

To gain this power, the first requisite is a resolute,
determined aim to do it. Mere wishing it or fretting
about it will not compass the end. Set about it in
good earnest, and be willing to make some sacrifices
in order to accomplish it. Entire, absolute familiarity with what you are going to teach is another
requisite. The teacher who wishes to control the
attention of a class must know the lesson so thoroughly as to be able to teach it without book. This
is an inexorable condition of success. Close your
book before you begin to teach if you wish to put
forth any teaching power. Thus only can you bring
your mind into living contact and sympathy with the
minds before you.

7. *How to Question a Class.*

Skill in the art of questioning is a qualification
for the teacher's office of the very highest importance.
In the long catalogue of things required there is
hardly one that should be set higher. It cannot,
therefore, be too much insisted on or too much dis-

14

cussed.   I shall offer a few thoughts on the subject
for the consideration of teachers.

1. In the first place, the teacher who expects to
excel in this particular must make up his mind that
the gift referred to is really a most valuable and important attainment.   No other quality can supply
its place in the peculiar power of awakening, guiding and moulding the minds of others.   Eloquence
and learned discourse can do much in producing an
impression, and of course are not to be underrated.
But the peculiarity of the influence exerted by skill
in the art of questioning is that it goes directly to the
very roots of the soul, so to speak.   It operates in
the formation of opinion, in the growth of intellectual power, and in the increase of knowledge, in a
way altogether peculiar to itself, with a directness
and energy unattainable by other methods of instruction.   The prodigious influence exerted by the late
Dr. Archibald Alexander, of Princeton, upon the
mind of the Presbyterian Church in the United
States was not due so much to his lectures in the
theological seminary, for he lectured comparatively
little, nor to his published theological works, which
are lamentably few, but to his wonderful power as a
catechist.   In the theological class-room it seemed
as if there was not a thought or a perplexity in the
mind of any student which did not lie open to the
penetrating ken of the professor, not a power of
thinking which the professor did not stimulate into
lively action.   He seemed to touch, as if with the

wand of an enchanter, all the hidden springs of
thought, and whatever of mental power was in a
man came forth. It was thus he moulded and developed all those great minds which have exerted,
and which are now exerting, such a controlling influence upon the destinies of the Presbyterian Church
in America. Dr. Alexander, like Socrates among
the ancients, has written comparatively little. But
his power as a teacher was second to none, not even
to that of Socrates, and it will go on perpetuating
and reproducing itself for ages to come.

It is not expected, of course, that every teacher
will have the gifts of Dr. Alexander. But his example is worthy of study as showing the kind of excellence desired, and also the prodigious results of
which it is capable. It is no ordinary matter, like
some of the mechanical details of the teacher's work,
but something of first-class importance.

2. In the second place, the teacher, after having
risen to a due sense of the importance of this gift
and a corresponding desire for its attainment, should
define clearly in his own mind the true object of the
art of questioning as a teaching power. It is not
uncommon to see teachers, in asking questions, proceed as if the sole object of the exercise was to find
out and record how much the scholar had learned
before coming to the class. Such a teacher unconsciously puts himself in the attitude of a public pros-
ecutor or of a detective policeman. His questions
are formed with a view to find out whether the pupil

has exercised due diligence in learning the lesson, and to know exactly how much of merit or demerit to mete out to him in the roll-book. Now this is to lower the whole affair—to mistake and ignore the true nature of the teacher's office. Of course, it is of prime importance that the scholars should prepare and study the lesson before coming to the class, and a proper record of faithfulness or unfaithfulness in this respect is among the legitimate means of stimulating scholars to study. I believe in recitation marks. Their influence, when rightly used, is pervasive and beneficent. But after all, they are to be reckoned as the mint, anise and cummin, and not among the weightier matters.

The true object in questioning in class is not so much to ascertain the present amount of their knowledge as to increase it. It is to awaken thought, to bring up suggestive inquiries into their minds, to deepen impressions of truth already received, to bring into clear and sharp outline what is now seen but dimly and obscurely. It is a sifting process, by which the pupils are enabled to let go the chaff and to hold fast the pure wheat. Questioning, properly conducted, produces a sort of intellectual ferment in the minds of the class which is very favorable to the acquisition of new truths. Mind is a curious machine, working according to laws of its own; and one of those laws is, that a certain amount of excitement is necessary to the rapid and sure apprehension of knowledge. A truth, a sentence, a single word dropped into the mind just at the right moment, when its powers of eager inquiry and lively apprehension are all in the highest state of activity, will produce a greater fructifying effect than any conceivable amount of dull, plodding ·routine over lessons.

Nor should the teacher make the mistake, which many make, of supposing that the mind of a child is merely a fountain, and the questioning process is a sort of pump, and that by a due working of the machine knowledge can be drawn out. Knowledge is never drawn out unless it has first been taken in Mind is a power, and the business of the teacher is to stir up that power. When knowledge has once entered the mind, it is indeed important that it should be again given out. The reproduction of our knowledge in intelligible form is as important to us as is the first taking of it in. We get an idea, and then we give it out. In all true teaching the two processes go together. The one is the complement of the other. Direct, positive inculcation should always accompany questioning. Pour in as well as draw out. Draw out what you pour in.

The main end, then, of questioning a class is not to register progress, but to promote it—to stir up mental activity and add to the pupil's stock of knowledge. No matter how studious a scholar may be, or how faithful may have been his preparation, he will come away from the recitation, if it has been rightly conducted, knowing more than he did. One hour

14 * L

of recitation ought to be worth three hours of solitary study.

3. How shall a teacher question a class so as to bring about this result?

In the first place, he must not limit himself to the questions in the question-book. To sit down before a class and read questions out of a book is about the dullest and most stupid, as well as most stupefying, process ever attempted. Better that every question-book in print were with Pharaoh's chariots at the bottom of the Red Sea than that such a process of hearing lessons should fix itself upon our schools. The question-book has its place. but that place is not in the school-room or the class. The sole object of the question-book is to help in preparing the lesson. Neither teacher nor scholar should be allowed to bring one to school ; or if brought to school, they should be gathered up and carefully piled away before the lesson begins. What if the teacher in catechising the class does forget to ask some of the questions, or asks them in a different order from that in the book, or asks them in different words? Ten questions springing up as the course of inquiry suggests, while teacher and scholars are engaged in earnest conversation, face to face, eye to eye, are worth fifty questions put and answered in the usual humdrum style.

In the second place, the teacher who would question his class with skill and effect must be thoroughly at home in the lesson. He must not only know the facts and truths which it involves, but he must be familiar with them. He must know them as he knows the road to school. It is on this point more than any other that teachers fail. They think if they go over a lesson and study out all its hard points, so as to understand them, they are prepared. It is a mistake. Study the hard points, of course. But what you chiefly want is familiarity with the easy points. In order to teach you must have your knowledge not safely laid away in some remote recess of the understanding—in some underground magazine of your intellectual fortress—but brought forward into the very outworks, ready for instant handling and use—on the tip of your tongue and the tip of your fingers, talking and chalking, asking and telling, just as the emergency of each successive moment calls for.

In the third place, get back from your scholars all you give them. It is implied in the very idea of teaching that you communicate to your scholars some new ideas—some facts or thoughts which they did not know before. Now this process is incomplete until you induce the class to reproduce and give back to you in some intelligible form what you have thus given them. The knowledge is really not theirs until they have reproduced it and given it expression. They may have some vague idea or transient impression in regard to it. But they do not grasp it with firm hold or with a clear and lasting apprehension until they have expressed it in language. This is one of the laws of mental action. We fix a thing in our minds by communicating it to another ; we make it plain to ourselves by the very effort to give it explanation. Or, to state the matter still more paradoxically, we learn a thing by telling it to somebody, we keep it by giving it away. The only way to be sure that your scholars are learning from you is to get them to tell you back all you have told them. The teacher who does all the talking, or even the greater part of it, is making a mistake. You may talk very well, your scholars may hang with rapt attention upon your lips, and yet you may be making a huge mistake. You are attempting to make a web that is all warp. Fill in the woof, if you would make a texture that will hang together. Let the long yarns of your discourse be constantly crossed and recrossed by the swift-flying shuttle of question and answer, if you would be a weaver worthy of the name.

In the fourth place, do not ask your questions regularly round the class, but skip about, taking first one scholar and then another, without following any regular order, only being sure to light down on any one that is inattentive, and being sure also to call on every one in the course of the lesson, the dull as well as the bright, the lazy as well as the diligent. Do not pride yourself upon puzzling your scholars and asking questions which none of them can answer. You may take this method sometimes, perhaps, to check a child that is forward or pert. But such cases are rare compared with those who are timid and who need encouragement. Be prepared, therefore, with easy questions as well as with hard ones, and have something to ask which any one in the class, even the dullest and the most timid, can answer. The questioning power is not perfect which is not able to unloose every tongue in the class.

8. *How to Conduct a Recitation.*

1. *Closing the Books.* Let the teacher begin by closing his own book, and by collecting and piling up all the books of every kind in the class. I have no objection to hearing a preacher or a lecturer read a discourse. But when it comes to teaching, no reading either by teacher or scholar should be tolerated. The teacher is there not to read something out of a book, but to tell the scholars something that he knows. The scholars are there not to read answers out of a book, but to recite answers which they have prepared. They are to tell the teacher their thoughts, either in language committed to memory from the book, or in their own language, in order that their answers may be canvassed by the teacher and compared with his views. The teacher may say, perhaps, that, in attempting to conduct a recitation without referring to the book, he is likely to omit many of the questions, or not to call them in the order in which they occur. I think this is altogether probable. But the questions, be it remem-

bered, are to study by, not to recite by. They help
the teacher to fill his mind with the subject; there
their function ends. Coming to his class with his
mind thus full, it is of little matter whether he follows the order of the book or not, or whether he
goes through all the minutiæ in the book or not.
He will find himself in possession of ample materials
to fill up all the time at his disposal. This hand-to-
hand encounter between scholars and teacher, in
discussing the meaning of a lesson, is unlike any
other mental process that we ever go through, and
is, of all our mental processes, the one most vital-
izing; neither solitary study, nor listening to discourses and lectures, is comparable to it in the
quickening effect which it has upon the mental
faculties. It is of the very essence of teaching.
Nothing else is teaching.

2. *Reciting the Verses.* Having closed his own
book and collected and closed the books of the
class, let the teacher next have the Bible verses recited which form the subject of the lesson. And
here will come a real difficulty. At first, especially,
the scholars will not know the verses. One of the
most difficult things, nowadays, in the whole work of
the school-room, whether in the Sunday-school or in
other schools, is to get the young to commit anything
to memory. The current seems to have all set the
other way, and whoever attempts the thing named
will find himself working his way up stream. Nevertheless, it is worth the effort, and if he persists, he

will in the end succeed. And in this matter of reciting the verses the teacher himself should set the
example. The first thing he ought to do, in preparing the lesson, is to commit to memory the passage
which he is to expound. The lessons, as marked
off in our question-books, seldom exceed a dozen
verses, and surely there is no one so busy or so dull
of recollection as not to be able to learn that much
in the course of the week. Let the teacher, in this
part of the exercise, set the example, not only in
committing the verses to memory, but in reciting
them. If they are recited verse about, each member
of the class saying one, let the teacher take his turn
with the rest. If he happens to have a class no one
of which has learned the verses, let him recite the
whole! Such an example will shame the scholars
into learning some verses at least. The first and
most earnest and most persistent effort of the Sunday-
school teacher should be directed to this end; that
is, to securing from his scholars an accurate and
prompt recital from memory of the verses which
form the body of the lesson.

3. *Hunting up the References.* Have some
method about hunting up passages or places which
are referred to in the lesson, or which come up for
remark or illustration in the course of the exercises.
A good plan is to have by you a Bible, a Scripture
atlas, and a Bible dictionary, and whenever a question arises in the course of the conversation between
the teacher and the scholars about some place or

person or passage of Scripture, and it is desirable to
have the matter settled by a reference to the book,
do not delay the class or yourself by stopping to hunt
up the thing referred to, but selecting some one of
the class for this purpose, and giving him the book
to make the search, go on to some topic until he is
ready to report. As soon as he has found the information required, a pause can be made in the recitation, and he or you can read or show to the class
the result of his inquiries. The task of making these
searches should not always be assigned to the same
pupil, but should be distributed, first to one and
then to another, so that all in turn may share in the
exercise. By such a process two important ends
are gained. The time of the class is economized,
and the members are gradually trained to familiarity and skill in the use of books of reference. It
would not be amiss to have by you, besides the
three books which have been named, a good English dictionary, such as the latest edition of Webster's
octavo. Questions often arise in a Sunday-school
class about the pronunciation or the meaning of a
word, and it is well to settle it authoritatively and on
the spot.

4. *Skipping About.* In every part of the exercise, whether in reciting the verses or in answering
questions, never go round the class in regular order,
but skip about from one to another, so that no or e
may know when he is to be called upon. Propoun d
a question first, clearly and distinctly, so that all

can hear, and try to make all hear it, and then select and designate the one who is to give the answer. If you see a scholar inattentive and listless, or giving his attention to something else, let that be an invariable reason for putting the question to him. If you do not succeed in getting an answer from him, you will succeed in recalling his attention. Have in your mind a number of easy questions which almost everybody can answer. In nearly every class are some who are timid, or who are slow of comprehension, or slow of speech, and they are apt to fall into the idea that nothing is to be done by them, nothing is expected of them. They need encouragement, and there is no way of encouraging them equal to that of giving them something to do which they can do. Do not let all the talking and reciting be done by a few bright scholars, but see that something is said or done by every one, the dullest and most timid as well as the most sprightly and forward.

5. *Keeping all the Class Engaged.* Aim to have the attention of all your scholars all the time. Do not make the mistake of some teachers who seem to think that they are to break up their time into little doses, giving first two or three minutes to one, and then two or three minutes to another, and so on round the class. Aim to keep your own mind and that of your class filled with the idea that everything which you say, and also everything which one of the scholars says, is said not to an individual, but to the class, that the whole thing, in every one of its

15

parts, is a class exercise, addressed to and belonging to the class as a whole, and not to any one individual. To this end always place yourself, whether sitting or standing, in such a way that your eyes can command every part of the class. Some teachers place themselves so close to the class that a part of the line of pupils overlaps them to the right and left, and so is out of the line of vision and of direct communication. Such a thing may seem to some to be a small matter, but it is of great importance in securing entire and undivided attention from the class.

6. *Making the Scholars do the Talking.* Aim to get your scholars to talk, rather than to talk yourself. Of course the teacher must have something to say. But many teachers err in doing all the talking. It is by telling a thing, by explaining it to others, by giving expression to it in words, that it becomes .clearly defined and fixed in our own mind. This is one of the laws of mental action, and this is one reason that people learn faster by reciting and by catechetical instruction than by listening to lectures. However fluent we may be in conducting a recitation, our scholars are learning little from us unless we manage to unloose their tongues as well as ours. In all good teaching there is the joint action of the teacher's mind and of the scholar's mind. It can never be a one-sided process. Give the scholar the needed information if he is destitute of it, but make him give it back to you in words. Be sure he has

not made it his own until he has thus reproduced it. Draw out and pour in. Pour in and draw out. This, as I have said before, is the sum of the whole matter.

9. *Teaching Out of Book.*

Imagine a company of soldiers, raw recruits, standing up to drill. The captain is undertaking to teach them the complicated bodily movements connected with facing, wheeling, marching and handling their weapons. Imagine him standing, book in hand, and perhaps spectacles on his nose, and finger on the line to keep the place, carefully *reading* the word of command, then looking off the book to see the movement of the soldiers, then looking back at the book to read the description of the movement and see whether it corresponds to the way in which the soldiers have executed it, then proceeding to the next movement, and so on through the whole manual of arms and book of military tactics. Is there any one that would not pronounce the whole proceeding absurd?

Yet this is precisely what may be seen in the school-room any day in the week, Sunday *not* excepted. Go into a Sunday-school, or into any other school. In nineteen cases out of twenty the teacher is before his class, *book in hand*, undertaking to teach exactly as our imaginary captain was undertaking to drill. The proceeding is just as absurd in the one case as in the other. All the difficulty of maintaining order, of securing attention, of making the children interested, of keeping every part of the class engaged at the same time, has its root in this method of teaching out of book. If the teacher is pinned down to his question-book, obliged first to read the question, then to look at his class, then to look at the answer in the book to see if it corresponds to that given by the scholar, he may perhaps be hearing a lesson, but he is *not* teaching. In real teaching there should be no book in the hands of either teacher or scholars. I do not mean that books should not be used in the preparation of the lesson. Some persons indeed go so far as to say that text-books should be dispensed with entirely, the teacher supplying the knowledge by familiar lectures, and then catechising the pupils upon it until they know it. This is a mistake in the other extreme. In my opinion the scholars should have a text-book, and should prepare their lessons by means of it. It is important for them not only to learn the knowledge or facts contained in the lesson, but to learn how to study. The object of the recitation, however, is to sift the knowledge acquired by the pupil in his private preparation, to bring it out for examination, to correct it wherever it is faulty, to round it and give it completeness by additions from the teacher's own fulness.

Nothing is so exhilarating to all concerned as real, live teaching. Scholars and teacher enjoy it alike. But to this end, while in the class, books must be entirely laid aside. Where the class has a room by itself, so that the teacher can be free in his movements, he should stand or walk about in front of his class just as a captain or a drill sergeant does in front of his company. Sitting down to teach is precisely on a par with sitting down while putting a company of soldiers through their movements. Teaching is a mental gymnastic, and while it lasts it should be conducted with such vigor and such tension of mind that at brief intervals, half an hour or three-quarters at the most, teacher and pupils alike will need a breathing-spell.

Most of the teachers whose eyes these paragraphs will reach will think it quite out of the question for *them* to attempt to carry this theory through with their classes. Suppose their class has a lesson in the question-book. How *can* the teacher remember all those minute questions? But is it necessary that you should? Is it *intended* that all these questions should be asked and answered in recitation, and exactly in the order put down in the book? Most decidedly, No. The true way to use a question-book is this. First, let all, scholars and teacher, commit thoroughly to memory the text or verses which form the basis of the lesson. If any of the scholars cannot as yet be induced to do this, let the teacher at least not fail to do it. Let him have the verses at his tongue's end, just as the captain has at his tongue's end the various words of command. The next step in preparing the lesson is to find answers

15 *

to all the questions in the book. This helps to bring out the meaning. The teacher would do well also to go over the subject in his mind and see how far he can recall the various points without referring to the book. Having thus studied the lesson, let teacher and pupil both when the hour for teaching arrives lay aside their books and come face to face as friend to friend when talking about some point of interest, as man to man when meeting in the street, as buyer and seller when driving a bargain.

There is a prevailing timidity on this point among Sunday-school teachers. It requires some nerve at first to undertake to teach without book. But a little extra exertion in preparing the lesson will secure you against failure, and when you have once achieved success and delivered yourself from the trammels of the book-method, you will feel such freedom and joy in the work that you will wonder how you could ever have worked otherwise.

That I may not be supposed to be advocating something entirely unattainable, let me quote an example or two to show what is done wherever the art of teaching has been made a study.

Professor Newell, the Principal of the Normal School of Maryland, before taking charge of that institution, went on a tour of observation to some of the leading State Normal schools of the country. In his report on the subject occurs the following remark : "Though I did not find exactly the same methods of instruction prevailing in all the schools visited, nor even in all the departments of the same school, yet a striking family likeness could be noticed among them all. *I never saw a teacher in one of those schools use a text-book* (other than a spelling or a reading-book), except for occasional reference. I was present at recitations in history in several schools, and *in none did the teacher use a book.* Every lesson seemed to be thoroughly mastered and systematically arranged in the teacher's mind before coming to class; and I have no doubt that many of the teachers spent as much time in preparation as their scholars did."

Horace Mann, in his report of six weeks among the Prussian schools, says: "During all this time *I never saw a teacher hearing a lesson of any kind* (except a reading or a spelling lesson) *with a book in his hand.*"

"I never saw a teacher with a text-book in his hand!" Will our Sunday-school teachers ponder these words? It is not meant that text-books should be discarded. The schools visited by Professor Newell were not taught on the lecture system. The classes and the teachers that he describes in almost every case had used books in the preparation of the lesson. But in reciting the lesson teachers and pupils alike laid aside all books. In fact, no book is allowed to make its appearance in the recitation-room. Teacher and pupil meet in fair and equal encounter, each dependent solely on the knowledge that has become *bona fide* his own. The teacher stands up before his class and questions them, or discourses to them from the fulness of his own mind, looking them directly in the face. The scholar's response, in like manner, is from himself, not from his book. This is live work, and it has a quickening influence on all concerned. It almost certainly secures that direct contact of mind with mind which constitutes teaching. A man may learn by solitary study. But if he is taught by another, it must be by having that other's mind brought into living contact with his own, and there is no bar to this contact so thoroughly effectual as a text-book in the hand of the teacher. A man might as well attempt to see his class through leather spectacles as to teach them with his eye on a question-book.

Will our teachers who have been all their lives in bondage to their text-book method of hearing a lesson be persuaded for once to try teaching without book? They will be amazed at the sudden feeling of emancipation that they will experience. There is a wonderful sense of freedom and enjoyment in thus teaching. The scholars enjoy it too. Recitation instantly loses its character of humdrum, and becomes animated and absorbing, like the exercise of some pleasant game. The ideas too that are evolved in such a process acquire a peculiar sharpness and definiteness, and they are stamped in on the memory in characters never to be effaced.

It may perhaps require some courage for you to go before your class the first time without your question-book. You will undoubtedly see a lion in the path. But, like Bunyan's pilgrim, you will find the lion chained. Your first lesson on this plan will be your hardest. Every succeeding lesson will be easier, and in the end you will wonder that you could ever have been content to teach in any other way. The Sunday-school teacher of course will always need to have his Bible in hand, for the purpose of referring to chapter and verse when parallel passages are needed for confirmation. But the text and the topics of the lesson itself should always be thoroughly committed to memory and the question-book should be left at home.

Such a method undoubtedly requires study and preparation. But it pays.

10. *Holding the Attention of a Class.*

The idea which some teachers have of their office is that their whole duty consists in hearing lessons. Until this idea is thoroughly scattered to the winds there can be no progress, not even a tendency toward improvement. Teaching and hearing lessons are different processes. A child recites lessons when it repeats something previously learned. A child is taught when it learns from the teacher something not known before. The two things often, indeed, go together, but they are in themselves essentially distinct. A class of children may come to school, and each in turn recite what it has learned from its parents at home, and the teacher, so called, may be

M

of some use in listening to the children, and in judging and recording the merits of each. In performing such a function as this, it is hardly necessary to have the attention of any member of the class except the one who for the time is repeating his verses, and the teacher would find it next to impossible to secure any greater amount of attention, even should he attempt it. In a class so conducted all that the teacher can hope for is that, by the help of library books, papers, coaxing and scolding, the several members may be kept from actual riot during that portion of the hour when each one is not going through his own individual performance.

But let the teacher once wake up to the idea of what teaching really is, and he will begin to see, first how vital it is that he should all the time have the attention of all his class, and, secondly, that this essential result is really attainable. Let it only be understood that the class go to the teacher to learn something from him, and that the teacher goes to the class to teach them, that is, to make them know something which they did not know before. Nothing can be plainer than that he must have the undivided attention of the whole class all the time. To proceed without this would be working to the greatest possible disadvantage. Suppose a teacher has a class of ten, and that the time of actual teaching extends to fifty minutes, which is an allowance reached in few Sunday-schools. If the teacher, instead of claiming the attention of the whole class at once, proceeds on the individual method, and takes but one pupil at a time, he will have but five minutes to give to each, and besides, instead of giving but one lesson, will have to give ten separate lessons. The practical absurdity of such a method is too apparent to require argument. The teacher who would accomplish anything worth the name of teaching must come to his class with one definite, well-prepared lesson or train of thought in his mind, and must then give his whole time and energy to the task of putting that train of thought into the minds of his youthful auditory. How this is to be done is another matter. But the one indispensable prerequisite is that he have this singleness of purpose, and that the class for the time shall be a unit, that is, that he shall have their undivided attention.

Such attention will not be given to one whose own attention is confined in any considerable degree to the book. I cannot too often repeat, *The teacher must learn to teach without book.* To be obliged first to look into the book for the purpose of reading out a question, then to look round the class and hear the answer, then to look into the book again and see if the answer is right, is to subject one's self to continual embarrassment, and practically to lose control of the class. We may compare it to a man driving a six-horse team who should drop his lines every few rods for the purpose of buttoning up his coat, or putting a cracker on his whip, or to examine a map or a guide-book. Every time the teacher stops to look into the book, except in the most casual way, he drops the reins, and the young coursers take the bit into their own mouths. If the teacher would hold the attention of the class, he must give the class his own attention. Whatever attention is given by him to the book is so much withdrawn from the class, and consequently so much of his power over the class is lost. There is no mystery about it at all. Any teacher who has the lesson thoroughly at his command, so that if he needs to refer to the book at all it will only be in the most casual and rapid way, can experience no great difficulty in securing attention.

The true secret of the whole matter lies in the preparation of the lesson. Here is the difficulty. What can we say to persuade teachers to be more diligent in this matter? Going over the questions in a question-book and hunting out an answer to each question is not enough. The question-book is intended to help in studying the lesson, but should never be used in teaching it. Before beginning to hear a lesson, let teachers and scholars all lay aside their question-books. Collect them and pile them up until the lesson is over. What if you do forget some of the questions? No great harm is done, and an immense gain is secured. Teacher and scholars are thrown directly upon their own resources. Knowing that the lesson is to be gone through in this way, you will not fail to make your preparation in an entirely different kind of way from what you have been accustomed to. You will find in each lesson certain leading facts and thoughts, and you will endeavor to fix these definitely in your memory, without reference so much to the particular form of words in which they are expressed. You will unconsciously make questions of your own or put the same questions in different shapes, and will continue to go over each point until you find the whole class familiar with it.

By being thus untrammelled with the question-books, you and your scholars will be left to the free use of your eyes, and the eye is as great a teacher as the tongue. The teacher must look right into the eyes of his scholars all the while if he would hold their attention. Scholars like this living, constant interchange of looks with their teacher. The influence of it is magnetic. It quickens thought as well as sympathy. It transforms the whole exercise and makes the recitation a season of exhilaration and enjoyment. But no one can be thus free to use his eyes unless the lesson is entirely at his command, so that the book may be closed.

Study the lesson. Teach without book. Use your eyes. Do these three things, and you will find no difficulty in holding the attention of your class. You will then really and truly teach.

Before dropping the subject I wish to express another thought, though it is to some extent implied in what I have said already.

If you want to hold the attention of a class, par

ticularly if the scholars be quite young, you must make them all actors in what is going on. Children, grown people too, tire of being talked at, or merely acted upon. None of us like to be in the passive voice. The indicative, active, first person, singular, is the favorite part of the whole verb. There must be question and answer in quick succession if the class is to be kept thoroughly wide awake. If even in sermon time it were possible to have occasionally some "answering back," instead of the congregation remaining entirely passive, there would not be quite as many sleepers as we now sometimes see in looking over the pews.

As I have said before, children are often kept wide awake by skipping about in giving out the questions, instead of passing regularly round the class. But in pursuing this method one caution is to be observed. Unless the teacher is himself wide awake, all the reciting will be done by two or three bright scholars, while the lazy ones will quietly slip out altogether.

One of the finest methods of waking up a class that I have ever seen was in the Girls' High School of Philadelphia. The exercise was what used to be known in that institution as "fast parsing." In this case the questions were not skipped about, but passed in regular order round the class, but passed so rapidly that the pupils had to keep their wits about them with as much intensity of attention as that of the player at sword fencing. To make this movement the more rapid, the parsing of each word was cut up into as many separate items as possible, each pupil being required to give only one single item, and give it in the exact order previously prescribed. For example. In parsing a verb, pupil number one says, "It is a verb," number two gives the principal parts, number three says, "It is regular," number four, "It is transitive," number five, "It is in the active voice," number six, "It is in the past tense," number seven, "It is in the singular number," number eight, "It is in the third person," and so on. If any pupil hesitates a moment, or says wrong, or says the right thing out of its right order, the teacher instantly passes it on to "the next," "the next," until the right answer is given.

A class must, of course, have already attained good proficiency in parsing, or in any other exercise, before this method could be applied to it. But this point once gained, the effect in keeping the attention upon the strain is marvellous. It is not recommended as a means of securing close and careful thought, or learning nice distinctions, but simply as a sort of mental gymnastics. If the pupil lets his attention flag for half a minute he is tripped up. And then it differs from the usual methods of tossing a question about according to the show of hands or the snapping of fingers. These methods produce a lively time for the spectator. But there is always a considerable part of the class that do nothing. These very pupils that thus sit quiescent and passive are the very ones that need to be waked up and put into the active voice, first person singular. But in the "*fast*" method, *every* scholar is stirred up. It has all the awakening and enlivening effect of a merry game.

The " fast" method is one to be used with caution and only as an occasional exercise. Quickness of perception, promptness of utterance and a thoroughly awakened attention are cultivated by it. But these are not the only mental qualities to be cultivated. We need the power to trace out and bring to light hidden analogies—a power that necessarily moves slowly, cautiously and inquiringly. We need that power of complete and continuous expression which comes from the topical method of recitation.

11. *Keeping the Children Busy.*

Among Mr. Fitch's celebrated maxims for Sunday-school teachers is this : " Never permit any child to remain in the class, even for a minute, without something to do and a motive for doing it." No one can doubt the excellence of the rule. The difficulty is in knowing how to keep it. It is like saying to a minister, Preach like Henry Ward Beecher and you will be sure of having a good congregation ; or saying to a clerk, Write like the Spencerians and you may be sure of a good salary ; or saying to a child just beginning to learn to walk, Hold yourself straight, put your feet out one after the other as I do and you will not fall. This keeping all the children in a school fully occupied all the time is just the very hardest thing for the teacher to do. It is the crowning achievement of the teacher's art. To point to it distinctly as an aim toward which the teacher should direct his efforts and his ambition, and to suggest means and devices by which he may be helped in reaching it, is all very well. But simply enjoining it as an elementary rule has always seemed to me somewhat absurd.

Every one who has taught in a common school, or in a Sunday-school, knows that one of the most difficult things to do is to keep one part of the class or of the school properly occupied while he is busy with the other part. Children are by nature restless, and none more so than those who are particularly bright and intelligent. Indeed it is often the brightest scholars in the school that give the most trouble. When the teacher, as it sometimes happens in Sunday-schools, has only one class, and the children composing it have all exactly the same lesson, the problem is comparatively easy. But this is rarely the case. Even in Sunday-schools, and under the best classification, the teacher is sure to have one or more scholars who require special and separate instruction, and while the teacher is attending to these the others need to be provided with work. In many classes, in mission-schools, almost every scholar is a unit by himself, requiring separate treatment. In the common weekday district-school the difficulties are greater still. There the teacher usually has from forty to fifty scholars divided into

16 *

at least a dozen classes, of which only one can be taught at a time. The others, it is true, have their lessons to prepare in the intervals between recitation. But to keep their little feet and hands and tongues all busy with their studies, not by terror and punishment, but by adequate motives of a better kind, taxes the ingenuity and the invention of the most skilful teacher. The common-school teacher, however, has the advantage of being able to use methods and subjects that would not be appropriate to a Sunday-school. Children, for instance, are fond of doing sums in addition, subtraction, multiplication and division, especially under the principle of emulation, striving to see who can do the greatest number of sums, and as this kind of exercise is in itself exceedingly valuable in making them practically expert in figures, teachers often employ this method of filling up waste moments, requiring the pupils first to study the appointed lessons, and then allowing them to acquire extra merit marks by doing as many of these sums as they can find time for. To facilitate this kind of exercise, ingenious methods have been invented by which a teacher may place upon the board any number of arithmetical examples of this kind, so constructed that the teacher knows by inspection whether the answer is right or wrong without having to work out the sum himself, although the pupil has to go through all the work in order to get the right result.

The Sunday-school teacher who aims to observe

Mr. Fitch's rule must become inventive. Invention, in fact. is one of the prime requisites in all teaching. No rule can be given which will apply to all cases. Every class has its peculiarities. The teacher must think of the character and disposition of each of his scholars, and during the week must say to himself, What is there that I can give to this child, what to that, what to the other, to do while the rest of us are otherwise engaged? The thing thus assigned should be something that the child will not look upon as a disagreeable and irksome command, but as something which will be attractive and interesting, and which he will enter upon with zest as a pleasure. It should be also something which the teacher can, without much interruption or loss of time, examine, that he may test the correctness of it, and make some kind of record of what each child accomplishes. Care should be taken that these little tasks should be of a definite kind. which can be exactly measured as right or wrong. that they should not be puzzling or complex, and that, instead of one long task to be done with greater or less degree of perfection, there should be a number of small and comparatively easy things, each complete in itself, so that every pupil may be able to do at least one, while none will be able to do all.

Suppose for instance a teacher, who had a class of suitable age and attainments for such a purpose, were to ask his pupils to open to the first chapter of Matthew, twenty-second verse, where it is said that the Saviour's birth was in fulfilment of prophecy, and after explaining the matter to them should say, While I am engaged in hearing the different parts of the class recite, I would like each of you to begin at this twenty-second verse and read on and see how many other places in the narrative you can find where it is said that prophecy was fulfilled. But keep a sharp lookout not to overlook any. I will give one credit mark for every example which you find, taking them in the order in which they occur, but will deduct one for every example which you may overlook. I have been examining the narrative myself during the week, and have the examples all at my finger ends; so you must look out that I do not find you tripping.

On another occasion, or with a different class, supposing the pupils to be furnished with a suitable map, he might point them to the thirteenth chapter of Acts, and might say, You see here that Paul and Barnabas set out from Antioch on a missionary tour. Suppose you follow the narrative with the map before you and see how far you can trace Paul's journeyings during the time which you will have to spare this morning, so that you can point with your finger from place to place each step in his journey, not omitting any.

There is in the Bible no end to the things which children may be requested to find out, and there is nothing that children like better than to hunt. They will hunt for Scripture facts and truths, if once their

curiosity is aroused and some little emulous excitement is produced, with as much pleasure as they
hunt for shells or flowers or squirrels. But it requires on the teacher's part a great deal of time and
thought bestowed upon invention. He must be all
the while hunting up something new. The examples which I have given are not in themselves particularly good, but they may serve, perhaps, to explain
what I mean and to put the teacher on the right
track.

12. *Gaining the Affections of Scholars.*

This is a hackneyed subject, and for that very
reason one to be discussed. It is mentioned so often
because of its supreme importance, and this supreme,
urgent importance of the subject makes it proper for
me to recur to it again and again.

The teacher who has not the love of his scholars
can do little toward promoting their advancement,
either mentally or morally. If, instead of loving
and respecting him, they have for him a positive
dislike, the task of teaching is almost hopeless. If
there could be a true record of school-room labor,
what a sad revelation would much of it be ! In how
many cases the chief end of the teacher is to detect
mischief, the chief end of the scholar to escape de-
tection ! In how many cases the lesson is not a
boon to be craved, but a task to be deplored and if
possible evaded ! In how many cases the teacher is
regarded not as a dear friend and helper, but as an

enemy, a taskmaster, a tyrant, an obstacle in the way of enjoyment!

Thank God, these cases are on the decrease. As the business of teaching is becoming better understood, as the number is increasing of those who enter upon its duties because they like the work and find it congenial, there are proportionally fewer who make it an intolerable burden for themselves and their scholars. There are teachers, and there are scholars, who are never more happy than when in the school-room—who look forward with longing to the hour when school is to begin, and back with regret upon the hour when it closed. There are schools which are more attractive than the play-ground or the social party. In all such schools LOVE reigns. There are rules, doubtless, and sometimes penalties, for children will forget, and they need restraint even under the best conditions. But the supreme power, that sits enthroned at the desk and that sways every will in that little kingdom, is a spirit of love.

Why is it important that scholars should love their teacher?

Not because it is pleasant to the teacher to be loved. No doubt it does add to the teacher's happiness, and this added pleasure is something which he may well covet. But no true teacher is so selfish as to wish and labor for the love of his pupils merely for the personal gratification it affords. Such a view of the subject degrades and belittles it.

A child's love for his teachers makes tasks easy. He is more ready to encounter toil in the preparation of lessons. He works hard without counting it work. He has no longer any motive for engaging in those petty tricks and annoyances which consume so much of some scholars' time. A desire to win the approbation of a teacher who is loved gives to study a zest equal to that which children find in their games.

Love and hatred have upon the understanding a singular effect which seems not to be appreciated by many persons, and which in fact has not as yet been fully explained. Hatred or evil passion of any kind has an effect upon the mind somewhat like that of stirring up the mud and sediment in the bottom of a fountain. The perceptions are obscured under such disturbing influences. No man can reason clearly when under the influence of anger or malice. Every bad passion stirs up the sediments in the bottom of the soul and makes it impossible for a man to see clearly or judge truly. The sun may shine brightly in the heavens, but it will reveal no gems of truth at the bottom of that fountain which is ever throwing up mire and dirt. Scholars will never learn much from a teacher who for any cause stirs up their feelings of animosity and dislike. Not only will they make less exertions to learn, but their very power of mental perception seems to be obscured. There is no clarifier of the understanding equal to that of a calm, serene, undoubting love. Mental perceptions, in other words, are helped or hindered by the state of the heart. We may not be able, perhaps, to explain it philosophically. But of the fact no teacher can well doubt who has had much experience in his work.

But the teacher has other functions besides that of making his scholars grow in knowledge. He is to mould their opinions, to shape their moral sentiments, to influence their habits. Here the power of love is still more marked than in the purely intellectual processes. Without love as a controlling motive, the teacher in all this important class of duties can do absolutely nothing. With love he may do what he will with the yielding and plastic materials before him.

How shall this love be gained?

Not by weak compliances. Not by foolish and unwise indulgences. Not by flattering words. Love, to be of any value as an educating power, must be based on respect, and children do not respect a teacher who grants to their solicitations what they know is not for their real benefit, or who seeks to ingratiate himself with them by ministering to their vanity and self-conceit. Love is the true price for love. Let no teacher expect the love of his scholars who does not truly love them. God help the teacher who has not this love in his heart! Most profoundly do I pity him.

But some teachers who truly love their scholars shrink from giving it manifestation. This is not so bad as pretending to a love which you do not have. Still, it is a mistake. Let your affection beam forth in your face and you will soon see a warm answering smile in the face of your scholar. Faithful, conscientious teachers sometimes err just here. They stand too much upon their dignity. They seem afraid of letting themselves down to the level of their scholars.

Prodigious is the power of pleasant looks and pleasant words in the school-room.

13. *Reaching the Comprehension of the Scholars.*

One of the last things that a teacher learns is, how little the scholars understand of what he says. A word which to him seems perfectly plain, the meaning of which he takes for granted they know, conveys to them no more idea than if it was Greek or Choctaw. It is only after long experience, and by many and painful trials, that he finds out that in teaching a lesson every word has to be questioned and challenged. I speak, of course, of young children and of primary instruction. Yet even pupils more advanced need watching. Scholars fifteen or sixteen years old often fall into the habit of hearing and of using words to which they attach no meaning. I knew a boy fourteen years old, who had grown up in daily attendance upon excellent public schools, who when questioned upon the meaning of the phrase, "Forgive us our manifold sins," said that "manifold" meant "pertaining to man." Another in the same class said that "atonement" meant "orthodox," and gave in illustration of it the phrase, "the Church of the Atonement." Another boy in the class explained the common word "deride" as meaning "to ride down."

I was once teaching a Bible-class consisting of young ladies, whose average age was certainly not less than seventeen, and most of whom were attending school during the week. They were not poor girls, but belonged to educated families. The lesson was on the gift of tongues on the day of Pentecost, in the second chapter of Acts. This verse came under discussion: "And there appeared unto them cloven tongues like as of fire, and it sat upon each of them." It was found on inquiry that not one young lady in the class, consisting of some twelve or fourteen, had the slightest idea of what was meant by "cloven." They had heard and read hundreds of times of "*cloven* tongues," but apparently had never given a thought to the question what the word meant, or whether it meant anything. Some guessed that it might mean "fiery," and that was about the nearest conjecture that was ventured.

In the case of young children, such as form the majority of those attending Sunday-school, examples even more striking than these might be adduced. The difficulty is that teachers mostly aim too high. In preparing a lesson they look for hidden meanings, for solutions of abstruse points of doctrine, which are deeply interesting to themselves, but are entirely above the heads of their children. The points needed in the instruction of children are for the most part those which are plain and simple, and which lie upon the very surface of the subject. The teacher is under the continual temptation to take for granted that a thing is plain to the children because it is so very plain to him. The more advanced a teacher is in knowledge the more he is liable to make this mistake. The expert accountant who can run up a long column of figures, and almost by a glance of the eye tell the sum, can hardly realize by how slow and laborious a process a young beginner arrives at the simple result that three and two make five. The man who has spent his life in the study of language receives on reading a sentence a distinct idea from each word as it passes under review, without his once giving it a thought. Very different with the child. One-half the words that meet his eye in an ordinary reading-book convey to him no more meaning than do the cabalistic signs of algebra and the higher mathematics to one just learning to count. Hear a class of children reading. You know by the very tones of their voices that the words which they read awaken no ideas in their minds. They spell a word out and pronounce it, but it evidently stands to them for a mere sound and nothing more.

Now in teaching a child the very first step is to gauge accurately his mind. You must first find out what he knows and what he does not know, and then there is some hope of your being able to minister to his intellectual wants. Children exert a powerful influence upon children, because each knows from his own consciousness what interests his fellows. Grown persons often fail to influence the young, because they forget what were their own views and feelings when young. We must get down to the level of a child if we would make effectual entrance into his mind. We must put ourselves in a position to understand exactly what his difficulties are. Unless a child feels that he is understood, he is soon discouraged; and though a compulsory obedience may make him appear to attend to what you say, your statements make no real lodgment in his thoughts. He may be looking at you, but he is thinking of something else. The intellect of a child must be reached, in a great measure, through his sympathies and his feelings.

We may learn in this matter a useful lesson from the methods pursued in the instruction of idiots. The following example will illustrate my meaning. It was told me by Mr. Richards, the gentleman who first introduced the subject of the training of the feeble-minded to the attention of the philanthropists of Philadelphia. Among the feeble-minded children that Mr. Richards had in his charge was one that interested every visitor. It was a boy about ten years old. This child, when first found by Mr. R., was in about as low a condition as a human being could well be and yet be regarded as human at all. It was a child six years old, incapable of almost

every kind of voluntary motion and apparently
knowing nothing. It did not know its own mother.
It took no notice of any one. It was dressed in a
loose sort of sack and lay on its back on the floor.
It could not chew or move the muscles of the throat,
except merely to swallow milk or other nutritious
liquid. It could neither walk, nor stand, nor sit, nor
turn over, nor lift its hands, nor move any of its
limbs. The only motion of which it seemed capable
was sometimes to turn its head and a portion of its
body a little over to one side. This mass of flesh
and blood in human form lived and breathed, di-
gested food, and performed the ordinary vital functions, but had thus far given no signs of containing
within it even the germ of intellect. Its eyes looked
out upon vacancy, seeing nothing. Its ears were
formed like other ears, but whether they heard anything no one knew. Its very sense of feeling was
almost wanting, a pin thrust into its leg to the depth
of half an inch causing no sign of pain. It seemed
below the level of the ordinary brute. No token of
will, of passion, of love, of hate, of recognition even
of the hand that fed it, had yet been given. Was
there really a human soul in that living body? Mr
R. believed there was, and determined to make the
attempt to awaken and develop its dormant energies.

When I first saw this child he had been about
four years under training. He could then walk
across the room, could speak slowly a few words,
and he repeated to me distinctly the Lord's Prayer.

17 *

Three years later he was running about the grounds, playing and enjoying himself with the other children, could read and spell quite well, and answered correctly many simple questions that I put to him on various subjects. The transformation seemed almost miraculous, and I asked for information as to the steps by which it had been brought about. It would take me too long to detail all these steps. But one remark made an indelible impression upon my mind. Said Mr. R., " On looking at this child, and considering the question how I should raise him to the ordinary conditions of humanity, I believed the first step to be to establish some connection between his mind (if he had a mind) and mine. This connection must spring out of sympathy. The child must be made in some way to feel that there was another being like itself. So, after pondering the matter for some time, and in the absence of all precedent to guide me, I made the following experiment, pretty much at a venture. About the middle of the morning I lay down on the floor alongside of him, and just as he was lying, and remained there an hour or two reading aloud from a book. I did the same thing in the afternoon, and so continued to do twice a day for about a fortnight, leaving him at the intervals quite alone. When this process had continued so long that I thought some impression must have been made, I went in one day and lay down as usual, *but did not read.* I wished to see if he would notice the omission. The moment was critical. I watched with the most intense anxiety. After three or four minutes of silence I saw signs of muscular action, and gradually he moved his head and face over toward me! He was actually waiting for me to begin the customary noise! I could hardly contain my joy. I felt that from that moment I had him! I had got down to his level. I had established a connection between his mind and mine. From that day I never began the reading until he signified his desire for it by turning his head over toward me. Thus my first step in raising him up to my level was to get down to his level."

14. *Variety in Teaching.*

A mistake sometimes made by teachers is that of proceeding exactly in the same way all the year round. I do not, by any means, count it as among the most common or the most serious of errors in teaching. Yet it is an error, and a serious one, and it is usually committed by teachers who in other respects are worthy of high commendation. They have in some way formed for themselves a model of the manner in which a lesson should be given, and they follow it with undeviating uniformity year after hear.

Such a course is at war with the constitution of the human mind. If order is heaven's first law, variety is the second. The very best method of presenting truth, if followed constantly without change, becomes tiresome and loses its attraction. It is so with our food. The most wholesome and delicious articles of diet pall upon the appetite when long continued. We require change and variety in what we eat, whether we consult health or pleasure. The soil requires rotation of crops, else it becomes impoverished and barren. What a marvellous change God has ordained in the seasons, giving us endless alternations of summer and winter, heat and cold, darkness and light, moisture and drought! How the birds and the flowers, the grains, the fruits and the vegetables come and go in endless succession and equally endless variety! All is change, yet all is order. Nature, in all her operations, seems equally to abhor confusion and monotony.

Let us learn a lesson from this in our teaching. Let us learn that the very best methods of teaching and training, of discipline and government, wear out. They lose after a while their effect. Modes of stimulating enthusiasm or of awakening attention, of securing punctuality or of enforcing order, which for a time seemed perfect, begin after a time to lose their power upon the youthful mind. Just as we think we have everything perfect, we are working after the latest and most approved pattern, our machinery is complete and moving without a flaw, just then somehow the propelling power gives way. The grooves and pulleys are all there, but the mind ceases to run in them. What a power in the Sunday-school the little blue and red tickets once were! Yet they wore out. Merit marks and demerit marks and averages for attendance, recitation or conduct, produce for a time prodigious effects, and an inexperienced teacher, seeing the effect in some particular case, jumps to the conclusion that he has found the universal remedy, and he settles down upon a system for life.

In so doing he forgets one essential condition of the material upon which he is acting. A worker in wood or metal or other material substance, having invented the best mode of fashioning it to suit his purpose, follows that mode with undeviating uniformity, or until some better mode is discovered. The more closely he sticks to his method and his pattern, the more sure he is of success. But it is quite otherwise with the worker upon mind. Here the material upon which we work is seldom twice in the same condition. We influence and mould the mind of a child only by securing its own co-operative action. We cannot teach a child by merely pouring out knowledge before him. Teaching, in its very essence, and in every stage of it, is a co-operative process. And there is no fact more patent to the thoughtful observer than that with children *methods wear out.* They tire of the same style of teaching and talking, no matter how good it may be, and when they tire of the method, and it ceases to interest them and to induce their active co-operation, the teacher's work is lost. He is working, but doing nothing. Hence the imperative necessity of his studying variety.

The teacher should study variety in his manner, in his topics and in his illustrations.

1. *The Manner.* As to manner, it is, indeed, not easy to attain the variety that is desirable. Every one almost imperceptibly and inevitably falls into a certain style or manner which becomes habitual, and which it is of all things the most difficult to change at will. One is habitually lively and buoyant; another grave and serious. One speaks in a quick, sharp tone; another speaks mildly and persuasively. One has the pleasant smile so attractive to children; another looks austere and forbidding. One in speaking gesticulates a great deal, his hands and features expressing his thoughts almost as fully as his words; another hardly moves a limb or a muscle in talking, but depends for effect upon his words only. One is calm, impassive, collected; another is ever boiling over with emotion of some kind. Now there is not a manner mentioned here, hardly a manner conceivable within the bounds of ordinary propriety, that has not its uses and that might not be adopted on some occasions with singular fitness and effect. On the other hand, there is no manner, conceived or conceivable, that is suitable for all occasions. There is no manner that, if adopted on all occasions, will not become tiresome. There is no one best manner. The teacher must cultivate the faculty of changing his manner from time to time to suit the occasion and to prevent monotony. It is not an easy achievement In no

one thing is it so difficult to be various, and yet perhaps no one faculty is so important. In the case of the worker upon dead matter, it is of no consequence whether he is gay or grave, whether he smiles or frowns. The wood or the metal is just as pliable in the one case as the other. Not so the child. If you would mould him according to your wishes, you must vary your own moods with his.

2. *The Topics.* The topics to be presented in teaching are literally infinite, and therefore the teacher has no excuse who travels on in one monotonous round of subjects. Variety even here, however, will not come unsought. The teacher must have the wants of his class on his mind and be on the lookout for fresh matter. All nature is full of subjects for instruction. God's word in this respect is as remarkable as his works. No book in the world is so various in its matter as the Bible. Teachers and preachers sometimes make it monotonous by their mode of handling it. They undertake to set forth a system of divinity, and then hunt up proof-texts to establish their system. Of course I do not object to systems of doctrine. The teacher must have his doctrinal scheme. But in teaching a class, if he wants to avoid running into a rut, he had better take texts or passages as he finds them, study them in their connection, and follow out each text or passage to its natural results in doctrine and practice. Studied in this way—that is, textually rather than topically—the Bible presents an endless variety. If

a preacher discusses from the pulpit in logical order
the subject of repentance, for instance, or faith, or
any other great doctrine, he cannot very easily renew
it Sunday after Sunday without repeating himself.
But he may expound on one Sunday the case of
Peter, on another that of Felix, again that of Saul,
and so on, taking each case with its circumstances,
and thus ever having something new and different
from that presented before.

3. *The Illustrations.* As with subjects, so with
illustrations. There is no end to the number of illustrations that may be had for the asking, and no limit
—almost—to the power which they give over the
youthful mind. But to most persons they do not
come unbidden. We must in this matter cultivate
the inventive faculty. In doing so it is well to study
the writings of those who are masters of the art,
and this not for the purpose of borrowing the illustrations made by others, but to get into the spirit of
it. There is a book called "Illustrative Gatherings"
from which much may be learned in this line. Read
every week a chapter from the pen of Dr. Todd or
Dr. Newton, and see how they enforce every point
by an apt illustration which makes the doctrine take
fast hold of the youthful mind. Dr. Guthrie, the
Scotch preacher, is admirable in this way. A mind
that has any inventive faculty of its own could hardly
fail to find out some good, fresh simile after reading
one of Dr. Guthrie's lectures on the parables. In
recommending the study of such works, I do not

advise the teacher to borrow or to imitate the similes which he finds. But by habitually reading works of this kind his own mind will gradually learn to think out apt comparisons.

4. *Freshness.* What the teacher needs is to keep himself always fresh. Principles are eternal, but methods change. *There is no one best method of teaching or governing.* Eternal vigilance must be the teacher's motto. Of course there must be some stability in the operations of a school or of a class. But be ever on the lookout; and when you find the little ones flagging in interest, and the methods which for six months or a year seemed to be working wonders now losing their hold, try something else. The teacher's business, more even than that of the mechanic, requires invention. The secret of the power exercised over young minds by such writers as Jacob Abbott and John Todd, and this new French writer, Jean Macè, is their marvellous power of invention. God has not endowed us all with this gift in an equal degree. But it is a faculty that we should cultivate, and we may all, by diligent reading and observation, keep ourselves familiar with the devices and ingenious thoughts of others.

One of the very best means for a teacher to keep himself from monotony and stupefying routine is to attend teachers' institutes and conventions. There he comes into contact with other minds and is made acquainted with other methods. His own mind is stirred up, and he returns to his work with new ideas.

18

These new ideas are not necessarily better in themselves than the old ones, but they are new, and by that very quality have a power and vitality which the old ones have ceased to have.

Another method by which a teacher may deliver himself from the bondage of routine is to take a teachers' paper. A paper like *The Sunday-School Times* is a sort of permanent institute. The teacher in reading it is every week brought into communion with other teachers from every part of the land, and made familiar with the various methods which the ingenious and inventive are devising for the improvement of schools; and though ninety-nine out of a hundred of these suggestions may be for him impracticable, yet even if the hundredth gives him a practicable improvement he is well rewarded. The Sunday-school teacher who neglects to take a teachers' paper must either think himself too wise to need instruction, or must be strangely indifferent to the wants of his class.

Some books are printed from stereotype plates, others from movable types, that is, the types are reset for each new edition. If the printers will allow me to take an illustration from their trade, I would say that the teacher's methods should never be stereotyped. Every new edition should be made from movable types.

15. *Giving a Definite Lesson.*

A few sections back I spoke of the difference between the Sunday-school and other schools. I will now notice one at least of the points of resemblance.

A school of any kind, so far as it is a school at all, is a place for definite work. It is not a sort of youths' mass-meeting, or a prayer-meeting, or a convention, or a religious sociable, but a place for teaching on the one side and learning on the other, where lessons are to be assigned and definite progress in knowledge is aimed at. In the daily school this knowledge is for the most part of a secular kind, and there is by the almost universal consent of educators a certain routine of studies to be followed. If a child begins his arithmetic and goes to school for a certain length of time, the parent expects him to be advanced from rule to rule until the subject is mastered, and then to take up whatever study is next in order. When the child comes home in the evening he has his lessons to learn for the following day. What would a parent think of the school if his children on being interrogated did not seem to know what they were studying in school—whether they were studying arithmetic, or geography, or grammar, or history ; or if history, whether it was the history of France, of England or of the United States—who did not know what part of the book they were in, but their teacher took up sometimes one part and sometimes another, sometimes talked about it, and sometimes entertained them by reading interesting extracts from the newspapers?

I am sorry to say this is no caricature of what is

done by a good many Sunday-school teachers. The
hour spent by the teacher with his class is nothing
more than a pleasant religious sociable. The little
ones have a good time. get their library books and
papers, enjoy the singing, and that is all. They
make no definite progress in religious knowledge.
They know no more about the contents of the sacred
volume at the end of the year than they did at the
beginning. A gentleman told me not many weeks
since that his children seemed very fond of the
Sunday-school and of their teacher, but he never
could find out from them that they had any lessons
to learn or any preparation to make. They did not
know whether they were studying in Matthew or
Genesis or Psalms. They had no question-book,
they were not required to commit any verses to mem
ory. When they came together on the Sabbath the
teacher selected a chapter, sometimes in one part of
the Bible, sometimes in another, and read it to them,
or they read it verse about. Then she talked to
them about it for a while, and when that failed she
read to them some of the pretty little stories from
the Child's Department of the *New York Observer.*
Any one going into the school where this teacher is
engaged, and looking casually at the class, would
gather the impression that they were legitimately
engaged in study and recitation. With the exception of the *Observer* part of the business, the whole
affair may have the appearance of a regular school
exercise.

I fear there are a great many such classes and teachers, and I desire to raise my voice against it in earnest remonstrance. This whole thing is wrong. It is an awful wickedness thus to allow the hours of religious instruction to run to waste. Every scholar who goes to Sunday-school should have some definite plan of study placed before him, and should have a definite lesson to learn for each session of the school. The teacher or the superintendent who has no such aim, and allows things to go at loose ends in the manner described, has yet to learn what a school is. The teacher may not always be able to secure from the scholar adequate preparation of the lesson assigned. Many parents are grossly derelict in this matter, and give no co-operation in regard to the Sunday lesson. But in the case to which I have referred, the parent was anxious to give this co-operation, and gathered his children about him on Sunday evening for the purpose of going over the lesson of the next Sunday with them and seeing that they had it duly prepared. But no lesson had been assigned. Nor was it a mission-school, with chance scholars attending irregularly, coming and going according to childish caprice, but a school of considerable celebrity, in a well-known and influential church in one of our large cities.

Definite lessons and a plan of study are the indispensable conditions of a school. Just so far as these conditions are wanting it ceases to be a school and becomes a mere social gathering. The highest state

18 *   O

of efficiency attainable in a Sunday-school is that in which all the school has one lesson, the higher and the lower classes studying it with varying degrees of minuteness, and the superintendent and teachers meeting weekly to go over the lesson together. When this point cannot be, or is not, gained, the next best thing is for all the scholars in a class to have the same lesson. There may be good schools, however, in some of the classes of which even this point is not secured. There may be classes in which every scholar is studying on his own hook and reciting separately. But even in this extreme case the individual scholar should have a definite lesson assigned him and a plan and course of study marked out. The teacher who neglects so plain a duty has no claim to the name of teacher. He is a mere social visitor, who comes to have a pleasant chat with the children. The superintendent is unfaithful to his stewardship who allows such things to be.

16. *Preparation for the Lesson.*

The temerity of undertaking to give a lesson to a class without making preparation for it is amazing. It is only equalled by the man who undertakes to preach without preparation. Teachers complain that they have such a hard class, that they have not the natural talents and gifts for the work which God has given to others, that they cannot keep the attention of their scholars, and so on through the whole catalogue of complaints, while the real difficulty half the time is that they are unwilling to bestow the labor needed for suitable preparation.

There are some teachers in almost every Sunday-school who have no regular class, or whose class is made up of odds and ends—children just brought into the school and not yet assigned to any class, or children whose regular teacher is unexpectedly absent. Such teachers are very useful. Their work is most uninteresting, but not the less important to the school. Every superintendent needs one or more faithful workers of this kind. Such teachers need a weekly preparation for their duties, but not of the kind I am now about to speak of. My remarks are intended for those who have regular classes and a common lesson.

There is a preparation of a general kind which every teacher needs. It is important that every teacher should be a person of general information and culture, that he should have a good address and pleasant manners, which come much more from care and painstaking than from nature ; above all, that he should have that preparation of the heart which comes from earnest, devoted piety. But it is not this general preparation which I have now in view. What I recommend to the teacher is that he make specific preparation for every lesson to his class.

The lesson *to* his class. The phraseology is not an inadvertence. The lesson *of* the class is that which the class are expected to learn. But teachers who mean to be good for anything must learn as soon as possible to get rid of the idea that teaching is merely hearing recitations. In this interview between the teacher and the class, called a recitation, not only the scholars must be prepared to bring something to the teacher, but the teacher must be prepared to bring something to the scholars. Scholars come to learn as well as to say what they have learned. Scholars who have a good teacher always come to the class in a spirit of expectancy. See to it that this expectant spirit never goes away unrewarded. See that you know the lesson more minutely and exhaustively than any of your scholars do. A teacher may conclude that he has reached the right idea on this subject if, when speaking of his work, he unconsciously talks of *giving a lesson to his class,* instead of saying that he is going *to hear the lesson.* The teacher who goes to his class without the specific preparation which this phraseology implies is just as derelict as would be the minister who should go into the pulpit without having a prepared sermon, or the lawyer who should go into court without having studied the case of his client or prepared the necessary papers.

Let us come to particulars.

1. *Committing the Verses to Memory.* The lesson, as now assigned in most schools, consists of a short passage of Scripture, with questions upon it, and references. The first thing to be done in the preparation of such a lesson—the thing absolutely indispensable, the thing which is the foundation of

everything else, and without which all other labor will be merely building upon sand—is to *commit these verses to memory*. That, and that only, is the solid rock on which all the superstructure must stand. The teacher who is not able, on coming before his class, to close his book and repeat the text of the lesson without hesitation and without missing a word or a syllable, is not prepared. He might almost as well undertake to teach reading without knowing the alphabet. The first exercise in the recitation ought to be for the class to recite the verses in this way to the teacher, and the teacher ought to be able to follow them in the exercise and correct their mistakes without looking at the book himself.

I have adverted to this topic several times already. But I am disposed to reiterate the remark and to emphasize it, because there is a widely-prevalent and mischievous mistake just here. Teachers sometimes bestow a great deal of labor and research in hunting up some far-fetched and perhaps fanciful illustration, or going off into some curious theological or antiquarian issue, while neglecting the plain truths which lie right on the surface. The first thing for scholars and teachers is to know the words of the lesson. Let this part of your preparation be done thoroughly, not as children often commit to memory, being barely able to get through a piece if you prompt them every few words. Learn the passage as you know the Lord's Prayer or the Ten

Commandments. The teacher should know the words of the lesson from beginning to end, so as to be able to say them or hear the children say them without having ever to look at the book. This, of course, will involve some labor. It is more difficult for grown persons to commit to memory than it is for children. We may learn a portion of Scripture after a fashion without much labor. But to make even a dozen verses every week thus thoroughly one's own requires time, toil and resolute determination. But no toil yields so sure or precious a reward. We all have a considerable amount of general information about the Scriptures. But how little is our stock of precise and thoroughly accurate knowledge of God's Word! The teacher who every week adds to his store only eight or ten verses of Holy Scripture, completely mastered and fixed in the memory, is insensibly but steadily growing rich in Bible lore. Such an acquisition is, in the first place, an unspeakable blessing to himself. But besides this, it gives him a power before his class that nothing else can give. It enables him to accomplish twice the amount of work in the way of instruction, besides the influence which his example will have in inducing the children to do the same thing. The verses are the foundation for the lesson. If teachers and scholars will learn these and have them in their memory, they have something to build on. Without this preliminary step all other preparation on the part of either teacher or scholar is of little account. It is making bricks without straw—almost without clay.

2. *The Parallel Texts.* The teacher should have some definite plan in his mind in regard to the parallel texts referred to in the question-book. Some teachers commit these to memory and require their pupils to do so. Of course there can be no objection to such a plan, if a teacher and a class will carry it out. But in ordinary cases I would not recommend it. Far better that the verses which form the main lesson should be thoroughly learned than that both the verses and the parallel texts should be half learned. The compilers of our question-books have not usually bestowed the amount of care upon the references which the importance of the subject requires. References are often made to passages that have almost nothing to do with the lesson, and to long paragraphs and even to chapters which neither teacher nor scholars can be expected to learn. Let the teacher examine carefully those parallel texts, see exactly how they illustrate the verse referred to, prepare himself to point out readily and clearly the analogy, and tax his memory with the chapter and verse and the exact place in his Bible where the parallel passage is to be found, so as to be able at once, without a moment's hesitation, to turn to it. This is the kind of preparation which I recommend the teacher to make, and to urge his pupils to make, in regard to the parallel texts.

3. *Use of the Question-Book.* Let the teacher

use the question-book and encourage the pupils to use it, for the purpose of aiding to understand the passage, or of suggesting some of its practical applications. This is the true and only design of a question-book. It is a book to be used in preparing a lesson, not in hearing or reciting it. The questions often suggest points that may escape the attention of the teacher. I would not discard the book, therefore. Only let it be properly used. To use it as is commonly done, however, is a great abuse. Nothing is more common than to see a class and their teacher confronting each other, each with question-book in one hand and the Bible in the other, the teacher reading the question and the pupil reading the answer. If those good men who first invented our question-books had dreamed that any such abuse would have grown out of them, I am sure they would have wished their invention at the bottom of the sea. Before beginning the recitation let the question-book (the teacher's as well as the scholars') be collected and piled, and not one of them be opened by teacher or scholar until the lesson is over. In anticipation of such an experiment as this, the teacher's preparatory study of the questions will be far different from what it ordinarily is. He will find it necessary to get the subject itself, not the mere verbal questions, in his mind. With his mind full of the subject, however, he can frame his own questions, if he cannot read those in the book. Be it ever remembered, the lesson is not the questions, but the portion of holy Scripture standing at the head. That is what we ought mainly to study.

4. *Additional Illustrations.* Let the teacher always aim to get some points of information and illustration not suggested by the question-book. The sources of these are numerous, and vary with the subject and the portion of Scripture under review. Commentaries, Bible dictionaries, books of travel in the Holy Land and Scripture atlases are the chief aids in this respect. What I advise is, not a large amount of such illustrations, but one or two well-selected examples for each lesson, enough to create expectancy on the part of the pupils, and let these illustrations be so thoroughly prepared and canvassed by the teacher in his own mind that there will be no hesitation or want of clearness in his mode of presenting them to the class. The fact that the teacher always has some fresh materials of this kind for the illustration of the lesson will gradually give him an authority and influence over the minds of his scholars that can be acquired in no other way. The children will feel that he is really a teacher, not a mere hearer of lessons.

5. *Critical Study of the Meaning.* The teacher should set himself to study out the meaning of every part by the aid of commentaries and works of reference. So much has been said on this point that I do not think it necessary to dwell upon it. But there is one feature in this part of the teacher's preparation which is apt to escape the notice of the inex-

19

perienced. The young teacher is apt to think it is quite enough for him if by study and research he actually discovers the meaning of a passage. In course of time, however, he awakes to the fact that many thoughts which seemed quite clear and plain to him at the time of study have somehow gone from him when he comes before his class. He finds that he must not only hunt up a thing, or think it out, but he must then ponder it and turn it over and over in his mind, and inquire again and again how he would present it to his class, so as to become perfectly familiar with it. This is the difference between ordinary knowledge of a thing and that knowledge of it which is needed for the teacher. We must be *familiar* with any thought or subject before undertaking to teach it. Knowledge which comes to the tongue only after hesitation and by a slow and measured process is of no avail to the teacher. Readiness is indispensable to a good teacher. What he undertakes to teach to a class should be at the tip of his tongue, and this readiness requires something more than going over the lesson once, no matter how careful that study of it may have been.

After studying the lesson, therefore, and satisfying himself that he understands it thoroughly, let him next go over the various points again and again, a hundred times if need be, until he knows all the ins and outs of the lesson just as familiarly as he knows the way to the school-house. This readiness is more easy and natural to some than to others, but it is within the reach of every one who will take the necessary pains.

6. *Practical Thoughts.* The teacher in the course of his preparation should fix upon a certain leading thought, or thoughts, on which to concentrate the thoughts of the class. The Sunday lesson should be something more than a mere intellectual exercise. It should always have a practical bearing upon the moral state and condition of the class. All Bible study has for its object not merely intellectual knowledge, but the improvement of the heart and of the life. No Sunday-school lesson is complete unless it conveys some truth which is to affect the heart and conduct of the pupils. This is the great difference between the Sunday lesson and a lesson in arithmetic or grammar. The teacher should ask himself, How can I make this a means of spiritual benefit to my scholars? What is there in it which has a lesson for them in their present condition? and how shall I so shape the course of the lesson as to bring out this point in an easy and natural manner?

The lessons assigned in our question-books usually contain several such practical suggestions. Some of these are more applicable to one class of scholars, some to others. The teacher will be most likely, in ordinary cases, to accomplish practical results, if each Sunday he will limit his exertions to some one point. After studying a lesson thoroughly, let him think what one of its many teachings is most especially suitable to his particular class, and let him lay out his strength upon that. Having made this selection, he will be surprised, on going over the lesson again, how many things he can find in it bearing upon that point.

The teacher fails in his preparation who does not mature some definite idea of this kind for each lesson, and who leaves this practical application to the impulse of the moment and the chapter of accidents.

7. *Beginning Early in the Week.* Nothing can be plainer than that the teacher should begin his preparation for the Sunday lesson early in the preceding week. The best time is on the Sunday evening previous. If the main preparation be made then, and the subject be thus early fixed in his mind, thoughts and illustrations will be occurring incidentally all the week long. Having thus prepared the lesson on Sunday evening, pondered over it during the week, and given it a careful revision on Saturday evening, with an earnest cry to the great Teacher for help and wisdom, let him go before his class on the Sabbath with a full assurance that his labor and study will not be in vain.

8. *Seeking Aid from the Great Teacher.* Lastly, let the teacher not fail to ask and entreat for the guidance of the Holy Spirit. In nothing do we so much need the aid of the Divine mind as in our attempts to influence a human mind. Private prayer should go hand in hand with private study in every stage of the teacher's preparation for his work.

17. *Getting the Scholars to Learn the Lesson.*

Many teachers are studious themselves, but they fail to make their scholars studious. . The teacher is becoming rich in biblical knowledge, but the scholar is learning nothing. Such an order of things obviously is a grave evil. While the teacher is benefited by his work, that benefit is only an incident, not the end, of Sunday-school instruction. The school fails of its main end if benefits do not accrue to the scholars. The school or the class is to a great degree a failure if the scholars do not habitually prepare a lesson. If they come to school merely to hear explanations, merely to be talked to, their coming is not absolutely useless, but they might almost as well stay away. Real improvement of any kind is not something to be received passively, not something which you can pour into persons as you would pour water into a vessel, not something which you can put on them as you would dress them up in fine clothes, but something which must grow up within them by the active exertion of their own powers. You might as well chew and digest the child's food as to undertake to do all his intellectual work for him. There is no such thing as learning without study and work on the part of the learner. If he studies and works for himself, then your work and study in his behalf will be a help to him. Otherwise they will be, so far as he is concerned, mere water spilled on the ground.

19 *

How can an idle, indifferent scholar be induced to prepare his Sunday lesson?

Not by railing at him. I have not much faith in scolding on any subject, and certainly I never saw an idle scholar made industrious by calling him hard names and heaping abuse on his head. You may thereby make him sullen, or you may drive him from school, but you will not make him love study.

There is nothing that children need so much as *encouragement.* One half the failures in school come from the idea which the child has got, that he cannot do the thing required. Perhaps he has attempted it once, and his awkwardness has been laughed at. Perhaps he is slow of speech. He has not the natural glibness of tongue which some of the other children have, and he is driven into silence, and then is discouraged altogether, because he thinks there is no use of his trying. A Government contractor, who had been largely concerned in the purchase and training of mules, informed me once that the sullen stubbornness of that animal, which is so proverbial as to have given a new word to the dictionary, is really a mistake in our estimate of the animal's character; that the mulishness of the mule is only his timidity and want of confidence in himself; that if you treat him with kindness, awaken in him confidence in yourself, try him at first on such things only as he plainly sees that he can do, and thus gradually educate him to self-confidence, you will find him in the end more tractable and docile

than even the horse. But he must have encouragement. He is by nature timid and diffident.

Much of the so-called mulishness of children is
only timidity driven into sullenness. What is needed
in such cases is not the sickening flattery in which
some teachers indulge, but ingenuity in creating in
the child's mind a spirit of hopefulness, a conviction
that he as well as the others can do something.
There is a fine thought on this subject in Virgil.
He is describing the glow of earnest enthusiasm
with which the Carthaginians, under Queen Dido,
are building the walls of their new city. Under
the influence of this hopeful spirit all the difficulties in their way seem to vanish; they achieve
what is apparently impossible, because it seems
possible to them. *Possunt, quia posse videntur.*
They are able because they seem to themselves to
be-able; they *could* do it because they *thought* they
could do it. Making a child think he can master a
task is half the battle.

How shall this feeling be created in the mind of a
child who is naturally timid, or who is really deficient either in mental training or in mental power?

One way is to find out something that the child
can do, and do well—if possible, something that the
child can do better than any one else in the class.
The depressing effect of a sense of inferiority is thus
removed, and in its place springs up hopefulness.
A most remarkable instance of this kind once came
under my own observation. A young lady seemed

entirely unable to learn the lessons of her class. Grammar, geography, arithmetic, history, whatever the subject of study was, it seemed equally beyond the reach of her capacity. As a consequence, she had almost ceased trying to learn. She became indifferent and careless, showed no ambition, and was rapidly falling into habits of recklessness and insubordination. The first thing that changed the current of her thoughts was the accidental discovery that she had a talent for *drawing.* The talent was at once fostered. Special opportunities were given for practice. Her efforts and successes were brought into notice by exhibition and commendation. Here was something that she could do better than any of her classmates. Her countenance, which had heretofore been dull and leaden, now lightened up. A spark had been kindled, and the heat gradually communicated itself to her other faculties. Before long it was noticed that in her other lessons she was making progress. She became gradually a respectable scholar in all her studies. More even than this. The mental impulse thus awakened communicated itself to her moral nature. Her feelings were touched, her heart was aroused, her conscience was softened, she became an earnest, hopeful, devoted Christian, and she is now practicing her profession as a public teacher with marked and signal success.

Children are always fond of doing anything to *help* their teacher. If you want help of any kind, do not call upon your brightest and most forward children, but make it a means of calling into notice some obscure and timid member of your class. The moment a child of this sort begins to feel that he is of some importance, and his ambition is roused, you have a hold upon him.

I have dwelt a little upon this point, of giving encouragement to the backward, because from a large experience in the matter I am fully persuaded that three-fourths of the indifference to lessons, whether in the Sunday-school or in other schools, may be traced to a feeling of discouragement or sense of mental inferiority. There is no stimulus to mental exertion so healthful, so uniform in its action, so certain of success, as a spirit of hopefulness growing out of actual success. Use your ingenuity in finding something to be done, some question to be answered which is within the reach of the dullest and most perverse child in your class, and when he succeeds fail not to reward his success with judicious notice and commendation. You will soon find him taking an interest and waking up.

But there are very many things to be done by the teacher who has a class that will not study their lessons. The first thing, however, for every teacher to do who is so situated, is to make up his mind that the evil *may* be corrected and that it *shall* be corrected. Remember for yourself the case of the Carthaginians just referred to. You *can* do the thing if you only *think* so. Or, forgetting the words of Virgil, remember those of the divine Teacher: "All

P

things are possible to him that believeth." Settle in your mind, therefore, that you can and will succeed in getting your scholars to prepare their lessons, and success is already assured; nay, is already half achieved.

18. *Acquaintance with the General Contents of the Scriptures.*

On one point Sunday-school teachers need to use their utmost ingenuity and skill, and that is, to make their scholars familiar with the contents of the Bible. This is no easy achievement. The Bible contains so much that few know it thoroughly. We may be diligent students of the Word all our lives and yet be constantly finding in it something new. But there is a kind of knowledge of it which every one may attain. Every one may and should know the general scope of the Scriptures. He should have their outlines so fixed and clear in his mind that he can know at once where to turn for any particular subject, event or book.

It is to be feared that this point is overlooked in many of our Sunday-schools. Most of the question-books in use enter so minutely into the examination of particular passages that the scholars lose sight of the general scope of Scripture. A large number of Sunday-school scholars do not remain in school longer than three or four years. Four years in the Sunday-school is perhaps the average length of a generation. Yet I have known a school spend two years in the study of one single book of the Bible. If they undertook to master the subject in the thorough and exhaustive manner prescribed in the question-books, they could not do it in less time, allowing for the weeks lost by vacations and other interruptions.

I do not wish to discourage this kind of careful and exhaustive study of particular parts of Scripture. It is in itself very profitable. But it should be alternated with another and quite different mode of study. Every child during the period of its Sunday-school life should go once at least through the whole Bible. We want a question-book or lesson-book of some kind, so general in its outlines that a class or a school using it will go through the Bible in a single season. Possibly there may be some book or books of this kind with which I am not acquainted. If so, and my attention were called to them, I would gladly help to make them known. I know some single volumes which thus go over the whole ground. But they are not sufficiently general. They require too much.

The Child's Scripture Question-Book is an admirable compend of Scripture truth, and comes nearer to the idea I have in view than any other book I can think of. But it is rather a compend of Bible *doctrine* than a compend of the *Bible*. We want something which shall make our children familiar with the Bible itself, so that if you speak to them of Samson, or Daniel in the lion's den, or the calling of Samuel, or the children that mocked Elisha, saying, " Go up, thou bald head," or the miraculous passage of the Red Sea, or the building of the Ark, or any of the various scenes in the life of our Saviour, if you refer them to any particular book in the Bible, to Exodus, or Ezra, or Nahum, or Proverbs, or Hebrews, they shall know at once where to find it.

A part of the course of study in every Sunday-school should be to have the children learn the order of the books in the Bible. Questions or exercises of some kind, having this object in view, should form a part of the small synoptical volume that I am speaking of. It is lamentable to see the manner in which some children, and some who are not children, go to work to find a text or a topic which has been referred to. They seem to know that the book of Psalms is somewhere in the middle of the Bible, that Genesis is at the beginning and Revelation at the end, but beyond that they are altogether at sea.

It used to be the fashion, as soon as children could read, to set them to reading the Bible through in course, and it was a matter of ambition to see how early in life this feat could be accomplished. It was even sometimes entered in the family record that Edward or James or Susan had read the Bible through when he or she was only eight years old, or seven, or possibly six. It became, however, in course of time, the fashion to sneer at these perform-

ances, and to ask how much of knowledge or benefit such youngsters gained by wading through the
long lists of hard names in the book of Numbers or
the mysterious utterances of the Hebrew prophets.
The sneer showed only how ignorant were those
who uttered it as to a true philosophy of mental development, and it has been a great misfortune that
parents and teachers had the weakness to listen to it.
There is no better way for even a young child to get
a knowledge of the general contents and scope of
Holy Scripture than to read the Bible straight
through in course. While much of what he reads
will be unintelligible to him, much also—more, indeed, than many persons imagine—will make a lasting impression, and the acquaintance it will give
him with the general outline of the Bible will be the
very best preparation for the special study of particular parts of the Bible.

I believe the scriptural knowledge of this generation would be greatly increased if this good
old custom could be revived. The benefit would
be still greater if, at stated intervals through life,
say at the end of every five years, each individual
should set apart a year for repeating the process;
that is, should read the Bible through in course at
the age of ten, at the age of fifteen, at the age of
twenty, and so on to the end of life. How at each
new general perusal would light flash upon the
pages from the special studies and experiences
of the intervening years! And how upon each

20

special study would help come from his increasing familiarity with the Scriptures as a whole!

19. *Irregular Attendance of Teachers.*

In the actual work of the Sunday-school few things are more disheartening than the irregular attendance of teachers. I cannot say from certain knowledge how extensive the evil is. But in every school with which I have ever been connected it has been one of the sources of greatest annoyance, discouragement, and even of dismay, with which the superintendent has had to contend.

It is rare to go into any large Sunday-school and not to find one or more teachers absent. The same men and women who would not absent themselves from a business engagement on a weekday for any cause short of sickness, or some imperative necessity, will stay away from their class on the Lord's day for causes too frivolous to name. The consequences are disastrous in the extreme. A class thus deserted by its teacher becomes disorderly and noisy, and is a source of annoyance to all the rest of the school. The children, feeling that their teacher cares little for them, lose interest in their lessons and in the school, and some imitate the example set them by staying away likewise. The superintendent, to prevent the growing disorder which two or three unoccupied classes produce in the school, sets some chance visitor, or some of the older scholars from other classes, to instruct the neglected ones. It is a great kindness in the persons thus called upon to undertake the work. But it is little usually they can do. They are unacquainted with the children and with the lesson, and so the time is pretty much lost to the class.

I fear there is among teachers generally an entirely too low standard of duty in this matter. The secret, unacknowledged reasoning in the case seems to be this: My undertaking to teach the class is altogether voluntary. My going to the school at all is a favor which I may give or withhold. My engagement to be there is quite different from that which binds a clerk to be at the office of his employer during the appointed hours of business. I may therefore exercise my own choice whether to go or to stay away.

Perhaps no teacher ever puts the case in this bold way. But it is to be feared, if the real truth were known, much of the absenteeism among Sunday-school teachers has no better foundation. The engagement to teach and to be present has no legal sanction. The violation of it brings no pecuniary penalties. And so it is treated lightly.

I say these words with sorrow. They imply a grievous dereliction of duty on the part of those who act thus. A teacher who absents himself from his class for any cause which would not make him break a business engagement, says in effect that the cause of Christ is less dear to him than the cause of his fellow-man; that displeasing Christ is of less import-ance to him than displeasing a fellow-man; that the loss of Christ's favor is of less value than the loss of money.

It should be to the teacher just as sacredly a matter of conscience to be in his place at the appointed time as for the minister to be in his pulpit, for the physician to be at the bedside of his patient, for the lawyer to be in the court when his client's cause is called, for the clerk to be in bank when bank-hour comes, or the workman in any worldly business to fulfil his engagement to his employer. The teacher who undertakes the charge of a class with any lower sense of obligation on this subject has no business there. He does a grievous wrong to the cause of his Lord and Master.

A teacher is sometimes compelled, by sickness or by other imperative and satisfactory cause, to stay away from his class. But in such a case he should take the same precaution that he does in any other business to prevent the evil consequences of his absence. The minister who is detained from his pulpit provides a substitute. The physician who is unable to pay the expected visit to a patient sends another physician to take his place. So with other engagements where temporal interests of any kind are at stake and a fellow-man is the contracting party on the other side. Shall we be less scrupulous where the interests are those of the soul, and where the party in whose service we are engaged and with whom we have entered into covenant is the Lord Jesus himself?

If the teacher finds that it will be impossible for him to meet his class, two things are binding on him. First, he should use his very best endeavor to procure a substitute, and the measure of his duty should not be less than that of the minister or the physician in a like case. If all Sunday-school teachers had a right sense of duty in this matter, it would be as much a cause of surprise and wonderment to see a school assembled and a teacher's chair vacant as for a congregation to be assembled and see the pulpit vacant. Secondly, when the teacher finds that he cannot be present, he should make the matter known to the superintendent, and at the earliest moment possible after the necessity becomes known to himself. Nor is this duty discharged by sending word to the superintendent by some scholar on his way to school. If the superintendent knows it a day or two beforehand, particularly in cases where the teacher can himself procure no suitable substitute, measures may be taken to prevent the injury which the absence is likely to produce in the school. But a scholar often comes up to the superintendent's desk after the school is opened, and says, "Mr. Smith requested me to tell you that he went to New York Wednesday last; will you please to get some one to take his class to-day!" Of what possible use to the superintendent is such a message?

20. *Visiting Scholars.*

The Sunday teacher is, in some respects, at a disadvantage, when compared with the ordinary daily teacher. The teacher of the weekday-school has his scholars five days in the week, five hours a day, sometimes more. The studies follow each other in regular course; study and attendance are compulsory, failure in either respect being visited by appropriate penalties. The school-room is furnished with maps, globes, desks, blackboards, scientific apparatus, and all the other means and appliances for teaching and study. The Sunday teacher on the other hand has the child but one day in the week, and on that day but one hour, or at the utmost one hour and a half. Indeed, if we take out the time spent in opening and closing school, in collecting and distributing books and papers, and in other miscellaneous business, the teacher rarely has left for uninterrupted instruction more than three-quarters of an hour. From a pretty large acquaintance with the subject, I believe this is fully up to the average of time actually given to direct instruction in the Sunday-school. That is, for teaching religious truth and knowledge of Holy Scriptures. which we profess to believe to be the most important of all concerns, we give three-quarters of one hour out of the one hundred and sixty-eight hours which make up the week. Nor does this state the case fully. Attendance. even for that brief period, and the preparation of the lesson, are for the most part considered entirely optional, and in point of fact are given with much greater irregularity than the attendance upon the weekday school and the study of the daily lessons.

Such being the state of the case, the Sunday teacher who is anxious to accomplish something substantial in the way of religious instruction naturally avails himself of all the accessory means by which his limited time on Sunday may be made as efficient as possible. Among these means none is more common or more effectual than the occasional visiting of his scholars at their homes. I do not mean by this that he should give instruction to the scholars at their homes, but by visiting them there he becomes better acquainted with their condition and their mental wants and difficulties. He finds out what hindrances they have to contend with, and he is enabled to invoke the influence of parents in securing regularity of attendance and the proper study of the lesson. The visit begets a feeling of kindness on the part of the child and of his friends, who naturally feel gratified by such a mark of attention and interest, particularly if the family are in the humble walks of life. The common experience of the Sunday-school teacher is that the Sunday lesson is very imperfectly prepared. Sometimes this lesson is not prepared at all, and very rarely is it prepared with that care and thoroughness which mark the lessons of the week. The same child that recites its lessons in grammar, arithmetic, geography and history without hesitating and without missing a word, will come to the recitation of its Bible lesson with only the most dim and vague recollection of its contents. The Sunday lesson usually consists of a certain number of verses to be committed to memory, with questions intended to illustrate and draw out their meaning and application. It has become very common for children to omit entirely committing these verses to memory. In this matter the parents are the ones to correct the evil, and in most instances would do so if the case were properly stated to them by the teacher on the occasion of his visit. It is not exaggeration to say that the amount of instruction given in the Sunday-school would be doubled if all the scholars would habitually come to the class with the Bible verses of the lesson thoroughly committed to memory. This is one way, then, in which the time of the teacher with his class may be made more efficient, and there is no means by which this can be so effectually brought about as by a visit from the teacher to the child, at his own home.

I have spoken thus far merely of religious instruction. The argument drawn from the personal influence acquired by the teacher in these visits is still stronger, but I have not time to dwell upon it. Suffice it to say that the teacher thereby gains numerous and most favorable opportunities for bringing home the subject of personal religion to the child and sometimes to the other members of the household.

No definite rule can be given in regard to the

frequency of these visits. It depends upon the circumstances of each particular class and scholar. Some scholars need visiting as often as once a month. In other cases a visit once or twice a year is sufficient. There is little danger, however, of over-doing the matter.

In regard to visiting scholars, the following points may be considered as 'settled: 1. Every scholar should be visited in case of his absence from the class, and this visit should be made as soon after the absence as possible. 2. Every scholar should be visited occasionally. 3. Teachers should make a business of visiting all their scholars immediately after the summer vacation.

21. *Keeping up with the Times.*

The Sunday-school man is essentially a man of progress. We feel at once an incongruity when we think of him in any other light. The institution itself was born of progress, and belongs to the new order of things. It is one of the subjects on which the church, dissatisfied with past shortcomings, has made a bold and free step in advance. Whoever is engaged in this advanced enterprise would seem, by the very nature of his occupation, to be committed to the principles and the spirit of progress. Yet there are not wanting among our Sunday-school people indications of a spirit, if not opposed to improvement, yet timid, hesitating, indifferent, retrograde. Of course, I have nothing to say against genuine

conservatism, meaning by that term the disposition
to hold on to whatever is good. But there is a conservatism which consists in holding on to whatever
has been once established, whether bad or good. If it
is only one of the things that used to be in the olden
time, that fact alone hallows it. Against such conservatism the earnest Sunday-school man feels bound
to protest and contend. He is what we call a live
man, one thoroughly wide awake. He does not re-
ject a thing without examination because it is new,
nor cleave to a thing against his judgment because
it is old. While projects and schemes never before
heard of are admitted to a hearing, and if they make
a reasonable show are admitted to trial also, methods
and practices that have been in use for generations
are not thereby exempt from respectful inquiry, and
if found on sober examination to be wrong, are not
exempt from reform.

The Sunday-school man, however, is not a de-
structive. On the contrary, he is as truly a genuine
conservative as he is a progressive. He aims on
the one hand to keep whatever is good and desirable
in that which has come down to us from the past,
and on the other hand to seize with eager welcome
whatever real improvement the present order of
things brings him.

The Sunday-school man, therefore, if he would be
true to the character which his position would seem
to impose, must be a man of the progressive order,
thoroughly wide awake to every real improvement

in his work. What are some of the ways by which he can aid himself in keeping up to the times?

1. *He should take a Teachers' Paper.* The teacher who takes no teachers' paper can hardly expect to keep pace with the current of opinion and improvement. This Sunday-school work has become an important department of human effort. The workers in it are numbered by hundreds of thousands Many of them are not mere men of routine, but are men of thought, originality, invention, enterprise Experiments of high moment are going on continually in every department of the work. Reports and discussions of these fill the columns of papers devoted to this particular subject. Almost every conceivable question that can be raised, either in regard to the work to be done or the manner of doing it, is there discussed. Can a teacher who would claim to be a live man afford to be without such a paper?

To state the question would seem to be to answer it. The proposition which it involves seems to address itself at once to the intuitive perceptions of men. Yet as a question of fact the duty is ignored by almost the entire body of Christian men and women who are engaged in the business of Sunday-school teaching. I do not believe that more than one teacher out of two hundred takes a teachers' paper. Should this be so? Is there not some duty in this matter? Does not a weekly paper, giving in compact form the latest and ripest thoughts of the wisest and most experienced workers in the cause, furnish a means of

self-improvement which a conscientious teacher cannot well forego? Do not the recorded experiences,
the suggestive anecdotes, the earnest appeals, the
useful hints as to improved methods for managing
libraries and class-rolls and for conducting the various machinery of a school,—do not these suggestive
and varied practical details with which its columns
abound from week to week furnish the teacher regularly and surely with matter which he urgently needs
and which he cannot get elsewhere?

Taking a religious paper of some kind does not
meet the case. Every man expects of course to take
the weekly religious paper of his own denomination.
But this does not fill his want as a teacher any more
than occupying his pew in church would render it
unnecessary for him to be in his place in school.
For his special work as a teacher he needs a paper
devoted to this specialty just as much as the intelligent farmer or mechanic, the florist, the gardener,
the builder does, each in his own special calling.
Our good brother Pardee used to tell us instances of
the mistakes of Sunday-school men on this subject
which would be ludicrous were it not for the seriousness of the consequences involved. After visiting a
village and spending three or four days with the
teachers, holding what is called an " Institute," and
explaining to them in his pleasant, practical way just
how this, that, or the other thing is done, the teachers
would gather round him full of enthusiasm, wonder-
ing that they had never heard of these things before,

and zealous to hear more. " Do tell us, brother, where we can find out more about these things?" " I have not told you a thing that you will not find explained and discussed all the year round in *The Sunday-School Times.* You take that paper, of course?" " Why, no. I take, you know, my own church paper, the ——, and one religious paper seems to be enough."

2. *He should have a Teachers' Library.* Besides reading a teachers' paper, there are many books devoted to the explanation and discussion of the Sunday-school work with which the Sunday-school teacher should be familiar. As a lawyer has a law library and a doctor a medical library, so a teacher should have a teachers' library. This library should include not merely books suited to give him progress in Christian knowledge and culture, such as all Christians need, not merely the commentaries and other books needed to aid him in preparing the lesson, but books on teaching, in which all that pertains to the art and mystery of the profession is discussed, and especially books written specifically about Sunday-schools, explaining their rise, progress, development, object and methods. We are beginning to be quite rich in our literature on this subject. The teacher who is up to the times will spend some money in stocking his shelves with the books pertaining to his business, and some time in stocking his mind with their contents.

3. *He should attend Conventions.* There is still

another means of improvement which the really wide-awake man will not willingly miss. By nothing are our faculties so soon quickened as by actual contact with wide-awake people. It is a great mistake for a Sunday-school man to shut himself up in his shell. Let him gladly embrace every fitting opportunity for meeting his fellow-laborers in Teachers' Institutes and Conventions. No doubt there is usually some chaff in these meetings, but there is also generally good, pure wheat. I never attended a Sunday-school Convention yet that I did not bring away from it some valuable thought. Besides, in many parts of the country, these meetings, under the name of Institutes, have become real practical, working affairs. I urge very strongly upon all teachers the duty and policy of mingling more than they generally do with other teachers for the purpose of comparing notes and of learning what others are doing.

Is teaching the only business in which no advantage is to be taken of the experience of others? Are teachers the only workmen who are above *or below* being profited by suggestion, advice and example? Are the teachers of our Sunday-schools generally so thoroughly skillful and so completely furnished for their work that they need no help from any quarter? Does no intelligence reach us from any quarter, of schools verging toward dissolution because of the irregularities and disorders which the teachers know not how either to quell or prevent?—of classes which are a nuisance to all the rest of the school to which they belong because of the rude behavior, the loud talking and the irregular attendance of the members?—of scholars who never learn their Sunday lesson, though perfect in the lessons of the weekday-school, and who do not attend the Sunday-school more than one-half or one-third the time, though never absent from school during the week?

CHAPTER V.

TEACHERS IN COUNCIL.

IN the previous chapter the discussion has been limited for the most part to those topics in which each teacher necessarily acts by and for himself. But many things in this great Sunday-school work require co-operative action. Teachers must confer together in various ways and in greater or smaller numbers if they would reap the full fruit of their labors. I propose, therefore, in the present chapter to consider some of those various meetings held by Sunday-school men under the names of Conventions, Institutes, Teachers' Meetings and Teachers' Normal Classes.

The object, in all such gatherings, is improvement in the means of carrying on the work, and especially improvement in the qualifications of teachers.

1. *Such Gatherings Needed.*

That there is need of some agency for the accomplishment of these ends is evident. Of the four hundred thousand teachers who are guiding

and sustaining this great work of Sunday-school instruction, probably less than one-tenth have ever had
any regular professional training for the business
of teaching. Let us think for a moment what this
fact implies. There are, it may be, at this very
time, in the United States, four hundred thousand
steam engines at work, propelling boats or drawing
trains of cars laden with human beings. Would it
not be accounted an act of suicidal madness and in-
fatuation if nine out of ten of the engineers by
whom these precious burdens are hurried along
were allowed to be persons not professionally trained
to the business of an engineer?—if they were taken,
in fact, haphazard from the passengers on the spur
of the occasion? Is the business of a teacher any
less responsible than that of an engineer? Is there
any less risk in guiding an immortal soul along the
path of eternal life than in guiding a steam engine
along its appointed track? Shall the children of
this world always be wiser than the children of
light? Shall worldly men be more careful of risks,
where only a few dollars are at stake, than the
people of God, where the stake is eternal life?

Why should not our theological seminaries make
some provision on the subject? A young man goes
to a theological seminary for the purpose of being
fitted and trained for the pastoral office. In the
providence of God and the practical working of
Christian institutions at this time, a large part of the
pastor's work—that part of his work, too, which is

21 *

most productive of results—lies among the young of his flock. There is not probably a really successful worker in the pastoral office, in any Protestant church in the United States, who does not feel that the Sunday-school stands second only to the pulpit among his agencies for carrying forward his Master's work. Do our theological students receive in the seminary any adequate instruction and training for this part of their duty? They are told there how to expound the word to the people, how to preach, how to manage the adult portions of their congregations; are they told how to manage their Sunday-schools? Are they told how to train up a corps of faithful and efficient teachers?

The pastors of several congregations, whether of the same denomination or of different denominations, might, by a little conference, get up among themselves, with the aid perhaps of one or more special lecturers from abroad, a systematic course of instruction for a local Normal Institute. However feebly or imperfectly carried out, such a plan could not fail of doing some good. The pastors would of course succeed better in such an enterprise, if themselves trained to it in the seminary, as they are trained to writing sermons and to preaching. But without such instruction they can accomplish much. If the pastors and superintendents of any one town, village, or neighborhood would come together and have a free conference as to the best means of improving the qualifications of their Sunday-school teachers—nay, if only the pastor and superintendent and two or three of the most thoughtful members of a single congregation would thus confer, and fairly set some plan in motion, no matter how incomplete the plan might be—good would come of it. What we are suffering from is patient indifference and quiescence in the present state of things.

Let me speak plainly. Our schools are taught by those who know not how to teach. Of course there are many brilliant exceptions. I speak only of the general fact. Yet these unskilled teachers, with all their imperfections as teachers, are among the noblest Christians in the land. No one knows so well as they themselves do the extent of their deficiencies and imperfections. No one longs as they do for the knowledge and the skill to do better. Their hearts ache for the longing they have to serve the Master efficiently in this glorious cause. There is no fear that they will not respond to any well-considered and practical plan by which their talents may be guided and their laborious services made more effectual. What the leaders in Israel, the wise men in the church, the ministers and superintendents, the working and thinking men of large hearts and long heads, owe to this cause, is the devising and maturing of plans for the improvement of our Sunday-school teachers. Our schools will never accomplish what they should do until our teachers know better how to teach and what to teach. Our teachers must themselves be taught. Whoever shall devise the means of doing this effectually will help forward the great cause as much as if he were to put a hundred missionaries in the field.

2. *State Conventions.*

Should our State conventions be denominational or should they be union meetings?

It seems to me that in this matter there is no necessary antagonism between denominational interests and the interests which are common to all. On the contrary, a right understanding of the subject will promote both—will make both union movements and ecclesiastical movements more effective.

In the first place let me say, I have always advocated and urged ecclesiastical action on the subject of Sunday-schools. How any church that has any proper comprehension of its mission as an agency for the propagation of Christianity, or of the place that education holds among the means for spreading and perpetuating true religion, can avoid taking action as a church in this work of the religious teaching and training of the young passes comprehension. I hold that every church (that is, every separate congregation) is bound to engage actively and effectually, in its organized capacity as a church, in this Sunday-school work. A church that neglects to provide for the religious instruction of the children is as truly guilty before God as if it neglected to provide for pulpit ministrations. The session, consistory, vestry, or whatever body is charged with the spiritual oversight of the congregation, is bound to see that there is a Sunday-school, and that it is rightly and efficiently managed and taught. In whose hands the management of the school should be is a question of time and circumstance. But the church as such should see that the work is done, and well done, and should throw the weight of its official character and influence into the work. Office-bearing in the church, in other words, should be seen in something more than in merely its negative character, its power of excluding measures or men of an improper sort. It should rather and mainly be felt as a positive propelling power in every good word and work.

In like manner the various ecclesiastical bodies in which the interests of many individual churches are represented, the Presbyteries, Classes, Conferences, Synods, etc., have other than mere rectoral or governmental duties. It is one of the pleasant signs of the times that at many of these convocations the wants of the Sunday-school are brought prominently forward, and a part of the sessions of the body have almost the appearance of a Sunday-school festival, —children, teachers, parents, whole congregations, meeting with the venerable body of pastors in some special service appropriate to the occasion. One of the standing committees in many of these bodies now is the committee on Sunday-schools, and many of the topics discussed are precisely the same as those discussed in a Sunday-school convention, such as the qualifications of teachers, methods of teaching, Sunday-school music, the early conversion of children, etc. I hope to see the time when, in every ecclesiastical council, of whatever name or magnitude, a part, and no small part, of its regular business, shall consist in action on Sunday-school matters, and its sessions shall be looked forward to and attended upon by Sunday-school teachers and Sunday-school children, by parents and by whole congregations, with that same feeling of personal interest with which a whole population will now turn out to a heart-warming, fire-enkindling Sunday-school convention.

But there are some who, in addition to this introduction of the Sunday-school cause into ecclesiastical convocations, would have each denomination hold a separate Sunday-school convention of its own, both of the State and the county, and on this point I am at issue with them. This is a multiplication of machinery entirely uncalled for and unnecessary. The Sunday-school workers of any denomination have in their regular ecclesiastical councils all the machinery they need for conference, and counsel and the prosecution of their work as a denomination. But in this Sunday-school work we naturally desire to profit by the skill and experience of those outside of our own pale. We therefore come together in State and county conventions in which all denominations are represented. Improvement in such matters comes by comparison. Few

ever attended one of these large union meetings
without feeling that he had learned something new,
and without having received a fresh impulse, such
as he would not have received in any meeting composed exclusively of those of his own particular way
of thinking.   No one can be much conversant with
the Sunday-school work of our day without feeling
that the Spirit has bestowed special gifts in this
matter to one and another, here and there, in
different churches, and that if we are to have
Sunday-school conventions at all, and derive from
them the full benefits that they are suited to
give, they should be union conventions, where the
best workers and thinkers of all denominations
may be brought together in holy and fraternal
counsel.

I would urge then these two things : First, let
each denomination, through all its official and organized agencies as a denomination, take up and
push forward the Sunday-school cause to the utmost
of its strength.   The more any church pushes its
own schools, the greater and more beneficial will be
the impulse it will give to the schools of other
churches.   Secondly, let the Sunday-school workers
of all denominations meet yearly in county and
State associations of a union character, for the purpose of discussing those questions of a general
nature which belong equally to Christians of every
name.   Denominational activity, through the regular
ecclesiastical channels, will help the union meeting.

The union meeting will react most kindly and benef-
icently upon the ecclesiastical council. There is no
antagonism between the two. On the contrary,
each helps the other.

But it will be in vain to attempt to have union
Sunday-school associations, whether for the county
or the State, if there are to be denominational associations for the same purpose. The majority both
of ministers and laymen have not the time, and cannot afford the expense of attending more than one
such meeting. If the denominational association is
maintained, it will kill the union association, and
between the two I certainly think the union meeting
vastly the more important and necessary.

My view of the matter may be summed up in a
dozen words. Church action in the Sunday-school
cause—union action in Sunday-school conventions.

3. *County Conventions.*

The first rule to be observed in regard to all such
gatherings is, make ample preparation. Those who
originate the movement must not imagine that a
mere announcement that a meeting is to be held at a
certain time and place will be sufficient. They must
bestir themselves diligently in making the thing
thoroughly known and talked of all through the
county. Ample time should be allowed between
the issuing of the call and the time for holding the
meeting. Handbills, circulars, pulpit notices and
newspaper notices should all be put in requisition.

The newspapers are always ready to co-operate in any such enterprise, and lend their columns freely, both in giving notice of the meetings and in reporting their proceedings. Get the ministers to urge their people to attend.

The convention should be held at a convenient and central place. The county town is a good place for the first convention. If the first is a success, there will be plenty of places eager for the privilege of entertaining the second, and others which may follow. Hold it in the largest church, and see that the church is well filled at each session.

Select such a time as will suit the greatest number of people, remembering that it is impossible to suit everybody, and that if you wait for a time which will suit everybody you will indefinitely postpone your convention. Two or three days will generally be found enough to continue the convention. In some places it is well to hold it in the middle of the week; in others at the end of the week, closing with a grand children's meeting and other public exercises on the Lord's day. In other places it is well to commence on Sunday with such sermons, children's meetings, etc., as may be thought best. The circumstances differ so greatly in different places that no outside suggestion in this respect is as good as that which the residents of the place where the convention is held can devise for themselves.

When the convention assembles let it be with a prayerful spirit of earnest devotion to the work, and

22

with a determination not to waste a moment in anything foreign to the purpose for which the people have been called together.

Select for officers the men who will best fulfil the duties required of them.

Very much depends on the Chairman. A dull chairman can put the convention to death in short order. An earnest man, prompt, decided, courteous, well acquainted with the rules of deliberative bodies, will contribute much toward making the convention a success. The chairman should keep the meetings moving briskly, confine speakers in discussion to the subject announced to be discussed, and have courage enough to stop, without respect of persons, any speaker who exceeds his allotted time, if a certain time has been allotted.

Much depends also upon getting a good Secretary. He need not be a man of great gifts as a speaker, but he should possess the pen of a ready writer, and should be a man of accurate habits; otherwise the minutes of the convention will be of very little use. If there is no newspaper reporter present, the secretary may make himself useful by furnishing a report of the proceedings to the newspapers.

The expenses of the convention should be met by subscription or collection, and not laid on any one individual. The amount of money required, even for a most excellent convention, is so small that it will hardly be felt if collected from all who are present. Always secure funds enough to save the gentlemen who get up the convention from the annoyance of outstanding bills. It is well, also, at each convention to secure a sufficient amount to put the County Secretary in funds for the work expected of him for the year. He will be at some expense for stationery, postage, travelling, etc., and it is right that he should not be asked either to incur these expenses himself or to advance the necessary amount from his own pocket.

Discussions of topics of interest in the various branches of the work may well consume a large part of the time of the convention. Select your topics with care and with a view to the most practical and profitable remarks. *One hour at each session* may well be spent in discussion.

Somebody should be appointed to open the discussion on each subject. Allow *him* ten minutes. The other speakers on the subject may be allowed less— say five minutes. But it is hard to say exactly how many minutes each man should speak. If a man discovers on rising that what he has to say will not hold out for more than two minutes, he is under no obligation to spin it out to five merely to consume the time. Three-minute speeches have been very much in vogue, but the fact is that there are very few people who can say a great deal in so short a time. Whether a speech is long or short, it is unwise to begin it with an apology; it is an unnecessary expenditure of precious time. The chairman should confine the speakers to the subject under discussion, and firmly but courteously cause each speaker to conclude when his time expires.

Bring out your home talent in discussion as much as possible, and let no man be afraid to speak on account of youth, inexperience or supposed lack of oratorical ability. It is very important that the discussion be thrown open as widely as possible rather than conducted by a few persons.

Statistics, if they have been carefully collected so as to be reliable, are very valuable. It is tedious business, however, to read them, and few people have such memories as to remember them on hearing them read. It is better to print and distribute them; and the Secretary, when he makes his report or speech about them, can give grand totals on the blackboard, with the certainty that this will be more acceptable to his hearers and more profitable than the reading of a long string of figures.

Children's meetings may profitably be held in connection with almost every convention. There is no trouble in filling the largest church with the children. Have plenty of good singing. Three or four speeches will be enough. It is very difficult to say how long they ought to be. While it is well to make them short, remember that brevity is not the only merit of a talk to children. Some men can interest children for three-quarters of an hour, while others have a way of putting them to sleep in five minutes. The latter may as a general rule be excused from addressing children's meetings.

Above all things try to make these meetings *profitable* as well as *interesting*. Amusement is well
in proper time and place, but *mere* amusement is
decidedly out of place at such gatherings. The
speaker who will give the children a practical religious talk, full of rich illustration, accompanying it
sometimes with a little exposition of some passage
of Scripture, will do little people more good than he
who merely entertains them with story-telling. Do
not weary them. An hour and a half is long enough
for a children's meeting. It is a sin to keep it over
two hours.

4. *County Institutes.*

An Institute is something different from a convention, and still more from a mass meeting. In a convention people meet more or less in a delegated capacity and for the purpose of mutual conference,
consultation and deliberative action. All the members are on an equal footing, electing their officers
and controlling their own proceedings. They meet
to tell each other what their experience in the good
work has been, to exhort each other and to pass resolutions. An institute is altogether a different affair.
It is rather a temporary school, in which a certain
number of speakers are present by invitation as instructors or teachers, and the others are learners.
They do not meet to deliberate and resolve, but to
teach and learn. The more rigidly the exercises
can be confined to this idea the more profitable as

22 *   R

well as distinctive the institute will become. All
"five-minute" speeches or "one-minute" speeches
or pop-gun exercises of any kind for the purpose of
letting off gas are out of place. Extempore talk, vol-
unteering, making apologies, speeches of welcome,
resolutions of thanks—resolutions indeed of any kind
—are all and equally at a discount. They are all in
place at a convention and out of place at an institute.
The institute is for instruction. Those who compose
it are divided into two classes, teachers and scholars,
and the exercises should be based on this idea. There
should be, as in a school, a regular and exact programme, fixed beforehand, and filling up the entire
time with a consecutive series of carefully prepared
lessons or lectures, and without even a minute for
any sort of extemporaneous fumbling.

While the institute and the convention are so unlike in object and in their methods of procedure,
there is one point at least in which they agree. Both
should be pervaded with a spirit of prayer. It is
well in both to begin each session with a definite
season, say fifteen or twenty minutes, for devotional
exercises.

The "question drawer" is a useful part of the machinery of an institute. It gives opportunity for
drawing out the opinions of the teachers or leaders
of the institute on many points not covered by the
regular exercises. The questions ought to be sent
in at one session and answered at the next, so that
the answerers may have time to prepare themselves;

and the answers should be simple, direct statements of opinion, without going into any argument or defence of the positions assumed.

The proper way to get up an institute is for some association of teachers or convention to resolve to have one, and to appoint a conductor and a suitable committee for carrying the project into effect. The convention or association which resolves upon an institute should also provide the means for holding it. An institute that is good for anything costs something. The teachers who give up their business for two or three days, besides being at expense for travelling, etc., for the sake of learning something about their work and how to do it, think it poor economy to lose their time and labor for the sake of saving a few dollars in the bill of expenses.

The proper time for holding an institute differs, according as it is held in the city or country. In a large city, where all the teachers who are to attend are present, it is best usually to hold the institute only in the afternoon and evening, and sometimes only in the evening. Six successive evenings, or four successive afternoons and evenings, make a good institute for a city. The members in such a case attend to their regular worldly business in the morning and to the institute in the afternoon and evening. In the country the case is different. The large body of those attending have to be away from home. In all such cases the number of days should be fewer. Two full days, with morning, afternoon and evening sessions on each day, make a good institute. Men who will give up their entire time for two successive days, having a session of three hours in the morning, three in the afternoon and two or three in the evening may learn a good deal if the programme is worth anything.

Institute Programme. In making up a programme no little judgment is to be exercised so as to have due regard to variety and to apportioning the time to the character of the several exercises. Some topics can be satisfactorily disposed of in fifteen minutes, others require thirty or forty minutes. The time table should be as definite and should be adhered to as closely as that of a railroad. Nothing should be at loose ends or hap-hazard.

One of the best programmes that I have seen of an institute was that held in Morristown, New Jersey, in November, 1867. The institute occupied two days. The sessions were from half past ten to twelve, from two to five and from seven to ten on Wednesday, and a like arrangement on Thursday except that on that day they began at half past nine. In all they were in session sixteen hours.

Each session began with a devotional exercise of twenty minutes, occupying two hours out of the sixteen. The remaining fourteen hours were divided into periods of varying length, from fifteen minutes to sixty minutes, there being, however, but one exercise of the latter length, namely, an infant class lesson by Ralph Wells. The following is an abstract of this programme:

Programme of an Institute held in Morristown, N. J., November, 1867.

WEDNESDAY MORNING.

I. 30 minutes.—*Opening Exercises.* Partly devotional, partly "address of welcome." The latter part might have been omitted without injury.

II. 40 minutes.—The work of the Sunday-school Teacher. Rev. Thomas S. Hastings.

III. 15 minutes.—The Superintendent. R. G. Pardee.

IV. 5 minutes.—"One-minute" speeches from five different persons, volunteers.

WEDNESDAY AFTERNOON.

I. 20 minutes.—Devotional. Hon. John Hill, conductor.

II. 40 minutes.—Lecture on Sacred Geography. Rev. Arthur Mitchell.

III. 40 minutes.—Various uses of the Blackboard. Ralph Wells.

IV. 40 minutes.—Order of exercises in Sunday-school. A. Baldwin and Ralph Wells.

V. 40 minutes.—Question Box. R. G. Pardee and Ralph Wells.

WEDNESDAY EVENING.

I. 20 minutes.—Devotional. Rev. H. A. Butts, conductor.

II. 25 minutes.—Principles of Infant Class Teaching. Rev. J. M. Freeman.

III. 60 minutes.—Infant Class Lesson. Ralph Wells.

IV. 30 minutes.—Teacher Preparation. L. P. Cummings.

V. 45 minutes.—Fifteen "three-minute" addresses.

THURSDAY MORNING.

I. 20 minutes.—Devotional. Hon. George T. Cobb, conductor.

II. 30 minutes.—Principles of Illustrative Teaching. Rev. J. M. Freeman.

III. 40 minutes.—Peculiar Wants of Sunday-schools in Rural Districts. A. Baldwin, Rev. J. M. Johnson and R. G. Pardee.

IV. 30 minutes.—Teacher Teaching. Ralph Wells.

V. 30 minutes.—Teachers' Meetings. Andrew A. Smith.

THURSDAY AFTERNOON.

I. 20 minutes.—Devotional. Rev. S. Smith, conductor.

II. 25 minutes.—Blackboard Uses and Picture Teaching. R. G. Pardee.

III. 20 minutes.—Relation of the Sunday-school to the Family. Rev. J. M. Freeman.

IV. 20 minutes.—Sunday-school Music. Lucius Hart.

V. 15 minutes.—Three "five-minute" Volunteers.

VI. 25 minutes.—How shall we interest our children to labor for Jesus?

VII. 25 minutes.—Question Box.

VIII. 30 minutes.—Address. Rev. C. S. Robinson, D.D.

THURSDAY EVENING.

I. 20 minutes.—Devotional. Rev. A. Mitchell, conductor.

II. 20 minutes.—Mission Sunday-schools. Rev. H. A. Butts.

III. 45 minutes.—Bible Lesson. Andrew A. Smith.

IV. 15 minutes.—Importance of Inducing the Scholars to commit Scripture Truths to memory. Rev. Sanford Smith.

V. 30 minutes.—Privileges and Rewards of Sunday-school Teachers. Rev. R. J. W. Buckland.

VI. 50 minutes.—"Ten addresses of five minutes each."

It is desirable, as a matter of theory, that there should be a variety and frequent change in the exercises of an institute, and that all the exercises should be short. But suppose at any particular institute circumstances enable the managers to have with them some very eminent worker in the cause who has come five hundred or a thousand miles, and who can stay only a day or half a day, would it not be absurd to chop such a man off at the end of twenty minutes because a programme crowded with a large variety and assortment of items looks a little better on paper? In large cities it is practicable to have a number of stars of the first magnitude. But in places remote from the great centres such a result is not easily attainable. If, in some interior town, in connection with a good assortment of local talent. it is practicable to obtain the services of some such man as Mr. Vincent, Mr. Reynolds, Mr. Wells or Mr. Peltz, it would be the extreme of folly not to make good use of him while there, even if the programme did suffer a little by the operation. The object of the institute is to promote the Sunday-school cause, not to make or even to carry out a programme.

In the rebound from the prosy, slip-shod, long-winded, humdrum ways of past times, we are in danger of going into the opposite extreme and becoming dapper and superficial. While it is important to cultivate the grace of brevity and to have things move at the tap of the bell, and while perhaps the majority of subjects and of speakers may appear to best advantage under a limitation of fifteen or twenty minutes, yet there are topics and men that require and deserve a more deliberate hearing. No institute can be considered as of first-class character which does not include in its programme at least one topic to which justice cannot be done in less than an hour, and at least one speaker in regard to whom the members would feel it to be a positive loss to let him off under an hour. To have all the exercises, or many exercises of this length, would, however, be as great a fault as to have them of the three-minute or pop-gun order. The managers of an institute should study variety as well in the length as in the subjects of discussion. To have all the exercises short and snappy is to turn the institute into an exhibition room. To have them all long is to put the concern asleep. The prevalent length undoubtedly should be about twenty minutes. But there should be a free range about this point, from five minutes all the way up to sixty. The first thing for the managers to do before making up a programme at all is to ascertain what materials are at their disposal, who are to be had for the occasion, and the peculiarities and gifts of each. There will be some five-minute men and some forty-minute men, and occasionally a big gun who ought to have an hour. Make the programme accordingly. Do not cut all your coats to fit either Daniel Lambert or Tom Thumb, but take some little measure of your men before you proceed with your tailoring.

A printed programme, to be placed in the hands of all the members, is indispensable to the thorough success of an institute. This programme should be in the form of a small pamphlet rather than a broad sheet. One page should contain the names and post-office addresses of the managers, conductor and teachers. The hymns to be sung should be printed as a sort of appendix. This is better than borrowing a big pile of music books for the occasion. The hymns and music should be such as are suitable for use in Sunday-school. They may not be perhaps as appropriate to adults as others that could be selected. But there is usually at an institute some first-rate musical talent, and the members, by singing together under such direction, get ideas about the manner of singing such pieces in their own school, and this is as important to them as any of the other exercises.

5. *Teachers' Weekly Meeting.*

The association of teachers for the purpose of mutual improvement is an agency for good second to none. It is a great mistake when a teacher, or a person in any kind of occupation, isolates himself from his fellows. If his own methods and plans are good, he owes it to the cause to communicate them to others. If he gains nothing himself by such intercourse, he imparts an important benefit to his fellow-laborers. But there is no one, no matter how gifted or accomplished, that has not much to learn, and that may not learn by the interchange of thought with others working in the same field. Nor is it only from the great and distinguished that we are to learn. The very humblest worker may contribute something to the common weal. He who has most to learn on his own account may yet have something to teach to others.

A teacher who communes only with his own thoughts, who keeps entirely to himself and his own class, is neglecting a most important means of growth. Improvement in all things comes by comparison. The wide-awake teacher never confers with another teacher, or visits another school, without getting new ideas and having his old ideas stirred up. A method that is different from our own, even if it is not as good as ours, sets us to thinking. It shows us often that we have fallen unconsciously into mere routine, and without drawing

23

us into another man's rut, it serves to drag us out of our own. If the earnest men and women who are carrying forward the Sunday-school movement wish to accomplish really great things, they must manage to have some stated times for conference and for the comparison of thoughts and plans. By these means poor teachers may be made good and the good may be made better, the weak may become stronger, and the strong may be enlarged, and the inventions of one become the possession of all.

I fear that in many schools the teachers have no stated meetings for conference and study. I know there are practical difficulties in the way of keeping up a teachers' meeting. Of the six weekday evenings, one is appropriated to the weekly lecture and one to the prayer-meeting, and it is rare in any congregation that a week passes without at least one extra meeting of some kind connected with the cause of religion and benevolence. Here are one-half of one's evenings already taken up. If the Sunday-school is to occupy a fourth evening of every week, have teachers ordinarily the leisure for it?

This question of time is really the gravest obstacle in the way of the superintendent who seeks to have a stated meeting with his teachers, and I have known more than one earnest, resolute man, who was full of zeal, and whose heart was much set on this very thing, who was yet obliged to abandon the project because he feared to multiply meetings in the congregation. Sunday-school teachers are expected as a matter of course to be at all the other meetings. They are at the lecture, the prayer-meeting, the missionary, the Dorcas, the ladies' aid and other societies. If, in addition to these and to the sessions of the school on the Sabbath, and the visitation of their scholars, one evening in the week is to be given to a special, extra service, where is their leisure to come from? What time are they to have for social claims and for duty in other directions? Will it not deter many from the work of the Sunday-school, if so much is exacted and expected of them?

I am stating the case strongly perhaps. But the best way of surmounting a difficulty is first to look it full in the face. We do not escape danger by shutting our eyes to it. Let us admit then that an undue multiplication of religious services is an evil, and that the Sunday-school teacher has already a heavy burden of duty upon his shoulders. But in undertaking this additional service, he is to consider whether it will not really lighten instead of increasing his burden. The help which the teacher gets from the weekly meeting with his fellows more than compensates for the time it costs. An hour thus spent often puts one farther forward in preparation for the Sunday work than two or three hours spent in solitary study. Moreover, at such a meeting, by a free interchange and comparison of thought, we often get views and ideas that no amount of solitary study would have given us, and we almost always get our hearts warmed and our consciences quickened by this contact with other live workers.

But in discussing this question, and every other question connected with the subject, let us bear in mind that the Sunday-school work is a great work—second only to that of the pulpit. The more we fix our thoughts on the incalculable good we may accomplish, the less will we think of the difficulties. Set before the teacher the brightness of the crown at the top of the long ascent, and he will not mind a few rubs and scratches by the way. If by spending an hour a week in prayer and conference with his fellow-teachers he can increase perceptibly the chances of his winning the souls of his pupils as stars in the crown of his rejoicing, he will rather rejoice at the opportunity than regard it as a hardship. Love lightens every labor. The way to meet this question is first to get our hearts warmed with the thought of our Saviour's great love for us and of the infinite preciousness of the work of saving souls. Certain it is that in many congregations the teachers do find a way of meeting statedly for study and conference, and where they thus meet they show less signs of being overburdened than where they have no such meeting. There may be cases in which it would be advisable for a teacher to absent himself from some other weekly service in order to gain the time for being at the teachers' meeting.

I cannot but think that in every congregation in which the Sunday-school teachers have no regular stated times of meeting, the pastor and the superintendent ought to take the matter into serious consideration, and not to let such a state of things continue if by any ordinary exertions, or even by some *extraordinary* exertions, it can be prevented.

The teachers' meeting—by which phrase I mean the teachers of one particular school meeting statedly by themselves as a class—bears about the same relation to one of these big conventions that the base of a pyramid bears to the apex. The latter is a more conspicuous object, but the former is by all odds the most important. It is important indeed that the active Sunday-school workers of a whole State, county or city should come together in general council once a year to compare notes and to devise plans. But it is incomparably more important that the teachers in each particular school all over the land should come together from week to week all through the year. Here in the single congregation is the true place for the Sunday-school normal institute. In those large institutes of which the newspapers have given us an account, principles may be discussed and methods may be illustrated by lecturers and master workmen, ideas may be disseminated and impulses given, but the carrying out of the scheme into practical results is a work for single congregations. Here the members are all acquainted with each other; they have a common interest, and may have a common lesson; the number is not so large but that all may take part; and by continuing to meet weekly,

23 *

year after year, there is a reasonable chance that they will acquire not merely knowledge and good theoretical views, but practical skill.

Teachers' meetings are no new thing. They date back almost as far as the Sunday-school itself. If I mistake not, they were more common thirty or forty years ago than they are now; but in the teachers' meeting as it existed in a former generation the ex-ercises were limited to prayer for the school and studying the lesson. In urging the maintenance of this meeting upon our teachers now these two ob-jects, prayer and study of the lesson, are still to be kept in view. But there is now an important addi-tion to the exercises imperatively called for. A thor-ough knowledge of the lesson is absolutely essential to all good teaching, and for obtaining such a know-ledge a teachers' meeting is a great help. While discussing the various topics of the lesson with our fellow-teachers, we gather up hints and ideas that we would never get from mere solitary study. But some-thing more than this knowledge is needed in order to teach. The teachers' meeting must be something more than a mere Bible class. It must be a normal class, in which the members, besides investigating the lesson, may study methods of teaching and gov-erning, and may each in turn give a practice lesson under the guidance of the pastor or superintendent and the kindly criticism of their fellows.

To see some one else give a practice lesson gives us new views. It improves our theoretical knowledge, but it imparts no skill to ourselves. We learn to do a thing *by doing it*. There is no other way. If it is not practicable at a teachers' meeting to have a class of children present to practice on, let the teachers practice on each other. This is constantly done in normal schools. One of the class takes charge of it as teacher, and goes through the lesson to the best of his or her ability. Then the regular teacher and the members of the class discuss in a friendly spirit the manner in which the instruction was given, offering suggestions and criticisms. The process is at first rather embarrassing, and it requires no little gentleness and tact on the part of the conductor. But after a while the parties become more at their ease and acquire greater freedom of action ; the exercise then becomes in the highest degree interesting and exciting. A teacher who has once fairly gone through the ordeal of teaching a lesson to his fellows feels a degree of confidence when coming before his own class that nothing else could give, and this confidence and self-possession is always an element of power when in the presence of a class.

Besides these two things, the study of the lesson and practice teaching, the teachers' meeting should set apart a regular portion of its time to the consideration of the numerous questions connected with the science of teaching. The literature of this subject is ample and is increasing, and Sunday-school teachers would do well to acquaint themselves with it more than they are in the habit of doing. Besides the books which discuss exclusively Sunday-school methods, there are excellent treatises on the general subject of teaching and school government, and the perusal of these could not fail to be of eminent service to the Sunday-school teacher.

A Sunday-school teacher who will acquaint himself with any considerable number of these works can hardly fail to derive benefit from them for the discharge of his own special duties. These works abound with suggestions which apply to Sunday-school teaching as much as to any other teaching.

But to return to our subject, the teachers' meeting. I hold that this is the true starting-point for all general and permanent improvement in our Sunday-schools. The teachers of every school ought to meet weekly by themselves as a normal class. The exercises of this class ought to be: 1. The thorough study of the lesson; 2. Practice teaching, in which there should be no mere spectators, but all in turn and equally should be actors; and, 3. A discussion of some of the general principles of teaching and school government.

CHAPTER VI.

THE SUNDAY-SCHOOL LIBRARY.

PART I.

HOW TO SELECT A LIBRARY.

THE subject of Sunday-school books and papers has assumed such proportions that the friends of Sunday-schools can no longer ignore it, if they would. The time was, and that within the memory of some still living, when Judson's Questions, Anna Ross, Little Henry and his Bearer, and some half-a-dozen other books, which could be counted on your fingers, constituted the entire encyclopædia of Sunday-school literature. Now the number of books clamoring for admission at the doors of the Sunday-school library is absolutely appalling. The number of publishing houses actively engaged in the production of this class of books, including the great religious publication societies, is not less than thirty-six, wielding a capital of at least five millions of dollars. The books already produced are numbered by thousands (seven thousand is probably a moderate estimate), and they are increasing at a rate that is really frightful. The number of new Sunday-school library books has for several years exceeded the rate of one a day, and it is all the while increasing. It was four hundred and thirty-four in 1868, and probably reached five hundred in 1869. Question-books, Record-books, Picture-cards, Maps, Reference-books, and Periodicals, weekly and monthly, have increased in a like proportion.

The church committee, therefore, the pastor, the superintendent, the librarian, or whoever it is that is entrusted with the duty of furnishing the Sunday-school with books and other supplies, is compelled to pause. He must perforce give the matter some thought, and determine, if possible, upon some principle of selection. No haphazard purchases will be satisfactory where there is such a vast variety from which to choose, and where there is of necessity so much that is mere trash, if not worse. Not only should the superintendent, or the committee-man, pause, but the Christian community should pause. Here is a practical question which we can neither ignore nor evade, and it has already assumed such proportions that we must either master it or be mastered by it. The reading which the Sunday-school library supplies forms no inconsiderable part both of the religious and the literary food of the community. Every child that attends the Sunday-school expects, as a matter of course, to take home

a library-book every Sunday, and this book is read
not only by the child that takes it home, but by other
members of the family. It is speaking within bounds
to say that not less than three millions of these
bright little volumes are carried home weekly, and
each of them is read by not less than three persons
on the average. The influence of such a fact, like
that of the dew and the light and some of the other
noiseless agencies of nature, is beyond the power
of computation or of statement. We have evoked
a power that will not be laid at our bidding. The
appetite for reading, like that for food or for drink,
when once aroused, will take no denial, and in the
case of the young it devours without discrimination
whatever is set before it. Food or poison, so it sat-
isfies hunger, it is eagerly swallowed.

What shall we do ?

First, we are not to raise a howl of lamentation
about it. As well might a farmer go about groan-
ing and grumbling because his acres yield such a
prodigious growth of weeds. The very rankness
of this growth only shows how fat is his soil, how
genial have been his skies. The very luxuriance of
this juvenile literature, while it necessitates increased
labor and care, is yet one of the hopeful signs of the
times. Only we must do as does the thrifty farmer
—we must spare no pains in the work of weeding.
If our children refused to read at all, or if there
were no books of any kind to tempt them, or if all
that the soil of literature produced were weeds, we

might well groan and howl.   But in the present case indiscriminate croaking is as unreasonable as it is useless.   In the face of such a state of things as we have described, mere grumbling has about as much effect as grumbling at the weather has; it does not make the number of books produced or the number read one volume less; and, like finding fault with the weather, it ignores the countless blessings produced by those very clouds and showers and dew and frost which we are so constantly berating.

What then shall we do?

I answer: The subject of juvenile religious literature must occupy more of the serious and deliberate attention of the Christian community than it has hitherto done.   It is not a subject to be estimated by the puny size of the volumes concerned, nor is it one to be left to the judgment of the youngest and least experienced in the congregation—the giggling, sentimental misses, who, not old enough to take charge of a class, are sometimes thought quite competent to have charge of the library, and who often really have more to say as to the choice of the books than have the minister, the superintendent and the librarian.   Verily, such things ought not to be. *Next to the choice of a superintendent, there is no graver subject of consideration for a Sunday-school than the selection of its library books.*   It is entitled to the best judgment of the soundest heads that the congregation or the church contains.

It should be made a prominent subject for examination and debate at every convention of Sunday-school teachers. It should be made a part of the standing order of business for every ecclesiastical synod or assembly. The three millions of Sunday-school books devoured every week in the chimney-corner and the nursery are of quite as much consequence to the health of the church as are the few hundreds or thousands of ponderous octavos and quartos which in the course of the year find their way to the shelves of the theologians.

But, once more, says the reader, what is to be done? What is your plan of operations? How are we to get at it, as a practical question? Suppose the case of a new school about to be organized, or of an old school about to renew its library, how shall they go to work to root out the weeds, or to select the pure wheat out of the vast mass that lies before them?

These are reasonable questions. I shall endeavor to give them an explicit answer.

How shall we select our Sunday-school books?

I take it for granted that there must be a selection. The number of books offering is so great that no Sunday-school can take them all, and if it could, it would be very unwise to do so, for out of this vast number of competing books very many are such as ought never to see the inside of a Sunday-school library. A school, therefore, which undertakes to

24

replenish its library, must make up its mind that something is to be done besides collecting money. Some thought and labor must be bestowed upon it.

This, then, is the first thing for the minister and the superintendent to do when a new library is to be bought. Let them make a stir about it, and keep on stirring, until a right feeling of the importance of the subject is awakened in the congregation. Unless the people first feel that it is really of some importance, and of very grave importance, to know what books their children shall receive from the Sunday-school library, there will be difficulty in getting the necessary help. These books preach to the children, silently, perhaps, but not the less effectively, and it behooves a people to know that this preaching is of the right sort, quite as much as that which is addressed to them from the pulpit.

Let the minister, the superintendent, or whoever is to engineer the matter, take his stand here, and say, *No book shall come into the library until it has been read and approved by some one in whose judgment on such matters the people have confidence.* Nothing like standing still to wake people up. When a locomotive meets an obstruction, and the train comes to a sudden halt, everybody is wide awake in an instant. If the superintendent finds the people in a sound sleep on this subject of the library books, let him close the library ; close the school if necessary ; bring matters up with a round turn ; **do** *something* to wake the people out of their sleep.

But suppose everybody wide awake, *what next?*
Let it be understood that work is required, and this
work is not of that kind which is to be done with a
hurrah and a flourish and under social excitement,
like that of getting up an anniversary, a pic-nic, or
an excursion, but is something to be done with slow,
patient, solitary labor—something that will take
time, and that involves no little of irksome drudgery.
There is needed, in short,

A Reading Committee.

The duty of the Reading Committee should be
to read and approve every book that comes into the
library; and if two or three hundred new volumes
are needed—which is no uncommon demand—it
will be seen that the position of the committee is no
sinecure. Yet is not this what is required and expected of those who are the guardians of our public
schools? Do not the books in use in those schools
have to pass a rigid scrutiny, each book in detail,
on its own individual merits? And do we not hold
to a strict accountability our school directors and
trustees for the manner in which they discharge this
trust? And are the books which are to be used in
our Sunday-schools of less importance than those
which are used in our week-day schools? Surely
there are in every congregation men and women
enough, and of the right kind, too, if the proper
means are taken for bringing this subject before
them, to undertake and carry through this work of

examining and passing judgment upon the books
which are to go into the Sunday-school library, and
which are to mould, to so large an extent, the religious views of the youth of the congregation.

The Selection of the Committee.

Who are to select this committee, and of what
kind of persons should it consist?

As to the power of selection or appointment, that
will of course depend upon the usages in each congregation. Whoever in the congregation has by
law or usage the control of the Sunday-school, has
the control of this matter also. Churches vary
much in their views in regard to the control of the
Sunday-school. In many cases this institution is
altogether at loose ends, being considered as a sort
of independent, irresponsible concern, and left to
manage itself in whatever way it pleases. I have
no sympathy with any such views. I am most
decidedly of the opinion that the pastor, the session,
the vestry, whatever man or men constitute the governing power of the church in its spiritual concerns,
should be the ultimate, controlling power of the
Sunday-school. The simplest and the safest organization for a Sunday-school is that in which the
superintendent holds his appointment directly from
the church authorities, and in his management of
the school is considered as representing the church
authorities—acting for them and carrying out their
views. That same authority, then, is the one to call

into existence the Reading Committee of which we are now in search. Practically, in most cases, the selection of the committee will rest with the minister and the superintendent, and these two officers will also have to do work as members of the committee. Often, indeed, the whole work is thrown upon these two officers, sometimes upon one of them. But such a plan is eminently unwise, and can rarely be necessary. No one man can find the time to do the whole work, and do it well and with the proper promptness, and that congregation must be exceptional indeed in which there are not some members competent to act upon such a committee besides the minister and the superintendent. It is a case in which, of all others, division of labor is desirable.

Having determined in some way, by whom this important committee is to be appointed—whether by a vote of the teachers, by the superintendent, by the minister, or by the church session, the next question, and one coming even more directly home to the very heart of the business, is, What sort of persons are needed for this committee? What are the qualifications desirable in those to whose judg-ment we shall leave the selection of our library books, and what rules should govern them in mak-ing the selection?

Without some clear and well-defined views on this point, we shall be in danger of making a most serious mistake.

24 *

To this point, then, I shall next direct the attention of my readers.

What Sort of Persons should be on the Reading Committee?

Not every one is fitted to choose books for the
Sunday-school library. Something more is needed
than piety, good intentions, and willingness to do
the work.

1. In the first place, the person appointed for this
purpose ought to be one who has some education
and literary culture. Of course, a book is not to
be selected merely because of its style as a literary
performance. But unfortunately, some of the books
now written for children have literary blemishes
which ought to exclude them from every Sunday-
school library. So long as we have such an abundance of what is unexceptionable in every respect,
there is no excuse for putting into the hands of our
children what is not good English — slang, bad
grammar, bad rhetoric, tinsel, sickly sentimental-
ism, or windy hifalutin. The persons entrusted
with the selection of the library ought to have sufficient literary taste and judgment to be able to exclude all such wretched stuff, and I assure my readers there is no little of it in the market.

2. In the second place, the committee ought to be
well acquainted with Christian doctrine, and especially with the doctrines peculiar to their own
church. Of course, it is not to be required of

ever, book that goes into the library that it teaches the distinct peculiarities of the church to which the school belongs, or that it teaches all the distinguishing doctrines of Christianity. What is required just here is a negative safeguard. We want some one competent to see that, under the guise of a pleasant sentimental story, impressions or thoughts are not conveyed prejudicial to the truth as embraced by Christians generally, or to the truth as held by that particular church. Some of our most popular works of fiction are in this way quietly sapping the foundations of religious truth. The evil is not absent entirely from the religious story-books written for children, and those appointed to examine these books with a view to selection should be clear-headed in doctrinal matters, able to detect all false teaching, no matter how much it may be sugar-coated.

3. In the third place, the committee ought to consist of those who have some sympathy with the wants and the tastes of children. It is of no avail that a book is in faultless English, and that its orthodoxy is above suspicion, if the book itself is dull, heavy, uninteresting, abstruse, or above the children's heads. Doubtless such a book will do no harm, but it will also do no good. Such books are perhaps a convenience to the librarian. They are always in their places on the shelf, they never are lost, they never want rebinding. I have seen scores and hundreds of such volumes holding their places

in the library, undisturbed year in and year out, and just as good and fresh in paper and binding at the end of eight or ten years as when first placed upon the shelf. The books may perhaps be very good in themselves, such as would interest and profit a different class of readers, but they do not interest children. The young cannot be made to read them, except only as they may be made to take rhubarb, or to do anything else that is disagreeable. No one, therefore, is suited to serve on the book committee who has not some practical acquaintance with the wants and the tastes of the young. No one, also, should be selected for such a service who has the impracticable notion that any book is fit for the library if only it is a good book. Edwards on the Affections is a good book, but it is not good for the Sunday-school library, though it is sometimes placed there.

What Sort of Books should be Selected?

First, negatively. No book should be admitted to the library which is in bad English, none which is unsound in doctrine, none which from want of attraction will not be read by the scholars.

Thus far the way is clear. But let us now advance one step farther. Not every book which is attractive to the scholars is necessarily a fit book for the library. A volume may be one of absorbing interest, one that the scholars will devour with greediness, and yet it may be no more

fit for the Sunday-school library than Uncle Tom's
Cabin or Old Mortality. The mere fact that,
a book is intensely interesting, and that it is especially interesting to the young, is no proof of its fitness for the library. *A book may be too interesting.*
The story may be of such an exciting and absorbing character as to create a false and depraved taste,
and so to unfit the youthful mind for reading of a
sober and healthful character.

The positive requirements of a Sunday-school
book are few and plain : 1. It should be sufficiently
interesting to secure a perusal from ordinary youth.
2. The interest should turn, not upon love and matrimony, or anything of that sort, but upon points of
duty and doctrine. 3. It should teach religion. 4.
The religion which it teaches should not be of the
sentimental kind, like that of Dickens's Little
Nell, which quietly ignores all that is peculiar to
Christianity, and sends people straight to heaven
if only the circumstances of their death happen to
be pathetic. The religion inculcated in the Sunday-
school library-book should be something distinctly
taught in the Holy Scriptures, and connected with
the way of salvation through Jesus Christ. A book
is not religious merely because it touches the feelings and opens the fountain of tears. Let the inexorable demand of all these authors who are flood-
ing the land with story-books for children be that
no story, how pathetic or thrilling soever, shall be
deemed fit for the Sunday-school, unless its manifest

aim is to set forth attractively the peculiar doctrines of the gospel—faith in the Lord Jesus Christ, repentance for sin, and a holy life, as that life is described in God's Word. The conversion, the repentance, the religious experience, the good deeds which are wrought up into the story, and constitute its substance, should be such as will bear the test of Scripture.

It is, I think, a serious mistake in these religious story-books, to describe the good children as all dying young. It begets in the minds of the youthful readers the idea that religion is a mere matter of deathbeds, and that if a youth becomes a Christian he will, as a matter of course, die early. Another mistake is to imagine that a story to be interesting should contain the whole life of any one. In both of these respects there has been of late years a great improvement. Some of the very best books now offering contain only a single episode or transaction in the life of the boy or girl described—the narrative of a single summer, or of a trip to the seaside, or something of that sort, the object being to bring out in narrative form some particular type of Christian character or duty. I cannot speak too highly of such a method.

How to Select a Library.

We will suppose a committee appointed for the purpose of choosing books for the Sunday-school library. We will suppose the committee to consist of persons competent and willing to undertake the work—persons of some education and literary culture, well informed in matters of doctrine, in hearty sympathy with the wants and tastes of youth, and having the necessary leisure. Suppose such a committee organized and ready to go to work. What is the first thing they should do?

It is obvious that the committee should know first of all how much money they have to spend. Next, they should take some precaution not to duplicate books which the scholars have had already. Thirdly, they should consider the proportion needed of each particular class of books. Some of the books offering are written for and suited to very young children, who are just beginning to read. Others are suited only to adults and those in Bible classes. Others are suited chiefly to youth of ten or twelve years of age. Then, again, some books are large, costing from a dollar to a dollar and a half or more. Others are small, costing perhaps only fifty to sixty cents or less. Scholars always choose large books. A big book pleases the child's vanity, and besides it gives him more reading. But it is not always practicable to indulge the scholars in this whim. If two hundred volumes are needed to go round the school, and there are but one hundred or one hundred and twenty dollars to spend, the purchase must include some small volumes. The committee, therefore, should look over the school and make an approximate estimate of the proportion of books needed of the different sizes and for the different ages.

Having gone through this preliminary work, the committee should next agree among themselves upon some principles of rejection and selection. It would be well, I think, and save time as well as trouble, to reduce to writing the rules which are to govern the members of the committee in making their decision, and each member should have a copy before him while reading. Of course, it is not necessary that these rules should be very elaborate. Something very simple and concise, like those which follow, might answer the purpose. It is agreed, for instance, to buy—

1. No book that is carelessly written.

2. No book that is weak and trashy in substance.

3. No book that contains erroneous doctrines.

4. No book that recommends or countenances what is of doubtful propriety.

5. No book that is dull and prosy.

6. No book that is above the comprehension of the scholars.

7. No book that requires coaxing to induce the scholars to read it.

8. No book the interest of which depends in any considerable degree on love and matrimony.

9. No book that is not distinctly religious.

10. No book whose religious teachings are not scriptural.

I give these, not as exhausting the subject, but as

specimens to show the way of getting at something tangible.

But suppose the committee organized, and the rules for the selection of the books adopted, what is the next step? Shall we go indiscriminately into a market containing seven thousand different books, and try them all?

Fortunately, such an impracticable plan is not necessary. The main part of this most difficult work is done to our hands. There are men engaged exclusively in this business, dealers in Sabbath-school books, having, it is true, a pecuniary interest in the matter, but yet conscientious, upright, God-fearing men, who are, furthermore, pledged to an honest endeavor in this matter by the fact that the success of their business as dealers depends upon their selling only books of the very best and most unexceptionable character—men who make the selection and sale of Sunday-school books their main if not their sole business, and who pledge themselves before the public that they will keep no book upon their shelves but such as they have examined, and are prepared from personal knowledge to recommend. The existence of such a class of dealers, while it shows the magnitude and complexity of the Sunday-school interest, offers also a practical convenience of incalculable value to purchasing committees.

Such a committee, having made all their preliminary arrangements, may be imagined to proceed as fol-

lows. Having found a dealer of this kind, in whose
integrity, judgment, and experience in the business
they have some confidence, they send to him a *con-
ditional order* for the number and amount of books
wanted, the condition being that any books may be
returned which, on examination, are not approved by
the committee.

The committee, in sending such an order, should
send with it a catalogue of the existing library, so
as to avoid duplicating, and should describe in general terms about how many volumes are desired for
the money, the proportion of large and small volumes, of books for adults and for juveniles, and so
forth.   There are dealers, well known, responsible
men, who, on receiving such an order, would be
willing to bestow the labor necessary for making up
a suitable assortment, and who, for the sake of the
custom, would accept the condition of taking back
such of the books sent as did not suit.   Such an arrangement as this would save the purchasing committee a vast amount of labor, and yet leave them
perfectly independent in their choice.

Two or three additional suggestions are needed to
close up this whole subject.   First, it is much more
important to a school to get books of the best character than to get them at a discount from the publishers' catalogue prices. A dealer who bestows
much time and expense in examining and certifying
each particular book that he puts into an invoice
cannot afford at the same time to sell largely under

the publishers' catalogue prices because the order happens to be of considerable size. Secondly, I would not as a rule, recommend to any school the books that come put up in paper boxes or made-up libraries. I have had some experience in this sort of thing, and found, to my cost, that generally, in such collections, a few good books are used to make sale for a large percentage of trash. Let each particular book that comes into the library be chosen by itself, on its own individual merits, even if it does cost a little more both of time and money to make up the collection. One hundred volumes, every one of which is a live book, are worth more to any school than one hundred and twenty volumes, forty or fifty of which are just so much dead lumber on the shelves.

PART II.

HOW TO MANAGE THE LIBRARY.

THE proper management of the library is one of those practical questions which every superintendent has to meet. The methods adopted are as numerous almost as the schools, and there is no method that I ever heard of that does not involve some practical inconveniences. I find inconveniences and difficulties in that which I myself recommend. Yet on the whole it seems to be the one involving the least trouble and securing the greatest practical efficiency. I propose to set forth briefly what some of the difficulties are and the ordinary methods of meeting them, and then to explain the plan which, after much experience and thought, has secured a more general verdict of approval than any other.

Difficulties in the Ordinary Methods.

1. *Books Disappear.* I do not mean to say that they are stolen, but through some leak in the mode of registration and distribution the librarian loses track of them, and they are gone past recovery. Replenishing a library is in too many cases like pouring water into a sieve. I think I do not overstate the fact when I say that on the average one-half the books which are furnished to Sunday-school libraries are lost. Some books will be lost under the most careful management. But, other things being equal, that system is best which with the least labor and friction secures the most complete responsibility for the books given out and is best adapted to ensure their safe return.

Some librarians charge the books to the teacher, and look to the teacher for their return. It is well, certainly, for the teacher to have some responsibility for the books given out to his class, as he comes more directly than any one else into communication with his scholars, and he has more than any one else the means of getting the books promptly returned. But teachers change from time to time, and when they do not change they are often absent. There is hardly a session in a school of any size at which some of the regular teachers are not absent. The temporary supply of course knows nothing about the books that were given out on the Sunday before. A teacher who is going to be absent, or who leaves a class entirely, *ought*, of course, to communicate with his successor or his temporary supply, and with the superintendent, and to place in their hands his roll-book and other memoranda pertaining to the class. But teachers are oblivious of this duty, as of many others, and we have to take things as we find them, not as they ought to be.

The librarian, who has no record of the books given out except the name of the teacher through whose hands they have gone, will find himself sadly strait-ened in the means of tracing and recovering lost vol-umes. If this ruinous disappearance of books is to be stopped, each volume given out must be charged directly to the scholar who takes it, and there must be some means both of doing this without much labor and also of knowing at a glance, when a scholar ap-plies for a book, whether there is one already charged against him. If in addition to this record against the scholar there is one against the teacher also, so much the better.

2. *The Selection of Books.* How, when and where shall the scholars make their selection of the

books which they wish to take each week from the library?

In some schools assistant librarians go round from class to class with a basket or tray full of books, and the scholars overhaul the load and pick out from inspection what they want, if perchance there happen to be in the lot any that they care about at all. The interruption and confusion which this occasions, besides its unsatisfactory results in other respects, make it unnecessary to dwell upon it.

A worse plan still is for the teachers to go to the library and select for their class from the shelves. While the teacher is at the library selecting books his class is running riot. Besides this, people the world over are careless about such matters, and Sunday-school teachers are no exception to the rule. Where this plan is adopted, the librarian will be fortunate indeed who has reported to him for record one-half the books taken out. The plan is as unbusiness-like as it would be for a grocer to allow his customers to weigh out and charge their own tea and sugar, or for a bank to allow its depositors to put their hands into the till and count out the change called for by the checks presented instead of receiving it from the hands of the teller. No one but the librarian should in any case take a book from the library. This should be the inexorable rule; any other rule ensures loss. The loss does not imply dishonesty. It is merely the inevitable result of doing business in an unbusiness-like way.

Another plan having many features to commend it is to have the library operations conducted at some different time from the session of the school—say on some day in the week or before church on Sunday, on that part of the day when the school is not in session. Some schools which meet in the afternoon have their library open on Sunday morning for an hour before church-time, and the scholars come in by groups as it suits their convenience, and going to the shelves, select a book and have it charged to them.

This plan avoids disturbing the school with the giving in and taking out of books; but the scholars thus collected about the school-room and the vestibule of the church for half an hour or an hour before service are apt to become noisy, and, moreover, the books received just before going into church are apt to be read in church instead of the children attending to the service. Besides this, if there is a proper lack of responsibility in the teachers' going to the shelves to make the selection, the risk is much greater in allowing the same privilege to the whole mass of the scholars. I do not deny that there is some advantage, in making a selection from a library, to be able to go to the shelves and look over the volumes for one's self; but the evils attending this mode of selection, whether made by teachers or scholars, are so many and great that I am persuaded the plan ought never to be adopted. Some method of selecting books must be invented besides that of actual inspection of them on the shelves.

I do not deny, also, that there are advantages in having the library opened at some different time from the ordinary session of the school, but the disadvantages on the other side greatly preponderate. Among these, one that ought never to be forgotten is that in our schools are many children, and those the very ones that we desire most to benefit, who could not come for books at any other time than during the regular sessions—children of the poor, children at service, mission children. If the library is to be of the greatest practical efficiency and value, its operations must be carried on during the time of the regular session of the school.

3. *The Interruption of the Lesson.* Teachers are so much annoyed by the continual interruptions from this source that they are disposed at times to vote the whole thing a nuisance. After the necessary deductions for the general exercises of the school, the time remaining to the teacher for direct instruction of his class is small at the best, and it should be kept absolutely sacred from intrusion. Neither secretary, nor librarian, nor superintendent, nor pastor, nor visitor, should encroach for a moment, unless on some special and most urgent occasion. If the teacher is to accomplish anything worthy of the name, he needs every moment of that precious time, and he needs it without distraction.

How is it practically in most schools? The teacher begins the lesson, and has just succeeded in getting the attention of the class fixed on some interesting point, when round comes one of the librarians to collect the books. Interruption number one. His own thoughts and those of the scholars are diverted. The librarian has to make some examination of the books returned, and see that they correspond to the registered account; he has to inquire of one and another for books not returned, perhaps to have a little chat with the teacher about the books or something else. Altogether, this preliminary visit rarely costs less than five minutes, besides the diversion of thought which it occasions.

Then comes—interruption number two—the choice of books. Whether this choice is made after the librarian's visit or before, the time for it comes out of that appropriated to the teacher. It cannot be done during the singing, or the prayer, or any of the general exercises of the school. It must be done, if done in school, in the teacher's time, and it takes a good deal of time. The scholars have to talk over among themselves the character of the different books, and to explore the pages of the catalogue, and then they hesitate, and weigh and balance the fancied merits and demerits of particular books, and then they come to a stand-still, unable to decide, until the teacher finally goads them to a conclusion, and with minds thoroughly distracted, they once more resume the lesson.

Interruption number three is caused by the delivery of the books. Sometimes the teacher requires the books to be placed in a pile at his seat, and does not distribute them to the scholars until the close of the lesson. But many a furtive glance at the coveted pile shows that its presence is a disturbing element. The evil is greatly aggravated when, as is the usual custom, the books are actually delivered to the scholars by the librarian. Every one is eager to see if the book brought him is the one he ordered, or if it is such as he expected it to be, and he can hardly help peeping into it to look at the pictures, or perhaps to see how the story begins, and he must needs whisper to his neighbor something about its contents, or he blurts out to his teacher that it is not the kind of book he wanted. Altogether, in many and many a class, the scene after the delivery of the library books is a Babel in miniature. Teachers and scholars equally are disturbed, excited, not unfrequently vexed.

What between the coming and going of the librarians, the collection and the distribution of the books, the worry of making the selection, and the expressions of satisfaction and of dissatisfaction at the result, I deem it no exaggeration to say that in a majority of Sunday-school classes, as matters are now managed, at least one-half the teaching-time is consumed by the operations of the library. Such a state of things surely calls for some remedy.

The Plan Proposed.

Having thus shown the practical difficulties attending the subject, and the objections to most of the methods of management in actual use, I shall now explain with some particularity the plan which on the whole seems to have the fewest defects and to secure the greatest number of advantages :

1. *A Printed Catalogue.* A printed catalogue of the books is indispensable, and a copy of it should be in the hands of every member of the school, whether scholar or teacher. Our plan contemplates that the selection should be made from the catalogue alone, and without an inspection of the books. It is important, therefore, that the catalogue should be so made as to give as much information as possible concerning the character of the several volumes.

It was at one time proposed to append to the title of each volume in the catalogue a brief description of the book. But a descriptive catalogue like this was found to require a large amount of skill and judgment in the preparation, and furthermore to be very expensive. Instead of a descriptive catalogue, therefore, I recommend a classified one. The books may be assorted into three general kinds, corresponding to three general kinds of pupils in every school. These we may for convenience designate as the Primary classes, the Main school and the Adult classes. Some of the books are suited to scholars just beginning to read. Other books are suited to those of mature minds—to the teachers and the members of the adult classes. Others again are such as form the main staple of our Sunday-school books, and are suited to the main body of the school.

If the catalogue contains the titles of the books all alphabetically arranged, and if after each title are appended the letters *Pr.*, *M.* or *Ad.*, to signify that the book is suited to one in the Primary, in the Main school or in the Adult classes, and if besides this the number of pages is given, the scholar has some considerable clue to guide him in the selection of the books.

Sometimes the catalogue is printed in three parts, with three separate headings. But this creates a difficulty. Whenever additions are made to the library, an entirely new catalogue would have to be issued. But under the plan which I propose all that is necessary, when new books are bought, is to issue supplementary slips.

Some check is needed to prevent the scholars from losing or destroying their catalogues. The best plan is to fix a small price upon the catalogue, and require the scholar who loses his copy to pay for the extra one.

The cost of printing a catalogue such as I have described will depend upon the size of the library and the style of the catalogue.

2. *The Scholar's Library Card.* Every scholar should be furnished with a library card, in which to enter the numbers of the books selected. Cards of various patterns have been designed for this purpose. The form most convenient is given on the next page.

This contains nine blanks, giving the opportunity for nine selections. The scholar may, if he chooses, fill up the whole number at once. If, when the card goes in to the librarian, the book first selected

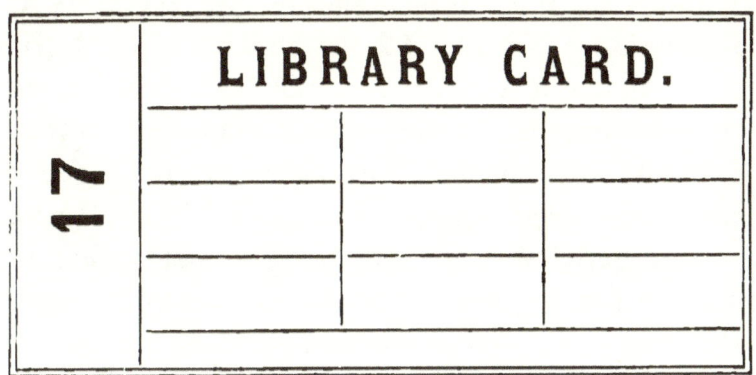

is out, the librarian will supply the applicant with some one of the others; and when all the numbers have been exhausted, a new card will be issued. These cards may be obtained at the very moderate price of fifty cents a hundred.

There is another form of card of larger size containing blanks enough to run through a whole year. The cost of this is $1.50 a hundred. The back of the card contains the necessary directions to the scholar, as: (1.) Write in the spaces on the other side of the card the numbers of the books which you wish to get; those numbers which you place first will be considered your first choice. (2.) Leave this card with the librarian as you enter the school-room; do not put it inside your library book. (3.) You cannot get another book while you have one out of the library, etc.

3. *Register Number.* Every member of the

26

school, whether scholar or teacher, should have a register number, by which he should be known on the books of the superintendent, the secretary and the librarian. Number **17** in the style of card given shows at once to what scholar or teacher it belongs. Only one person in the school has that number. An admirable and most complete form for a general register has been prepared, providing for all possible emergencies and guarding most effectually against mistakes, and is at the same time exceedingly simple and easily worked.

4. *Selection at Home.* The scholar is expected to keep his catalogue at home and to make his selections there. This is an essential feature of the system. The catalogue gives him all the means for making a choice, and while at home during the week, with ample leisure for the purpose, he prepares his card just as he prepares his lesson. He has the opportunity of consulting his parents, his brothers and sisters, or any members of the school whom he may meet, and he makes his choice with the fullest deliberation, instead of doing it in the haste and confusion of a brief interval in school.

5. *Returning Cards and Books.* The librarian or his assistant has a table at the door of entrance of the school-room, and each scholar on entering the school, before going to his class, hands his card and his library book to the librarian. That is all the scholar has to do with the matter until he is dismissed at the close of the school.

6. *Receiving Cards and Books.* At the close of the school the librarian and his assistants stand at the door of exit and give to each scholar as he passes out the book selected for him, and his card with it. The superintendent of course has to watch the operation, and to dismiss the classes only as fast as they are disposed of by the librarian. The plan, however, is so simple in its working that the books and cards can be given out as fast as it is proper for a school to be dismissed.

By this plan of taking in and giving out the books it will be seen that all confusion in the school and interruption of lessons arising out of the operations of the library is absolutely excluded.

7. *Numbering the Books.* Some cheap, convenient and effective way of numbering the books is needed, whatever mode of registration and distribution is adopted. For this purpose nothing with which I am acquainted is comparable to "*Geist's Adhesive Labels.*" In the State Normal School under my direction, I am sure that the use of these labels saves the institution the loss of books to the value of two to three hundred dollars a year.

It remains that I explain

The Work of the Librarian.

It is obvious that the plan described for selecting, taking in and giving out the books has advantages in itself, without any reference to the librarian's work. Whatever way the librarian may take for executing his difficult task, it will still be very greatly to his convenience and to that of the teacher that the books should be selected by the scholars at their homes, that they should be handed in at the door on entering school, and given out at the door on leaving. This gives the librarian the entire time of the session for putting away the books returned, getting out the books ordered and making the necessary records.

The most time-consuming part of the whole operation is that of the registration, and for this a plan has been invented that is truly marvellous in its simplicity and its completeness. The plan referred to is known as "*The Check System Library Register*" (Ray's patent). I will endeavor to give my readers as clear an idea of it as I can by a mere verbal description:

1. *The Checks.* These are small slips of tin, of the size of the accompanying engraving:

At one end of the slip is a circular shield with a number painted on it, and near to where this shield is placed the slip has a double bend or curve, creating a sort of shoulder, and giving the slip, when seen edgewise, this appearance:

The tin slip, or check, as it is called, is to be inserted at the top of the book, between the leaves, in this manner:

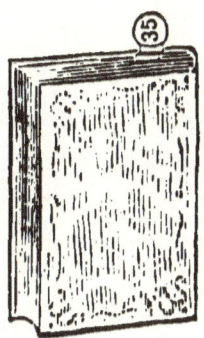

and the object of the shoulder is to prevent the check from slipping down too far and to keep the number · up full in sight.

The librarian needs as many checks as there are volumes in the library. The checks are numbered from **1** up, to correspond to the number of the books. Each book when placed in the shelf has its check inserted in the top, as above.

2. *The Register.* This is something like a big portfolio, each of the pages being divided into five rows of twelve compartments each, making sixty to a page. The cut on the following page represents a section of a single page of the Register.

Each compartment is numbered, and represents one scholar or teacher. Compartment No. 17, for instance, belongs to scholar or teacher No. 17, and so of the others. The Register is made with two, four and six pages, according to the size of the school.

Section of the Library Register.

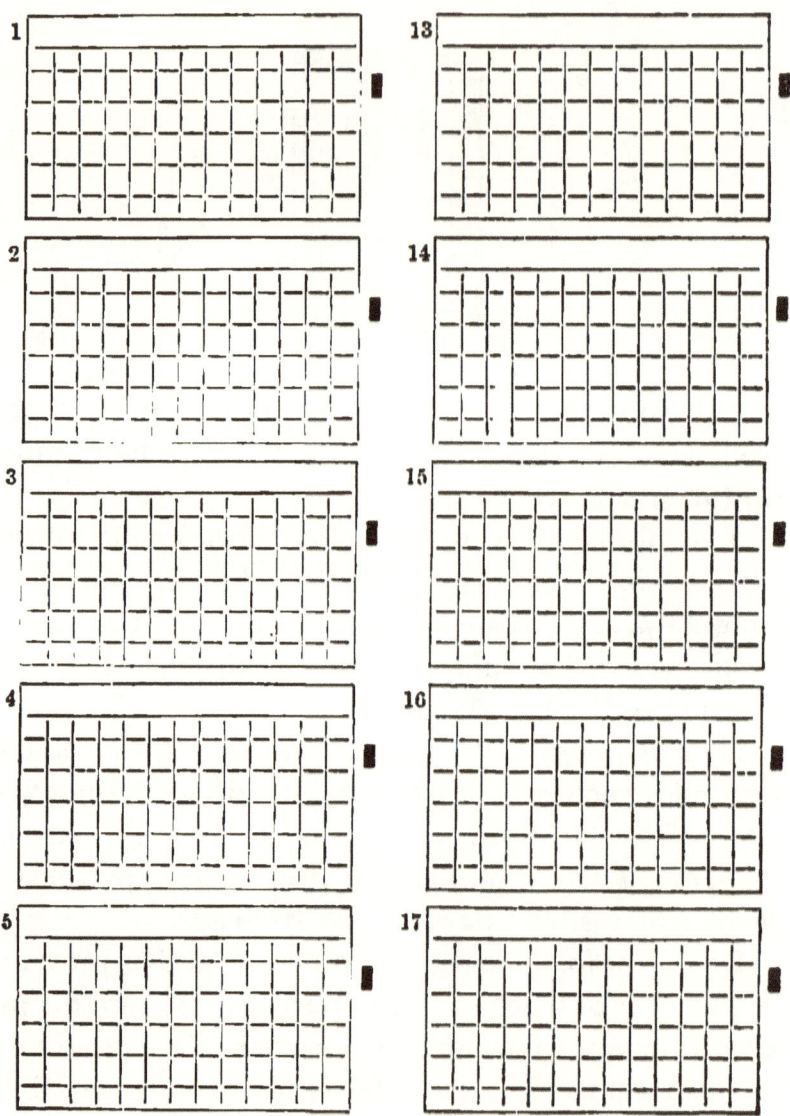

Here is a single compartment of the actual size used in the Register:

The perpendicular lines divide it into twelve spaces, one for each month in the year. The horizontal lines divide it into five spaces, that being the greatest number of Sundays that ever occur in one month. There are blank spaces, therefore, for every Sunday in the year. On the right margin is a slit for inserting the flat part of the check.

This slit forms a very important part in the economy of the business. It is the means by which the librarian charges a book or cancels a charge. If pupil or teacher No. 17, for instance, has called for book No. 35, the librarian, on finding said book, takes the check from the volume and slips it into the slit, as in the figure. There it remains as a charge against the representative of that compartment. When scholar or teacher No. 17 returns the book, all the librarian has to do in order to cancel the charge is to take the check out of the slit, put it into the book, and put the book back into the library.

The whole thing is the work of a moment, and it requires the use of neither pen nor pencil. Besides this, it enables the librarian to see at a glance whether the applicant, No. 17, has or has not a book charged to him, and so to carry out with entire ease the important rule of giving no one a new book until the old one is returned.

The object of the blank spaces is this: When the librarian finds that a particular scholar is irregular in his attendance, or negligent about returning his books, it is sometimes important to record the time when a book is given out. In such a case, all the librarian has to do is to draw an oblique line through the appropriate space. Thus in the figure it is shown that No. 17 not only has out book No. 35, but that he took it out on the third Sunday in July. This particularity of date helps sometimes in the recovery of a missing volume. When a book thus doubly charged is returned to the library, the librarian not only removes the check (which cancels the general charge), but also draws a slant line across the other in the opposite direction; or, if the line is made with a lead pencil, he may erase it with a rubber.

Some librarians enter the date in all cases, but this is not recommended.

Now, let us see what the librarian has to do:

1. The books and the library cards are collected at the door at the opening of the school.

2. The books being brought to the library table, he takes up one volume at a time, looks at its num-

ber, and then at his Register, to see against whom (or rather against what number) it is charged; removes the check from the Register, puts it into the book, and puts the book in its place in the library. So he goes on, book after book, until all the books brought in are disposed of.

3. Next, he takes up a library card; sees what volumes are ordered on it; selects one of them (the first that happens to be in); takes the check from the book and puts it into the appropriate slit in the Register, and puts the library card into the book with the number of the applicant sticking out at one end, to show to whom the book and card are to be given. Thus:

He proceeds in this way, card after card, until all the orders are executed.

4. The books thus selected are then assorted into heaps for delivery, each heap representing a class.

5. The heaps are taken to the table or shelf at the door, and finally the books are handed by the librarian and his assistants to the individual scholars as they pass out.

It has taken a good many words to explain this process, but the process itself is one of the simplest and least embarrassing that it is possible to conceive.

CHAPTER VII.

RELATIONS OF THE SUNDAY-SCHOOL TO OTHER RELIGIOUS INSTITUTIONS.

 HAVE failed entirely in my purpose if I have not, in a great variety of ways, made known my opinion that the Sunday-school is not an institution standing by itself. On the contrary, according to the view of it advocated in these pages, it has numerous most important, some of them organic, relations with the other leading institutions of religion. Some of these relations will occupy the present chapter.

1. *The Sunday-school and the Church.*

The Sunday-school could have no more dangerous enemy than one who should persuade its friends that they were or could be in any way antagonistic to the church. Who support, cherish, establish and keep alive the Sunday-school? The church. Who are its superintendents and teachers? The members of the church. Where is the school ordinarily held? In the church, or in some building belonging to the church. Whence does it take its name? From the church to which it belongs. It is the school of the Tabernacle Baptist, of the Epiphany, of the Tenth Presbyterian, of the Green Street Methodist, or of some other church. A school is considered and spoken of as belonging to some particular church, just as a boy or a girl is thought of as having a father and mother and as belonging to some particular family. There are indeed orphan children and street children not thus blessed, for whom public philanthropy must in some way provide. But these are the exceptions. So there are schools in out-of-the-way places, where there is no one church to care for them or own them, and they must be cared for, if at all, by godly men and women of various denominations uniting in the good work. These are the union schools of frontier regions. Some of the mission-schools of our cities are of the same character. But even these soon cease to be orphans, being adopted by some church, and thus brought into the family relation. Go through the length and breadth of the land, and nine-tenths of all the Sunday-schools to be found are the schools of some particular church. The proportion of schools which hold no such relation, which are independent organizations, is smaller than the proportion of children in the community who have no parents of their own to look to.

The Sunday-school is the child of the church. It springs from the church It is only one of the church's modes of acting, in evangelizing the world. The church, in endeavoring to carry out the Master's command to indoctrinate society with the precepts of the gospel, takes this among other modes of doing it. It proclaims the gospel from its pulpits. It draws the reins of parental responsibility, thus propagating religious truths by means of the family organization. It sends forth Bibles, tracts and books, to reach those not touched by the pulpit or the family. It gathers the young into Sunday-schools, still further to supplement the teaching given by other means.

The church with all her efforts is unable to secure, even from godly parents, the amount of religious instruction which their children require. Then there are the countless numbers of children whose parents are indifferent and irreligious. The church feels, therefore, that she has need of every legitimate means, and that she must push them to the utmost if she would fully execute her trust in the work of evangelizing society. The church does not regard the Sunday-school as antagonistic to parental and family instruction, any more than a general would regard his cavalry or his artillery as antagonistic to his infantry. All means are needed in this great work.

I have yet to see the first Sunday-school teacher who is not delighted when he finds parents giving their children instruction in addition to that received at the school. I have yet to see the first teacher whose heart does not bound with joy on seeing his pastor and elders and other officers of the church taking hold of the school, mingling actively and efficiently in its affairs, and showing that they consider it as theirs.

Whenever I see any one working himself up into a suspicion that the Sunday-school is a something that is going to override or supersede the church, or arming himself with ecclesiastical legislation against it as against an enemy that needs bridling, I cannot but feel that the wiser course for such a person would be to enter into the cause itself with a little warmer sympathy.

Persons holding opinions of this kind, I am happy to believe, are much fewer now than they were some years ago. A healthy sentiment has been awakened in the public mind in regard to the true relation of the Sunday-school to the church. There was at one time not exactly a definite theory, but a vague, undefined feeling, that the Sunday-school was an institution by itself, like a temperance society or a hospital. As the institution has grown in importance and efficiency, a clearer apprehension has arisen in the minds of Christian people in regard to its true position. There are few thoughtful Christians now who do not recognize the Sunday-school as one of the agencies of the church, and who do not theoretically hold the church responsible for maintaining such an agency. A church that did not maintain a Sunday-school would be in the popular estimation almost as great an anomaly as a church that did not

27

maintain public worship. At the same time there is in some of our largest and most influential denominations a want of definite, official action on this subject, which is withholding from the institution its most natural and powerful means of growth and efficiency.

Why should a cause of such vital importance be left at such loose ends? Is the religious training of its youth a matter to be left to casual impulse or to individual caprice? Has not the Sunday-school a right to a place in the ordinary business of ecclesiastical assemblies as much as has the theological seminary, the education of ministers, church extension, domestic missions or foreign missions?

What I urge upon ecclesiastical bodies is that they take some action which shall make the consideration of the Sunday-school interest a part of the standing order of business, both for the supreme judicatory itself and for all the subordinate church courts for which it legislates, in regular succession, down through Synods, Presbyteries, Sessions, Consistories, Vestries, and so forth. Only let it once be established that Sunday-school operations are a part of the church doings which are to be reported for review by the appointed church authorities, and a great point will be gained both in checking irregularities and extravagances on the one side, and on the other side in giving strength, solidity and comprehensiveness to the whole system.

It is not far to go to find topics which in the present aspect of the Sunday-school movement require grave consideration at the hands of the ablest and wisest men of every church. The enormous—it is not too strong to say, the appalling—multiplication of Sunday-school library books is one of these topics. Four or five millions of these little volumes are taken home and greedily devoured every week. How much of this reading is beneficial, and how much of it is debauching? Is not the question one of as much interest as whether Turrettin still holds its place in didactic theology? Should the temperance question and temperance organizations and pledges enter into the Sunday-school movement? Should the Sunday-school be made the nucleus for missionary collections? and if so, for what purposes? Should the training of youth to the habit of giving and the instruction of them in regard to the objects on which to bestow their benefactions be left entirely to chance or to the smartness of enterprising and often irresponsible agents? or should this whole subject be under some wise and responsible guidance from the recognized authorities of the church? How may we secure more complete and reliable Sunday-school statistics? Ought not the annual returns from churches and parishes to embrace a column devoted to this subject, showing the number of scholars, teachers, conversions, etc.?

The Methodist denomination a few years ago took the right ground on this subject, making the Sunday-school operations of their churches the object of systematic ecclesiastical supervision and control, and they are reaping the benefit of this course in the greatly accelerated growth of their schools.

Bishop Stevens, of the Episcopal church in Pennsylvania, in his charge to the clergy of his diocese some years ago, said : " It is the duty of the minister to put himself at the head of his [Sunday] school ; not, indeed, as its superintendent—that perhaps had better be a lay person—but he should be its controlling and governing power. He should select his superintendent and teachers, should direct the studies and the school with all the appliances necessary for its largest usefulness."

The Presbyterian General Assembly (New School), before the late re-union, in a report on Sunday-schools, used the following language :

" The danger is that the Sabbath-school may become detached from its proper connection with the church and its authorities, and assume an independence which must prove in the end injurious both to itself and the church.

" This severance has, we learn, actually taken place in some instances, and the proper shepherd of the flock can appear before the lambs only by the sufferance of the superintendent ; and so the young, cut off from their appointed guardians, are exposed to influences which cannot be brought under proper supervision and control."

In accordance with this report the Assembly passed a resolution in these words : " That it belongs em-

phatically to the pastor and elders of each congregation to direct and supervise the whole work of the
spiritual training of the young, and that it is an important part of the functions of their office both to
encourage parents to fidelity in bringing up their
children in the nurture and admonition of the Lord,
and also to secure the co-operation of all the competent members of the church in the religious education of all the children and youth to whom they can
gain access."

The Presbyterian Publication Committee (New
School) also issued a tract on this subject, in which
the relations of the Sunday-school to the church are
set forth with clearness and force, and are placed on
precisely the same ground as that which I have here
advocated.

The united body signalized their happy reunion
by some judicious action on this subject. The
matter was brought forward under the auspices of
Dr. McCosh, and after some opposition and an
earnest debate resulted in the adoption of the following resolution :

"That the Board [of Publication] at as early a
date as possible consider the propriety of establishing a *Department of Sabbath-schools*, whose office
it shall be to promote the number and efficiency of
Sabbath-schools throughout the congregations of the
Presbyterian church."

I congratulate this great re-united church on the
important movement thus auspiciously begun. The

27 *

resolution of the Assembly, it is true, is not imperative, but only recommendatory. Yet so decided a
recommendation will hardly go by unheeded. I
take it for granted, therefore, that this great and
prosperous church will soon have a recognized and
responsible agency of its own, for giving direction,
life and system to this important part of its operations, and that hereafter, in every church court, from
the highest to the lowest, the Sunday-school will
have its rightful place, just as much as the cause of
Theological Seminaries, and that of Home and Foreign Missions.

2. *The Minister and the Sunday-school.*

I do not agree with Dr. Tyng and some other
high authorities that the minister should be the acting superintendent of the Sunday-school. The
amount of work to be done is too much, and it
would lead in almost every case either to a neglect
of the school or to a lowering of the standard of the
pulpit performances. At the same time, I most fully
believe that the minister should be the chief animating soul of the school. The superintendent should
be his right-hand man, his counsellor and co-worker
in all his plans for sowing the seed in the hearts of
the young of his charge. The minister should spend
some time—not less certainly than half an hour—in
his school every Sunday. He should know all that
is going on in it. He should know every teacher
and every scholar by face and by name, and what

influences are at work in each department and in every class, and he should find the means to make his own influence felt in every movement of the school. Every scholar and every teacher should feel that the pastor is cognizant of his or her doings in the school—not, of course, by any system of espionage, but simply by the fact of his constant and pervading presence. The school, in short, should be thought of and spoken of *as his*.

Am I laying upon the ministry too great a burden? If an efficient working of the Sunday-school brings two souls into the church where the labors of the pulpit bring one, if the minister's heart, all aglow with fire in the school, burns thereby with increased brightness and intensity in the pulpit, should not the minister consider the Sunday-school a part of the burden that the Master has put upon him?

Our conventions, our institutes, our religious journals, are doing much for adding to the efficiency of our Sunday-schools. But our main hope, after all, is in the ministry. Our Sunday-schools will become what they should be, and will accomplish the mighty results which they are capable of, when our pastors come fully up to the work, and not before. Here and there is a superintendent who has the fitness and the consecrated talent to work up and mould the materials of a congregation so as to make out of them a thoroughly efficient Sunday-school. But these are the exceptions. So here and there is a teacher thoroughly competent to the work.

But in the great majority of cases, all over the land, superintendents and teachers *have to be made.* The raw material exists in the greatest abundance in all churches. I never saw a church yet, big or little, in country or city, that did not contain in itself the materials, the men and women, capable of fitting out a school with a first-rate corps of teachers and a good superintendent. But usually these materials bear about the same relation to the actual work that cotton growing in the field bears to the finished fabric. The man who is to pick the cotton, gin it. sort it, spin it and weave it into cloth ready for use is the minister. He must select the men and women of his flock who have the natural fitness for taking care of the lambs. He must enlist their sympathies in the work, and know how to counsel and direct them in it. He is not to do the work of the school himself, but he should be the animating spirit of those who do it. To do all this he must, however, be himself practically familiar with it. A housekeeper who has made bread herself can train a domestic to make bread. A farmer who has himself sown and tilled the field can train his boys to do it. A master mechanic whose own fingers know how to wield the tools of his craft can alone make other craftsmen.

In all our congregations are the materials, the men and women, in abundance ; but who shall convert them into teachers? This is the one desideratum for making schools.

Some congregations, here and there, are blessed with a man, a layman, whose education, training, talents, choice and actual experience mark him out for this service. These, however, are the exceptions. But in every church where there is a settled pastor there is *one* man whose office ought to include this idea, just as much as that of preaching sermons.

The minister ought to be an expert in Sunday-school matters. He ought to be what the graduates of a military school are to unskilled volunteers at the outbreak of a war; and if ever the noble four hundred thousand willing workers now engaged in the American Sunday-school become a conquering army in the Master's service, it must be by an adequate infusion of experts into the mass to organize and guide them to victory.

Our military schools are the theological seminaries. Our young ministers must be trained to the Sunday-school work as well as to the business of writing sermons.

Some of our writers seem to be under the apprehension that the Sunday-school work is in danger from the interference of ministers. They speak of it as a work peculiar to laymen—one in which clerical interposition would be a sort of intrusion and impertinence. Such notions are utterly alien to every idea that I have formed of this work. If at times I have been disposed to utter a sharp criticism upon ministers in regard to the Sunday-school work, it has been for their indifference, not for over-interference.

V

I have known pastors—not many, but here and there one—who did not seem to realize the immense power of the institution for carrying out their appropriate work, and who practically stood aloof from it. There are perhaps no ministers who would be willing to admit that they stand in this position. But they do not throw themselves heartily into the movement; they catch no inspiration from it; they give no inspiration to it, any more than they would do in regard to any ordinary philanthropic enterprise. They look on with approbation, and even with some degree of interest, but it is as spectators rather than as actors. When I have seen such a pastor I have felt at times like stirring him up, and, if necessary, with sharp words.

I do not think it desirable, ordinarily, as I have said before, for the pastor to superintend the Sunday-school. There is not one minister in a thousand that has the physical strength to do so. A man needs to go into the pulpit with his energies fresh and in full vigor. If he rises to preach after exhausting himself mentally and bodily in the school-room, and with his voice husky by use, he would be doing a serious wrong. But he cannot by any possibility be an intruder in the Sunday-school any more than he could be in the prayer-meeting or the lecture-room. There is no one whom superintendent, teachers and scholars so universally delight to see in the school-room as the minister. The minister neglects an important duty and misses a great privilege who does not visit his Sunday-school habitually, and, if possible, every Sunday, who does not keep himself thoroughly acquainted with what is going on there, and who does not promptly interpose, if need be, to correct or prevent abuses. The Sunday-school is not something outside of or apart from the church; it is the church itself. It is one of the ways in which the church is putting forth its spiritual life and fulfilling its divine mission. It is the creature of the church, and should be under the control of the church as much as the weekly prayer-meeting.

It is one of the best features of the Sunday-school work that all classes can engage in it. More than any other operation in which the church is engaged it enlists laymen. It furnishes a field in which every one may find something to do for the Master. But there is no motive or warrant for a layman to work in the Sunday-school which does not apply with equal and even greater force to a minister. Who, if not the minister, is interested in the religious training of the young? Who, if not the minister, is under obligation to see that the lambs of the flock are cared for?

No pastor who is wise will meddle with the small details of the school-room. If a superintendent is to get along comfortably and efficiently, he needs to enjoy largely the confidence of those above him as well as of those below him. But then the superintendent should not shrink from recognizing the fact that there are those above him; any other theory

than this will lead to inevitable confusion and disorder in our Sunday-school affairs. We cannot
safely have an *imperium in imperio* in religious any
more than in civil matters. In each particular
church there must be one general centre of authority,
whether pastor, session, consistory or congregation.
Whatever that power is which controls the teachings
of the pulpit and the exercises of public worship in
the church, the lecture-room and the prayer-meeting,
it ought to and must in the last resort have the control
of the Sunday-school also. To set up the Sunday-
school as an independent and self-existent organization is simply monstrous.

3. *The Sunday-school and Parental Responsibility.*

In the agitation of the Sunday-school cause and of
the duties of pastors and teachers to the children,
there is some danger of forgetting entirely the existence of parents. I would go as far as almost any
one in urging upon the church the duty of looking
after the religious interests of the young. Just so far
as a man is a Christian at all will he seek to promote
Christ's cause, and one of the most efficient ways of
promoting that cause is to indoctrinate youth in the
principles of religion. This is a plain, direct, con-
clusive argument for Sunday-schools, and for the
duty of the church as such, and of every individual
member of the church to support the institution. A
church is guilty which allows any child to grow up
in irreligion whom it has the means of reaching and

reclaiming. What is true of a church is true of its members individually.

But this responsibility of the church to look after a child by no means relieves the parents from responsibility in regard to the same child. If the child is lost and God holds the church guilty for the loss, it does not follow that he will hold the parent guiltless. It is a case of double responsibility for the same object. The object—the salvation of the child—is so important that God would put it under double guard. It is like taking two endorsers to a note; the failure of one endorser does not exonerate the other. The holder has his remedy equally against both, and thus the fulfilment of the obligation is better secured.

The duties of teachers to the children are the theme of constant discussion and illustration. I would not have it otherwise. But let us not ignore the fact that parents have even a greater stake than teachers have in the same issue. The relations of the teacher to the matter are only inferential and secondary; those of the parent are primary and paramount. No duty of one human being to another is more direct, positive and intransferable than that of a parent to educate his child religiously as well as intellectually. The mistake that many parents make practically, and that we are all in danger of making theoretically, is in supposing that this duty can be delegated. Some portions of a child's education can be given by strangers, but other, and by far the most important portions, can be given only by the parent. If

28

the home education of a child is deficient, the school, with all its means and appliances, will never educate him. He may be taught many things, but his education can never be complete.

Just here it is that parents otherwise judicious and thoughtful make a mistake. They think that if they secure for their child a good school, their duty in the matter is ended. Business men, merchants, often make this mistake. They cannot spare time from their business to look after their children. They will pay liberally for a good teacher, but, having done that, they expect the teacher to relieve them from all further care in the matter. Hundreds and hundreds of times, in my professional labors, have I encountered this fact. A laboring man sends his child to a good public school, and because it is a good school he is disappointed if his child does not turn out well. A man of wealth pays his hundreds to a private teacher, and he is vexed to find that his boy does not become a pattern of all that the circular holds out. The poor man has his daily labor to attend to, and he thinks he has no time to be troubled with looking after his children. The rich man has his business enterprises, that absorb his time and his thoughts, so that nothing is left for home duties. Rich and poor alike forget that a part of the price for the education of their children *is to be paid by personal service.* No amount of money expenditure, whether from the public or the private purse, can pay this debt. The man who brings a child into the world puts himself under a perpetual obligation of personal service to that child. A man might as well expect to keep himself in health by paying annually a doctor's bill, while not observing personally the laws of health. A parent should lay it to his account that he owes to his child a certain amount daily, and that by no means a small amount, of his time, thoughts and personal care. The parent who ignores or neglects this, and who hopes to meet the case by invoking the instrumentality of the state or of the church, or by spending freely his thousands upon schools and teachers, is surely laying up for himself multiplied sorrows.

What can the Sunday-school teacher do for a child during the one hour and a half on Sunday, if during all the remaining hours and days of the week at home the Sunday lesson is quietly ignored? If the Sunday-school teacher, who has no interest in any child beyond the promptings of Christian benevolence, is willing to endure the labor of teaching him, and of preparing himself for that teaching by long hours of study during the week, and is willing to step aside from his worldly employments to attend meetings, Institutes and Normal classes, in order to fit himself for the task of giving my child skilful religious guidance and instruction, shame on me if I am not willing to give some portion of my time, labor and thought to the same end! Shame on me if I do not see personally that my child goes to school thoroughly prepared in his lesson! Shame on me if I do not myself read and study and think on the subject, in order to be thoroughly efficient and skilful in the work of co-operation with the teacher of my child, and if I do not myself attend meetings, institutes and conventions as a learner, that I may better know how to do my part in the work of his education!

4. *Attendance of Children in Church.*

I sympathize fully with those who deprecate any arrangement that tends to draw away children from the house of God. The Sunday-school is no substitute for the church. Indeed, the greatest argument in its favor, in my estimate, has always been, that it brings the young to the church. It is a feeder for the church. If in any instance the school is so conducted, with respect to its teachings or its sessions, or any of its arrangements, as to lead either young or old away from the church, to diminish the stated attendance upon the regular services of the church, or to become regarded by scholars or teachers as an equivalent for the public worship of God in his sanctuary,—assuredly in such a case there has been a sad mistake.

This attendance upon church is not a question of one session or of two. I have known schools holding two sessions whose children in large numbers attended the church services. I have known other schools holding but one session whose children absented themselves from church. So far as my own personal experience and observation go, children who attend Sunday-school twice a day are just as likely to attend church as those who go to school but once. Teachers in arguing this matter make the mistake of judging of the children's feelings by their own. To the teacher, especially to one whose health is at all delicate, it becomes an exhausting labor to attend two school sessions and two church services. If I have ever had any misgivings about the propriety of two sessions, it has been on account of the teacher, not on account of the children. The school, which to the faithful teacher is necessarily laborious and exhausting, is to the scholar almost a recreation. Look at the scholars as they issue from any well-conducted school. You see no jaded looks among them. They are as full of life and buoyancy as when they left home in the morning. They are just as ready and as fitted, physically and mentally, for attending the church service, as if they had come fresh from home. Sometimes more so. For there is a stir and a social excitement in the school-room which cannot always be found at home, and this stir and excitement awaken the faculties and make them more ready for new mental occupation.

Let us apply a little arithmetic to this subject. The morning session usually occupies one hour and a half, the church service an equal time. Here is a confinement of three hours before dinner, not continuous, however, but relieved by the transition from the school to the church, and by numerous changes

28 *

of occupation during the three hours.   In the afternoon, the session continues usually one hour, and the
church service one hour and a half.   Here then are
five hours and a half hours of confinement, all told.
This, it is said, is too much for childhood and youth.
It is more than they can bear, and when compelled
to give full attendance upon school both parts of the
day, they are so jaded that they cannot and ought
not to attend church.   How is it on Monday, and
on every other day except Sunday?   These same
children in the weekday-schools attend regularly
five and six hours a day, and no harm done.   Three
hours in the morning and two or three in the afternoon, often five or six hours continuously, unrelieved
by change or transition, and with very brief and pre-
carious intermissions.   Would the writers who contend that the children are so fagged out by attending
Sunday-school an hour and a half in the morning
and an hour in the afternoon, that they are physically disqualified for the church service, be willing
to limit the attendance of children upon the weekday-school to two hours and a half daily?   Is the
importance of secular instruction so much greater
than that of religious instruction that while we give
to the former thirty hours a week in school, we can
afford to whittle down the latter to a bare allowance
of an hour and a half in school?

I repeat, the attendance of children upon the
church service is not a question of sessions.   When
the children leave the school, they are in just as

good a condition for entering the church as if they were fresh from home—in many cases, more so. In a great majority of cases, those children who on being dismissed from school do not enter the church would not have gone to church if they had not been at school. The church is not attractive to them. With all respect to some who have argued on the other side, I do not think the church is to be made attractive by making the school repulsive. Continue to the school all the attractions it has, and give it manifold more. But let the church itself have some attractions for the young. If children are driven from the school into the church, like sheep into a pen, by mere naked authority, the effect cannot fail to be disastrous.

Children ordinarily have nothing to do in church. They are not allowed to join in the singing; it might disturb the quartette in the gallery. They are not required to follow the minister in the reading of the Scriptures. There is nothing in the sermon addressed to them, and usually little in it which they can understand. They are merely required to sit still and do nothing. Truly, it is a hard task. Flesh and blood cry out against it. Pounding stone in the street is nothing to it. No wonder that children are rebellious on the subject.

People, old or young, are interested in a service in proportion as they have an active participation in it. I cannot but think it a great mistake, in arranging any public service, to have it so ordered that the

mass of the people should be mere passive recipients
or spectators. In proportion as one single func-
tionary becomes a mere factotum, do the rest of the
congregation lose interest. I know that it is not the
theory of any church service that the minister and
the choir are to be the active, and the congregation
merely passive, participants in it. In theory, when
the minister reads the Scriptures, the congregation
are supposed to read with him, though not always
audibly. When he prays, it is not that he prays
for them, but they all pray through his one voice.
All likewise are supposed to sing God's praises, the
choir acting as a sort of support and guide to voices
not so well trained. Something like this may perhaps be the theory. But we are now inquiring for
facts, not for theories. It is a fact which no one
will probably call in question that in some churches,
during the public services, the mass of the congregation do nothing. They may do mental acts. But
so far as material, bodily acts are concerned, they
are simply passive.

Now grown persons, with minds matured and dis-
ciplined, may be able, by a process of mere mental ab-
straction, to enter somewhat into the various services.
But it is not so with a child; and I have often
noticed that children are much more inclined to attend church in those congregations in which either
the custom of the people, or the prescribed order of
the service, gives to the congregation an active participation in what is going on, as in giving responses,

in reading alternate verses of the Scripture, in general congregational singing, and so forth. Let parents and teachers who wish children to become interested in the church service see that they take as active a part in it as the prescribed order of the church will permit. Let the seats which they occupy be furnished with Bibles and hymn-books. When the minister reads a chapter, let each child be required to find it in his Bible and follow the reading, the parent or teacher setting the example. When the hymn is announced, let each child find it and follow the reading when it is read, and join in the singing to the best of his ability when it is sung. Let children be trained to assume a devotional attitude during prayer, and taught to endeavor mentally to follow the prayer and join in it. If the prayer be extemporaneous, some petitions specially suited to the thoughts and the wants of the young will aid wonderfully in giving the young an interest in the prayer. Let them, of course, be required always to turn to the text when announced, and make a note of it.

Beyond this, I know that I am on ticklish ground. But will not our clerical brethren listen for once to a short sermon from a lay brother? Not every minister has the gift to preach sermons to children as Dr. Newton does and as many others do. But this is not necessary. Indeed, except only as an occasional service, it is not expedient or wise. But may not every minister in every sermon put in something which shall be level to the capacity of the child-part of his audience? May not every minister in the composition of his sermon remember that children are to be among his hearers? Though he cannot perhaps make his whole discourse such that they can follow it, yet surely he can bring some of its paragraphs within the range of their intellectual vision. And let him be sure of one thing : no part of his discourse will be so acceptable to the whole congregation or receive such universal attention as those passages which were intended especially for the little ones, and which the little ones appropriate as their own. Will not our ministers think of this? Do, brethren, say something every Sunday to the children. The children will then feel that they have something to come to church for.

Some consideration of the bodily comfort of children should find its way into the brains of those who plan and build our church edifices. Church architects and building committees have much to answer for. A house of worship should not be built for the purpose of illustrating some particular style of architecture, or as a pattern card of some particular architect or builder, but for the convenience and accommodation of the worshippers in attending upon the public service of God. Whatever of ornament or of architectural device can be had in connection with this, and subordinate to it, is well. But, after all, the accommodation of the worshippers is the main design, and should ever be kept uppermost in the

thoughts of the builders. Yet when, in the consultations of a building committee of a church, was the
question ever asked, How far will our children be
made comfortable and find their places pleasant and
attractive in this house which we are planning? It
is not uncommon in these days to spend a hundred
thousand dollars upon a church edifice. Does a dollar of these hundred thousand ever go directly or de-
signedly toward making the seats or the furniture or
any of the appointments of the building convenient
and pleasant to children? If we were to require our
children to go to church in the clothes made for their
parents, it would not be a whit more absurd than
what we now do. Father's boots and long-tailed
coat and steeple hat are just as suitable and comfortable to little six-year-old Johnny as are the seat and
the benches which were made to suit the persons
and the limbs of adult people. If our grown-up
folks could be obliged for a few Sundays to occupy
for a couple of hours, twice a day, seats three feet
wide and five feet high, so that during the whole
service neither their feet could once rest upon the
floor nor their persons lean against the back of the
pew, they might begin to understand one of the reasons why children so often find the church a burden.

5. *School Accommodations.*

If our Sunday-schools are ever to be what we are
aiming to make them—a great instrumentality of the
church in doing her appointed work of evangelizing

the masses—we must give them better accommodations, and building committees and church architects
will never rise to a proper comprehension of the
wants of the case until Sunday-school men take the
matter seriously in hand and agitate the subject.
This should be a standing topic at every gathering
of Sunday-school teachers. I must be allowed to
express some surprise that it attracts so little attention. Look over the programme of topics for almost
any convention, large or small, whether of city,
county or State, and you will rarely find this subject
on the list of those to be discussed.

One reason probably why Sunday-school teachers
do not agitate the subject is that each one considers
the matter settled so far as he is concerned. His
church is already built, and it is too late to make
changes. If the school is properly accommodated,
well and good ; if not, the thing is done, and all that
is left is to make the best of what they have. Go on
with the school in the gallery, or in the pews, or in
the basement, or up in the belfry, or wherever it has
been held hitherto, because it is out of the question
to think of tearing the church down in order to re-
construct it with reference to the wants of the Sunday-school. This feeling of the hopelessness of the
case puts a quietus upon all plans for improvement.

But is this right or wise? See what prodigious
improvement has been made in the construction of
houses for the weekday-school. And how was this
brought about? By teachers and the friends of edu-

cation keeping up a continual din on the subject, exposing the shabby condition of the old-fashioned school-houses, and clamoring for something better, until a public sentiment was created which compelled a better state of things. New churches are going up every year all over the land, and they are all being built, and they will continue to be built, in the old stereotyped way until, by talking, discussion and agitation of various kinds, we make it impossible for church architects and builders any longer to ignore the wants of the Sunday-school.

Let me give in a few words my idea of what a Sunday-school does need for its accommodation. If I were about to embark in an enterprise having for its object to gather and build up a large, strong, working congregation, and had to construct the necessary building or buildings for such a congregation, I would say to the architect, Remember in your plans that the audience-room where the preaching is done is not the whole church, or all that is to be looked after. There will be as many people to be seated in the Sunday-school rooms as there will be in the church. The Sunday-school rooms should occupy as much space,—length, breadth and height —and should cost as much money, as the main audience-room of the church.

Why not? Why should we give a style of palatial elegance and comfort to the apartment which is to be occupied from half-past ten to twelve, and thrust the same number of people, and to a great extent the same identical people, down into some dismal basement from nine to half-past ten?

If the main auditorium of the church is to cost fifty thousand dollars, and we wish to maintain a due proportion in the arrangements, we ought to spend another fifty thousand dollars on the school-rooms, and twenty-five thousand more on the lecture-room and its appertainings. Or, to vary the phrase, if the whole structure and furnishing are to cost one hundred and twenty-five thousand dollars, let twenty-five thousand go for the lecture-room, fifty thousand for the school, and fifty thousand for the church. Or, to generalize the problem, divide your money into five equal parts, and spend one-fifth on your lecture-room, two-fifths on your school-rooms, and two-fifths on your audience-chamber.

I am in sober earnest in these statements. I believe most thoroughly that the money bestowed upon a church enterprise, if expended in about these proportions, would yield better results, would sooner gather a good congregation and a flourishing and healthy church, than if expended in the usual way. For the religious wants of a congregation the audience-room, or preaching-room, should bear about the same proportions to the remaining part of the edifice that the parlor of a dwelling-house bears to the other apartments. In building our churches we imitate some fashionable people whose houses are all parlor.

In large Sunday-schools, such as we have, or might

have, in cities and in inland towns and villages, and in some country congregations, in a school numbering, say, three hundred scholars or more, we want, first, a large room, where all the school can be assembled for opening and closing services, and where a majority of the scholars can be taught, divided into classes. This room should be light and airy, suitably carpeted, the walls supplied with maps and blackboards, and the ceiling in no case less than twenty feet high. There should be a separate room of about one-third the size for the infant school. The ceiling of this also should be not less than twenty feet high. The infant school-room should be furnished with a rising gallery and supplied with pictorial illustrations in great numbers and variety. There should be also several small rooms, nicely carpeted and furnished, for the Bible classes and the normal class. It would be well, also, though not essential, that the library should be kept in a room by itself.

I do believe that, with the earnest spirit of improvement now manifested by Sunday-school teachers, a great and wonderful stride forward would be made by the institution if our church builders would fairly recognize its claims and provide for its material wants.

CHAPTER VIII.

MISCELLANEOUS TOPICS.

1. *Sunday-school Music.*

ALL children love music, and almost all children love to sing. This instinctive desire has been wisely subsidized in aid of religion, and especially in aid of the Sunday-school. Singing makes the school attractive. In many districts children are literally sung into the school by hundreds. Music is made also the vehicle of direct religious teaching and impression. The words sung ought always to convey, and usually do convey, important and weighty truths, and these truths thus find a lodgment in the mind. Sacred song also is expressive of emotion. The child in singing gives by his voice expression to this emotion, and the mere act of giving it expression reacts upon the mind itself just as a man in uttering the strong language of scorn works himself gradually into the feeling of scorn. In every view of the subject, therefore, I cannot but regard with interest and hope the very general attention that is now paid to singing in our Sunday-schools.

340

Music-books for this special purpose have been greatly multiplied, and though there is necessarily much difference in these books as to merit, I have never seen one that did not contain some sweet and beautiful tunes. These facts are of good omen. They ought to encourage the Sunday-school laborer and make him hopeful.

In teaching children in the Sunday-school to sing there are some common-sense rules to be observed. First of all, the pieces selected should not contain anything light, irreverent or vulgar, either in the words themselves or in their associations. I have heard not a few pieces sung in Sunday-school that savored very decidedly of the circus and the negro minstrels. The argument for it with the superintendent was that it seemed to captivate the children. There was a stir and a movement about it which was pleasing, and the children sang it with a will. The argument would be just as good for introducing a game of base-ball or of marbles into the Sunday-school; no doubt the children would go at it with a rush. I go as far as any one for pleasing the children. There is no use of trying to sing anything in school unless the children are pleased with it. But that is no reason for singing there everything they like. The thing sung must be devout, religious and elevating in its character. This is indispensable.

But it by no means follows that either the words or the tune should be glum and chilling. On the contrary, our second rule is that the prevailing tone both of the words and the music intended for the Sunday-school should be of a cheerful and buoyant character. There must be life and movement about it. Expressions of gladness and exhilaration, of joy and hope, of love and desire, always take with the children. The movement of the song also should be quick and lively like the physical activity of children. Some schools go to an extreme in this matter; their singing is at full gallop. The more common error, however, is on the other side, expecting children to sing in the slow, stately and solemn style suited to adults. It is essential to excellence in children's singing that it be childlike. Softness and gentleness in music are qualities that always please the little ones. These qualities also have a fine effect upon the order of the school, soothing asperities, quieting the tendency to noise and producing in some indescribable way a feeling of contentedness.

The following cautions are to be observed:

1. *Mere noise is not singing.* In some schools the children sing with a will—at least they go through with a vocal performance which can be heard a good way off, and which is called singing—but no one who has an ear for sweet sounds would call the performance music. There is a great deal of earnestness about it, a great expenditure of vocal power, but no melody, no harmony, nothing that can be truly called song.

2. *Mere song is not sufficient.* What we want in the Sunday-school is sweet sound employed to

express and to cultivate religious emotion. Some of the pieces sung in Sunday-school are beautiful in their vocalization; the ear is delighted and charmed, but the heart is not satisfied; they express nothing, or, at best, something comparatively mean and trivial. No piece should find a place upon the Sunday-school programme unless it is devotional as well as musical. It should express scriptural and religious sentiment,—holy joy, gladness, penitence, hope, godly fear.

3. *The music of the school should be such as will be continued in the music of the sanctuary.* Nothing is more common than to hear in the Sunday-school very excellent singing, every voice joining in and all enjoying the service; but ten minutes later, in the same building, in a room separated from this by only a single wall, you shall see a congregation, composed largely of these same persons, sitting silent listeners to a quartette club performing in the gallery the music of the church. Why is this? Why can these scholars and teachers sing so well and so heartily in the school, while they can only sit dumb in the church? It is not all their fault. The choir often sing pieces which none but a choir can sing. But this is not always the case. Some of the pieces sung in church are such as are suited to congregational singing, and yet the members of the school never join in. The reason is that the church hymns and the church music are not sung in the school. This I hold to be all wrong. While some few of

the things sung in school should be such as are suited to the school only, yet the great majority of the hymns and tunes should be such as the children will sing in church when they become men and women. The Sunday-school service will thus become an important auxiliary and preparative to the church service.

A superintendent who knows nothing about music himself, and who cannot sing at all, may yet secure excellent singing in his school if he has any one of even ordinary ability to lead. To accomplish this end, however, he must reserve to himself the selection of the tunes. Let him only keep his eyes open and observe the effect of each tune upon the scholars. If it is one that produces wild excitement, and creates a tendency to noisiness after the singing is over, or if it is one that after fair trial the children will not take to and that evidently is a drag, drop it; no matter how fine the music teacher pronounces it to be, *drop it.* It may be very good for a choir, or for professed musicians. But for the Sunday-school it is simply *nil.* There is no use of worrying the children with a tune that is a drag and a bore. An indispensable requisite in a Sunday-school tune is that it is one that the children themselves will love and will sing with pleasure, and of this fact the superintendent can judge just as well as the chorister, generally better. If a tune is a favorite with the scholars, you see it in their eyes the moment that it is announced, or that you begin to sing it. By this simple rule, of admitting no tunes but those that prove themselves favorites, the exercise soon becomes pleasurable and attractive, and the children get into the way of singing with their whole soul.

It helps very much the learning of a tune for the children first to commit the words to memory. This should be secured partly by the labor of the teachers in the several classes, but also, and perhaps mainly, by a general concert recitation. Let the whole school *say* the words in concert, at the dictation of the superintendent, before they undertake to *sing* them. Some superintendents seem not to know how to secure entire harmony and thoroughness in a concert recitation. The main secret is in the manner of giving out the words to be repeated. The leader in such an exercise should give out a very small portion, only two or three words, at a time. He should keep his eyes on the smallest and dullest child in the room, and gauge his movements by the manifest capacity of that child. If the number of words given out at once is more than that child can readily take up and repeat, let him proceed more slowly, and shorten the portions. This rule is particularly important in introducing a hymn that is quite new. Go over it in this way very slowly and thoroughly the first few times, securing a full and complete response from every voice in the room. After a while, he may proceed more rapidly, giving perhaps a whole line at a time, and finally the school, on being started with the first word, will go through the whole hymn without missing a word, and without a voice dropping out. This reciting a hymn thus in concert has other advantages besides merely securing that it shall be perfectly remembered. The voices of the whole school learn to move together. They learn to blend smoothly and harmoniously, and they acquire a precision and uniformity of vocal action which are half the battle when they come to sing. This training the children to commit the words to memory and to recite them in concert is the work not of the chorister, but of the teachers and of the superintendent. According to my observation, it is very generally neglected, and much of the failure in Sunday-school singing is attributable to this cause.

2. *Sunday-school Anniversaries.*

Some superintendents and pastors disapprove entirely of Sunday-school anniversaries, and discountenance them in every way practicable. It is feared that the children will get their heads full of excitement, and that the show and bustle and slight irregularities of various kinds connected with a public celebration will divert attention from study and disturb the sober proprieties suitable to God's holy day and house. It is not to be denied that anniversaries may be so managed as to produce frivolous thoughts and behavior, and to make children vain and conceited. But so may the school itself, in its ordinary sessions, produce these same evils. The argument from the abuse of a thing is not valid against any right use of it. An anniversary in a Sunday-school may be so conducted as to promote directly and efficiently every right aim of the institution, and at the same time it may secure certain important results which cannot be reached by the school in its ordinary operations.

An anniversary should always be of a memorial character. It is an occasion for recounting and recording the mercies of the year. These mercies occurring singly, from week to week, fail to make the proper impression. When brought together and aggregated in the annual report, in the form of statistics and of narratives, they stand out in relief, and have an emphasis not accorded to them otherwise. Even a school that seems to have been languishing and feeble will find on reviewing its own history for a year, and putting down carefully its own experiences, that there has been much to be thankful for.

The anniversary strengthens the hold of the school upon the church. It brings many persons into sympathy with the work who are never reached in any other way. It gives an impetus to the school itself, stirring up both scholars and teachers to new zeal. It furnishes an occasion for the pastor and for other speakers to appeal to scholars and teachers on many points of a general character which ought not to be neglected. It is a favorable season for urging the duties of benevolence, of punctuality, of order, of diligent study of God's

word.   So far from the anniversary being a sort of
frolic, I know no better time in the whole year for
pressing upon the unconverted the duty of repentance and conversion.   I have known serious impressions often produced by the anniversary exercises,
and I think, in arranging these exercises, a place
should always be reserved for this important topic.
Let the children have music that will gladden and
please them.   Let them be cheered and entertained
by various little ceremonials connected with the
annual collections, the distribution of premiums, etc.
But let there always be at the right moment a few
plain words of direct counsel and warning on the
subject of the salvation of their souls.   The topic,
if rightly handled, will be all the more impressive
on account of the general good feeling which prevails on anniversary day.

There are modes of holding Sunday-school cele-
brations which it is difficult for any sober-minded
Christian to approve.   Sometimes particular children are showed off in a manner that is very injurious to themselves and that creates envy and ill-feeling
in the minds of others.   There is at times a levity in
the proceedings entirely unsuited to the service.
The exercises, of course, should be of a glad and
joyous character.   Let the children shout their ho-
sannas, as of old, from hearts alive with love and joy.
But nothing so really kills this true and holy gladness of heart as rudeness or levity.

The most objectionable feature connected with a

Sunday-school celebration is turning it into a dramatic entertainment. I have never seen a performance of this kind, but have heard of such, and I have before me a published account of one which I have read with sincere sorrow. This celebration did not take place in the church, nor on Sunday. Still it was a celebration of the Sunday-school, so regarded and so called. The exercises consisted almost exclusively of " performances" by the children. There were speeches, dialogues, songs, tableaux, and finally a " regular drama," with " actors" dressed in appropriate costume and with scenic display. I give a few extracts, and let my readers judge for themselves whether a word of caution is not needed :

" Single pieces, such as ' The Best Use of a Penny,' ' I'll Never Use Tobacco,' and ' Willie's Temptation,' by some of the smaller boys of the school, were remarkably well delivered for children of their age. The dialogue of ' The Two Dimes' contained an instructive moral that all could appreciate, and the ' Eleventh Commandment,' a dialogue between three of the girls, was as perfectly rendered as anything we have ever seen anywhere. The other exercises embraced the recital of ' The Better Land,' from Mrs. Hemans, recitation of the twenty-third Psalm by the whole school, song, ' I Ought to Love my Mother,' by three very small girls, whose voices blended in sweet accord, dialogues entitled ' God is Love,' by two little girls, and ' The Rabbit,' by two boys, presentation of gifts by the superintendent to scholars who had, as missionaries in our midst, been most successful in bringing new scholars into the Sunday-school, some beautiful tableaux representing ' Incidents in the Life of a Boy who had neglected the Sunday-school,' and then in contrast with it, ' Incidents in the Life of a Sunday-school Scholar,' from which the moral was easily drawn. ' Faith, Hope and Charity,' and the representation of ' Night and Morning,' constituted the most perfect and beautiful tableaux we ever remember to have witnessed. Perhaps, however, the great piece of the evening was a scenic representation of ' Joseph and his Brethren.' It was dramatized from the Scriptures, divided into acts and scenes : the characters were all dressed in Oriental costume and exhibited the Oriental styles of salutation and manners, and the effect was to impress this most interesting portion of the Scriptures upon the minds of the children in a manner they can never forget. We were first introduced to the old patriarch Jacob as

30

he is sending his sons to Egypt to buy food ; next we are in Joseph's palace, and the sons before him, unconscious in whose presence they stand ; then the sons in prison, and the entry of Joseph and his permission to all of them to return to Canaan except Simeon ; their return and story to Jacob ; their second visit to Egypt, with all the incidents ; the discovery of Joseph to his brethren and their final return and account of it to Jacob. We are not extravagant in saying that but few persons of any age could have rendered these parts better than the boys of this Sunday-school, and the whole performance certainly reflected great credit upon those who had the management of it in charge."

As to the season of the year for holding the anniversary, schools differ according to the customs prevailing in each congregation ; but the majority of schools have their anniversary in the spring or early summer.

There is, of course, no absolute rule as to the best part of the day for holding the anniversary. I object, however, most decidedly to having it at night. In most congregations the afternoon is found most convenient. Whatever part of the day is taken, the anniversary should take the place of one regular service. To have preaching morning and night, and the anniversary in the afternoon in addition, is wearisome and unprofitable to teachers and scholars, who constitute no inconsiderable part of the congregation, and it for the same reason prevents the other part of the congregation from attending the anniversary. The anniversary exercises occupy the full time of an ordinary regular service of the sanctuary, and it ought to be understood that they take the place of such a service and that all the congregation are expected to attend..

It is well for the pastor, in the regular service for

that day, to preach on the subject.   There are many points connected with the religious training of the young on which the pastor desires to address his people, and the anniversary Sunday furnishes a suitable occasion for the purpose.   Knowing that such a sermon will be expected of him has its effect on the pastor's own mind, keeping him in fuller communication with the operations and the necessities of the school. The preaching of such a sermon on the day of the celebration marks the day out with greater distinctness in the Sunday-school calendar, and makes the occasion in all respects more imposing and significant in the minds of the young.

The superintendent should present a short but carefully-prepared report containing a business-like statement of the condition and history of the school for the past year and its wants and prospects for the year to come.   This report should consist mainly of facts, giving accurate statistics of attendance, of benevolent operations, of the library, of the teachers' meetings, and so forth.   The report should always be in writing and fully written out, not a few written memoranda for the superintendent to expatiate on.

The superintendent's report should be followed by an address from the pastor, and that address will naturally take its tone and topics from the report.   The facts of the report furnish indeed the points on which the pastor will want to talk to his people.

Some schools make a point of securing for the anniversary speakers from abroad.   It is a mistake.

These gentlemen who thus go about making speeches say many good things, doubtless, and give an extra brilliancy and glitter to the occasion, but this very extra brilliancy and glitter only make the regular routine of the school more tame and humdrum. Whatever speeches are to be made let them be made, so far as possible, by persons connected with the congregation. There is hardly any congregation which does not contain some gentlemen capable of performing such a service if they are properly set in motion, and the very fact of a gentleman's thus addressing the school makes him more interested in it ever afterward.

Two speakers are enough, one to the scholars and one to the teachers, and neither speech should in any case exceed ten minutes. While it is well to have the speeches enlivened with anecdote and illustration, let them never degenerate into buffoonery or into mere story-telling. Scholars are willing enough to be amused, and are very prompt to laugh at any tolerable joke that is offered, but they know at the same time that they come to the school for no such purpose, and they will give respectful attention to any stranger who gives them plain, brief, well-considered counsels concerning the best means of improving their advantages as scholars.

The anniversary will be a dull affair without some good singing. By this I do not mean that the choir should get up some high-wrought, artistic music. The music wanted for the anniversary is Sunday-school music—whole-souled, sweet-voiced singing by the entire school. Five or six pieces are needed of an animated sort, and the school should be well and thoroughly drilled on them for some weeks in advance.

There should be a printed programme of the exercises to be distributed among the audience as well as in the school, and the hymns to be sung should be printed on the programme, so that all may join in the singing.

It is customary in many schools to give Bibles, Testaments, hymn-books, and other rewards of this kind to pupils who have recited the catechism or certain portions of Scripture, or have been specially meritorious in other respects. Sometimes a book or other present is given to every scholar who is a regular member of the school. This whole matter of making presents to the children, besides the heavy expense it occasions, has other serious drawbacks, and needs extreme caution. Kindness, good will, liberality, shown to the children, are all very well; but let us do nothing that looks like bribing them to attend. A gift is not the only way to the heart of a child. The distribution of presents is not the only way of making the anniversary interesting and pleasant to the children; on the contrary, it often produces heart-burnings, jealousies and discontent. A pretty certificate of membership or of attendance, neatly printed in colors and awarded publicly to all who during the year have complied with the condi-

30 *   X

tions, is inexpensive, and forms an agreeable item in the proceedings of the anniversary. Bibles, Testaments, etc., awarded in a like way to all who have accomplished certain required studies of the school, form another item to which there can be no reasonable objection, but beyond this there is need of very great caution. Greater latitude of course is proper in mission schools than in church schools.

Shall there be in the anniversary any performances by the children?

Why not? Is not child-nature the same on Sunday that it is on other days? I would not get up dialogues and debates and declamations as in the weekday exhibition. But there are certain things which can be done by the children at the anniversary that will be perfectly in keeping with the occasion, and that will add greatly to the interest. Suppose thirty young girls, say about ten years old, rise in a semicircle on the platform in front and repeat in perfect concert the twenty-third Psalm, not missing a word, and as many boys immediately thereafter repeat in the same way the Beatitudes. The whole performance occupies less than five minutes, yet it has given to those sixty performers and to their five times sixty friends in the congregation a lively interest in the occasion; besides that, the preparation for it has engraved indelibly on their minds a precious portion of God's word.

But I have not the space to enlarge. Suffice it to say that in my opinion recitations of portions of

Scripture and of hymns by the scholars, either singly or in groups, form a valuable part of the proceedings of the anniversary, and just that part that will most surely bring out a full house.

In seating the children for the anniversary always put the smaller children in front, near the pulpit. See that the pews occupied by the young children are supplied with high benches on which their feet may rest. Nothing is more common than for the exercises to be disturbed by a continual knocking of little heels against the seat of the pew, and the superintendent gets up and berates the children for "kicking" and "making a noise," whereas the noise is no fault of theirs. The pew seats are made to suit grown people, and when little shavers five or six years old sit in them, their legs hang dangling in the air in a manner that is painful to them, and that necessarily leads to the distracting noise spoken of.

4. *Closing Schools in Winter.*

The Sunday-school is subject to two evils, of a kind exactly the opposite of each other, yet alike in their pernicious effects. City schools are very generally closed for a couple of months in midsummer, country schools for a like, sometimes even for a longer, period in winter. This latter practice is not perhaps as general as the other. But where it does prevail, the habit is usually inveterate, and it requires no little resolution and energy to break it up. In many neighborhoods in the country, it is assumed as a thing certain, and not to be called in question, that the Sunday-school cannot be maintained in winter. The people would as soon expect to raise a crop of corn or of peaches in winter as to keep the Sunday-school open. They expect, as a matter of course, to close it about the middle of November, and not to open it again until spring.

How this practice originated it is difficult to say. Perhaps it was in those old times, which some of us can remember, when the churches were not warmed in winter, and when consequently there would be some practical inconveniences in holding the school. This cause, at least, no longer exists. The rooms where the school is held may be made as comfortable in winter as at any other season. For that matter, indeed, the school-room may be made more comfortable in midwinter than in midsummer. It may be warmed in the coldest weather, but it cannot always be cooled in the heats of July.

Will not the teachers and superintendents and other Christian people, in those districts where this periodical Sunday-school hibernation takes place, give the subject a respectful reconsideration? Is there any valid reason why the schools should be thus closed for three or four months in the year? The church is not closed in winter, why should the school be? The weekday-school is not closed, why close the Sunday-school? The children can go out to skate, and ride down hill, and build snow-forts, from Monday to Saturday; how is it that they become all at once so delicate and tender on Sunday morning? Winter in the country is the season above all others when social gatherings of all kinds are opportune and rife; why should the weekly gathering of the children in their loved Sunday-school be the only exception?

There are weighty reasons, physiological, social and domestic, why a country Sunday-school should be maintained in winter more than in any other season of the year. In the long winter evenings in the country there is more leisure for study and for preparing lessons than at other times. The teachers of country Sunday-schools have then more time upon their hands, particularly the male teachers, and can with less sacrifice of business engagements prepare themselves for their Sunday duties. Farmers have winter work, it is true, but it is not so pressing and imperious in its demands as the work of "seed-time and harvest." Then there is no time when mental operations are so vigorous, when the business of learning and teaching can be conducted with so much effect, as in the crisp, frosty days of winter. The cold is a mighty tonic both to the mind and the body.

So well is this physiological fact understood that all institutions of learning the world over have their main season of study in the winter. Is there anything in religious truth that should make its study particularly suitable to the sultry and relaxing heats of July and August? Why should the children of this world be more wise in such matters than the children of light?

One thing which gives the argument special point is that in very many country districts the Sunday-school is kept in the same building in which the weekday-school is kept—that is, in the district school-house. If, in any of these districts, the common school is not kept up all the year round, the time selected for keeping it is always the winter, as being the best season for school purposes; and the strange anomaly is often seen of the school-house being open all the rest of the week for the weekday-school, but closed on the Sabbath because then it is too cold for the children—those children, too, being the very same boys and girls who have been going there all the rest of the week!

When a custom like this has long prevailed in a neighborhood, there is always a certain amount of *vis inertiæ* to be overcome before a change can be brought about. But it will yield, nevertheless, to persistent pressure. All that it requires in any particular case is one resolute mind. Let there be but one teacher who will make up his mind to go right on with his own class through the winter, whether others do or not, and he will be surprised to see how many, both of teachers and scholars, will follow his example.

If these paragraphs meet the eye of any teacher so circumstanced, I hope that he will not dismiss the subject lightly, but that he will weigh well the re-

sponsibility of continuing a practice so entirely unreasonable and so fraught with evil.

5. *Closing Schools in Summer.*

Midsummer is a hard time of the year for city
superintendents. From the first of June the exodus
of teachers begins, and by the first of August less
than one-half of the regular corps of laborers are to
be found at their posts. In many large city schools
more than three-fourths of the most efficient teachers
are absent from the city from one to three months in
midsummer. I do not blame them for going. The
strain upon the vital energies, caused by the present
methods of city life, makes this annual period of
relaxation an imperative necessity to such people as
constitute the mass of our Sunday-school laborers.
They have no choice but to get this annual relief,
or to abridge, if not abruptly to terminate, their active usefulness. But this does not make the case
any the easier to the superintendent. The great
mass of the children, particularly in schools which
partake at all of a missionary character, remain in
the city. They are on his hands to be cared for, and
the burden is not light. It is not an infrequent experience for a city superintendent, in midsummer, to
meet in his school-room from two to three hundred
children, and not more than half a dozen of his
regular teachers. I have myself, on occasion, had
two hundred children on my hands, and not one
regular teacher, the few laborers who were present

to help, being special aids picked up for the day wherever they could be found. Such a state of things needs remedy, if it can be had.

Many superintendents, in view of the difficulties of the case, suspend their schools entirely during July and August. Some schools are suspended for a period of three months. This shifts the difficulty without removing it. The real difficulty is that nine-tenths of those children who most need the religious instruction of the Sunday-school do not leave the city. During the time that the school is disbanded they mostly wander about the streets, unlearning the good they have received, and receiving on the other hand lessons in irreligion, Sabbath-breaking and vice; and when the time for reopening the school has come, it requires several weeks of industrious visitation on the part of the teachers to reclaim all these youthful stragglers and bring them once more into orderly habits and regular attendance. A school that is disbanded in the close of June will not be brought to full working order before October. One-fourth of the year is lost. More than this: the cultivator finds that there has been in the mean while a rank growth of weeds which it will require time and toil to extirpate. The garden is not found as it was left. The fences are out of repair. The evil seed always present in the soil has grown apace. The good seed unprotected has been choked.

I do not advise, therefore, the closing of our city

schools in midsummer. There are, indeed, evils attending the keeping of them together. But the evils of suspending the schools are still greater. Let superintendents then keep up their organization all the year round, if possible, and meet the exigencies of the summer season in the best way they can.

Where nothing better can be done, the exercises of the school may be changed. The regular studies may be suspended until the return of the regular teachers, and a course of special studies and exercises be introduced. More of the time than usual may be occupied in addresses and instructions to the whole school from the superintendent's desk. The temporary teachers, so called, are often quite incompetent to give instruction. But they can keep the classes together and keep them in order while the superintendent, or some one from his desk equally competent, addresses the whole school. There are many special topics that are never devoid of interest which may well occupy the attention of the school on such occasions. The evils of drunkenness, of swearing, of Sabbath-breaking, may be dwelt upon, the person who addresses the school having prepared himself with instructive and interesting facts suitable to the character of his audience. Another fruitful topic for instruction on such occasions is the work of Christian missions. Often a foreign missionary may be present, and a narrative by him of what he has seen among the heathen will greatly interest the

31

children. Where a missionary is not to be had, suitable reading and preparation on the part of the superintendent or speaker will enable him to gather facts in regard to the missionary work that will be equally valuable. But besides missionary addresses and addresses on other special subjects, the Bible is full of topics. A parable may be expounded. The biography of some Bible hero may be sketched. If the superintendent has no particular skill in such addresses, he might read a portion of one of those admirable children's sermons that have been prepared by Dr. Newton, Dr. Todd and others.

A part of the Sunday-school machinery that should be kept specially active in the summer months is the library. Some schools take this occasion to close the library. There could hardly be a greater mistake. Doubtless there will be during this interval some irregularities and some loss of books. But remember, it is not the main object of the library to preserve the books, as some librarians seem to think, but to do with them the greatest amount of good. I would not discourage a faithful librarian in his efforts to lessen the loss and waste of books that take place. But in the summer-time, when the regular teachers are absent and the ordinary course of instruction is very much interrupted, the use of the library is needed more than at any other season to supplement the teaching and to keep the school together; and if the keeping of the library open during this season of general irregularity does occasion the

loss of a few volumes, the end is important enough
to justify the expenditure.

What is true of books is equally true of Sunday-
school papers. During the summer months, if during no other season of the year, the superintendent
should be prepared *every* Sunday to give each scholar
an attractive paper. Most of these papers are published only monthly. But there are now so many of
them that there need be no difficulty in having one
for each week. He might give them, for instance,
the *Child at Home* on the first Sunday in the month,
the *Child's Paper* on the second. the *Child's World*
on the third, and so on. Some schools do thus supply their children with a paper every week all the
year round; ordinarily, however, a paper is distributed only once a month. What I now urge is that
during the two or three months of summer when
the regular course of study is so much interrupted
the superintendent should make arrangements to
distribute a paper *every* Sunday.

The burden of providing temporary teachers for
the summer season should not be thrown upon the
superintendent. On this subject there is a degree of
thoughtlessness and inconsideration on the part of
teachers that is perfectly amazing. I have never
been disposed to censure teachers for leaving the city
during the hot months where their circumstances
enabled them to do so, but to go away for two or
three months without giving any thought what in
the mean time is to become of their classes is, I think,

to be guilty of a great sin. There always remain in the city adult members of the church enough to supply all the classes temporarily with teachers. These persons are not, perhaps, thoroughly competent; we would not choose them for regular teachers; but they are better than none. Some of them have engagements or physical infirmities that prevent them engaging as teachers all the year round, but they can safely engage for a few weeks. Now, to hunt up such persons and secure their services and make all the necessary arrangements and explanations require time and labor, but this time and labor each teacher should religiously give. It should be a part of his regular preparation for leaving town. Each teacher, having only his own class to provide for, may without difficulty do it. But when it is all thrown upon the superintendent, and he alone has to furnish substitutes for twenty-five or thirty teachers, it becomes a labor of Hercules. The teacher, in making provision for his or her class, should of course confer with the superintendent; but this is very different from throwing upon him the whole burden of the arrangement. The teacher who leaves the city for the summer without having fairly tried to provide a substitute is just as guilty as the physician who without notice should leave a patient dangerously ill and go off to Long Branch or Saratoga. The charge of souls is not the less a serious responsibility because no pecuniary reward is involved in its observance or neglect.

6. *After Vacation.*

A large number of Sunday-schools, particularly those in cities, are virtually disbanded in midsummer. The teachers and many of the scholars leave town for recreation and health, and the classes are depleted and disorganized where not actually disbanded. When the first of September comes, few schools in our large cities are to be found in active operation. I am not going to argue the question now whether or not this is a bad state of things and one admitting a remedy, but taking the fact as I find it, I wish to address a word of exhortation to superintendents and teachers.

This is the season for a fresh, vigorous, decided effort. You have come back to your homes strengthened and rested. Quite possibly in your summer rambles or reading you have met with books or people that have given you new ideas in regard to your work; you have seen and heard many things likely to interest your scholars; your mind is full, your pulse beats healthily; your scholars, whether they have remained at home or whether like yourself they have been travelling, are all just in that condition in which they will be glad to resume their old places and studies in school. Do not make the mistake of many, and let these genial influences all die out. Do not leave matters to readjust themselves gradually and slowly in the course of the autumn, but make a bold, prompt push the very first week you return to

31 *

the city. You will find it operating powerfully in
favor of your class and your school. Scholars who
are neglected at such a season by the teachers of
their own schools stray off into other schools that
are more active, or stray off from school altogether.
A superintendent or a teacher who is in his place by
the first of September should not be content to let
matters drift on easily and composedly until the first
of October. Determine to have a full school at once.
Let every teacher the very first week of his return to
town visit every scholar on his roll ; it is an excellent
way of beginning the fall campaign. A thorough
general visitation on the part of all our teachers on the
first week of September would in many cases double
the results of the year's work. Many a school, many
a class, instead of continuing to be a drag for months,
would start out with full, fresh energies from the
first.

Nor should teachers confine their visits and inquiries to their own scholars. During the summer
many changes have occurred. Other families have
come into the neighborhood. The season is one
especially favorable for getting new recruits. There
are few schools that might not add fifty per cent
to their numbers if on the first week of September
their entire corps of teachers would sally out, and
while calling on all their own scholars make inquiries as they went for new ones. Is it not worth a
trial? If concerted action in any particular case
cannot be obtained, let each one try the experiment

individually. Let each teacher for himself determine to signalize the first week of his return to town by calling on every scholar of his class, and by a bold, resolute effort to win new recruits. How pleasant, how refreshing, to enter your school-room the first Sunday after your return and see your own little circle of bright faces all complete, besides a goodly outside circle of new-comers drawn within the precious place by your own kindly influence and solicitations! Could you in any way make a more suitable return for the goodness and the gracious protection which you have experienced during the late season of repose and recreation?

The most beautiful natural phenomenon that I ever witnessed was seen one summer afternoon at the Profile House, among the White Mountains of New Hampshire. It was a rainbow stretching across in front of that perpendicular wall of rock which stands directly before the hotel. The huge background of rock brought the rainbow so near to the spectators at the hotel that we could see the separate drops of rain as they glittered, millions of sparkling diamonds, softly descending through a mist of radiant gold. Not only was every color of the rainbow marked with a distinctness and perfection of which the spectators had before never witnessed any parallel, but the bow itself was complete through its entire semicircle, without a break or a faintness even, from end to end. More than this. The reflected or secondary bow seen outside the other, though not so brilliant as the primary phenomenon, was yet equally full and complete in its every part.

Not less beautiful than this crown and glory of Nature's loveliness will be that Sunday-school class which on its first reassembling in September shall present to the eye of its teacher and its superintendent a circle equally complete, with at the same time its full-orbed complement of new recruits standing round the inner circle as a halo of reflected but ever growing glory. Who will show such a phenomenon in his school on the first Sunday after his next vacation? Will you?

7. *New Scholars.*

The Sunday-school is often called a garden. The comparison is as suggestive as it is beautiful. Notice the care bestowed by a skilful gardener upon a plant that has just been taken from some other soil and replanted in his garden. How particular he is to see that the ground where he places it is properly prepared and just of the right kind ; that every little rootlet and fibre shall come into contact with some portion of warm, nourishing earth ; that the soil shall be loosened deep enough and wide enough to allow and invite the roots to send out their taps freely in whatever direction the nature of the plant inclines it to grow ! How promptly he removes from the neighborhood of the young stranger any weeds or plants that may be likely to hinder its growth and prevent its forming a strong and healthy attachment to the soil! With what watchfulness he sees the first indications of sickliness or drooping, watering it in drought and giving it his daily care and attention, until its every leaf and limb shows that it has firm possession of the soil!

With equal care should the teacher and superintendent watch and nurture the child just transplanted into the Sunday-school garden. The new scholar requires for a time twice or three times the attention given to the others. The superintendent in the first place should see to it that the child is placed in the class best suited to its wants. The gardener would not plant a rose in the same position in which he would put an ivy. The different classes in school are so many garden-beds, each suited by the varying circumstances of sun and shade, light, heat and exposure, for a particular kind of plant. When the gardener receives from abroad some new and curious specimen, he does not at once set it out into the first vacant piece of ground he finds, but he sets himself to work to study the nature of the plant, makes himself acquainted with its habits and wants, and then places it intelligently where it will be most likely to thrive. It is no sufficient reason for the superintendent to place the new-comer into Miss Smith's class that Miss Smith's class is nearly empty and there is plenty of room for him there. The first duty that the superintendent owes to the new scholar is to get acquainted with him, to find out something about him, before selecting for him his school companion-

Y

ship and his caretaker. The opportunities which the superintendent has for making this acquaintanceship are few. But that is only a stronger reason why he should use more carefully the opportunities which he has. In a well-ordered school, when a scholar is registered, questions are asked as to his age, residence, the name and occupation of his parents, and so forth. All these items help the superintendent who is wide awake in forming an estimate as to the social circumstances which surround the child. He learns the nature of the soil from which the plant has been taken. A new scholar is usually introduced by some teacher or Sunday-school worker who has found him and visited him at his home, or perhaps by some one of the other scholars. The superintendent should not fail in such case—which is almost every case—to exhaust this additional source of information. He may thus usually learn all about the external relations and condition of the child. Before placing a new pupil into a class the superintendent needs to know something of his mental capacity and attainments; he must, therefore, make an examination more or less formal. In nothing is there greater room for tact and skill than in this. At the idea of being examined on admission to a Sunday-school a proud child becomes restive, a sensitive child shy and embarrassed, one overgrown and awkward very likely revolts or is sullen. The superintendent must know how to examine without any appearance of an examination. He gets the child to read a little, and has a little conversation about what is read or about any topic that may be suggested, he all the while gauging the child's mind. Thus, by one means and another, the superintendent endeavors to find out where to place the new pupil so that he will be under influences most congenial and most suited to his particular case.

The proper placing of new scholars on their admission into school is one of the most difficult, as it is one of the most important, functions of the superintendent's office. Yet I have seen superintendents of no mean ability in other respects who in this matter were utterly deficient, who on receiving a new pupil seemed to think their only business was to fill up certain classes that had become small and weak ; and I have not been surprised in such cases to notice that, however great the number of new recruits, the school never seemed to make any permanent growth. I have known schools in which there was an average of four or five new scholars every Sunday, and yet at the end of the season the general attendance was no greater than at the beginning. It was pouring water into a sieve. The new plants had been put into uncongenial soil, and after a brief and sickly growth had died out. Such is the history of a great deal of the missionary work that is done to extend the benefits of the Sunday-school.

Having selected a class and a teacher according to the best judgment he could form of the case, the superintendent should then in all cases communicate privately to the teacher all the information obtained in regard to the child. Without this knowledge the teacher may make mistakes still more mischievous than those of the superintendent. In acting upon this knowledge, and in attempting to get upon a more intimate and confidential footing with the stranger, the teacher should not rush upon him with sudden and overpowering attention, as is the manner of some. A child is to be approached very much as you would approach a horse—quietly, and by giving it opportunity for observation. Of course you will speak to the child when introduced, and show him some little civility. But to press your attentions upon him so as to make him the continued centre of observation is embarrassing, and leads him to be reserved. Better let the exercises of the class run on in their accustomed course until the scene becomes familiar to him and he begins to feel a little at home, and to feel an interest in what is going on, before you question him much personally. A moment's conversation with him at the close of the school, after the other scholars are dismissed, will often be of service. Nothing is of so much importance, however, in setting the teacher upon a right footing with a new scholar, as visiting him at his own home. This visit should be made by the teacher the very first week, if possible, after a child is introduced. Such a visit is an act of kindness that is always appreciated. It places you at once in your right relation to him as a friend and acquaintance, and enables you in the class to accommodate yourself to whatever is peculiar in him.

Children are more influenced by each other than they are by their teachers or those much older than themselves. The companionship selected for the new scholar is therefore a most important item. It is in fact the soil into which the new plant is set. If it has been wisely chosen and the classmates among whom he is placed are congenial, he will not find much difficulty in getting acquainted. Yet even here, so important is this matter, the teacher should not leave it to chance. Let him see to it that the little stranger ceases from the very first day to be a stranger. The teacher who has any tact at all will find opportunity, before the hour is over, to make him acquainted with some of his young companions, and will select for the purpose those that will be likely to make the most agreeable impression. It is very chilling to a young heart, on the first day of one's admission to a large school, to walk home alone. Some teachers perhaps may think these things of small importance, unworthy of such grave consideration. If so, I have only to say, their experience has been very different from mine. The impression made upon the mind of a child on first entering a Sunday-school often determines the question of his return to it. It should be the study of all concerned—superintendent, teacher and classmates—to make him feel that it is a pleasant place, where he will find friends and meet with kindness,

32

and where hearts are beating in sympathy with his own.

Care, in short, in the treatment of new scholars is quite as important as zeal in hunting them up.

8. *Absenteeism.*

It is necessary that some distinct provision should be made in relation to the absence of scholars. Absenteeism, or irregularity of attendance, is the weak point in the Sunday-school system. It is impossible that a scholar should be making any distinct progress in religious knowledge, or gaining substantial benefit of any kind, so long as he comes or stays away, according to the caprice of the hour. Such scholars get no good themselves, and they hurt the cause by giving occasion to opponents to say, "See how little comes of your Sunday-school labors!" Now, in my opinion, this absenteeism may in a great measure be cured. But to this end the teachers must take hold of the matter resolutely. Let them have the courage to resolve that in every case, without exception, where a scholar is absent, he shall be visited by some one during the coming week. If his own teacher is so situated as to be unable to make this visit, let it be done by some one else. But in all cases and at all risks the visit must be made.

This brings up the next point to which I would advert, and that is the necessity of teachers visiting their scholars. On this point, I think, there is a misapprehension in the minds of some conscientious and most excellent teachers. I have known several instances of such teachers, who really desired to discharge this duty, and had no disposition to shrink from the labor involved in it, but were deterred solely by a mistaken view of what was really required. If any pious Sunday-school teacher has the gifts and the experience necessary to visit the home of a scholar in such a way as to make it a direct means of spiritual counsel and edification to the household, if he has the gift and the prompting of heart, while visiting a member of his class, especially if it be in a home where God is not honored by the heads of the family, to lift up his voice in prayer, to read to the assembled household God's holy word, and to give to the family, or to any member of it, spiritual exhortation and advice,—I bid him Godspeed. May we all see the day when we can do this wisely and profitably! But there is much visiting that is content with a lowlier aim than this, and is at the same time exceedingly useful. Go to the homes of your children, if for nothing else, that you may see where they live, and how they live, and the influences around them—that you may become acquainted with their families, and make them feel that you have some interest in their welfare. Fear not that you will be regarded as an intruder. I know the heart of the parent, and I know that nothing sooner gladdens a father or a mother than the face of one who has the charge of their child. Go then with the assurance of a welcome. Go, too, expecting to learn something valuable yourself. When you return from a friendly conference with one of your scholars at his own home and with his parents and family, if there is a right spirit in you, you will come away a wiser man or woman than you went. You will know better than you ever knew before how to gain the attention and the affections of your scholar. You will see better than you have ever seen before the difficulties that were in your path. More than all, you will have broken down the wall of partition that existed between you and your scholar, and you will have established a bond of sympathy that will turn teaching from a drudgery to a delight.

There is one view of this whole subject which often presents itself with great force to my own mind. If by some special dispensation it could be granted to you to see personally the Lord Jesus Christ, in his human nature, as he appeared in the synagogues of Judea eighteen hundred years ago, how attentive you would be to the words which fell from his mouth! If it should appear that he was now living upon the earth, and that he was destitute of comfortable apparel, or that by fatigue and want of food he was in a suffering condition, how glad and honored you would be to minister to his personal comfort! Suppose it could be certainly made known to you that he was now to be seen in some suburb of the city where you live—that in some dark upper room, in a remote alley, he lay sick of a fever, and that he had sent to your school a message requesting some one to watch with him and visit him, and look after his personal wants—who would not leap for joy to be entrusted with the precious mission? Suppose he were as he was a few years after his birth at Bethlehem—a child, a poor mechanic's son—and yet it were certainly declared to you that this poor, obscure child were the Lord of Glory dwelling in flesh, humbly and meekly, who would not be eager to have that child in his class, to visit him weekly, to look after him, to be kind to him, to clothe him if he were naked, to feed him if he were hungry, to exercise toward him all that patience and forbearance and love which the weakness and dependence of childhood require?

Christian friends, where is our faith? Has not Christ expressly taught us that children are the objects of his special care, and that kindness to them is kindness to *him?* We wrest the Scriptures from their plain and obvious meaning when we explain away entirely all literal application of those remarkable passages in which he speaks of little children. Undoubtedly, we are to love and honor all, of every age, who have a childlike and Christian temper. But our Saviour loved not merely the child*like*, but *children.* So should we. Little children, as such, are objects of special regard to our dear Redeemer ; and when we minister to the wants of such because they are dear to Christ, we minister to *him.* What

32 *

though the act be no more than giving a cup of water, or speaking a kind word? what though it be done in some hidden alley, where no human eye sees it, and no human tongue shall ever tell it, yet if it be done to please and honor Christ, and to do good to an immortal spirit for which he has died, he will see and honor the act just as certainly as though it had been done to himself personally. Martha and Mary and their brother Lazarus were doubtless greatly privileged by the visits which our Lord frequently paid to their lowly dwelling, and the Scriptures tell us with what assiduity they waited upon him, and how Mary, who loved him much, washed his feet with her tears and wiped them with the hairs of her head. But when we see a pious disciple now who has leisure, or cultivation, or an abundance of this world's goods, going about noiselessly and assiduously, doing good to all who need, out of love to Him who died for them, can we doubt that the eye of the great Master is upon such a one just as certainly as it was upon Mary?

Teacher, where is your faith to receive this great doctrine? • If you really, truly believed that the ministrations of mercy, and in some special manner the caring for children, were services done to Christ, *could* it be that of the "little ones" belonging to our schools we should see so many statedly absent? Where are these stray lambs? What account can you give of them to the great Shepherd? Whence that vacant seat in your form? Perhaps that scholar

may be confined to a sick chamber, perhaps he may
be running the streets, perhaps he may have parents
that care nothing about religion, and he may be
staying away from mere indifference, and a friendly
visit would bring him back within the sympathies
and the precious influences of the Sunday-school.
Do you really believe that it is " not the will of our
heavenly Father that one of these little ones should
perish," and that what you do to bring them to
Christ is as truly gratifying to him as were the affec-
tionate and grateful personal attentions of Martha
and Mary and Lazarus and John, and will you any
longer forego such an unspeakable joy and privilege?

9. *Uniform Lessons.*

Although the minds of most of our active Sunday-
school workers are now made up in favor of having
a uniform lesson for the whole school, yet there are
many schools in which there is still no concert of
action as to the study of a particular portion of Scripture. There are so many arguments in favor of the
uniform lesson system that it may with great propriety be urged on all our schools.

Let us glance at the other system for the sake of
illustration, or perhaps it might be safe to call it, in
most instances, a want of system. In the majority
of cases it is rather from thoughtlessness than from a
thorough consideration of the merits of the question
that each class selects its own lesson and studies on
its own account, instead of acting in concert with the

rest of the school. It is safe to say that where there is a lack of uniformity in the lesson there is a poorer style of preparation and a lower grade of teaching than where the whole school is at work on the same lesson. In the appearance of the school there may be little or no difference. There may even be much the same apparent interest in the classes as the teacher hears the lesson, but the difference in result is apparent at the end of a year's teaching. In the school where various lessons are studied at the same time, each class is independent of every other class. While independence in a general way is exceedingly desirable, yet this kind of independence is pernicious. In a well-ordered Sunday-school the teachers are made to realize that we are " members one of another." We must all help each other, we must all labor for one purpose, and we can help each other better, and better labor with a view to a common end, if we intelligently and systematically labor at the same thing. If of four oarsmen in a row-boat each pulls his oar at such time and in such manner as best suits himself, the vessel is likely to be jerked in various directions and with a result anything but convenient or profitable ; but when all pull together, their labors being directed, too, by the man at the helm, the course is straight onward, and the result is just what was aimed at.

Pursuing the independent plan, there is little opportunity for a teachers' study meeting. True. the teachers may meet for prayer, or they may hold business meetings. They may, for the sake of holding meetings, make frequent amendments to the constitution or additions to the by-laws; or they may meet to hear the report of the treasurer, or of some committee which would give account of the progress it has made since the previous meeting; or the meetings may be for purely social purposes, or with a view to the cultivation of the musical ability of the teachers. While it is good to a certain extent for teachers to meet occasionally for almost any wise end, yet it is the experience of almost all who have attended teachers' meetings that no meeting is so profitable as that which is held for the diligent and prayerful study of the lesson. Too much business degenerates into routine and parliamentary formality. Too much of mere social gathering turns the teacher's work into profitless festivity. Independently studying what each teacher pleases, what shall we study at the teachers' meeting? On whose lessons shall we prepare ourselves? There is no way of meeting the wants of each teacher in this respect, no concert of action, no united study, consequently, none of that invaluable help which teacher can impart to teacher when those who are studying the same passage with a view to the same result are exchanging thoughts and comparing ideas.

School being opened, the superintendent, instead of introducing the teachers' work with a few pertinent remarks as to what the lesson is and where, announces, " The school may now go on with the lessons." And when each class has in its individual and solitary way plodded through its verses, he brings the teaching to an end with a tap or two of the bell, gives out a closing hymn, and without a word of practical application or enforcement of what has been taught, he lets the school go.

The classes in the school whose teachers are absent are put to severe inconvenience. No two teachers having the same lesson, there is confusion in what is taught when a substitute is put in charge of the absent teacher's class or when two classes are temporarily thrown together. As teacher and scholar have prepared, or are supposed to have prepared, different lessons, there is a want of fitness in the teaching and its results which is undesirable.

When the teaching is over, the lack of a practical application from the desk leaves the work pointless and incomplete. The nail of truth, if any has been driven, has not been clinched, and is likely to drop out.

Now for the other plan—everybody in the school bending his mental energy to the consideration of the same passage. The teachers' meeting can be held regularly and to some purpose—not for the ordinary routine of business, but for the better business of hard study and diligent preparation of the lesson. Teacher helps teacher in the most efficient way, and the mental, moral and spiritual stimulus which each receives from each is a valuable element in making the school move along successfully. The superintendent or the pastor presiding at the study meeting gives direction to the exercise, and becomes committed not-only to a general interest in the affairs of the school, but to a particular and intimate co-operation with the details of its work.

Let us look at the school while in session. The teachers, having prepared the lesson together, naturally feel the bond which springs from having a community of thoughts and interests. The superintendent is not on duty merely in the capacity of an officer. His work is not only to see that the school opens and closes at the proper hours and that no unseemly noise is made in carrying it on. He can enter into the spirit of his labors with a greater zeal and efficiency than if his duties are merely the official ones of maintaining order and keeping people up to time. He has some central idea of the lesson, the keynote thought of it, already on the blackboard in the shape of a short, pungent text of Scripture, or a motto, to catch the eye and to fix the thought as teachers and scholars enter the room. He gives out a hymn which, as nearly as possible, bears upon the truths taught in the lesson. In reading a portion of Scripture he does not stumble at random on some chapter which has no particular connection with the lesson, but selects either the lesson itself or something which helps the school to understand it. He does not start the school at the study of the lesson with the barren announcement that the time has come at which that exercise may be proceeded with, but helps the lesson

with a pleasant word or two as to where it is and
what it is about.

And now the teachers and their classes proceed
with the lesson. If a teacher is absent and a substitute
is in his place, or if two classes are consolidated under
one teacher, all moves on smoothly. The hour of
teaching being over, there is room for a little talk
from the desk. Pastor or superintendent may now
apply the truth which the teachers have been inculcating. There is no danger of the work being done
at cross purposes when all have been studying the
lesson together. The blackboard is brought into
service, and some of the leading ideas of the lesson
are chalked upon it. Ten minutes or so may profitably be spent in this exercise. The closing prayer
may well add another clincher to the nail of truth
in asking God's blessing on what has been taught.
Then, when the teachers and those whom they have
labored with go home, they go warmed with the
enthusiasm proceeding from a well taught and harmoniously learned lesson.

I would urge on all who have never adopted the
uniform lesson system a fair and thorough trial of it.
If the school has been successful under the other
plan, depend upon it the success has been in spite
of the independent system rather than an evidence
of its excellence, and if there has been an attainment of successful results without a uniform lesson,
there is hardly any measure to the success to be
hoped for when the whole energy of the school is

concentrated in the co-operative work of studying one lesson.

It is just as appropriate to have a uniform lesson for one and the same school as to have a uniform meal for one and the same family. And what is a Sunday-school but a family? and what is their Sunday's meal but a blessed Sunday's feeding upon the Bread of Life?

10. *How to Start a New School.*

Any earnest Christian whose heart is in the work can start a Sunday-school, should his lot be cast in a neighborhood where no such school exists. There are such neighborhoods scattered all over the land and many thousands of Christian hearts earnestly longing to engage in the most blessed work, but they know not how to set about it. I propose to offer a few plain, practical suggestions on the subject. I have in view a destitute neighborhood in the country where there is no regular church organization and no stated preaching of the gospel. In the establishment of a mission-school in the city, or of a school within the bounds of an organized congregation, the steps would be somewhat different, though the spirit and the governing principles would be the same.

1. The first step for any one who would begin such a work is to seek guidance and aid from above. "Except the Lord build the house, they labor in vain that build it." This is true, indeed, of every

undertaking, but it seems especially applicable to such a work as that of the Sunday-school. The man or the woman who meditates engaging in such an enterprise needs to begin with earnest, importunate prayer. Pray to have your own soul baptized anew with holy zeal and energy; pray for special guidance, that you may be led to adopt the right measures and to seek the best co-operation; pray that the Holy Spirit would move the hearts of those whom you will need as fellow-laborers in the work; pray that the children whom you wish to bring into the school may be inclined to come, and that the parents may be inclined to send them, and to co-operate with you heartily in your plans; pray that those who have the worldly means needed may have their hearts warmed toward the project, so that whatever money may be necessary shall be forthcoming as it is required. The hearts of all are in your Father's hands, and he moveth them whithersoever he will. Go to him, then, with the utmost confidence, but also with the most importunate and persevering request, for help in what you are about to undertake. This is your first step.

2. Make up your mind that you will give cheerfully of your time, strength and worldly means to the forwarding of the work. You will not succeed unless you enter upon it with a willingness to make sacrifices. You must be willing to give up something of ease, to make concessions to the wishes and the prejudices of others, to be deprived of certain

hours heretofore given to leisure and quiet retirement. You must make a fresh, special consecration of yourself to the Master's service.

3. Prepared thus to enter upon the work in a right spirit, and with an urgent cry for divine help and guidance, seek next for human guidance. Periodicals are now published devoted to this special work of the Sunday-school and containing practical hints and suggestions in regard to its management. Books have been published for the same purpose, such as Pardee's *Sabbath-School Index*, Eggleston's *Sunday-School Manual*, House's *Sunday-School Hand-Book*, Packard's *Teacher Teaching*, Hart's *Thoughts on Sabbath-Schools*, etc. Take some one or more of these Sunday-school papers and get one or more of these volumes, and give some time to reading on the subject. If in this reading you do not find exactly the directions needed by you in your particular case, you will at all events get your heart more and more interested, and you cannot fail to meet with many suggestive and wise thoughts on the general subject.

4. Before making any public move in the matter look around you thoughtfully and see what materials for a school exist; who there are in the neighborhood that would be suitable persons, in respect to age and character, to act as teachers, and that would be likely to be willing to engage in the service; what children there are that are of suitable age, and that might probably be induced to at-

tend. Make an inventory of these, putting down every one that you can think of, until you feel that you can form some reasonable estimate in regard to the prospects for a school. Among the preliminary subjects of inquiry that should thus occupy your mind is the question of a place for holding a school. Is there a school-house in the neighborhood? Could it be used for a Sunday-school? If not, what other building or room is to be had? You may not be able by yourself to solve all these questions, and you should by no means undertake to solve them without consultation with those who are to be your co-workers. But the more carefully and thoughtfully you revolve the whole subject in your own mind, before asking help and co-operation from others, the more ready will you find them to listen to you, and the less danger will there be of your falling into discouragement when you encounter, as you doubtless will encounter, difficulties and obstructions.

Having thus laid your case before your heavenly Father; having consecrated yourself to the work by some special, private act of voluntary self-devotion; having given time and thought to preparation for it by reading some of the books and papers that treat of the subject; and having endeavored to make a sober and intelligent estimate of what is to be done,— you are now prepared to go forward and make an actual beginning. In so proceeding, what is the first thing to be done? What are the specific steps to be taken in collecting and organizing a school?

What is your next step?

5. Get together in some way those who are willing to help as teachers. Who these are you can find out only by actual inquiry. You must go and see them individually, one by one, and talk the matter over. Having found the necessary helpers, get them together, and after prayer for divine guidance and help in your enterprise have a free conference, laying before them all the plans you have to suggest and all the information you have gathered, and then agree among yourselves upon some plan of proceeding. In this conference you will obtain much fresh information. No matter how well you may suppose yourself to be acquainted with the neighborhood, you will find that every one knows, in some nook or corner, some family that you have overlooked. You will also probably receive valuable suggestions. Perhaps to your surprise you will find some one who in other days and in some other place has been a regular Sunday-school worker and knows all about how the work is to be done.

6. Every family should be visited. This part of the work should be divided among you at the conference just spoken of. Make written lists of the families assigned to each worker, with the understanding and agreement that the visit shall be made within a week, if possible, from the time of the conference. A certain promptness and simultaneousness of action in the matter arrests attention and creates a stir. This systematic and thorough family

33 *

visitation is essential to success. No other kind of advertising—posting of notices and handbills—will answer. You must go from house to house, explain what you are going to do, ask the co-operation of the parents, and invite every child personally. If this part of the work is well done, you cannot fail to have a school.

7. A place for holding the school will have to be secured. In most neighborhoods, even in the most destitute, there is usually some place where people congregate occasionally for the purpose of religious worship. Very often it is the district school-house. Get whatever place you can that is most central and most convenient. In some cases the only opening will be in a private house. One of the most successful schools I ever knew was held in a barn. Make a beginning somewhere, in the best place you can get. When you are once under way and people become interested in your work, places now closed against you may be opened.

8. Sunday-schools cost something—not much, indeed, but still something. There is no tuition to pay, which is the chief cost of the weekday-school, but books and other things are needed, and they cannot be obtained without money. Every scholar as well as teacher will need a Bible or a Testament. Most of the scholars will have Bibles or Testaments of their own, and those who have should be told when invited to come to the school to bring a Bible or Testament with them. For the supply of those

scholars who are destitute application should be made to the nearest depository of the American Bible Society, and the books obtained either by donation or purchase. After the Bible each scholar will need a hymn-book and a question-book or lesson-book of some kind. These are now published in great variety. The teachers in their preliminary conference will have to agree upon the hymn-book or question-book to be used, and order a supply to be in readiness when the school opens. At the same time each one should determine to take a teachers' paper at his own expense. Scholars should be induced, so far as possible, to purchase their own question-books and hymn-books. The cost to each will be but little, and it is better, as in the case of the Bible, for each to have his own. Besides Bibles, hymn-books and question-books, the school will need a supply of children's papers, a blackboard, one or more wall maps and a library. The cost of these will vary of course with the size and the means of the school. But if the school is to be made interesting and profitable, something considerable must be expended in this way. A proper outfit, in addition to the supply of Bibles, hymn-books and question-books, will cost not less surely than one dollar a scholar, and a like amount ought to be expended yearly in replenishing the stock.

Any dealer or publication society that makes a specialty of this business will, on application, cheerfully furnish estimates, with lists of books and other requisites. I give below a sample, such as I would recommend for a school of forty scholars :

1	Superintendent's Roll-book................	.25
1	Librarian's Record....................	.40
8	Teacher's Class-books....	.48
12	Primers :...........................	.48
1	Bible Dictionary......	$1.50
1	Pardee's Sabbath-School Index...........	1.25
1	Map of Palestine......................	1.50
1	Blackboard Paper.....................	1.60
40	Children's Papers, yearly................	5.00
1	Select Library, from 40 to 60 vols.........	27.54
		$40.00

The books and other requisites being provided, a place of meeting secured, and the scholars and teachers assembled, how is the school to be organized? What is the next step?

9. Probably the teachers will have agreed beforehand among themselves which of them shall be superintendent. If not, they must do so now. A leader is the first thing needed, and usually there is not much practical difficulty in determining which of them it shall be. In most cases the prime mover in the matter, the one who first set the enterprise in motion, will be the one most suitable for superintendent.

10. The superintendent having been designated, he will proceed to call the meeting to order. We can imagine him addressing the meeting as follows: "My friends, we have met to form a school for the

purpose of studying together God's holy Word on this his holy day. We shall not succeed in our undertaking unless we have his blessing upon it. To this end, then, let us call upon him in prayer."

11. After a brief prayer by the superintendent, or by some one else that he may call upon, he proceeds to divide the scholars into classes. This one step converts the little assembly from a mere meeting into a school. The classification is the first specific act of a school organization. In making this classification the first thing is to ascertain which of the scholars cannot read. These of course will form a class or classes by themselves. Next, of those that read, some will be found who read very imperfectly, having to stop frequently to spell out the hard words. These will constitute another class. Of those that read fluently there will probably be enough to form two or three classes, and these will be sorted according to age, sex, size and general indications of intelligence.

12. The superintendent, before beginning to classify, will do well to agree with the teachers which kind of scholars shall be assigned to each. Those who do not read at all are to be assigned to A; those who read imperfectly, to B; those who read fluently, to C, D, E, etc. He will then proceed to call the scholars to him one by one, and by asking each one to read a little in the Testament which he holds in his hand, and in case the scholar reads fluently, by asking him two or three questions as to

his studies and his general knowledge, he can determine pretty soon to which class he ought to belong, and can at once send him accordingly to A, B, C, D, etc. It will take the superintendent half an hour probably to classify in this way a school of forty scholars.

13. While the superintendent is thus engaged in examining and classifying the scholars, the teachers should employ the time in making themselves acquainted with the scholars assigned to them. As each scholar comes into the class, the teacher should make a careful and minute record of his name, residence, parents' names, and any other information which the scholar may give in regard to himself or his family, and of the neighborhood in which he lives. These particulars help the teacher wonderfully in his intercourse with the scholars, and they should be in such form as to be available to the superintendent, secretary and librarian in making up the general register and records of the school. The half hour spent by the superintendent in the classification may be very profitably spent by the teachers in making these preliminary inquiries and recording the results.

14. In a school numbering not more than thirty or forty scholars the general oversight need not occupy much of the superintendent's time. He should expect to teach a class, as well as to superintend the school, and provision for this should enter into his plans in making the classification.

15. The case is different in regard to the duties of librarian and secretary. The office of librarian particularly requires a considerable time, even in a small school, and unless there is some one who can give to the business nearly his whole time during the school-hours, the library will not have that efficiency which properly belongs to it, and besides, the books will very rapidly disappear. In a school of the size now contemplated, the librarian may, without difficulty, discharge the additional duties of secretary. There can almost always be found some young man or young woman who is not willing to teach, or perhaps not fitted to teach, who yet can perform admirably the duties of librarian and secretary, and who would be gratified in being thus honorably and usefully connected with the school. In case no one can be found for librarian, one of the teachers should undertake the duty, and the superintendent should take the duty of secretary.

16. When the classification has been completed, the teachers will severally proceed to instruct their classes in whatever lesson has been agreed upon or has been assigned by the superintendent. After a suitable time spent in this way, the superintendent will give a signal for the lessons to cease, and will then make a few remarks to the scholars urging their punctual attendance and asking their co-operation in bringing in other scholars, and also pressing upon their attention some of the truths contained in the lessons upon which they have been engaged.

The school should close with singing some pretty Sunday-school hymn of a kind likely to take with the children. If a library and a supply of children's papers have been procured, make a distribution of these just before dismission.

17. I have said nothing about a constitution and by-laws. In fact, I have not much faith in this kind of trumpery. I would not say that no Sunday-school should have its constitution and by-laws. Perhaps they may be necessary in some places and for some people, but oftentimes schools are killed by constitution making. A school such as I have described is a very simple affair, and the less machinery there is about it, the greater ordinarily will be its motive power. Instead of meeting to puzzle their brains over a constitution, let the teachers meet to warm their hearts in earnest prayer for the conversion of their scholars.

11. *Are we Making Progress?*

The Sunday-school cause is moving; no one can question that. The evidences of activity and of motion are too many and too palpable to be ignored or denied.

But all motion is not progress. There is such a thing as moving backward, or moving in a circle, going round and round, but not going forward. The boy's arrow is no swifter than his top. The activity of some people is that of the top. They make a great fuss, they bustle about and spin around here and there and are tremendously busy, but they have no well-defined aim, and you find them after a twenty years' absence just where you left them. Every now and then some new improvement in the Sunday-school machinery is brought out, but on examination it proves to be only the revival of what was in use thirty or forty years ago. Such things necessarily raise the query whether we really are only moving in a circle. Instead of pooh-poohing at the question—a method of arguing which often silences people without satisfying them—let us for a moment look soberly at some of the broad facts in the case.

1. In the first place, thirty years ago the idea still lingered in the minds of many good people that the Sunday-school was only for the children of the poor. Robert Raikes in the Sunday-school and Joseph Lancaster in the weekday-school did incidentally this great mischief. The controlling idea in the minds of both these good men was a scheme for the amelioration of the destitute. The idea took such hold of the public mind that it required at least two or three generations to grow out of it. The idea had not yet died out thirty years ago. To-day it is practically dead both as regards the Sunday-school and the weekday-school. The two have grown side by side, and have reciprocally helped each other. There is to-day a much sounder public sentiment in regard to both than there was a generation back. The cases now are exceedingly rare and exceptional of

those who think that either the Sunday-school or the common weekday-school is of the nature of a charity, like the almshouse, for the exclusive benefit of the poor and the vicious. Here, then, is substantial progress, about which there cannot be much question. The community has been educated to a more correct theory of the work to be done.

2. In the second place, the relation of the church to the Sunday-school is more clearly defined and more generally accepted than it was thirty years ago. The change here has not been so complete as in the preceding case. There are still those who regard the Sunday-school as a sort of outside, independent organization, like, for instance, an association for preventing cruelty to animals. I do not refer to the union of Christians of different name in what are properly missionary fields, where no one denomination is strong enough by itself to sustain a school. In such cases—and they are very numerous, and they always will be—God-fearing men, not as Presbyterians, Methodists, Episcopalians, Baptists, and so forth, but as Christians, come together and unite in gathering the children of all classes into a school on the Sabbath and teach them the great common doctrines of salvation. May the day never come when duty like this shall become an obsolete idea! The case to which I refer is different from this. It is that of the Sunday-school belonging to a particular congregation or parish. The time was when a few of the members of such a congregation—usually of the

younger portion—formed a coterie by themselves, and were regarded as specially constituting the Sunday-school people, the remaining and far larger portion of the congregation looking on, with approbation perhaps, but still only as spectators. If the pulpit was to be lowered, the pews to be remodelled or cushioned, the church to be painted or repaired, or a new minister to be called, it was a matter in which all had an interest and a voice, but the Sunday-school belonged to the teachers. Such was the theory. I am sorry to say the idea is not dead, but it is dying. In this matter we certainly have made progress, and the day, I believe, is not distant when the church and congregation as a whole will feel the same interest and the same sense of obligation in the organization, management and support of the Sunday-school that they do in the maintenance of public worship or in the settlement and support of a pastor.

3. Perhaps the most marked evidence of growth and progress in the Sunday-school work is in the multiplication of books, maps, charts, plates and apparatus of various kinds. There are, as I have already observed, hundreds of teachers still living who can remember the time when "Anna Ross," "Little Henry and his Bearer," and a few other books of the same sort, that could almost literally be counted on one's fingers, constituted the entire stock of books, and a few sheets of red and blue tickets were about all the apparatus of the Sunday-school. The writer of these paragraphs was himself a pupil in a large

mission school in which the entire stock of supplies of every kind was brought weekly by one of the lady teachers in her reticule. There was then no map of Palestine, big or little, which could be made available for the instruction of a class; there were no prints, colored or uncolored, coarse or fine, by which a teacher could illustrate to a class the manners and customs of Bible times; there were no class-books or school records; there were no Sunday-school papers either for scholars or teachers; there were no rooms specially fitted and furnished for the use of the school, but the sessions were held universally, as in many places they are still held, in the body of the church; there were of course no such things as blackboards in the school; indeed, they were not then known to any extent in the weekday-school, and their introduction into the Sunday-school hardly dates further back than five or six years. In all this—that is, in the means and appliances of various kinds for making Sunday-school instruction effective and interesting—we have unquestionably made great progress. In some of these things we have perhaps gone too fast and too far. We are going into an extreme, for instance, in the production of library books. More new volumes of this kind are now produced in a single year than the whole number which were in existence a little more than one generation back; and among this vast multitude of religious books for the young there is without doubt a large amount of which the most favorable opinion that can be expressed is that it is trash. But that does not detract from the substantial merit of that large number of books which are perfectly unexceptionable and whose influence upon the minds of the young is good and only good. In the means for inculcating Bible truth and producing sound religious impressions the teacher of the present day has unquestionably advantages vastly superior to those of the previous generation. Only, where the number of these appliances is so great—and some of them are of doubtful character—it behooves him now to exercise a degree of caution not needed formerly when he had almost nothing to choose from, good or bad.

4. In the fourth place, there has been a great advance in the matter of Sunday-school music. Instead of the dolorous, dismal, joy-forbidding strains which once dragged their weary length along at the opening and closing services of the school, tunes have been created better suited to the nature of children. As a consequence this part of the service, instead of being a solemn bore, to be submitted to with as little rebellion as possible, is now the bright spot in all the holy day. The children are fairly jubilant when the exercise is announced. There is nothing ordinarily that gives a mass of children greater pleasure than singing, when the exercise is properly conducted, and it was a great advance in the right direction when advantage was taken of this source of innocent enjoyment to make it a means of religious service and improvement.

5. The machinery for improving the character of the work has been very greatly increased ; " created" would perhaps be a more appropriate word. For awakening an interest in Sunday-schools, and especially for kindling an enthusiasm for the work in its missionary aspect, we have had, almost from the beginning, an admirable agency in the American Sunday-School Union. But for improving the character of the school itself, by teaching and training teachers, we are indebted to agencies not yet ten years old. That there is a prodigious advance yet to be made in this direction no one doubts, certainly not those who are on the top of the advancing wave. They feel as never before how wretchedly the very best Sunday-school teachers come short of the ideal standard now set before them ; yet that very great improvements in Sunday-school teaching have been made in the last ten years, and even in the last five years, is too plain to require illustration or proof. The whole idea of forming associations for improvement in Sunday-school teaching, such as normal classes, normal institutes and the like, is absolutely new. It is a creation of the present times. The agencies of which we are speaking have already produced a marked improvement in the style of teaching in the Sunday-school. This change of course is not yet general. There is a vast number of schools not yet reached by its influence. But the movement has been inaugurated. It is a movement in the right direction, and it is destined to go on. The great

want of the Sunday-school system as a whole is good teachers. *The teacher is the school,* and there is no better evidence that the cause has made and is making progress than the steps which have been taken in the last five years for improving the qualifications of the Sunday-school teacher.

6. Another point that merits special consideration is the gradual development of what Mr. Woodruff of Brooklyn is wont to call " The Sunday-school idea." By this he means the opportunity which the Sunday-school offers for the employment of laymen in the work of making known the gospel and bringing men under its influence. Every Christian, equally with the ministers of the gospel, it is believed, is bound to pray and labor for the coming of Christ's kingdom, and the Sunday-school opens a field in which every disciple may do something to further this great end. It is the very best field for private individual effort. Ministers in the pulpit can do many most important things toward the upbuilding of Christ's kingdom which laymen cannot do. But ministers, even if multiplied tenfold, could not do the tenth part of the work that is to be done. Besides this, the fact of laymen working in this way to bring others under the influence of the gospel is the very best means of developing the graces of private Christians. The Sunday-school would be a noble thing for the church if it accomplished no other good than this. As teaching is the very best way of learning, so doing good to others is the best way to get good

for ourselves. The Sunday-school is the agency beyond all others for increasing and developing the working talent and the Christian graces of the church.

The utility of the Sunday-school in the matter now suggested is indeed no new idea of the present generation. It lies at the corner-stone of the American Sunday-School Union, now half a century old. All the managers and most of the officers and working agents of that society are and always have been laymen, and the doctrine that laymen may wisely be employed in the management and prosecution of this blessed work, not to the disparagement, but to the relief and the assistance, of the ministry, has ever been maintained and exemplified by that institution. The idea was expressed with great clearness and force some years ago in a sermon preached for the society by the late Dr. Potts of New York, on "The Sunday-school as a Means of Developing the Lay Talent of the Church." But this idea, though advanced in a previous generation, and maintained throughout with an unbroken continuity, has received a large and unwonted development in the last twenty years. There never was a time in the history of modern Christianity when laymen were doing so much as they are now doing in the direct work of evangelization, making known the unsearchable riches of Christ and bringing others under the influence of Christianity, and all this mainly through the Sunday-school. In the development of this idea, therefore, there has undoubtedly been unmistakable progress.

7. One of the most hopeful signs in regard to the Sunday-school work is the spirit of restless uneasiness everywhere manifest in regard to it. We all see in this institution capabilities which we have hardly begun to realize. We all feel that our schools are sadly below the standard to which we are looking. Look over the columns of any Sunday-school teachers' paper for three or four successive numbers and notice the remarks of the various correspondents and contributors, and see how constant the demand is for something higher, something better, than anything we have yet reached in Sunday-school attainment. We want better books for our libraries; we want better question-books for our classes; we want Bibles filled with the right kind of maps; we want a better style of music—something that shall enable the children not only to sing sweetly and with a will while in the Sunday-school, but to keep on singing when they grow up and form part of the great congregation; we want better schoolrooms and more efficient and varied means of visible illustration—wall maps, charts and blackboards; we want trained teachers, capable of commanding attention and of making Bible truth plain and attractive; we want parents who really care more for the religious training and welfare of their children than for their secular education or their advancement in worldly condition; we want a church thoroughly

alive to the command of her Lord, "Feed my lambs;" we want pastors who can push forward and intelligently guide and control this noble movement—men who know how to take hold of the willing lay element to be found in every congregation and utilize it; we want more missionary work in bringing in the millions who are yet outside of the Sunday-school.

But there is no end to our wants, as there is none to our shortcomings. The fact, however, that Christians are to some extent alive to these deficiencies is among the hopeful signs of the times—more hopeful, assuredly, than a spirit of self-complacency or of easy indifference. The Sunday-school worker cannot better begin each new year than with the earnest aspiration after improvement in his work, or, to vary the expression, with a spirit of fixed, resolute, hopeful discontent.

INDEX.

Absenteeism of scholars, how to be remedied, 374.

Accommodations for the Sunday-school, 335.

Affections of a class, how to be gained, 189.

Age, how far to be considered in classifying scholars, 71.

Aggressive work, 22; Christianity aggressive, 23.

Aims important, 136; aims of the Sunday-school teacher, 138-149.

Alexander, Dr. Archibald's reading of the Scripture, 111; his powers as a questioner, 158.

American Sunday-School Union, its importance as a missionary agency, 31; the duty of giving it a liberal support, 31.

Anniversaries, 346.

Apparatus for Sunday-schools greatly increased, 400.

Attendance of scholars should be aimed at by the teachers, 138; irregular attendance of teachers, 230.

Attention of a class, how gained, 177-184.

Basis of Sunday-school organization, 35.

Bell, ringing the bell a bad way of stopping noise, 55; never to be used for arresting disorder, 83.

Bible Knowledge, the great means both of conversion and of growth in holiness, 16; the general contents of the Bible to be learned, 226; Bible to be read through in concert, 229.

Books to be closed during recitation, 165; teaching out of book, 171-179; the enormous number of Sunday-school books now published, 273-275; how to select, 277-291; modes of distributing, 291-310; multiplication of Sunday-school books, 399.

Busy, how to keep scholars busy, 164.

Card, library, 300.

Catalogue of library needed, 299.

Children to be trained and educated in the beliefs of the gospel, 17; this training to be accomplished in great measure by means of a school, 18; more than half the children out of the Sunday-school, 30; children's meetings at Conventions, 256; attendance in church, 328.

Child's Scripture Question-book, 227.

Chorister, necessity of having one in the school, 42.

Christianization, to be accomplished in great measure by education, 17.

Church, the church bound to indoctrinate the young in Christian knowledge and principles, 18; an organization for propagating the truth, 25; bound to be aggressive, 25; bound to look after neglected children outside of its pale, 27; church court ought to take supervision of this matter, 28; has properly the control of the Sunday-school, and should appoint and direct the superintendent, 35, 36; church action not needed in Conventions, 250–252; relation of church to Sunday-school, 310; the church should control the Sunday-school, 312–318; attendance of children in church, 328.

Class teaching, 153–157; questioning a class, 157–165; keeping class all engaged, 169; how to hold the attention of a class, 177–184.

Classification to be made by superintendent, 69; difficulty of the subject, 70; rules to be observed, 71–76; classifying a new school, 393.

Comprehension of the scholars, how to reach it, 193.

Conventions to be attended by teachers, 241; State Conventions, 248; County Conventions, 252.

Conversion of scholars the first aim of the Sunday-school teacher, 14; converts to be built up in holiness, 15; winning souls, 128–131; aiming at their conversion, 147.

Cost of opening a new school, 391, 392.

County Conventions, rules for conducting them, 252.

Deficiencies in the work accomplished, 20.

Definite lessons should be assigned, 206.

Denominationalism needed and not needed in the Sunday-school work, 249–252.

Devotional service, allotment of time for it, 94–96; of what it should consist, 96.

Disorder, wherein it consists, 80.

Doctrine, scriptural, the means of building up young converts in holiness, 16; doctrine of the Sunday-school to be scriptural, 145.

Doors to be closed and locked during the opening service, 97.

Dull scholars not to be overlooked, 144.

Earnestness needed in reading the Scriptures, 110.

Encouragement to be given to the dull, 224.

Evangelization by means of Sunday-schools, 16.

Every scholar to have a share of the teacher's attention, 143.

Example of prayer, 117, 118.

Executive ability wanted in the superintendent, 54.

Expulsion as a means of government in Sunday-schools, 90.

Eyes, how to be used in reading a hymn or a passage of Scripture publicly, 107, 114.

Fast parsing, 182.

Fitch, his rule about keeping the scholars busy, 184–187.

Formality in reading the Scriptures, 109.

Freshness in teaching, 205.

Fretful, fussy, disqualifications in a superintendent, 54.

Gardiner, Mary, worthy of imitation, 130.

Geist's adhesive labels, 303.

Government to be exercised in Sunday-school, 87.

Green, Ashbel, anecdotes of him, 119.

Guthrie, his skill in illustration, 204.

Help from the Great Teacher, 131–135.

Hymn, mode of giving it out, 103; waiting for the scholars to find it, 103; care in announcing the right number, 104; grammatical blunders in announcing the hymn, 106; object of reading the hymn before reading it, 106; looking at the scholars while reading, 107.

Idiot child, a remarkable instance, 196.

Illustrations in teaching should be varied, 204; additional illustrations, 207.

Individual peculiarities, how far to be observed in classifying a school, 76.

Institutes, County, different from a Convention, 257; programmes, 260–264.

Instruction to be scriptural, 145.

Intellectual progress, how far to be considered in classifying scholars, 75.

Irregularity of attendance, 230.

Knowledge of scholars and teachers and of what is passing in the school important to superintendent, 60–63; knowledge of the lesson, 64.

Lancaster, Joseph, his mistake, 397.

Last resort in Sunday-school government, 87.

Lateness encouraged by waiting for the laggards, 99.

Lesson, the teacher should aim to secure the study of it by the scholars, 138; to be studied by the teacher, 180; should be definite, 206; preparation by the teacher, 210; lesson *to* the class, 212; getting the scholars to learn the lesson, 221; lessons interrupted by the librarians, 296; uniform lessons, 379.

Librarian, his appointment and qualifications, 41; his work, 303; librarian in a small country school, 395.

Library for teachers a necessity, 241; Sunday-school library, how to select it, 273–291; how to manage it, 291–309; library card, 201; library Register, 306; use of library books in the summer, 362.

35

Love for souls the first qualification of the teacher, 124–127 ; power of love in teaching, 189–193.

Mann, Horace, report on Prussian teaching, 175.

Manner in prayer, 119; manner in teaching should be varied, 202.

McCosh, his position in regard to ecclesiastical supervision of Sunday-schools, 317.

Meditation needed as a preparation for reading the Scripture, 112.

Meeting, teachers' weekly, 265.

Memory, Scripture to be memorized, 146–167 ; the memory especially to be cultivated in Sunday-school, 152 ; teachers should commit the verses, 212 ; how to get the scholars to commit to memory, 237.

Methods wear out, 200.

Methodists, their position in regard to Sunday-schools, 315.

Minister, his relation to the Sunday-school, 318.

Mission work of the Sunday-school, 21 ; more than missionaries needed, 23 ; the Sunday-school a missionary agency, 29 ; missionaries for pioneer regions, 30 ; the missionary work of the American Sunday-School Union, 31 ; mission work everywhere, 31 ; mission work to be done by church schools, 32 ; missionary collections, 97.

Morristown, N. J., programme of Institute held there, 261.

Music in Sunday-school, 340 ; improvements in Sunday-school music, 401.

New scholars, how to be disposed of, 77 ; new school, how to start one, 385.

Newell, report on normal school teaching, 174.

Newton, Dr., referred to, 104.

Noise, how to avoid it, 55 ; sources of noise, 81.

Normal Institutes should be got up by the pastors of the place acting in concert, 296 ; the teachers' weekly meeting should be a normal class, 270.

Notices, rules to be observed in regard to them, 101.

Numbering books, 313.

Objects of the Sunday-school, 13–33 ; first object the conversion of the scholars, 14 ; building up the young converts in holiness, 15–20 ; second object, a mission agency for the unevangelized, 21–33.

Opening school punctually, 99.

Order, difficulty of maintaining it in Sunday-school, 79 ; doing things quietly, 80 ; doing things at the right time, 83 ; keeping things and persons in place, 84 ; order popular with the scholars, 91 ; the teacher should aim to keep order, 139 ; how it is to be done, 140, 141.

Organization of the Sunday-school, 34 ; the Sunday-school not an independent concern, but a branch of the operations of the church, 35, 36 ; appointment of superintendent, 37 ; other officers, 40

Out, going out rarely to be allowed, 85.

Paper, a teachers' paper needed by every Sunday-school teacher, 239.

Parallel texts, how to use them, 215.

Parents, their relation to the Sunday-school, 324.

Pastors should concert together in getting up a Normal Institute, 246 ; relation of the pastor to the Sunday-school, 318.

Pause before and after prayer, 120.

Penalties, the ordinary school penalties unknown in Sunday-school, 150.

Personal influence to be exercised by the superintendent, 57.

Piety the first qualification of the superintendent, 51, 52.

Place, things and persons to be kept in place, 84.

Power to be exercised in Sunday-school when necessary, but no show of it, 89.

Prayer, rules for the opening prayer in Sunday-school, 115 ; an example, 116 ; another example, 118.

Practical thoughts to be prepared, 219.

Preparation for the opening service, 100 ; preparation for the lesson by the scholar, 180 ; preparation by the teacher, 210–220.

Presbyterians, their action on Sunday-schools, 315–318.

Programme, importance of having one, 93 ; should be supreme, 94 ; a test of the superintendent's idea of what the school is, 94 ; allotment of time, 95–97 ; sample programme, 98 ; programme of Teachers' Institute, 260–264.

Progress in the Sunday-school cause, signs of it, 396.

Punctuality in opening, 99, 100.

Question-books, their true use, 162, 173, 180, 215.

Question drawer, its use at Institutes, 258.

Questioning a class, 157–165.

Quietly, doing things quietly, 80.

Reading hymns and Scripture, 107–115.

Reading committee for selecting library books, 279.

Recitation, how to conduct it, 165–171.

References, how to be used, 167.

Register number, 301 ; library Register, 306.

Religious teaching best effected, like other teaching, by means of schools, 18 ; more practical than ordinary teaching, 150.

Richards, how he reached the understanding of an idiot, 196.

Robert Raikes, his mistake, 397.

Salvation of the scholar the great end of the teacher, 14–20 ; 124–131.

Scholars to be kept busy, 169, 184–189 ; to do most of the talking, 170 ; gaining their affections, 189–193 ; reaching their comprehension, 193–195 ; getting them to learn the lesson, 221 ; treatment of new scholars, 368 ; absenteeism, how to be remedied, 374 ; duty of visiting them, 375–379.

Schools needed for religious teaching as much as for other teaching, 19.

Scriptures, mode of reading them in school, 108; formality to be avoided, 109; earnestness, 110; previous study required, 111; meditation on the passage, 112; alternate reading, 114; to be committed to memory, 146, 167.

Seat, scholars not to be allowed to leave their seats, 85.

Secretary, his appointment and duties, 40.

Size, scholars', 74; how far to be considered in classifying scholars, 72.

Skipping about in reciting, 168.

Social condition, how far to be considered in classifying scholars, 74.

Spirit, Holy, his help needed by the teacher, 125; how to be obtained, 127; the Great Teacher, 131; his influence a great mystery, 133; seeking his aid, 220.

Spy, superintendent should not play the spy, 62.

Squeak-leather not wanted in the superintendent's boots, 82.

State Conventions should be union, not denominational, 248.

Study needed as a preparation for reading the Scriptures in opening school, 110–112; study of lesson by the scholars, 136; critical study of the meaning, 217.

Summer, closing schools in summer, 359; what is to be done in the summer months, 361.

Sunday-school, its objects, 13–33; first object, the conversion and sanctification of its scholars, 14–20; second object, a means of Christianizing the masses, 21–33; organization, 34–47; not an independent institution, but a department of the church's work, 34–36; appointment of its superintendent, 37; of its other officers, 40; appointment of teachers, 43; qualifications of superintendent, 48–123; earnest piety, 50; executive ability, 52; things not wanted, 54; personal influence, 57; knowledge of the school, 61; and of the lesson, 64; bestowing attention upon all, 65; sympathy with all, 67; classification, 69; maintaining order, 78; exercising government, 87; making a programme, 93; punctuality in opening, 99; preparation for the opening, 100; giving out notices in school, 101; reading the hymn, 103; reading the Scriptures, 108; the opening prayer, 115; two examples of prayer, 117, 118; the teacher, first qualification, 124; winning souls, 128; help from the Great Teacher, 131; having an aim, 136; difference between teaching in Sunday-school and in other schools, 149; class teaching, 153; how to question a class, 157; how to conduct a recitation, 165; teaching out of book, 171; holding the attention, 177; keeping scholars busy, 184; gaining their affections, 189; reaching their comprehension, 193; variety in teaching, 199; having a definite lesson, 206; the teacher's preparation for the lesson, 210; getting the scholars to learn the lesson, 221; securing acquaintance with the general contents of Scripture, 226; irregular attendance of teachers, 230; visiting scholars, 233; keeping up with the times, 237; necessity of teachers meeting in council, 244; State Conventions, 248; County Conventions, 252; County Institutes, 257; weekly meetings, 265; the library, how to select it, 273–297; how to manage the library, 297–309; relation of the Sunday-school to the church, 310; relation to the minister, 318; to the parents, 324; attendance of the scholars upon church, 328; school accommodations, 335; Sunday-school music, 340; anniversaries, 346; closing school in winter, 355; closing in summer, 359; after vacation, 365; treatment of new scholars, 368; absenteeism, 374; uniform lessons, 379; how to start a new school, 385; is the Sunday-school cause making progress? 396; evidences of progress, 398.

Superintendent should be appointed by the church, not elected by the teachers, 37–40; superintendent should select the secretary, librarian, chorister and teachers, and displace them when necessary, 40–45; importance of the office, 48, 49; example of incapacity, 49; earnest piety the first qualification, 50; executive ability, 52, 53; should not be fussy, 54; nor fretful, 54; nor noisy, 55; nor a great talker, 56; personal influence, 57; should put forth his sympathies, 58, 59; should awaken his sympathies by making himself acquainted with the condition of the scholars, 60; should know what is going on in his school, 61; should know the lesson, 64; should bestow attention on all, 66, 67; should bestow his sympathies upon all, 68; classifying the school, 69; difficulty of classifying, 70; age as a ground for classification, 71; size, 72; social condition, 74; intellectual progress, 75; individual peculiarities, 76; maintaining order, 78; doing things quietly, 80; doing things at the right time, 83; keeping things and people in place, 84; exercising government, 87; making a programme, 93; opening school punctually, 99; preparation for the opening service, 100; giving out notices in school, 101; giving out the hymn, 103; reading the Scriptures, 108; making the opening prayer, 115; manner in prayer, 119; pausing before and after prayer, 120.

Support of Sunday-schools entirely inadequate, 19; compared with the support of the secular schools, 20.

Sympathy a power in the superintendent, 58; should be bestowed upon all, 67.

Talkative superintendent a nuisance, 56.

Teachers to be appointed by the superintendent, 43–46; inconvenience of any other mode of selection or displacement, 44; teachers not to be interrupted while giving their lesson, 84; the amount to be guarded in the programme, 95; first qualification of the teacher, 124; duty of winning souls, 128; seeking help from the Great Teacher, 131; having an aim, 136; securing regular attendance, 138; securing the study of the lesson, 138; keeping order, 139; teaching something, 142; teaching something additional every Sunday, 143; teaching something to every scholar, 143; making the teaching scriptural, 145; getting the scholars to commit Scripture to memory, 146; aiming to secure the conversion of scholars, 147; difference between teaching in Sunday-school and in other schools, 149; class teaching, 153; how to question a class, 157; how to conduct a recitation, 165; teaching out of book, 171; holding the attention, 177; keeping the scholars busy, 184 gaining their affections, 189; reaching their comprehension, 193; studying variety, 199; assigning a definite lesson, 206; preparing for the lesson, 210; committing the verses to memory, 212; plan in regard to the parallel texts, 215; use of the question-book, 215; preparing illustrations, 217; critical study of the meaning, 217; beginning preparation early in the week, 220; how to get the scholars to learn the lesson, 221; acquaintance with the general contents of Scripture, 226; irregular attendance of teachers, 230; visiting scholars, 232; keeping up with the times, 237; taking a teachers' paper, 239; having a teachers' library, 241; attending conventions, 241; necessity of meeting in council, 244; State Conventions, 248; County Conventions, 252; County Institutes, 257; Institute programmes, 260; weekly meetings, 263; teacher should provide for his class in summer before leaving the city, 363.

Text-book, how to be used in teaching, 171–177.

Theological Seminaries should educate their students in a knowledge of the Sunday-school work. 245.

Time, doing things in time, 83; apportionment of time to the different parts of the services, 94–98.

Todd, his skill in illustration, 204.

Topics in teaching should be varied, 203

Uniform lessons. 379.

Vacation, important work to be done in September, 365.

Variety important in teaching, 199–209.

Verses to be recited from memory, 166, 212.

Visiting scholars, 233, 375–379.

Wellington, Duke of Wellington's mode of intimidating a mob. 89.

Winning souls the great end of the teacher, 128.

Winter, closing schools in winter, 355.

Work, the work of Christians to Christianize the world, 17.

THE END.

HEAVENWARD—EARTHWARD.
By HARRIET B. McKEEVER.   4 illustrations............. ....$1.25

HELEN MACGREGOR; or, Conquest and Sacrifice.
By MRS. C. Y. BARLOW.   4 illustrations............... ..... 1.25

JOHN BRETT'S HOUSEHOLD.
By MRS. C. E. KELLY DAVIS.   3 illustrations........... 90

LIFE-SCENES FROM THE FOUR GOSPELS.
By REV. GEORGE JONES, M.A.   25 illustrations......... 2.00

LIFE-SCENES FROM THE OLD TESTAMENT.
By REV. GEORGE JONES, M.A.   25 illustrations......... 2.00

MISTAKES OF EDUCATED MEN.
By JOHN S. HART, LL.D.......... ....:. 50

ONE HUNDRED GOLD DOLLARS.
By MRS. J. E. McCONAUGHY.   3 illustrations........... 90

SEQUEL TO FRIDAY LOWE.
By MRS. C. E. KELLY DAVIS.   4 illustrations........... 1.25

STELLA ASHTON; or, Conquered Faults.
By MRS. C. Y. BARLOW.   3 illustrations......... 90

THE HOME VINEYARD: Sketches of Mission Work.
By CAROLINE E. KELLY.   3 illustrations...... 80

THE SABBATH-SCHOOL INDEX.
By R. G. PARDEE, A.M.   With Portrait on Steel....... 1.25

THE SUNDAY-SCHOOL IDEA.
By JOHN S. HART, LL.D........................... .... 1.50

THE TEACHER'S GUIDE TO PALESTINE.
By PROF. H. S. OSBORN.   With a Map................... 65

TILMAN LORING; or, Minister or Merchant.
By REV. J. K. NUTTING.   3 illustrations.................. 90

TOM MILLER; or, After Many Days.
By MRS. M. E. ROCKWELL.   4 illustrations............. 1.25

☞ Descriptive Catalogue and sample copy of THE SUNDAY
SCHOOL TIMES free on application.

www.ingramcontent.com/pod-product-compliance
Lightning Source LLC
Chambersburg PA
CBHW030814110726
47900CB00006B/1620